RIVALRY

BETWEEN

TESFOM & HABTOM

Story of

Justice, aggression, betrayal & steadfastness

TESFAY MENGHIS

GHEBREMEDHIN

Cover design by Ermias Zerazion, beteZION Info@betezion.com

www.betezion.com

*Contact Information (*ንሓበሬታ መወከሲ*):*

Tesfay Menghis Ghebremedhin. Email address: bagolu75@ yahoo.com or tes_men61@yahoo.com

Address in Eritrea: Ruba Haddas Street, House No 27, Asmara, Eritrea- Zip 186 Or Cathedral Pharmacy, PO BOX 12, Asmara, Eritrea. Tel. 291-1-127188.

Address in the US: Springfield, Virginia, Zip 22152 and Pittsburg, California, Zip 94565

Printed by Amazon KDP, USA, ……2022

1st edition 2022

ናብ ጴጥሮስ ፈለቑን፡
[illegible] ርሑስ ሓድሽ ዓመትን
[illegible]
[illegible]
ታሕሳስ 2022

ህልኽ
ተስፎምን ሃብቶምን

ዛንታ

ፍትሕን ዓመጽን፣ ጥልመትን ጽንዓትን

ተስፋይ መንግስ ገብረመድህን

Contents

Reader's comments to the Tigrinya version

Habte Tesfamariam-Virginia, USA.

From the title and the exterior story line, this novel might seem to be a simple story of rivalry between individuals. However, when we delve deeper into the story, we discover this fascinating novel to also be about progress and backwardness, decency and evil, victory and defeat, and steadfastness and betrayal. To describe life and fathom its depths requires a rare and unique gift. I have seen this talent and endowment at work in this intriguing, interesting and pulsating novel. It is a great leap forward in Eritrean literature.

Yibrah Solomon-Boston

In your first book, "**ህልኽ ተስፎምን ሃብቶም**," you reminded us that we don't live in a perfect world - the pros and cons of trust, betrayal and the virtue of tolerance are valuable lessons. I just read your 2nd book, "**ሕድሪ መድህንን ኣልጋነሽን**." In my opinion, calling the book a story is too modest. It is like reading the Book of Proverbs where you encounter take-away lessons in each narrative. The constructive messages and counseling on lifelong commitments, listening and generational respect, and letting go, etc. are all deeply educational. Thank you for your contribution.

Author Dawit Ghebremikael Habte

Author Tesfay Menghis has transformed his characters into living beings, by breathing life into them through love, hate, anger, jealousy and many other deeply human emotions. This is an amazing book that will continue to impress generations. I call on all book lovers to read and enjoy and appreciate this great book.

Yordanos Ataklti

This is a well-written, amazing and inspiring book! It is a heart-warming story of two families who went through a lot to keep their families together in spite of unbelievable hardships. I enjoyed both books from beginning to end! If you are looking for something to read for the summer, I highly recommend these two great books.

Tedros Tecle-London-U.K.

A book that entertains and teaches the young and sends the old down memory lane. An engaging, engrossing and gripping story that is difficult to put down. It seeps into every reader's mind and consciousness and arouses one's appetite for reading. Congratulations

Ogbai Ghebremedhin-Cambridge-Massachusettes

The size and content of the twin books the author has written reminded me of the great book, "War and Peace" by Leo Tolstoy. The author has used two great extended families to represent a microsome of highland Eritrean community and society. He has managed to balance the good and the bad in the daily interactions within families, communities and the society at large. This enables the old to ponder and question long-held traditional habitual behaviors and traits while encouraging the young to learn from them. The books are so well written, the characters so alive and the events so pulsating, that one practically forgets one is reading a novel but rather watching a mesmerizing play being enacted live. Once one gets into the thick of the story, it is very difficult to put the books down.

Amazon Reviewer's comment:

Entertaining, captivating and informative Tigrinya book!

This is a beautifully written, thought-provoking and intriguing story of two families. It is full of suspense, love, loss, rivalry and greed and it has been a while since I came across a Tigrigna book that drew me into the story and made me feel part of it. I felt so connected to the characters that I found myself wanting to intervene!!! I promise you will get hooked and will not regret reading this"!!!! Highly recommended!!!

The first book published in 2019-"ህልኽ ተስፎምን ሃብቶምን"

The second book published in 2020-"ሕድሪ መድህንን ኣልጋነሽን"

Note

"The novel "Rivalry between Tesfom and Habtom," is a work of fiction. Hence, all characters and their names are fictional personalities that I created. None of them represent in name or in act, anyone dead or alive.

Dedication

This book is dedicated to our grand-children, Sina, Noah, Simon and Heeyab, who have filled our lives with joy and happiness. They have recharged our old batteries and have enabled us to enjoy and appreciate anew, the beauty, sweetness and innocence of infanthood and childhood. I wish them long, healthy, fruitful and peaceful lives.

Tesfay Menghis Ghebremedhin

Preface

BOOKS AND RADIO became my best friends and my main sources of joy, inspiration and fulfilment, very early on. This was mainly because discovering new things and learning about new ideas were the two things that gave me the greatest satisfaction and gratification. I soon became aware that I had great respect for words - the power and depth of their meaning and their vital importance in our relationships and lives.

Whenever I wrote a letter or a short composition, I would continually change and edit it until I was satisfied that the words and sentence structure exactly represented the ideas and messages I was trying to convey. As I matured, I started appreciating the vital role communication played in our peaceful coexistence, both within our family structure and the community at large. I thus started developing extremely keen interest and a passion for the correctness of the spoken and written word.

After graduation, I had the privilege of working as a community pharmacist in Cathedral Pharmacy, Asmara, Eritrea, where I found out that communicating with a sick patient was particularly an even more demanding and challenging task. Despite the difficulty, when one masters the art of humble active listening and the correct use of words and general communication skills, then the reward is extremely gratifying.

Generally, community pharmacies in Africa, and Eritrea in particular, attract virtually every kind of person in the country, making them virtual laboratories of people. One has an opportunity to interact with every sector and cross section of the society. In my 45 years of service, I have probably interacted with about half a million people. I was therefore fortunate and blessed to find a wealth of wisdom and knowledge in my workplace.

This not only enabled me to grasp and appreciate our differences as human beings, but also had a profound impact on my personality. It promoted deep changes in my thinking and the way I saw the world, the community and myself. The breadth of things I learned in Cathedral Pharmacy during the nearly half a century of working with the community was far greater than what I learned from 18 years of school.

Meanwhile, my passion and ambition to write was intensifying. But my 11-hour, six-day work week did not permit me much time. Later on, came marriage and the responsibility of raising four children. Combined with my pharmacy responsibilities, this made it impossible even to think about writing. By 2008, two of my children had already graduated from university and the other two had already joined college. I felt that was the right time to start my writing in earnest.

After a few months and a 100-page draft, I was not satisfied with the result. As it stood, this first draft was not successfully transmitting the ideas, thoughts and the message I wanted to convey. That was when I realized that there was a huge mountain to climb between my desire and passion to be a writer and my novel writing skills.

It therefore became clear to me that I needed to learn the art of novel writing from scratch. I knew I had to depend on myself, since there were no books or courses that could help me learn. A friend gave me an electronic book titled, "Novel writing for dummies," which opened my eyes. Then I started collecting material from the Internet and took the job of learning seriously. This self-education took me a year and half. By the time I was done, I recognized that, though what I had learned might not make me a great writer, I was confident that I had acquired enough knowhow and tips to write a first novel.

I started my writing anew in early 2010. After three years, in 2013, I finished the first draft of a 900-page manuscript. I was elated that I was nearly done. I thought what remained was merely editing the manuscript twice or thrice. That was when I learned the depth and wisdom of what great writers meant when they said, "Books are not written, they are rewritten."

After my first draft, it took me another five years and 25 editions to be satisfied with the final format of the 1st book, "**ህልኽ ተስፎምን ሃብቶምን**" and the 2nd book, "**ሕድሪ መድህንን ኣልጋነሽን.**" These two books written in Tigrinya were published and printed in April 2019 and May 2020 respectively.

After the books were published, I pondered for a long time whether to write a 3rd Tigrinya sequel or whether I should translate my novels into English. After consulting with family and friends and listening to my heart, I finally decided on translation.

The target audience of my Tigrinya novels are Tigrinya speakers in Eritrea, Ethiopia and the diaspora. After 2016, I had an opportunity to meet and observe Habesha and African youth, who were born or raised outside of their home countries. The target audience for these translated works are all English readers in general and Eritrean, Ethiopian and African readers in particular.

During the translation, I have tried to maintain the identity of the story, the story line and the cultural background intact. However, I have also tried to delete some sections and add other new scenes to make the novel relatable and pertinent to the English reader.

The novels have thus been adapted and translated so they could be enjoyed by all English readers irrespective of their ethnicity or cultural background. It is my ardent desire and hope, that all readers will find the novel enjoyable, interesting, thought provoking and impactful.

Tesfay Menghis Ghebremedhin

Chapter 1
Ospedale Regina Elena

Tesfom was hurriedly finalizing his work. This was usually his favorite time of the day, when he could work without any interruption from customers or co-workers. While checking and sorting every file, he was about halfway through and was thinking about his steady progress, when the phone rang. His watch read 4:30 pm. He lifted the phone with exasperation and nearly shouted, "Hello?"

"Hello Tesfom *Hawey*?" said a voice he knew very well. However, at that moment, the voice seemed strange and distant, and it immediately captured his attention and unnerved him.

"Hello Medhn? Are you ok? What is wrong?!" he said, with a clear sign of worry in his voice.

"I am ok, but I have not been feeling well in the last hour or two. Since the doctors have already warned me, I am worried. I want you to take me to the hospital now, rather than later, lest I regret the decision."

He didn't wait for another word, nor did he ask further explanation. He quickly said, "I am coming right away!"

Immediately cradling the phone, he stood up. Picking up his

coat, he strode past his secretary's office, and without interrupting his steps, told her he was going out and would not return for the day. He didn't wait for a response.

Leaving the office, he half-walked, half-jogged to his car, which was parked nearby in the *Vialle Regina* street, in front of *Bar Vittoria*. He opened his car, threw his coat on the seat beside him, and started driving towards *Settanta Otto zone.*

While driving, he started thinking about the train of events that led to his rushing out of the office. He thought about the condition of her health during the last few months. Medhn was by nature the kind who would never easily admit to being sick or in pain. Tesfom thought, "If Medhn openly admits feeling ill, then she must be seriously sick!"

In the last few months, Medhn had developed hypertension. This was new to her. The doctors continually advised her to come for regular check-ups, and although she complied at the beginning, later on, she began to slack off on her appointments. Her excuse was always, "I am ok, I do not feel anything!"

In the preceding three months, Medhn's hypertension had started to climb up. Her doctors became concerned and again warned her to come back for regular check-ups. Nevertheless, she kept missing appointments, always insisting that she felt nothing and was ok.

Tesfom shook his head from side to side and said, "Oh boy, I hope she is ok. The problem with Medhn and her kind is that they never listen to professional advice. They only think, 'If there is pain, it is serious. If not, then it should be something minor'. He acknowledged that this logic was not unique to Medhn, but rather was very prevalent among the general population."

Sighing again, he said, "Well, nothing can be done now, except pray that God will help her. I hope this is nothing serious." He suddenly realized that while talking to himself, preoccupied by Medhn's illness, he had already arrived. He turned his car from the main road into a short alley.

He stopped his car and practically ran into the courtyard leading into the two-room house. The moment he entered; he saw that Medhn had already finalized her preparations. She was wearing a long wide dress (*kemish*), that fell past her knees to her ankles, with a white wide scarf (*netsela),* on top of her dress. She had covered her hair with a white headscarf (*shash*).

Tesfom was sure that Medhn would not show any outer sign of the pain and the condition she was in. Since he was already worked up and worried, he didn't bother to ask her how she was feeling, knowing he would only get, "I am ok," as a response.

To avoid wasting precious minutes, he only said: "Ok, let's go." He stepped towards her to hold her arm.

Medhn immediately moved away from him, saying: "Hey, I am ok, and don't worry. I don't need any help to walk."

"Ok, Ok," said Tesfom, with slight irritation towards her attitude of, 'I don't need any help.'

He ran back to open the car for her and started the car after making sure that she was seated comfortably. They drove from the alley towards *Addis Alem* Police Station and passing Bar *Torino* and *Cinema Croce Rossa* drove down towards *Comboni* College and soon arrived at *Regina Elena* Hospital. Tesfom looked at his watch and saw that it had only taken them a few minutes to arrive. The gate was opened for them and they drove into the urgent care department of the hospital. After a brief examination, the doctor decided to admit her immediately. They took her to the in-patient department and assigned her a bed.

The room where Medhn was admitted was not large, but it still had four beds. As soon as Tesfom went into the room, his nasal cavity was filled by the typical combined scent of drugs, disinfectants, and health institutions. Tesfom had detested these since early childhood. He stayed with Medhn for about 30 minutes until the hospital staff asked him to leave. They told him to return in the evening to bring her dinner. He left Medhn reluctantly.

It was a Thursday afternoon in January, 1952. In the highland area of Eritrea, particularly in the capital city Asmara, the month of January is comparatively one of the coldest months of the year.

As soon as he got out, Tesfom immediately felt the intense cold. He was wearing a thin white shirt with a pink tie, grey trousers and a black light coat and told himself, "When I come back to bring dinner, I have to remember to put on a sweater and a scarf."

Tesfom was very particular about the clothes and shoes he wore. Everything had to match perfectly. He bought imported expensive Italian clothes and shoes. Today though, his mind was not on his attire, but rather on what he feared was a grave danger to Medhn. All his thoughts were on her. He was truly worried.

* 2 *

That same day, Alganesh had been experiencing extreme discomfort and intense pain. She had a very low threshold and little resistance to pain, but that day, she was trying her best to resist and control it. As the day went by, the pain worsened and became even more intolerable. By 3pm, she couldn't resist it anymore and decided to send children from the neighborhood to call Habtom.

She was not wholly comfortable sending the children to call Habtom, as she knew he did not like to be interrupted at work. He would be displeased and might even yell at her. On top of that, he also believed that dashing to hospitals and doctors for anything big or small, was a weakness and unnecessary.

The last time she went for a check-up, the doctors had warned her to be vigilant and seek immediate assistance, if she noticed any changes. When she told Habtom of this, he had brushed it aside, saying, "Oh come on, what do you expect them to say? Don't you know that doctors and health care providers exaggerate even simple things?" Habtom was thus always discouraging Alganesh from seeking medical advice.

Alganesh knew that the consequences of inaction would affect her life as well as her family's life. She also realized that if anything went wrong, everyone would be quick to make accusations in hindsight like, "It is her fault! The doctors had properly warned her. She should have been more careful. She brought all this upon herself, etc." After weighing and carefully considering everything, she decided it would be better to accept the fury of Habtom, rather than face the rest of the consequences.

Habtom was very dedicated to his work. He never wanted to waste even a few minutes on other life events. For him, life was only work. When he received Alganesh's message, he became extremely angry and frustrated. After debating with himself awhile, he reluctantly ultimately decided to go home and see Alganesh.

Habtom was used to going everywhere with his coverall on, and despite the suggestions of family and friends, he stuck to this habit. He was about to go out wearing his coverall when an inner voice whispered to him, "Come on Habtom, don't forget that you are going to a hospital where anything can happen. At least take off your coverall just this once. Although he rarely listened to his inner voice, he immediately complied with it now and took out his coverall. He put his khaki coat and put it over his khaki shirt, put his sandals and left.

As he started to mount his bicycle, he realized that to take Alganesh to the hospital, he would need transportation. Scratching his head, he instantly decided that instead of taking transportation from the central market area (*shuk)*, he should go home and check for himself if she needed to go to the hospital. If he thought she was ok, he would just return to his shop without wasting money unnecessarily. Satisfied with his reasoning, he mounted his bicycle and rode off.

On the way home riding his bicycle, he remembered what the doctors had told Alganesh. As he started to think calmly about the matter, his anger and irritation started to diminish. "What if their warnings were real and had dire consequences?" he thought. "What if she does need to go to the hospital? Instead of regretting a wrong decision later, it would be better to err on the side of caution."

After going through all possible scenarios, Habtom was now much calmer. He arrived at home without even realizing it. He got off his bicycle and went into a very large compound, where many families lived side by side. As he entered the house, he found Alganesh in more pain and distress than he anticipated. "You don't look good. How are you doing?" he asked.

Alganesh's face was contorted and her jaws were clenched. She was breathing heavily, moving her body from side to side. Showing that she was indeed in intense pain, she emitted an anguished sound of pain, "Oww! Oww!"

She waited until she got a respite from her anguish and then said, "I am not ok at all Habtom. I am dying of unbearable pain. Please take me to the hospital immediately."

Habtom was shocked by the scene in front of him. "You are indeed in intense distress! I will be right back with transportation." He immediately rushed outside.

* **3** *

After ten minutes, Habtom returned with a horse and cart. With the help of a neighbor, they helped Alganesh on to the horse cart and, riding alongside on his bicycle, Habtom instructed the driver how to take the shortest way to the hospital.

Pulling the stirrup slowly and putting his tongue into his palate, the driver made a regular clicking sound familiar to his horse, slowly directing him from the alley onto the main side road. The care with which he was handling his horse and the patient showed that he was not only taking his responsibility seriously, but also understood that he was serving as an ambulance and emergency transportation.

From the side road, they merged into the *Haz Haz* road. They passed the roundabout at Bar Tiblets, *Satae B*us garage, Hansenian (leprosy) clinic, and arrived at a busy intersection where they stopped for a while. The driver directed his horse cautiously across the intersection and instantly arrived at the gate of the *Elena Regina* Hospital.

From beginning to end, the driver of the cart and his horse maintained a constant speed and rhythm. The horse instantly complied with the driver's regular sounds and hand movements, and together, they resembled a well-oiled machine. The horse seemed to know that if he did a good job, he would be rewarded by his master. He performed his duty gracefully and seriously and seemed proud of the rhythmic *Qua, Qua, Qua,* sound his metal heels were making on the road. Together they managed to transport Alganesh safely and comfortably.

During the journey, Alganesh sat crouched to one side, visibly in intense pain. Recognizing the familiar *horse cart* with a sick patient, the gateman immediately opened the gate for them. Habtom alighted from his bicycle and followed them. Along with the driver, they helped her into the urgent care department, where the nurses took charge of her. The nurse asked them to wait outside until she was examined by the doctor. Upon returning, she said that she needed to be admitted urgently. Habtom went and informed the driver that they would not be needing a return trip. He thanked him and returned to Alganesh

Alganesh had already been assigned a bed. Habtom noticed that there were eight beds in the room and noted that six of the other beds were occupied. Alganesh seemed more at ease than she had been. Her mood and condition slightly relaxed him. But soon, a doubt started to creep into his thoughts: "Maybe she did not really need to come to the hospital in the first place." He immediately brushed the idea aside and kept it to himself, saying, "Well it is ok. What is done, is done, there is no going back."

The truth differed considerably from Habtom's doubts. Nothing about Alganensh's condition was better. Her mood had improved only because she felt reassured that she was already in a hospital, where she could get help.

If Habtom had asked the hospital staff about her condition,

he would have learned that a medical assessment was a complex process. In a profession that one doesn't know, making subjective judgments and arriving at uninformed conclusions is especially dangerous and often wrong. In such instances, the wisest step is to ask those who know. Had he asked, Habtom would have learned the meaning of the *Habesha* proverb, "Hatati Iyu Felati," meaning, "Those who ask, know!" Unfortunately, Habtom, by character and temperament, was not inclined to thought processes that require deep inquiry.

Suddenly remembering that his shop was closed, Habtom woke from his internal monologue. He was concerned that his shop was closed and that he was wasting valuable time sitting alongside Alganesh, doing nothing. He told himself, "Soon the nurses will come and ask me to leave." With his reasoning thus reinforced, he was satisfied with his decision. Standing up instantly he said, "I have to go now. I will come in the evening and bring your dinner." With that, he bid Alganesh farewell and went out.

* 4 *

Tesfom had stayed with Medhn for about 30 minutes. After bidding her farewell, he went straight to where his car was parked, walking with his head down, deep in thought. When he reached his car, he raised his head, and found himself face to face with Habtom.

Habtom had gone to the parking area to fetch his bicycle. Both were surprised to see the other in the same hospital. Tesfom was the first to overcome his surprise and peppered Habtom with questions: "Wow Habtom, how come you are in the hospital? Are you ok? Is everybody ok?"

"I am ok. Alganesh was in extreme pain and I had to bring her to the hospital. They insisted she needed to be admitted. How about you? Are you ok? Is everybody ok?" Habtom shot back his own series of questions.

"Whaaat?! Alganesh is now in the hospital?! What kind of a

coincidence is this? Wow! You know that Medhn also became sick and called me from the office. I have brought her here. She has been admitted as well!" said Tesfom, incredulous at what had happened.

It was Habtom's turn to be amazed and he said, "Whaat?! Medhn is now in the hospital?! That is impossible! What is going on?!" He couldn't believe the coincidence of events.

After the initial astonishment, they agreed to go back to the wards to see both of them. They first went to Alganesh's room. She was surprised to see Habtom and Tesfom enter the room together. They quieted her curiosity and surprise by informing her that Medhn had also been admitted to room number four. Despite her ongoing pain and distress, Alganesh couldn't hide her immense surprise and disbelief that both of them were admitted to the hospital at the same time.

They quickly exchanged brief details of both women's health issues. After Alganesh was satisfied, they bid her farewell and went out to see Medhn, who was equally surprised, not only to see Tesfom, but also see that he was followed by Habtom. When they informed her that Alganesh was also admitted to room number eight, she was incredulous. Habtom briefly explained to her Alganesh's condition. After a short while, they bid Medhn farewell and left.

When Tesfom realized that Habtom had brought Alganesh with a horse cart, he felt bad. He said that, had he known, he would have helped. Habtom thanked him for his thoughtfulness. Tesfom expressed his hope that both would come out of the hospital safe and sound and promised Habtom, that he would take Alganesh back home, at any time of the day.

He asked Habtom if there was anything else, he could help him with. Habtom hesitated for a moment. Tesfom noticed his hesitancy and, without waiting for him to respond, said, "If you wish, instead of shutting your shop to bring dinner to Alganesh, I can pass by your place and pick it up for you."

Habtom's face immediately lit up and said, "That would be

awesome and extremely helpful. I could then go to Alganesh after I close the shop."

"No problem, I can do that with ease. Is there anything else I can help you with?" enquired Tesfom.

"If it is not a problem and if it wouldn't inconvenience you a lot, it would be very helpful if you could pass by my parents' house and inform them that Alganesh has been admitted to the hospital. I don't of course mean now. I mean after the office is closed," Habtom added, as an after-thought.

Immediately and without any hesitation, Tesfom said, "Sure! I have no problem with that. I am now going to go back to the office to wrap up a few things and then I will do that."

After agreeing on that, they bid each other farewell and went their separate ways.

* **5** *

While driving back, Tesfom's subconscious mind was in charge at the driving wheel, but his thoughts were on the events and coincidences of that afternoon. He arrived at his office immersed in deep thought. He worked at the State Bank, which was situated near the Government House (formerly The Commando Truppo). He telephoned the department of agriculture and talked to his father, Grazmach Seltene, briefly explaining to him the events of Medhn's admission to the hospital.

Since there were only a few minutes left before the office closed, he signed some urgent documents and started putting his files in order. He then drove directly home, where his father Grazmach Seltene and his mother Woizero Brkti were already waiting for him.

Grazmach was by now 50 years old, with bunches of grey hair above each ear lobe. He had attended the Italian school system and had attained the highest educational level available to natives at the time. During the Italian rule, natives were not allowed to progress beyond 4th grade. The Italian colonialists wanted educated natives to serve the system by being translators and small functionaries but they feared that if they proceeded beyond 4th grade, they might compete with the rulers and disprove the fallacy of "the black race being inferior to whites." Furthermore, they also feared that if natives were "too educated", they would become conscious of the abrogation of their rights and those of their countrymen, and might foment resistance to colonialism.

Grazmach was a government functionary. He thus had a comparatively comfortable middle-class life. He and W/ro Brkti had four children. Tesfom, like his mother, was lighter in complexion but in all other respects he looked exactly like his father. His mother, W/ro Brkti, was now 46 years old.

His parents were sitting in the second room, which they used as a living room. As soon as he came in, both hastily and simultaneously asked, "Is Medhn Ok?" with a clear sign of worry in their voices.

"I was with her a while ago. She is ok," said Tesfom calmly, wanting to reassure and calm their fears.

"How is her blood pressure?" asked Grazmach.

"Her blood pressure had gone up, but they have already started her on medication."

He could clearly see that his parents were truly worried. He wanted to reassure them further and said, "Anyway, there is nothing to worry about now, since she has already been admitted to the hospital. They will do everything that is needed."

His parents were clearly not very reassured by the words of their son. With a heavy sigh, both said in unison, "We hope the Lord himself will help Medhn."

Tesfom wanted to distract his parents from worrying about Medhn, so, he started recounting to them how he had encountered Habtom at the hospital and how Alganesh had also been admitted to the hospital. Momentarily distracted from Medhn's predicament, both showed utter surprise at the coincidence and started peppering him with questions.

While answering their questions, Tesfom kept darting his eyes towards the kitchen. As soon as they finished their questions, he stood up and told them he had asked the maid to prepare dinner for Medhn and he was going to check on her.

His parents wanted to go with him to visit Medhn, but he explained that visitors were not allowed at that hour. He promised that he would take them the next day at noon. He asked them to inform his brother Araya and his sisters, Msgana and Selam about Medhn's admission.

He went to the kitchen and got Medhn's packed dinner. He stood up, explaining that he had to leave immediately to take the food to Medhn, before it got cold and spoiled. At the time, people had no refrigerators, thermos flasks, Ice boxes or any other cold storage apparatus.

"Ok son, go in peace. Go with God," said his father.

"Don't worry son, with God's help, she will be ok," said his mother. She understood that below the calmness he was trying to portray, her son was deeply worried.

"Amen, father, Amen, mother," he said and immediately left.

* 6 *

As soon as he got into his car, Tesfom started to chart out his itinerary. He started thinking, 'If I first go to Habtom's parents and tell them what has happened, they will want to see her right away and will give me a hard time". He reasoned, "The best would be to go to Habtom's house, pick up Alganesh's dinner and then go to the hospital and deliver it. Then, I can tell Habtom's parents on my way back." He made his decision and was satisfied with his strategy.

Habtom's father, Bashay Goitom, was now 55 years old - five years older than Grazmach. Nevertheless, he didn't as yet have a single white hair. Even the goatee that he maintained on his chin was pitch black. With no formal education, he was a low-paid worker under an Italian baker. His wife, Woizero Lemlem was now 49 years old. They had five children.

Tesfom went to the hospital and delivered dinner to Medhn and Alganesh, and then he drove back to Bashay Goitom's house. After properly greeting Habtom's parents, he hesitated for a while, not sure where to begin. He quickly decided it was wiser and would be less of a shock to start with Medhn's admission. He started telling them about Medhn's urgent admission. They showed their concern by asking him questions about what happened, when, how serious it was, how she was doing, etc. He explained her condition calmly until they were satisfied.

He thought, 'so far, so good.' He then went on and started telling them about Alganesh's illness and her urgent admission to the hospital. As soon as he uttered the words hospital and urgent admission, W/ro Lemlem nearly stood up and instantly interrupted him by shouting, "Whaat?! Alganesh has been urgently admitted to the hospital?"

"*Adey* Lemlem, admission to the hospital is not necessarily a dangerous thing by itself," said Tesfom, trying to reassure her.

"Tesfom *wedey,* Lemlem is worried *proprio* because Alganesh has gone through so much the last few years. That is why Lemlem reacted the way she did," said Bashay Goitom, pulling his goatee.

Tesfom said that he knew what Alganesh had been going through the last few years. Despite her past condition, he assured them that she was doing fine, because he had just seen her in very good condition. He had made that statement to reassure them. The reality was, Tesfom was not sure of her medical condition.

The elders were not convinced by Tesfom's assurance. Despite that, they changed the subject and passed on to their next concern. They started insisting that they had to go and see her that evening. He explained to them that visitors were not allowed at that time. He convinced them that they could go and visit her the next day. He realized that Habtom's parents were much more worried about Alganesh than Habtom himself.

His errand accomplished, he stood up and said, "Allow me to go now. It has been quite an afternoon. Please inform your sons Dermas and Abrhaley and your daughters Lielty and Brur, about Alganesh's admission to the hospital." They nodded their heads.

Both parents wanted to stand up to see him off but he insisted that they sit. Both said, "Ok *Zwedey.* Go with God. Let's hope for the best."

Tesfom bid them farewell and drove back to his home.

* 7 *

The next day, Friday morning, Tesfom drove to work. As soon as he arrived, he heard of a very tragic accident that had happened on the Asmara-Mendefera-road. Two buses, each carrying more than 50 passengers each, had collided and rolled off the road into the valley below. Many lives were lost and many were seriously injured.

The highlands of Eritrea are mostly mountainous, lying between 2000 to 3000 meters above sea level. Most roads in highland Eritrea are carved out of the sides of chains of mountains. Menguda is a narrow and winding road and lies about 22 kilometers from Asmara. The roadway drops suddenly about 500 meters in altitude, in a mere 3-5 kilometers. On one side, it is bound by a huge rocky mountain, while on the other side, it is completely open, without a guardrail and bound by virtually nothing. One can only see a frightening 90-degree drop downhill. The roadway has a grim history of claiming lives.

The dead and the wounded from the tragic accident had to be picked up from the valley below and carried to the road above by people and donkeys. Since there were only two ambulances in Asmara, most victims had to be transported by trucks to the city. This caused further injury and suffering to the injured.

The number of people with serious injuries was beyond the main hospital's capacity. They had to distribute them into the two remaining small hospitals. Even then, the hospitals and their staff could not cope with the emergency. On top of that, the hospitals were overwhelmed with people rushing to enquire about their loved ones.

Generally, hospitals are places where people move about quietly and calmly. On that day, the hospitals were more like disorderly markets with people shouting and hurrying about. Ambulances and trucks constantly came in and out of the hospital, carrying the injured and the dead. Relatives and friends of the injured and dead were rushing in and out as well.

Diametrically opposing emotional scenes were evident everywhere. Some, who had already been told of the death of their loved ones, were wailing and crying violently and sending their frustration and anguish to the skies, with as much noise as they could. Others, who found out their loved ones were seriously hurt and critical, were wringing their hands and pointing up to the skies, begging their angels and the Almighty to preserve their loved ones.

Still others, who had no news of their loved ones, were running from one corner of the hospital to the other, trying to find out their fate. A few who saw that their loved ones had been miraculously saved with a few scratches, were practically jumping with joy and pointing toward the skies to thank their luck and their God. Amid all this chaos, the hospital staff were running from one place to the other, trying to be in two places at the same time.

The different emotional scenes playing out at the *Regina Elena* Hospital made it seem as if the three important stages of life: hope and happiness, suffering and pain and desperation and death were all being played out at the same time and place. But these are inseparable parts of the contract and package of life itself. Unexpected pleasant events in our lives make us ecstatic. Unexpected and unpleasant events make us numb and sad. Although we know from birth that these are part of the package that comes with the gift of life, we still never learn to accept and live our lives in peace with these impostors. That makes taking everything in our stride and living in happiness and peace much more difficult.

* 8 *

That same day at noon, Habtom and his parents went to the hospital to visit Alganesh. At nearly the same time, Tesfom and his parents also arrived at the hospital. They greeted each other warmly.

Grazmach Seltene and Bashay Goitom had been born in the same village and had lived as neighbors for many years, in one big compound, in *Igada Hamus* zone. The larger house on the right side of the compound, was occupied by Grazmach and his family. It had two rooms, one bathroom and a kitchen. Bashay lived on the left side of the compound in one large room, while sharing a bathroom in the compound with the other tenants.

Both families had already heard about the tragic accident that had happened, as the news had traveled by word of mouth, far and wide throughout the country. But what they had heard, did not even remotely prepare them for the confusion they saw, when they arrived at the hospital. Bashay was the first one to break his silence, "What can anyone say about such a tragic devastating accident? In our youth, such calamities happened only during wars, earthquakes or extended drought and hunger but now...." He, seemed unable to continue his train of thought, shaking his head left and right.

"Well, what can one say Goitom *Hawey.* So many families have been severely hurt and devastated. When such things happen, it shows us the vanity of our life and our world. We all tend to track and pursue only our own narrow private lives. Whenever we are fine, we are oblivious to the fact that others might be experiencing an unexpected tragedy. Otherwise, the good and the bad are always hanging over us and are housed within us," said Grazmach, shaking his head gravely.

"Absolutely! *Proprio*! That is how the world is. It reminds us of the vanity of life itself. Everyday a new life arrives into this world, while another one departs at the same hour," added Bashay, shaking his head.

"That is how it is!" sighed Grazmach., "By the way, what a strange coincidence that both our daughters-in-law have been admitted to the hospital at the same time!", he added. slightly changing the somber subject of life and tragic death.

"*Veramente*, truly that is indeed surprising and astonishing. We hope God will help both our daughters," said Bashay, looking upwards towards the skies.

Thereafter, both families went in and visited Alganesh and Medhn in their rooms. Every room was overflowing with visitors. Even the wards where there were no injured persons from the accident were full of people visiting their loved ones. In Eritrea, the high number of visitors is one of the main complaints of hospitals and their staff. Noticing this, Grazmach thought, "This is an indication of how much our community supports each other in times of sickness and adversity."

While Grazmach was engrossed in his own thoughts, both Aganesh and Medhn were in pain. Although they were surrounded with loving and well-wishing family members, it was clear to everyone that they were in severe pain. It was evident that Medhn was trying her best to fight the pain and not show it. Alganesh on the other hand, did not try to hide her pain and suffering. She was grimacing severely and making noises whenever she felt the pain.

Tesfom and Habtom were told by the nurses that their wives were in stable condition. Both started to slightly relax after they saw that every care was being given to their wives. They were informed that visiting hours were over, but if they wished and had the means, they could call and ask about their wives by telephone. All bid the two women farewell and wished them the best. The elders gave them their blessings and the two families departed to their respective homes.

* 9 *

To cope with the emergency, all doctors, nurses and other hospital staff were assigned to the emergency room and operation theater, leaving a bare minimum of staff in the rest of the wards. Even Obstetrics and Gynecology departments and the Children's Ward were left with a skeleton staff.

As would happen at such a time, these two wards were suddenly inundated with pregnant women at term and children admitted as emergencies. The influx soon exceeded what they could handle, but they continued working hard, as there was no point in panicking or asking for help, given what their colleagues faced in the emergency and surgical wards.

The entire hospital staff worked throughout the day without respite until, as the sun set, they were at a breaking point. Suddenly heavy rain began to pour, accompanied by rumbling thunder and lightning, which continued for 30 minutes. At that point, a power outage encompassed the whole city, and the entire hospital fell into complete darkness. In those days a power outage was extremely rare. Their only old generator started up and functioned at its best for about 2 hours, until it overheated and stopped completely at 9 pm.

With the loss of the generator, the hospital again fell into complete darkness, forcing staff to use candles and kerosene lanterns to concentrate on extremely urgent cases. There were no other lighting aids at that time.

No one at that time could have foreseen that, for many years to come, this tragic accident and the events that happened on that fateful day would have crucial effects on many lives.

* 10 *

Tesfom was at home when the power outage occurred. He called and learned that the hospital too, was in total darkness. Extremely worried, by 9:30 pm he dashed out to his car and drove to the hospital. As he stepped from the car, he realized that it was extremely cold and that he had again forgotten a sweater or overcoat.

He didn't feel the cold until he started shivering. Thinking only of Medhn, he failed to realize that he might be exposing himself to risk. Since he was of no help to anyone, the hospital staff advised him to leave and by 11 pm, they insisted that he leave. If he had a means of calling the hospital, they promised that they would respond to his calls and update him, if there was anything new in Medhn's condition. Finally, he left reluctantly.

* 11 *

At home, Tesfom was still restless. After about an hour, he called the hospital. No one responded to his repeated calls. He tried to appease himself by reasoning that it was difficult for them to respond to calls, given the darkness and the urgent unrelenting responsibility they had. Though he tried to reassure himself, he still felt restless.

He tried reading to himself to pass the time, but with poor lighting, he couldn't read much and immediately felt sleepy. He lay down on the bed, but the sleepiness that had engulfed him a few minutes ago, now eluded him. After about an hour of tossing in bed, he fell into a slumber.

At 2 am, he jumped out of bed. He thought he heard the phone ringing and hurriedly picked it up, but it was as silent as the darkness that engulfed him. He understood that, given the state of his mind, the phone had rung only in his imagination. Disappointed, he crawled back in bed.

But soon as he was under the blanket, the phone rang. This time, he was sure it was not his imagination. He ran back to the phone and, with his heart pounding, answered hastily, "Hello, hello!"

"Is this Tesfom's residence?" asked a voice.

"Yes, this is Tesfom," he answered hastily.

"This is Regina Elena Hospital. I am calling because it is urgent, otherwise I wouldn't be troubling you at this ungodly hour," said the courteous female voice calmly.

"Did you say urgent?! What kind of urgent?" asked Tesfom, his anxiety surging.

"Medhn has to undergo surgery and...,"

"Surgery?!" he shouted back in alarm.

"Please, don't be alarmed. The Doctor has decided that your wife will require surgery and...,"

"Wow, oh my God! surgery?!" he shot back again.

"Please understand that surgery is not necessarily dangerous. Oftentimes, surgery saves lives," she said firmly but calmly.

"I understand. I am sorry, I was alarmed by the mention of surgery. I overreacted, because I had not expected she would need surgery."

"It is ok, it is understandable. Anyway, since she will undergo surgery, we want you to come right away and sign for her. In addition, also tomorrow please bring two persons who can donate blood, in case she requires a blood transfusion. We need blood to replenish our stocks. Is that clear?"

"Yes, it is clear, thank you. I will come now." Saying that, he hung up the phone and said, "Oh my God, what kind of an unexpected complication?!" Tesfom slid into further worry and fear.

* 12 *

Tesfom could think of nothing but Medhn's condition. He picked up the clothes he had worn earlier and started putting them on. Suddenly, he remembered the cold that had earlier sent shivers down his spine and shaking his head at his absent mindedness, hastily put-on warmer clothes. He grabbed his overcoat and threw it on hastily as he hurried out the door.

Arriving at the hospital, he signed the necessary forms and asked permission to see Medhn. They said he could only see her for a minute, since they were preparing her for surgery. After thanking them, he saw her for only a moment and had to come out immediately.

Tesfom was reluctant to leave Medhn and go home to an empty house again. He collected enough courage to ask the nurses, if he could stay until Medhn was out of surgery. Though they did not grant him permission to stay, they promised to update him by telephone.

Leaving reluctantly, Tesfom suddenly remembered Alganesh. Feeling guilty and selfish for forgetting to ask about her condition, he returned to the ward. When the nurses saw him coming back, they thought he was going to give them a hard time. They asked why he was back and were relieved when he said, "I came back to ask for an update about Alganesh's condition. She was admitted yesterday at the same time as my wife. She is in room number eight."

The nurses smiled and said, "Oh Alganesh?! Everyone knows Alganesh well. She is doing fine, and we do not expect anything untoward in her condition. But she is giving everyone a hard time, because she doesn't have much resistance to pain."

He thanked them and bid them good night. He left the hospital with his head bowed down, deep in thought and full of worry. While he left the hospital, Tesfom felt as if he was seeing Medhn for the last time.

* 13 *

As soon as Tesfom arrived home, he went straight to bed. He tried his utmost to close his eyes and sleep, but the more he tried, the more sleep eluded him. It seemed as if sleep that is normally supposed to recharge our batteries, rest and relax our bodies, was purposely avoiding him. He tossed and turned until he felt as if he were sleeping in a stone bed. He struggled for what seemed like an eternity.

After 4 am, he could not take it anymore. He got out of bed. Extremely worried, he started repeatedly calling the hospital for about an hour. But, no one answered the phone. He told himself, "There must be something wrong, otherwise they would have called me by now. After all, they promised to call. It is nearly dawn; it is better if I go immediately." He was about to go, but decided to call one last time.

The phone rang. But still no answer. When he was about to put the cradle down, he heard a tired voice with a yawn say, "Hello."

"Hello, hello," he said frantically, adding, "Good morning," as an after-thought.

"We are thankful it is already morning. Let's hope it will be a good morning. The night, to say the least, was certainly not easy," said the voice firmly.

"I understand, you are absolutely right. I can imagine how overworked you have been and are. If you don't mind, please I want to enquire about Medhn, who is in room number four," he said, apprehensive and on edge.

"What is she to you?"

He felt his heart pounding and his mouth drying up and responded in a low voice, "I am her husband."

"Give me a minute," she said and heard her putting the phone down. He heard his heart pounding in his chest, his saliva dried up and his body was awash with cold sweat. After about two minutes, which for him seemed an eternity, he heard the cradle being lifted. His heart nearly stopped.

"Hello, congratulations, your wife had a successful surgery and delivery."

"Oh! Thank God! Thank you, thank you very much," he said, nearly jumping up.

"I am sorry we didn't call you earlier. We were extremely busy."

"It is ok. With everything that is going on, how could you?! Thank you again."

"I also have far sweeter and joyous news for you. You deserve double congratulations. Your wife gave birth to twins. A boy and a girl"

"Whaaat?! What did you say? Did I hear you right sister? Did you say a boy and a girl?" he nearly shouted.

"Yes, twins, a boy and a girl," she repeated calmly.

"Oh my God! Oh my God! Thank you, thank you so much sister," he said profusely, nearly bursting with relief and happiness.

"You are welcome. Well ok, I have to go now, *ciao*" she said, hanging up the phone.

As she was hanging up the phone, he remembered something and nearly shouted, "Hello, sister, hello, hello." The phone had already gone dead. He started to blame himself for forgetting to ask about Alganesh again. He started to dial the hospital number. He immediately heard, "Hello." It was the nurse he had just talked to.

"Hello sister. I am sorry for inconveniencing you further. This is not fair with all the emergency stuff that you guys are handling."

"It is ok. What is it?" she asked.

"Previously, you had given me great news about my wife's safe delivery and our being blessed with twins."

"Are you in doubt that I might have made a mistake?' she asked.

"No, no. Not at all. I just called to ask you about Alganesh, who is in room no eight. She was admitted yesterday. She is my friend's wife."

"Oh, everyone knows Alganesh by now. Did you say both were admitted at nearly the same time?" she asked again.

"Yes, at exactly the same hour!" he responded emphatically.

"Wow, that is surprising! What a coincidence!" she said.

"What do you mean sister?" he asked, confused.

"Amazing," she repeated and added, "Alganesh also gave birth to twins, a boy and a girl, at exactly the same time as your wife!"

For a moment, he couldn't believe his ears. Incredulous, he asked, "Whaaat? Did you say twins; a boy and a girl?!" he shouted anew. He added, "Are you joking sister?"

"We don't joke about such information!" she said sternly. Ok, I have to leave you now. The doctor is still with Alganesh, massaging her placenta, which is due any moment," saying that, she hung up the phone.

As she was hanging up, he said, "Thank you," not certain whether she heard him or not.

Medhn and Alganesh both had difficult pregnancies. Because of that, they had been examined by various doctors on different occasions. Medhn conceived three months after she got married. Alganesh did not conceive for two years. When she didn't conceive a year into her marriage, people started to talk. At that time, if a couple didn't give birth, it was considered evidence enough that the woman was infertile; the fertility of the man was in no doubt.

Alganesh was scared, because she knew the consequences of being infertile and the stigma attached to it. It might mean the end of her marriage and being sent back home to her parents. She started going to churches and monasteries praying and begging God, Jesus, Mary and all the angels to intervene on her behalf and bless her with a child.

She had started taking offerings to all the churches, convents and monasteries. She knelt and prostrated herself for hours in deep prayer. When her prayers were not answered into her second year, she and every family member was alarmed.

Alganesh stuck to her belief and persisted in visiting far away churches and monasteries where it was said miracles were performed. Finally, her prayers and her perseverance were answered and she was able to conceive. But because she had conceived so late and after so much effort, she was apprehensive lest anything went wrong with her pregnancy.

The doctors who were examining Medhn and Alganesh had instructed them to have regular check-ups and had warned them to go to a hospital for delivery, since it was their first pregnancy and both had certain complications. At that time, it was the norm to deliver at home. More than 90% of women in Eritrea used to deliver at home with the help of their mothers, relatives or neighbors who had previous experience.

After Medhn conceived, Tesfom had extensively read about pregnancies and delivery. His anxiety and worry increased after she developed hypertension and even more with the doctor's repeated warnings.

And now, after all this ordeal, Tesfom was being congratulated and told he was blessed with twins. At first it seemed unreal. He didn't change his position or move from the chair he was sitting on. It took a long time to sink in. When he was sure that he was not dreaming, he stood up abruptly, and, shooting his fisted right hand up into the air, repeatedly shouted, "'Yes! Yes! Yes!"

He sat down suddenly, scolding himself for shouting like a child at a victory that really did not belong to him and in which he had only a small part to play. He shook his head, chastising himself for acting like a child. After reminding himself to thank his God, he began to make plans to inform family and tackle other priorities. He took a paper and a pen and started to scribble notes.

* 14 *

The first item on Tesfom's list was to go to Habtom's place. It took a few minutes to arrive at the house, but the door was firmly shut. He looked at his watch and told himself, "He must be sleeping. He can't go out at this hour. It is impossible."

He knocked three times, with no response. He started to wonder whether Habtom was at home. He knocked harder for the last time and heard a slight movement, followed by a distinct male voice calling, "Who is that?"

"It is me, Tesfom!"

The door was immediately opened. Habtom stood before him

looking half-asleep. "I have been knocking repeatedly. Don't tell me you slept that deeply. How is that possible?"

"Of course, I did. Why not? I slept very well until you woke me up!"

"Man! you are lucky. Sleep was impossible for me. The whole time, I was worrying about the wives we admitted urgently to the hospital."

"Come on now! You are exaggerating! You know well enough, that about 95% of our sisters and mothers give birth at home. Why would you worry and lose sleep over two women who are in hospital, under the care of doctors and nurses?"

"Well, I guess we are not the same. Anyway, I am glad that at least one of us slept well. By the way, you will not believe the news I have!" said Tesfom, with excitement in his voice, purposely changing the subject.

"Did you call?" asked Habtom.

"It is a long story. I called. I went. I called again. I went again. I will tell you the whole story..." Habtom did not allow him to continue.

Habtom interrupted him excitedly by saying, "Did you get news?!"

"News? I have the greatest and the most fascinating update! Both of us have been blessed with a boy and a girl."

"Who got a boy? You or me?" asked Habtom, hurriedly.

"You!" said Tesfom jokingly, knowing well how important the subject of gender was to Habtom.

"Then why are you still addressing me simply as Habtom?", said Habtom, inflating his body and his ego.

Tesfom was about to respond when Habtom hurriedly added, "From now on, you should start addressing me as '*Abu Weled*,' Father of a Son! Or is it because you only got a girl?" said Habtom, laughing heartily and putting on an expression of pride.

"Man, you are always something. For you, anything and everything is always a competition you have to win!" Tesfom shook his head and added, "Have you understood that you also got a daughter?"

"Whaaat? What are you saying? Didn't you just tell me that I had a son. Why are you trying to mix things up?" asked Habtom, a little confused.

"I guess you are not wide awake yet. What I am telling you is that Alganesh has given you twins- a boy and a girl!"

"Whaaat? Wow this is great! Then from now on you have to address me as, Habtom, Father of Two!" Habtom laughed heartily again.

Tesfom again shook his head and asked, "If so, then how are you going to address me?"

"Well, what else can I call you, except Tesfom, father of a girl!" said Habtom. He again went into a frenzy of laughter.

Tesfom noticed that Habtom was uncharacteristically in a great mood that morning. Tesfom himself was also in a great mood and since he was enjoying the whole show, he decided to continue. "What would you say, if I also told you, Medhn has also given birth to a boy and a girl?" asked Tesfom.

"Whaaat? Come on, *Teal Yaho*! That is impossible! Don't tell me you have been pulling my leg the whole morning? Come on now, please tell me the truth," said Habtom earnestly.

"My dear, I told you the truth from the very beginning. It was only because you wanted to believe what you wished. Anyway, though it is hard to believe, the true fact is Medhn and Alganesh have both been blessed with twins!" said Tesfom seriously.

"Come on Tesfom, please, is that the real truth?" said Habtom, who by now felt uncertain of the facts. As an after-thought, he stretched his right arm towards Tesfom, with palms pointing upwards. Then he asked Tesfom to swear by striking his hand. Tesfom immediately brought his right hand and slapped Habtom's hand saying, "I swear by my father's name". This is a common form of making an oath in highland Eritrea.

"That is the truth and the whole truth, so help me God!' said

Tesfom sarcastically. Then he became serious and added, "Seriously though, that is the truth! Congratulations, to both of us!" said Tesfom and extended his hand to Habtom. They locked and shook their hands firmly.

"Wow! this is indeed amazing and great news!" said Habtom.

"Indeed, it is. Alganesh had no complications, however Medhn had to undergo surgery."

"Surgery?! Oh, poor Medhn. Anyway, we should be thankful that both are now safe and sound."

"Yes, absolutely. Anyway, let me go now. Let us tell our families the good news and then let's meet at the hospital," said Tesfom. He stood up, bid Habtom farewell and headed straight to his parent's and sibling's homes and gave them the good news.

Tesfom had only known that Alganesh had given birth to twins, but at the time he got this information, Aganesh was not yet out of the delivery room. He hadn't understood the significance of the nurse's mentioning 'massaging the placenta.'

Both new parents had no clue that soon after delivering the twins, Alganesh had fallen into mortal danger. At the same time Tesfom hung up the phone, the doctors were fighting to save her life. If both parents had this information, that morning's festive euphoric mood would have been different.

* 15 *

On Saturday morning, after informing their respective families, Tesfom and Habtom hurried to the hospital, eager to see their wives and newborns. But, when they asked permission, the nurses said that no one would be allowed to see them until further notice, because both women were still very weak. Their disappointment and anxiety were evident in their body language.

The nurses asked Tesfom if he had made the arrangement for blood donation. He told them that when he was informed that Medhn had a successful surgery and delivery, he had assumed there was no need for blood. The nurses told him the blood was needed for Alganesh.

Both fathers were confused and looked at each other. The nurses explained that after safe delivery of the twins, Alganesh had encountered a complication from a retained placenta and as a result she had lost a lot of blood. Her life was in immediate danger and had only been saved after a speedy and instant transfusion. The nurses emphasized the need for blood to replenish their stocks and care for Alganesh.

Both immediately went to the laboratory and donated blood, after which they were permitted to see the newborns through a designated window. Looking through the assigned window, they saw two nurses, each holding two tiny babies wrapped up in clothes.

Each father tried to identify which ones were his. Habtom immediately pointed at the ones on the right and told Tesfom, "Those seem to look like mine." Tesfom made hand signals to the nurses, who understood what he meant and indicated that the ones on the right were Tesfom's. The men laughed profusely, expressing their joy and happiness. They stood there smiling, laughing and shining with pride at being first-time parents. They did not want to leave the window until the nurses indicated that the show was over.

As they reluctantly walked away, their thoughts immediately turned to their wives. Since both were still not out of danger, the worry and anxiety they previously felt came back anew. They returned to their homes with mixed feelings and updated their two families, who were preparing to rejoice and celebrate. As soon as they heard the update, a cloud of uncertainty spread over both families.

* 16 *

The next day, Sunday, both Medhn and Alganesh made good progress and their husbands were permitted to visit them. The nurses also informed them that other visitors could visit the mothers during lunch break. Both women were still weak but in a stable condition, and although their bodies showed the trauma they had gone through, their faces glowed with relief, gratitude and pride. The newborns were bundled up, sleeping heartily and soundly.

The hospital was still overworked and under immense pressure because of the tragic accident. Most women with normal deliveries were immediately discharged, but the nurses said that Medhn and Alganesh will stay in the hospital to receive care and regain their strength. The nurses informed the new fathers of the things they needed to bring to their wives and the newborns.

When the noon visiting hours were over, everyone was reluctant to leave. They were herded out by the hospital staff. As parents and families were going out, the newborns were sleeping comfortably, unaware of their surroundings and impervious to the fact that the day and horrendous circumstances that announced their arrival into this world might have an impact in shaping their future.

* 17 *

The *Regina Elena* hospital was still overflowing with visitors from the countryside and the surrounding towns and cities, who had come to see their many seriously injured relatives and friends. The visitors were from all over Eritrea, with various cultural backgrounds and representing all age groups.

Those visitors who came from rural areas and were new to the city and the hospital, could be seen rushing from one place to the other, trying to locate their loved ones. The clothing they wore and their hair style set them apart from those living in towns. Although a few of them had some sort of crude sandals made from old car tires, most wore no shoes at all.

On Monday, many well-wishers and family members from villages and towns came to visit Medhn and Alganesh and to express their happiness at the safe delivery of the twins and to wish the best to the two families.

Tesfom's mother, *W/ro* Brkti and Habtom's mother *W/ro* Lemlem, had their hair braided in the *Albasso* fashion. They wore long wide *Kemishes (dresses)*, that stretched down to their ankles with a *Nexela (*shawl*)* on top. Their faces glittered with joy and pride at being first-time grandmothers.

Grazmach's younger sister, whose husband died a few months ago, was standing beside W/ro Brkti. Tesfom's aunt had come from her village and was staying in Grazmach's house with her adolescent daughters and two younger boys. The boys' hair was partly shaved, denoting their pre-adolescence status. One had a *Kuncho-Kuncho* and the other a style known as *Telela,* comparable to hair styles that later became popular among youth in the U.S. In memory of her recently deceased husband, their mother had braided and then tied her hair. This was a style known as *Mdrmam,* worn by women in mourning. Her daughter wore her hair in the *Game* fashion, typically worn by young unmarried teenage girls. Females braided their hair in different styles, each of which denoted their age and status in the society.

Habtom's uncle who lived in a nearby town wore *Khaki* shorts and shirt with a *Nexela* top. Both of his adult sons also wore Khaki shorts and shirts on top. Among the visitors were two Muslim families. Their women wore colorful kemishes reaching down to their ankles. One had her nose pierced with a ring in one nostril. The men wore full white gowns (jelebias) with a scarf. One of them wore a colorful turban, (Meememya), the other just a white turban, (Kuffyet).

Grazmach and Bashay greeted and congratulated each other, sharing their praise, "God has helped us. He is kind and gracious." They then proceeded to thank all the people who had come to express their happiness and good wishes. Tesfom and Habtom were ecstatic. They were going from one person to the other, thanking everyone and beaming with happiness.

* 18 *

Tesfom and Habtom were now respectively 23 and 25 years old, while, Medhn was merely 18 and Alganesh 21 years old. After a week, both Medhn and Alganesh were discharged from the hospital. As promised, Tesfom first took Alganesh, her twins and Habtom to their home and then came back for Medhn and the infants and happily and proudly took them home.

The time when Tesfom was joyously and proudly taking the twins home was extremely significant. The twins were born at a very critical and historic juncture in Eritrean history. It was the year of the beginning of the U.N. enforced Federation between Eritrea and Ethiopia. The British Administration which lasted ten years had just wound up its mandate. The federation was later on unlawfully and unilaterally dismantled by Ethiopia and Eritrea was declared a 14th province of Ethiopia. This led to a bloody, destructive and prolonged 30-year war, which finally ended up with the independence of Eritrea in 1992.

* 19 *

When after going through the rigors of a complicated labor and surgery, Medhn returned home, her complexion looked darker than normal. As far as physical features went, her endowments were all above average. She was neither too tall, nor short, neither too dark, nor too light and her facial features were all above average. She wouldn't be referred to as extremely beautiful but she was definitely attractive. In fact, Medhn was often referred to as a captivating woman, not only because of her physical endowments, but rather more because of her sweetness, thoughtfulness and natural likability.

Tesfom on the other hand was tall, light skinned, with dark silky wavy hair, a straight nose, large round eyes and beautiful teeth that matched all the rest of his features. His white teeth were lined up in exact rows, proportionally mindful of their size and place. Tesfom's smile and laughter captivated everyone around him. He was an extremely handsome and elegant young man. It was as if he was made with the utmost care to ensure every part was made in the exact size and proportion and fell into the perfect place.

As soon as Medhn arrived home, she knelt and thanked God for not only saving her life but also blessing her with twins. After her safe delivery and surgery, Tesfom had been busy shopping around town. He had been counting the days for Medhn to return home, so she could appreciate all the wonderful things he bought.

When Medhn did start to look around, she realized that their bedroom looked different. She couldn't believe her eyes and started admiring everything that was new. Moving from one item to the next, she was expressing and showing her appreciation for every single item.

"How did you manage to buy all these and where did you get the time?" she asked incredulously.

"Time was not that much of a problem. I bought most of the things by myself and the rest with the help of my brother Araya. The problem was not the logistics of buying. The hardest part was not having a list of the things we needed to buy; and when I asked you to get prepared ahead of time, you declined and flatly refused!" he reminded her.

"Well, I didn't want to prepare anything before I knew if I was going to deliver safely and come out of it alive!" She said firmly.

"Well…," said Tesfom. She did not let him finish, she instantly interrupted him.

"My beloved Tesfom, giving birth is not an easy feat; especially with a pregnancy like mine that carried added complications. You need to consider the many unexpected things that could go wrong. I was not sure whether I would come out of it alive and even if I did, I was not sure whether I would deliver a live healthy baby. I never believed I would come out this safely and or that I would be blessed with twins!" said Medhn smiling softly.

"Oh my God! you never give yourself peace of mind! You should understand that, however much you worry, there will always be so many things beyond your control. Why do you have to torture yourself worrying about what might or might not happen!" said Tesfom, smiling sarcastically, but also making a serious point.

"Well, my dear, a woman has to think of everything!" said Medhn emphatically. Her attention suddenly shifted and she started looking again at all the things he had bought. "Wow Tesfom! you actually didn't need a list at all. There is nothing you missed," she said, appreciating Tesfom's efforts and thoughtfulness.

"Oh, come on! This is not a big thing. Even if we are men, it is not something beyond us. You women go through nine months of pregnancy and then face the rigors and dangers of child birth and give life. As if that was not enough, you go on to breastfeed, pamper, feed and raise men and women," said Tesfom seriously and pensively.

"Well...," said Medhn. Tesfom was not finished.

"When we got married, I did not appreciate the role women play in our lives and society. I started to understand your important role only when you became pregnant and were going through its rigors. And when you were admitted to the hospital and I saw how much you suffered and nearly sacrificed your life, I felt very bad. I felt useless. If our responsibility as men is just to sit around like roosters, mate occasionally, stand on a pedestal, blow our horns, doing and contributing nothing else, then we are practically useless!" he said, with a serious expression in his face.

"That is a responsibility and a privilege given to us females by nature and God," replied Medhn equally seriously. "If one is graced with such a huge role and privilege, then one should also take the responsibility that goes with it! Women only need someone who truly understands, appreciates and cares about their role and contribution. Above everything else, that understanding and sympathy is all that we women need," she added, equally seriously.

She instantly relaxed her pensive face. Then her attention shifted again and she started going over all the stuff Tesfom had bought. There was a baby crib, mattress, sheets, washtub, baby blanket, caps, socks, cotton diapers, clothes, etc. She saw that everything he bought was expensive and of high quality. She told herself, "If Tesfom was responsible for purchasing everything we needed, our expenses would have skyrocketed and been beyond our means." Everyone in the family believed that was Tesfom's weakness, while he always believed that was his strength. She decided to broach the subject in passing.

"Everything is amazing. But Tesfom hawey, if you were the one that purchased all our stuff all the time, we wouldn't be left with any money!" she said smiling sarcastically.

"Medhn, come on! I have repeatedly explained this to you. People only live once. I don't like to live my life miserably, only counting money!"

"Well, there is also what we call 'average' Tesfom. But I guess, that is not in your nature."

"Come now Medhn! Tell me truthfully. Are you not happy that everything I have bought is high quality stuff?" he asked.

"Who can ever doubt or deny that you would buy otherwise, and of course I am happy!" said Medhn emphatically.

"That is, it! Nothing else matters!", saying that, he jumped up and kissed her on the cheeks.

"God bless you, Tesfom *Hawey*!" she said. Suddenly, she grimaced with pain.

"You are still in pain, right?" asked Tesfom concerned.

"It is ok. This is normal," said Medhn, reassuring him.

As Tesfom was about to say something, their heartfelt conversation of love and thoughtfulness was interrupted by neighbors, who came to express their good wishes. Tesfom received them in the sitting room.

* 20 *

Habtom was a well-built muscular man. He had a darker complexion, with a flat nose, large lips, small furtive eyes, short black hair and teeth that stood wherever they chose and grew however they wanted. His teeth were extremely uneven. He had excellent physical features in his torso and the rest of his body, but his forehead was always furrowed and he seldom smiled.

Alganesh, on the other hand, was an extremely beautiful woman. She was tall, light skinned, with long, shiny, silky, wavy hair, large eyes, beautiful teeth, and a nose and a mouth that perfectly matched all the rest.

When Habtom got married, his best friends' joke was always accompanied with roaring laughter. "Our friend Habtom was smart! He specifically chose Alganesh with the intention of improving the genes in his family tree!" they said, alluding to his facial features. He was always uncomfortable with those jokes and comments, because he had no answer to them.

After being blessed with twins, Habtom was filled with immense happiness and pride. He felt and believed that it was his manhood that gave him twins. He was constantly amplifying his part and minimizing Alganesh's role in the arrival of the twins.

One afternoon, Alganesh was lying in bed. Habtom was seated in front of her, and they were chatting with Habtom's friends, who had come to visit. The subject slowly moved towards giving birth.

One of his friends, addressing Habtom said, "It is amazing! After lying low for a long time, you finally brought twins."

"You know me!" Habtom said, inflating himself. Then he added, "When other men couldn't even father one, I made sure my wife got twins!" he said, sitting tall with an air of pride.

Habtom had been repeating the same statement to all the men that came to visit. Alganesh had listened patiently for days, but this time, she was exasperated and could not take it anymore.

After his friends left, she said sourly, "My God, Habtom! Instead of thanking God for his grace, you make it look as if you manufactured the twins by yourself! Don't forget, that I am the one who gave birth to them."

Habtom was momentarily disconcerted; he couldn't come up with an appropriate answer. So, he tried to wriggle out by saying, "Well, the real truth is, you were able to carry twins only because of me! That is the real truth!"

Alganesh was furious, but was still able to control herself. She calmly said, "If fathers can claim that, then what are we mothers going to say? How can any man in his right mind ever claim total responsibility for a human being that a woman carried within her for nine months?! How can you dismiss the fact that we not only go through the rigors of pregnancy, but also finally shed our blood and put our lives on the line, to deliver a human being?"

Normally, this irrefutable logic would have been more than enough for anyone to bow, accept and admit defeat. But not Habtom! He wouldn't be perturbed by logic, rationality or reality. He still had the courage and the impertinence to say with an air of pride, "Even so, it is I, who made it possible for you to carry and deliver not one, but two babies!"

"Ok, let it be! No problem. I should have known better than to argue with you. I know that once you make a statement, no logical argument would ever persuade you to change your mind. However, no matter what you or anyone else says or thinks, no one can ever take away the reality of what all of us women bring to our families and our societies!"

As Habtom was opening his mouth to answer back again, new guests arrived and they dropped the subject.

* 21 *

While they were in the hospital, Alganesh and Medhn were swamped with visitors and well-wishers for a whole week. This stream did not decrease even after they were discharged.

Three days after going home, a porridge ceremony was organized by the two families. In the highlands of Eritrea, it is customary to invite female neighbors and family members to a porridge (Geat) party or ceremony. Food in Eritrea is not traditionally eaten on individual plates, but is rather eaten communally from a large plate in groups. This is known as eating in a *Meadi,* which does not only represent food, but more broadly represents the sanctity of communal life.

Women neighbors, friends and family members in both households were invited to the porridge ceremony for Alganesh and Medhn. Upon finishing, the women-folk give thanks to God, Jesus Christ, Mary, the Angels and bless the parents and newborns with wishes for long healthy lives. After everyone is satisfied, the large porridge plate is taken away by the hosts. At this point, all the guests show their appreciation and joy by shrieking '*Eiliilileeee*' in unison.

The porridge ceremony that was held on the same day in both households was successfully concluded with joy and happiness. Meanwhile, the twins were gaining weight and becoming stronger by the day.

* 22 *

Since becoming a father, Habtom had started to spend more time at home. Even when he was at home, Habtom would never think of lending a hand or assisting in a household chore. For him, that would be an affront to his manhood.

Since Alganesh understood his beliefs well, she never expected any help from him. Alganesh did not actually expect him to physically help her with household chores. She knew this very well, since her childhood; she was already accustomed to the assigned gender roles. The only thing Alganesh expected and wanted from her husband was a simple recognition and acknowledgement of her contribution. But even such a simple recognition was never forthcoming from Habtom. He had the firm belief that was how it always was and should always be!

Along with caring for the twins and her household responsibilities, Alganesh would at times be swamped with too many chores to do. Under the circumstances, she sometimes felt on edge. Occasionally she would utter a few words or phrases that denoted her frustration and disappointment.

Habtom was chatting with his parents who had come to visit, while Alganesh was busy washing clothes, diapers, cooking, bathing, breastfeeding, cleaning and arranging the house. All morning, she was rushing from one chore to the next. As if all that was not enough, Habtom interrupted her occasionally, asking her to bring something for him and his parents.

At one point, Alganesh couldn't take it anymore, "Your son brags day and night about having twins and yet he never lifts a finger to help, even when he sees my two hands full and overwhelmed," she blurted impulsively.

"My dear Alganesh *Gualey*, a man should be a man! A man must not do a woman's chore. It should be each one to his own responsibility. After all, that is how we raised our five children!" said W/ro Lemlem, with a critical tone in her voice.

"Your mother-in-law is right dear Alganesh *Gualey*, said Bashay, airing his support for his son and his wife's viewpoint. "*Proprio*, nothing else is required of a man, if he works hard enough and succeeds in bringing enough money to satisfy his family's needs. As you very well know, Habtom in that regard is a *leone* (lion) to his home and family,"

"Do you know why she is raising this issue? It is because she heard Tesfom helps Medhn in washing the infants and getting up at night to help her hold the twins!" said Habtom sarcastically, pleased by his parents' support and feeling vindicated.

"No! No!" said W/ro Lemlem vehemently, at the mention of what Tesfom was doing. It was as if she heard a profanity being uttered in front of her. Moving her mouth from side to side, with a contorted face, she added, "My God, this is totally foreign to us. This is not in our culture nor in our upbringing!"

Alganesh quickly understood that she had made a huge mistake. She reminded herself, that if her own husband, who was much younger and supposed to know better didn't understand her, it was unreasonable to expect his parents to do so. She rebuked herself for being hasty. She knew there was no way of unsaying what she had uttered. She said to herself, "Damn Alganesh, you very well know that when you talk, you should before-hand examine and choose the time, the place and especially your audience," she said biting her lips. She started thinking fast about a strategy for retreat.

At that point, she heard her father-in-law say, "You see Alganesh dear, a woman gains respect when she acts like a woman," and putting the final nail into the coffin he added, "and a man is respected when he acts like a man!"

"I have repeatedly tried to explain to her the wisdom of what you said," said Habtom, already starting to taste the sweet victory he was being crowned with, more certain than before of his principles.

At that point, Alganesh knew there was nothing she could do, except let them be with their misguided views. So, she heard herself say, "My intention from the start was not at all to persuade you to see my point of view. I think it was my exhaustion that led me into unreasonable and illogical expectations. I am sorry. After all, even if I labor or become exhausted, I am only working for my babies!"

Bashay and W/ro Lemlem were very happy that Alganesh immediately saw her folly and accepted their logic quickly. Thanking her, they both said, "Thank you *Za Gualey!* We have always known how intelligent and perceptive you were."

Habtom was ecstatic in his victory. He smiled profusely, showing his uneven teeth and stretching his small eyes until they seemed to pop out. That was the end of the discussion. Alganesh made a promise to herself that she would never raise the subject again.

* 23 *

Grazmach's children were all born and raised in their rented house, in *Idaga Hamus* zone. When Tesfom and Araya were in elementary school, Grazmach had the financial capacity to rent a better house in a better neighborhood. He was not the kind who spent his savings on what he considered untimely and unnecessary expenses. At the same time, he was also not the kind who would put his wife and children through a miserable life of thrift, just for the sake of hoarding money.

Grazmach had a guiding principle, which he considered a cornerstone of his life. In a nutshell, he referred to it in Italian as, '*Tutto in moderazione*,' meaning, "Everything in moderation." He repeatedly would say, "Everything, including life itself, should be lived in moderation. People should eat, drink, dress, speak, spend, and save moderately and be content with moderate gratification. If we live moderately, and become thankful and gratified with what we have, then our lives will have contentment and balance."

To expand on his principle, he repeatedly asserted that the world and life don't ever provide 100% of what we desire; if we are lucky, we might end up with 90%, but we should be thankful for even just 70% or 80%. We should be satisfied with what we have and enjoy life to the fullest, instead of ruining and wasting our lives by constantly complaining about what we lack.

When Tesfom and Araya were finishing elementary school, Grazmach had saved enough money to buy a small house. However, he decided against doing so, because he first wanted to save enough money to ensure his family's future financial needs in health and education.

When his eldest children were finishing middle school, Grazmach decided it was time to improve their lifestyle by investing in a house. So, the family moved from their rented *Edaga Hamus* house, to a new house situated in an area known as *'Geza Banda Tilian,'* meaning Italian infantrymen's houses. This was later renamed, *'Addis Alem'*, although it is still sometimes referred to by its original name.

Their new home had its own courtyard, a veranda, two bedrooms, a sitting room, a kitchen and one bathroom. The area was comparatively sparsely populated so it was a peaceful and quiet neighborhood.

* 24 *

Grazmach was sitting in the living room, deep in thought. Over his clothes, he was wearing a (*Gabi*), a hand woven thick white cotton wraps to make sure that none of the biting cold would find a way in. But, at that very moment, Grazmach's thoughts were not on the cold, but rather on the circumstances of Tesfom's life.

Grazmach was happy and thankful that he had been blessed with grandchildren. His thoughts went back to Tesfom's younger years. Since childhood, Tesfom had always been a hard-working student with an exemplary character. He was very kind and responsible and used to advise his siblings to follow his example. But there was one important detail about Tesfom that Grazmach did not appreciate. He insisted on having only the best quality materials in what he wore and was extremely interested in his appearance. Grazmach did not believe much in outer looks, but he was not too worried about his son's minor 'weakness,' because he felt that it would disappear as he matured.

Tesfom maintained his outstanding success and personality, until he finished middle school. In Eritrea at that time, there was no high school, and the highest grade anyone could attend was the eighth grade. He was therefore sent to Sudan, to pursue his education at the Comboni College in Khartoum.

While in Khartoum, Grazmach later came to learn, Tesfom began to change some of his good habits and character. Although he still had no problems with his studies, he had started indulging in alcohol, smoking and going out with too many friends.

At the age of 19, Tesfom successfully completed what was then referred to as higher education in Eritrea. He came back to his country and his home and started a job. Grazmach knew that after his return, his son had quit smoking, but he still associated with the wrong kind of friends and continued drinking. Tesfom was trying his best to hide this side of his life, because he knew that it would disappoint his father.

After over a year into his employment, Tesfom informed his father that he wished to buy a car. Grazmach was not happy with this decision. Guided by his life principle, he felt Tesfom was being hasty, impractical and irresponsible by wanting to invest in something he didn't need.

He tried his best to convince his son to drop the idea, telling him, "Come on Tesfom, Asmara is a small town, why do you need a car and where would you go with it? Or is it because you want to show off? If that is so, you'd better think twice, my son." He recounted to Tesfom what his own father used to tell him in his youth: "Those who go around trying to impress others with what they have and possess, might eventually, after they have spent it all, find themselves wanting to hide from everyone!"

Tesfom had been riding a well-known British model bicycle, made in the U.K. Back then, those few Eritrean natives who owned bicycles were considered like car owners. At the time, most natives did not even own a bed to sleep on, let alone a bicycle or a car. As a result, natives who owned bicycles were very few. Even the total number of cars in town was very small. Anyway, notwithstanding his father's advice, Tesfom stuck to his desire. Grazmach gave in and Tesfom bought a German made Volkswagen beetle, on loan.

Grazmach started to contemplate about Tesfom establishing a family of his own. After serious consideration, Grazmach thought, getting married would be a good idea and now was the right time for Tesfom. Despite this, Grazmach believed that marriage should take place only when his son wanted it and was ready for it. Nevertheless, he wanted Tesfom to start thinking about it, so he started to indirectly throw in the idea of marriage intermittently within conversations, without directly expressing his wish.

Three years elapsed after Tesfom's graduation. Tesfom was now ready to settle down. He decided to marry. He chose his own bride and wed Medhn to be his future wife and partner.

* 25 *

Grazmach became increasingly gratified by the changes Tesfom made after his marriage. After the twins were born, he started to notice even further positive changes in his son. One afternoon as he was immersed in deep thought, reminiscing about his son, W/ro Brkti interrupted his thoughts by coming in with tea and bread.

"I was just thinking about the changes Tesfom has made since his marriage. Since the birth of the twins, I am so happy to notice even further positive changes in him. Have you noticed these changes?" asked Grazmach, expecting agreement and support.

"What changes are you talking about?! Even before his marriage, there was nothing wrong with my son! He didn't need any changes. It is only because you have always been too strict. At his age, staying out late and going around with friends to have a good time is normal," said W/ro Brkti, going straight to the defense of her eldest son.

"Come on Brkti, don't get defensive! Don't forget he is also my son. But we have to face the truth. It is true, as a student he was exemplary and superior to his peers, but after acquiring good-for-nothing friends, he was close to drowning. At one point, I was not even sure if he was ready to assume the responsibility of establishing a family. But now from what Medhn is telling me, he helps her wash the twins and even gets up at night to help. It is an encouraging and amazing development."

"It would have pleased me, if you had expressed your admiration for his many other good qualities. However, I don't like it when I see you try to give him recognition for doing petty stuff. In fact, washing the twins and getting up at night is not something he should be doing. He is a man and should only do manly chores, otherwise he is going to be looked down upon," muttered W/ro Brkti, seriously and a little angrily.

"Brkti please, don't forget that they are raising twins!"

"What if they are raising twins?! She has domestic help. Don't forget that I raised our children without any help!" she reminded him, stressing the "I."

Grazmach could not deny the veracity of what she was saying. With a trace of apology he said, "You are absolutely right. In our era, we never understood that we needed to help. Let alone help your wife, it was also considered demeaning for a man to perform a woman's chore."

"So, how can you now encourage and support Tesfom to perform something you have never done your entire life?"

"Well, now the times have changed Brkti. Just because we didn't do it in our times, it doesn't necessarily make it right now. To tell you the truth, we men became spoiled only after we started living in towns working for others, instead of working for ourselves. Otherwise, in our villages, except for a few particular chores that fell strictly to the man or woman, our parents were performing and sharing the rest of the chores equally."

"I have no opposition to his taking care of his children and family. What I don't like is, his performing female chores. He could help with other duties," said W/ro Brkti, sticking to her position.

"Brkti, washing your children and getting up at night is not necessarily only a woman's chore!"

"My main worry is that, if he does this today, then later he will be asked and expected to do more and more of his wife's tasks."

"I perfectly understand your worries Brkti," said Grazmach with serious concern. "I hope Medhn will be intelligent and thoughtful enough to understand and appreciate this without demanding too much from him. After all, we should be grateful to those who go out of their way to be helpful. We should not demand the impossible from them, just because they were helpful in the first place. If possible, we need to reciprocate and hold such persons in high esteem. If we abuse their thoughtfulness and trust, it demonstrates our unworthiness!"

"Well, Grazmach, you know very well that, in the end, it is the people who have been used to getting our assistance that become disappointed in us."

"What do you mean?" he asked, not sure of what she meant or where she was heading.

"So many relatives and friends, whom you have assisted in different ways, have forgotten your role and turned their back on you, simply because you have not lived up to their expectations even on unimportant matters and issues. Isn't that true?" asked W/ro Brkti, turning the subject into a very serious societal issue.

"You are right there. I guess it is because we have higher expectations on some rather than others. Whenever we encounter a few shortcomings and faults, we tend to forget all the good things they have done and rush to condemn them. It is like we tend to judge and condemn them not on the 80%-90% of their performance, but rather on the 10-20% of their shortcomings or failures. Conversely, we don't judge or condemn those who never care or do anything for others, because we have no expectation from them and accept their behavior as their nature. It is truly irrational and illogical, but I guess that is how we human beings are!" said Grazmach, shaking his head gravely.

"Exactly! that is what I have been saying all along!" said W/ro Brkti, encouraged that her argument had finally won the day.

"But Brkti, there is one important issue we have to understand. It is always a great grace to be blessed with plenty and be able to give, rather than to receive. Furthermore, it is also important to realize that help is not only about material or monetary help. More importantly, it is about encouraging, reassuring, inspiring, uplifting and giving hope whenever someone is in difficulty. It is about being there for people in need."

"Well..." said W/ro Brkti. Grazmach raised his hand to his wife, indicating that he was not finished.

"Many fall to the destiny of needing assistance, simply because they were not blessed to be on the giving end. It is a great blessing to be able to give and share", said Grazmach with emotion in his voice, stopping to catch his breath. "When we complain because we happen to be on the giving end, we should ask ourselves, would it have been better if we had not been blessed and were on the receiving end? It is not easy, nor is it comfortable and pleasant to always need and receive assistance. Therefore, irrespective of the attitude of people we have helped, we should be grateful that we have been given plenty and have been blessed to assist others."

"That is right, but ..." started Brkti.

"Excuse me Brkti, please allow me to finish." W/ro Brkti nodded and Grazmach acknowledged her permission with a nod.

"As I was saying, the other important issue to understand here is that, whatever we give to others, we are in reality not doing it for them, but rather for ourselves and for God, who initially blessed us with what we have. We will get the recognition we aspire to and the rewards we deserve, not from our fellow humans, but from God himself. We should not be disappointed or sad that we didn't receive recognition and thanks from those we have assisted. It is enough that we ourselves and the All-mighty God know that we have done a good deed. As much as we can't be what we are not, or claim deeds we have not done when we somehow got admiration that we don't deserve; similarly, no one can ever erase or take away from us whatever we have done by saying or acting otherwise," he concluded. Saying that, he sat back and smilingly added, "I am sorry that I strayed from the subject of Medhn to a far more serious issue."

"Well, Grazmach, that is your characteristic trade mark. Anyway, it is because of all of what you have just said that I expressed my reservations and worries about Medhn."

"I hope she doesn't change," he added. "So far, Medhn has not been the kind who would overexploit her husband's willingness to co-operate. Don't worry about it unduly."

Although W/ro Brkti agreed with his general ideas, she still was not convinced about Medhn. She did not acknowledge Grazmach's confidence and stand. She didn't try to hide her feelings and her position was evident in her body language. She collected her utensils, got up and went back to her kitchen without making any comment. That was the end of the conversation.

Grazmach did not explicitly and clearly explain to his wife that his worries were not about Medhn. Although he was telling his wife how satisfied he was with his son's progress, he still had huge worries whether the signs he was seeing in his son were transient and temporary or would actually be permanent.

* 26 *

Grazmach and Bashay had lived as neighbors within one compound for years. People living in compounds, live a communal life. Neighbors are a very important part of everyone's life. So much so, in Eritrea, one's neighbors are considered one's closest relatives.

The twins in both households continued to make good progress. The date of baptism of the boys was near. According to the tradition of the Coptic Orthodox church, baptism for boys is conducted on the 40th day, while that for girls on the 80th day.

Grazmach and Bashay were full of gratitude that their children were blessed with twins. They felt God was rewarding them for all the years they stayed together as neighbors in love, peace and brotherhood. They believed that God was sending them a message. They discussed what they could do to respond to God's message and to cement their love and friendship. Finally, they came up with the idea that the best thing to do would be, for each of their sons to be God fathers to the other's offspring. Tesfom and Habtom did not hesitate to accept the suggestion of their parents.

Medhn and Alganesh started to prepare for the baptism. With the help of their mothers in law, they started buying the best provisions and best quality white *Taff* grain, butter, *berbere* (pepper), and various other ingredients necessary for making *Swa* (traditional light beer).

At the time, monthly general expenses like food, house-rent and other expenditures were extremely affordable and within the means of everyone. These were comparatively easy times for town dwellers, and most people were not aware of the many blessings they had. It seems like human nature to not realize and appreciate good, easy and peaceful times until after they are gone.

However, even if the times were comparatively easy and life expenses affordable, most natives, including those who could afford it, were not benefitting from it. Every family, rich or poor, was stuck in preparing the same traditional village dishes, devoid of much nutritional value. It was only the Italians and other expatriates, who were benefiting from the extremely affordable proteins, vegetables and fruits.

The food culture in the villages was even worse. Most villagers who lived near towns used to haul the most nutritious part of their produce to the urban population, without leaving any of it for their children and themselves.

One illiterate villager, who was a relative of Grazmach, was naturally extremely intelligent and perceptive, despite his lack of formal education. He used to tell Grazmach, "We villagers are immensely foolish and stupid. We bring and sell to you chicken, eggs, goats, sheep, milk, butter, honey, pepper, fresh vegetables and grains. After handing all that over to you, we buy from you salt, tea, coffee, sugar, oil, flashy and colorful clothes, and the rest we guzzle up in *Swa* (traditional light beer) and *Mies* (traditional liquor). Then we return home empty-handed."

He used to conclude his statement by saying, "We hand you all the best and nutritious healthy food and take from you all the unhealthy stuff, just to satisfy our taste buds."

Grazmach always acknowledged his perception and observation by saying, "You are absolutely right there." He was always impressed at the natural intelligence of his relative. After he left, Grazmach always said, "If he had had an opportunity for formal education, this youngster would have gone very far and achieved great things."

It was at just such a time of culture, market and employment conditions that Tesfom and Habtom were preparing to celebrate their first sons' baptisms.

* 27 *

All preparations for the baptisms were finalized. As mutually agreed, Tesfom and Habtom had agreed to be God fathers for one another's son.

Tesfom was worried that his infant son might catch cold or another respiratory ailment due to the cold baptismal water and air exposure during baptism. He asked his pastor if he could bring warm water for the baptism, but the priest was angry at his suggestion and his lack of faith. He admonished him by pointing out that higher education abroad should not mean questioning long-held traditional practices and losing one's faith in God.

He explained that this tradition of baptizing with cold water has been going on, without any ill effects, since John the Baptist. He further stressed how Tesfom should hold unflinching faith in the God that sends his angels to stand by and protect day and night, not only defenseless children, but also all other human beings.

Though not totally convinced, Tesfom didn't want to antagonize the priest further, so he reluctantly accepted the priest's viewpoint. Despite that, his nagging worry wouldn't go away. He decided to seek the advice of his father, who reiterated what the priest had said and confirmed the validity of his logic. To prove his point, he gave an example. He told him, "Your mother and I were both baptized in the same manner, we grew up, married and gave birth to you and to your siblings. You and Medhn were baptized in the same fashion, grew up and have now given birth to twins. What better proof do you need?!" Tesfom could not find any counter argument to his father's explanation and had to accept the logic and drop the subject altogether.

On the day of Baptism, both Medhn and Alganesh braided their hair and wore *Henna* on their hands and feet. As recommended therapy for their body and skin, they also took the *Tish* ceremony, a traditional smoke and vapor bath of various medicinal roots and plants. They then wore identical traditional dresses, the *kdan Habesha*, which Grazmach had bought for both of them for the occasion. The elders, Grazmach, Bashay and their wives also wore traditional clothes for the occasion, while the two new fathers and God fathers-to-be, wore their best suits for the baptism.

Both families arrived at St. Mary Coptic church of Asmara at 5 am. After what seemed, especially to Tesfom, like an extremely long religious ceremony, at about 8.30 a.m., it was time for the baptism of the babies. Tesfom held Samson and Habtom held Bruk and after promising to assume the role of being God fathers to each other's baby, the church ceremony was over.

Both families returned to their respective residences to celebrate with guests. In Grazmach's household, the norm was to limit such occasions to a few selected guests, while in Bashay's household, the norm was to host large gatherings. So, the number of guests in Tesfom's house were few in number, compared to the larger crowd in Habtom's house.

After another 40 days, it was time to baptize the girls in both households. On their 80th day, the girls were baptized in similar fashion. Tesfom's daughter was named Timnit, while Habtom's daughter was named Kbret.

* 28 *

Both Tesfom and Habtom were born and raised in Asmara and had lived their entire lives in the native (*dekebat*) section of the city. Although institutional Italian colonialism, racism and seclusion had long gone, there were still areas where most Habeshas (natives) lived and areas predominantly inhabited by Italians.

Natives predominantly lived in one or at most two-room houses. At the time, there was no source of outside entertainment or pastime for any family. When the family gathered together for the common meal or prior to bed time, members had to depend upon themselves for entertainment. There were no radios, tape recorders, CDs, television, internet, satellite dish or any other invention that invaded the household's privacy from outside. There was nothing that disrupted the family's precious time of togetherness. This was the kind of environment in which Tesfom and Habtom grew up in *Idaga Hamus*.

Evenings were spent telling stories, anecdotes, sharing daily experiences, cracking jokes and chatting. In short, there was nothing to undermine and break up the strong human family foundation that can threaten the very existence of a family. This freedom from outside interference was greatly beneficial for the cohesion, strength and health of the family unit, which is the core building block for healthy communities and nations.

At mealtime, every family would gather in a circle around the meal (*Meadi*), or if mealtime was over, then around a coal burning stove (*Fornello*), or, if in the country side, around a bonfire, and chat until late into the night. Eritrean families at the time could not afford delicious nutritious foods, clothing, furniture and accommodation in large comfortable houses. Despite the lack of all of the above, it was this togetherness above all else that gave native families the strength to stand by and support each other. It enabled them to enjoy a special bond of love, thoughtfulness, understanding and unity, which was the cornerstone of family strength in the Eritrean society.

Twenty years after, even now, when Tesfom and Habtom became parents, the setting had not changed much. They had slightly comparatively better houses, furniture, food, and accessories, but the rest was still the same. The newborn twins continued to make steady progress day by day. The days became weeks and the weeks became months, until the months became a year. They celebrated their first birthdays together in an extremely joyous and extravagant fashion.

Everyone present marveled at the astounding luck and blessing of the twins, to have been born at such a time, in such a fashion and to such parents. One thing that they failed to observe was that each of us is born — to a limited extent — with our own destiny, which destiny follows us through life. We can - to a limited extent - make either a positive or a negative dent in it through our own efforts and exertion. Every well-wishing guest present at the twins' birthdays had no idea, nor could anyone predict, the kind of luck or destiny each twin carried within him or herself.

Chapter 2
Panificio Pace

When Grazmach and Bashay raised their children in the same compound, they were closer to each other than to the other neighboring tenants. This was because they were both from the same village and their acquaintance went back many years.

Grazmach had much more income than Bashay, and his children ate better food, wore better clothes and shoes, lived in a larger and better house and even went to better schools. Sometimes Grazmach's children would put on an air of superiority over Bashay's children. All the children naturally felt this bite and sting, but it was Habtom who most felt this arrogance. From among all the children of the two families, the two most fiercely competitive, stubborn and obstinate were the eldest two, Tesfom and Habtom.

Though Habtom was not endowed with good looks, he had no real problem with his looks. But he hated that Tesfom often took every opportunity to remind him of his limits by showing off his own good looks. On top of this, whenever his father got mad at him, he would always call him names referring to his looks. He mostly used words like *Gnay, kifue* (ugly)! These constant reminders and references to his looks negatively affected him, and over time, made him inclined to hold grudges.

Tesfom on the other hand, was very much aware of his good looks. Since childhood, every visitor would always comment on the unique good looks of the child. This had its exalting and elating effect on him and his feelings about himself. Such comments gave his mother immense happiness and pride. But Grazmach did not approve of such comments and was not happy about it.

He used to say, "Beauty and looks are not traits we achieve by our own efforts and exertion. We should not feel proud of a natural endowment that we were gifted with."

"That is an exaggeration Grazmach and you know it. There is nothing wrong in feeling pride of our natural endowments." W/ro Brkti would argue vehemently.

"Brkti, Beauty is something that has been given to us. It is not something we get because we deserve it. It is not something that should be given importance. It is especially harmful to growing children to comment on either their good or bad looks. Both have different but damaging consequences on their personality and character. Most importantly, looks and beauty are temporary and transient. They can fade and change with age, illness, accidents and other circumstances," Grazmach stressed.

"True, but despite its being temporary and transient, what is wrong with feeling proud about it while it lasts?" W/ro Brkti would ask.

"I feel if we put too much value on our good looks, we are bound to feel we don't need to work on anything else. While showing off our looks, we will neglect other areas that require attention and exertion and will weaken our drive to build our character and intellect," Grazmach would say, with conviction.

"Grazmach, why do you have to always complicate and twist arguments and ideas?" she would retort angrily.

"I'm not twisting or complicating things, Brkti. If you would carefully listen to the essence of what I am saying, you would understand it. The truth is that good looks, or even the money, property, education, and status we attain after years of hard work are not all ours. Only a part of it is due to our effort and exertion. A big part of it is due to destiny, luck, or blessing, or whatever you want to call it. Many who have exerted as much and sometimes even more than us, fail to attain the outcome they deserve. We should at least acknowledge this and be thankful for it," Grazmach would argue passionately.

"I don't see anything wrong with feeling proud of something that is yours. But that is not the problem, Grazmach. The problem is that you always insist that everyone see things only the way you see them. In that case, there is nothing I can do to convince you. So, suit yourself!" After saying that, W/ro Brkti would get up and stride angrily to her kitchen.

Grazmach used to offer such delicate and deep insights to everyone around him, but he was not gaining any fans or followers. Nevertheless, he continued to air his views without getting discouraged. Whenever he encountered strong emotional opposition and condemnation, he would sympathize with the limitation of his listeners and accept it quietly without much argument.

Though Grazmach worried that wrong parental attitudes might have real negative effects on their upbringing, in realty, they didn't observe any discernible immediate negative effect on the children. As children, showing off and intentionally making the other child jealous was normal behavior. Although their competitiveness, obstinacy and fighting were a daily occurrence, so was their playing, laughing and enjoying their days together. Tesfom and Habtom like most children, spent their childhood as friends one moment and enemies the next.

* 2 *

After completing his secondary school education abroad and returning to Asmara, Tesfom was employed at the state bank. After a short while, he was promoted to a position of responsibility.

On the other hand, Habtom quit school after the fourth grade. He had to start work to augment his family's income. Bashay bought a small shop with the money he had saved for years, and Habtom started to run the shop. He was extremely hard working and thrifty and had an eye for trade and business. In a short while, he was able to meet and cover the family's living expenses and make some savings. Habtom had a goal which he kept only to himself. He was determined that one day, he would make himself and his family equal to, if not better than, Grazmach's family.

Since his early years, Tesfom was very particular about the clothes he wore and the way he looked. After starting work, his level of care about how he looked and what he wore went to another level. The cost never mattered to him, as long as he satisfied his taste and looks. Habtom on the other hand, had to be content with clothes tailored to his father's limited income. Even after starting work, Habtom did not care much about clothes. He always put a coverall or a work jacket over his clothes.

It was following these two very different life paths that these once immensely competitive children became parents of twins on the same day. Suddenly, when their paths crossed each other's, they came to be God fathers of one another's sons. Thus, their lives became close and intertwined again.

* 3 *

Bashay and his family had stayed in the same one-room rented apartment in *Idaga Hamus* for many years. By the time Grazmach and his family were finalizing their plans to move to a new house,

Bashay and Habtom were making enough money to make changes to their accommodation. As soon as Grazmach moved, they rented the larger house that had been occupied by Grazmach's family.

A few weeks later, Bashay Goitom's employer and boss called him aside and gave him some important information. Bashay thought about the matter hard and long. He decided to share the information with someone he trusted. After seriously thinking about it for over 24 hours, he finally made his decision.

Bashay had not slept well that night. He had tossed and turned the whole night. He was worried about the correctness of the decision he had already made. He got up early and started for his destination, immersed in deep thought.

At that time, walking was the normal form of transportation. There were bicycles, but they were too expensive for many to own. Nevertheless, the next highest mode of transport was still a bicycle. There were practically no taxies, except the very few, used by the very rich on a contractual basis. Horse drawn carts and a few buses were available. The charges were a few cents, but at the time, those cents were very precious. If one had to go somewhere within the city, no one would even think of any other form of transportation other than walking. Let alone within towns and cities, it was very common for people to travel on foot for days, from one town to the other. It was considered crazy and irresponsible to waste, even that little money, when you had been blessed with two healthy feet.

Asmara at the time was a small city. It was only slightly bigger than other corresponding towns. The population was estimated at about 150,000, with an expatriate community of about 17,000, mostly made up of Italians. The whole population of Eritrea was then estimated as not exceeding 1,500,000. The Italian population in Eritrea was at its highest near the end of the 2nd world war, but when Italy was defeated, this number dwindled dramatically as did the number of other expatriates. Many Italians were already selling their houses and businesses and going back to their country.

Bashay Goitom was so immersed in thought, that he didn't

even realize which way he took from his house in *Idaga Hamus* to *Geza Banda Tilian* (*Addis Alem*). In such instances, when one's mind is elsewhere, the eyes and feet take over and guide us to a destination that is already familiar. Bashay's eyes and feet did not fail him, because even though his mind was elsewhere, they were able to land him at Grazmach Seltene's residence. It was after he arrived at the gate, that he realized his whereabouts. When the door was opened, he hurriedly and clumsily blurted, "Good morning Brkti."

"Good morning Bashay. Is everything ok? How come you are here so early?" asked W/ro Brkti apprehensively.

"Everything is ok Brkti. I am sorry if I alarmed you. I came early because I want Grazmach's advice on something important. Is he up?"

"Yes, he is already up. Please come in. I will tell him you are here."

Bashay took several steps towards the main door. As soon as he was by the door, Grazmach opened the door and they met face to face. It was Grazmach who reacted first, "Good morning Bashay. I heard a voice and was just coming out to see who it was."

"Good morning Grazmach. I came early so I could catch you before you went out. I want your advice on something important."

"It will be my pleasure. Would you care for tea now?"

"I would prefer to first finish our talk and then we can have tea."

"Ok, good," said Grazmach and walked back to the door. He called W/ro Brkti and told her that they would call her when they were ready for tea. He closed the door and sat in front of Bashay, on the brown sofa which he surrendered to no one.

"We haven't seen each other for quite some time. You never fail to remember to visit your friends and relatives periodically. You know that I am not as good as you in that regard. How come you disappeared for so long?" asked Grazmach.

"You are right Grazmach. But lately a group of us took responsibility to embark upon a reconciliation between family members that had gone into bitter dispute. You remember Aboy *Ghebreamlak's* children from our village back home?"

Grazmach nodded. Bashay continued, "The dispute that had flared up between them was fierce and would have resulted in disastrous consequences for the whole family, but though it took a lot of time and effort, we finally managed to reconcile them."

"That is an exemplary good deed. This is the kind of deed that rewards the spirit and brings peace to our souls. It is great that you finally succeeded. The fact that you spent a lot of time and effort and were all exhausted was nothing, compared to what you achieved. Whether we exert ourselves beneficially or spend our days uselessly, our body's final resting place is the soil. It is therefore nobler to make an effort and do something worthwhile. You see Bashay Hawey, instead of working to bring peace among men, many of us spend precious time backbiting, creating discord, and fomenting enmity and hatred. So, what you did is indeed a great and noble deed!" said Grazmach, with admiration.

"Thank you Grazmach. Only the few who are blessed and noble themselves understand and appreciate this. Many look down at such cultural practices, as a waste of one's time. They think it is foolish to engage themselves and waste time and effort in affairs that do not directly affect them."

"Great men and great books tell us, "'Whenever you can, try to do something good for others; if you can't, at least provide them with good advice and send them good thoughts."' God did not command us to be good to our fellow human beings so he can benefit himself. There is nothing God requires from us. But if we become good, it will bring goodness, peace and love to us, to our families, our societies, our countries and even our world. That is why God commanded us to be good to each other," Grazmach said passionately.

"You are right. *E' vero, e' vero*, Grazmach," nodded Bashay gravely.

Encouraged by his friend's response and appreciation, Grazmach continued, "You see Bashay, you hear many of us repeatedly complain about 'this world' and 'this life' all the time. The truth is, 'this world' is not the problem, nor is 'this life' the problem. The problem is us human beings. This beautiful world has been created with enough resources for everyone. We destroy the world and our lives by our selfishness, greed, shortsightedness and the injustices and crimes we commit against each other," said Grazmach. He then sat back as if he had finished. Then as an afterthought, he smiled and continued, "When I am with you, I get a little carried away and passionate. I think it is because you give me your full attention. Pardon me for straying."

"No, no, it is ok Grazmach. Even if you go on a tangent, it is always pertinent to the subject and occasion. You do not waste words for nothing. Your expressions are always instructive and profound," Said Bashay.

Grazmach was by nature never comfortable with compliments. Thus, he quickly said, "Thank you. Now please let us proceed to the subject that brought you here."

"Ok, *va bene*. You know very well that you and I have come a long way together. Though I am older than you, due to your natural endowment and education, you are more perceptive and possess a wider perspective. Because of this, whenever I needed it, you have always provided me with appropriate advice. That is why I came today, to seek advice on a subject matter I didn't even discuss with my children or my family."

"I thank you for the confidence you have in me. Please continue," said Grazmach humbly, bowing his head.

"*Bene*, good. As you very well know, *proprio* my Italian boss does not pay me much. But because I have no education or other vocation, I had to bow my head, accept the situation and raise my children with whatever I could get. However, since we bought the shop, our lives have slightly improved. For the first time, thanks to Habtom, we have even accumulated a small saving."

Grazmach nodded his head in appreciation and understanding and said, "I am very glad to hear that. Ok continue."

"My boss, the owner of the bakery, is planning to sell the establishment and return to his country. He called me in private and told me that since I had served him faithfully for many years, he would give me priority and even a discount, if I would be interested in buying the business. He has given me one week to think about it and respond."

"Ok good, go ahead," said Grazmach.

"The money we have saved is not enough to allow us to buy the business on our own," continued Bashay. "The other option we have is to find someone, who would be willing to partner with us to buy the business. I don't have anyone whom I trust as much as you. I have therefore come to ask you, if you would be willing to partner with us to buy the business," he finished, with a sense of relief that he had finally shared his plan with someone he trusted.

"That is very good. The fact that you came to me with this important proposition is a measure of the friendship and confidence you have in our relationship. So, I thank you for it. Secondly, the fact that it is a business in which you have spent your entire life and know very well is also important. Did he tell you for how much he is intending to sell the establishment?" asked Grazmach.

"Not yet, but he has promised me, he would tell me the price, after I assure him of my intention and ability to buy the bakery."

"That is fair enough. In principle, I have no objection to the idea of buying the bakery in partnership with you. For the rest, let's first see what he is asking and then we will take it from there. What do you say?" Grazmach asked.

"*Bene, benissimo*! That is very good," said Bashay, with pleasure spreading across his face, gratified that he had successfully accomplished his goal for the day.

They agreed to meet in two days' time, at Bashay's residence. After they finished their consultation, W/ro Brkti came with bread and tea and the friends took breakfast together.

* 4 *

At the time, most craftsmen, artisans, professionals and business owners in Eritrea were Italians. There were also other expatriates like Yemenis, Sudanese, Indians, Turks, Jews, Armenians, and others who were - to a small degree - active in commerce and business.

The British nationals who were in Eritrea during the British Administration, occupied positions of leadership in education, public administration, justice, the police force and security. The Jews and the Greeks had their own synagogue and church. The Indians had also their own resting place for the dead, in *Biet Giorghis*, just at the outskirt of Asmara. Most of the expatriates were engaged in commerce and business

Most small and large business organizations and factories were owned by Italians. Most of the native Eritreans living in urban areas worked under Italian employers. The majority — who had no education — worked as laborers and assistants in various enterprises. The Italians were not easy masters. They were racists and white supremacists. The native Eritrean bread earner had to endure harsh and vulgar language as well as physical abuse to bring bread to his family.

The Italians never taught or showed the techniques of their trade to their native employees. In fact, as much as practicable, they actively hid the techniques of their vocation and their accumulated work experience from the natives. Nevertheless, with endurance and perseverance, the natives slowly managed to master the arts of their trades. Bashay Goitom was one of those who, through self-discipline and perseverance, managed to master the art of bakery.

On the third day, Grazmach arrived at Bashay's residence at exactly 6 pm. They exchanged warm greetings with W/ro Lemlem. Grazmach immediately started to observe the place that had housed him and his family for years. He noticed with admiration, that W/ro Lemlem was taking good care of the house.

After W/ro Lemlem left, they delved straight into their topic. Bashay informed Grazmach, that his employer was planning to sell the bakery for 11,000- krshi; that he was prepared to grant him a discount of 1,000- Krshi, for his years of services; and that if we agreed on the deal, then he will be ready to finalize all paper work and hand over the bakery within a month. Bashay further told Grazmach, that he had actually expected a higher price quotation and expressed his opinion that the price offered, reflected his employer's urgency to sell and go back to his country as soon as possible.

Grazmach agreed with Bashay's observation and conclusion. He explained that he himself had been assessing prices for similar enterprises and that the offer was extremely fair and reasonable. Finally, in principle, they agreed to buy the bakery in partnership.

Bashay then proceeded to another important issue he wanted to address. He informed Grazmach that he would not be able to raise the full amount of money required to pay his share. Grazmach had not expected this and was taken aback, but did not show his surprise. He nodded to Bashay to continue.

Bashay then told him that he had 2,000- krshi in savings and would be able to raise another 1,000- krshi by selling the shop, but that he would still be short by 2,000- krshi. He explained the impossibility of finding anyone willing to lend him that much money. He asked if Grazmach could possibly put in 7,000- krshi, instead of 5,000- krshi. Then he would contribute the 3,000- krshi he could secure and they could buy the bakery. He explained that if they agreed to do that, the partnership and share-holding could be split into two to one, instead of one to one.

After listening attentively, Grazmach said, "I can't do that at all!" Bashay's face fell and became ashen. His hope was dashed to the ground. Grazmach noticed this and immediately said, "I am so sorry Bashay. Let me explain what I mean. I have agreed to your proposal - that we buy the bakery with the money we both could raise. But I will never agree to split the shares into two to one! Don't forget that from the outset, we had agreed to work in equal partnership!"

Bashay's face showed relief but also confusion. He said, "I completely agree Grazmach. I am proposing this solution, only because at this moment, I can't contribute equally to the partnership."

"Don't worry about that. Leave that to me. After all, you can't be partners, if you can't support each other in circumstances of need. I will myself advance the 2,000- krshi you require. You can pay it in due time, when we make profits together," he said with a smile.

"I thank you very much for your generosity, Grazmach, but I can only accept your offer with gratitude under one condition. As you graciously proposed, advance us the 2,000- Krshi; but until the time we finalize payment of the advance you make, let the partnership shares be two to one. Then, when we finish payment, we can revert the shares to one to one."

"No Bashay, I will never accept that. Listen my friend, partnership is primarily built on trust. We are becoming business partners now, because we had long years of close neighborliness and became close friends and confidants. From the start, the idea of this partnership was yours. The bakery is also an establishment you have worked on, for your entire life. Now, just because I have more money, how fair and just would it be in the eyes of anyone or God that I take two parts and you take one part? This is not something either man or God would like. So, we will only proceed in the manner I have suggested to you. That is final!" said Grazmach emphatically.

Shaking his head, Bashay said with gratitude, "Wow Grazmach, you are so kind. Thank you!" He shook his head emphatically again and said, "*Va bene, grazie* Grazmach! I know that you are a God-fearing, fair and just man. That is why I desired your partnership. Otherwise, partnership is a very delicate and problematic affair."

"Partnership is not the problem Bashay. We, human beings, are the problem. We become greedy, we double cross each other, we forget, and after a while, we completely change and become different people. If you and I proceed with love, correctness, thoughtfulness and fairness, then this partnership will bring everlasting friendship, love and strong cohesion even to our children and families," he said with hope and strong conviction.

"Amen! God is great! *Dio grande*! Everything is possible with him," said Bashay, looking upwards and pointing both his hands to the sky. They went on to discuss the details of implementing their plan, concluding by agreeing to meet as needed to review new developments.

* 5 *

They immediately paid the Italian a deposit, as a guarantee of sealing the sales agreement. After finalizing all paperwork, they paid the remaining balance and the Italian officially handed them the bakery.

The name of their new bakery was, "*Panificio Pace*," meaning 'Peace Bakery'. The two friends were grateful that they were able to become business partners just two years after their children had become God-fathers to each other's sons.

They agreed to share the work and divide the responsibility between themselves. All technical aspects of production were to be managed by Bashay, while Habtom would be responsible for the purchase of raw materials and sales. Grazmach and Tesfom took the responsibility for finance and accounting.

Grazmach had no problem in managing the accounts himself, but he wanted to include Tesfom in the arrangement. He believed Tesfom's involvement, would eventually bring multiple benefits to Tesfom and the family.

* 6 *

Grazmach was sitting comfortably on his brown sofa and taking his habitual daily afternoon nap. W/ro Brkti checked on her husband and saw that he was awake. She had concerns she wanted to raise with her husband.

She sat down and started explaining her concern that involving Tesfom in the bakery might inadvertently put too much weight on his shoulders. She reminded him that their son already had enough responsibilities, as an official of the bank and as a father with a wife and two small children.

Grazmach assured her that before making the decision, he had taken everything into consideration. He assured her that he believed the experience in commerce and business would eventually be invaluable for their son. He reminded her that they were advancing in age, and that as the eldest, it was appropriate for Tesfom to be prepared to take over the affairs of the family. As an after-thought, he added that the extra responsibility after office hours, would keep him from going around to bars every evening with friends.

W/ro Brkti brushed aside the other valid points he presented and focused on the last point that referred to her son's weakness. She started defending her son by saying, "The going around with friends you often refer to, is not unique to Tesfom. It is normal with most youngsters of his age and his contemporaries!"

"It is true, he could be like some of his contemporaries. My concern though is with my son, not others over whom I have no influence. Tesfom has now become a husband and a father. What good does it do to leave his wife and children at home and go around drinking, throwing away money and eventually hurting his health? I made this decision, not because we have any problems with the accounts, but because I know it will eventually benefit him on all fronts. Otherwise, I can easily handle the accounts by myself," he said angrily.

W/ro Brkti understood that the argument she was pursuing would not lead anywhere. She decided to try from another angle and said, "Anyway, do you also really believe they will work in peace and harmony with Habtom? Habtom is extremely jealous, obdurate and vindictive. You remember how they were at each other's throats when growing up as children?"

"Well, that is because they were children. Now as adults, they don't even remember that. They get along very well."

W/ro Brkti was not satisfied and was not done, so she added, "You also know very well that Habtom is a miser. He never likes to spend a single cent. Tesfom on the other hand is generous, spends freely and is kind."

"Well, Habtom's character might be described by some as miserly, while by others as thrifty and careful. While Tesfom's character might be described by some as benevolent and generous, while by others as extravagant and irresponsible."

Whenever she found it difficult to respond to her husband's rationale, W/ro Brkti always reverted to a strategy of departing from the actual subject matter and going on a tangent. She thus retorted angrily, "Oh my God Grazmach, why do you have to always spin words and phrases around to serve your purpose?"

"Brkti, this is not spinning," said Grazmach calmly. He added, "The best strategy in most life instances is to always take the middle ground. Even in the instance we just discussed, it wouldn't hurt Tesfom, if he adopted some of Habtom's traits."

W/ro Brkti couldn't control her anger. She retorted back, shouting, "Why should he take traits from Habtom, when he has his own fine qualities?"

"Let alone adopting traits from Habtom, who is his childhood friend and neighbor, borrowing good traits from anyone, even your adversaries and enemies is never a bad thing and is always advantageous. Anyway, don't overly worry and stress yourself about this. For any and every eventuality, Bashay and I will be with them all the time."

"Ok, as you wish," said W/ro Brkti curtly and unhappily.

W/ro Brkti was not happy with how the whole conversation went. That was evident in her facial expression and body language. This was clear to Grazmach. He wanted to deflate the situation and appease her. He also wanted to conclude the subject amicably, so he said, "Come on Brkti dear, now is a perfect time for that delicious coffee you brew. Please indulge us and let us enjoy our precious coffee time together."

W/ro Brkti's features instantly brightened. She said, "I was just waiting for you to finish. Otherwise, I was also thinking about going to make coffee." She stood up with brighter features and went to the kitchen.

When W/ro Brkti left, Grazmach fell into deep thought. He started having second thoughts and debating whether his wife might be right about throwing too much responsibility on Tesfom's shoulders. He acknowledged to himself that parents generally expect too much from their first-borns and that expectation eventually tends to hurt them. While debating thus, he started day dreaming about the memories of his dead father and his childhood.

Grazmach was the eldest son. As a child, his father had inflicted harsh punishment on him. His younger siblings by comparison were not subjected to the same discipline, and he had firmly believed that his father was not fair, because he was too soft on the other siblings.

When he was 14 years old, his father had somehow understood and noticed this. He thus one day called him and told him, "Listen Seltene, my eldest son, we have disciplined you harshly and made you shoulder far greater responsibility than your siblings, because we believed we were setting an example. It was not because we had less love for you, it was only because we believed, if you became disciplined and correct, your siblings would follow in your footsteps. Our forefathers have a beautiful saying to describe this, '*Itom Neashtu Ahwat, Beta Bokri Zefresa Quana Iyom Zimelalesu,*' Literally translated, this means, "The younger siblings will cross into their neighbor's yard through the short cut already established by the eldest." In essence, it means, the younger siblings generally follow the footsteps of the eldest."

He remembered his father explaining the details of what that meant, as if it were yesterday. He smiled at the sweet childhood memory. He felt as if he was 14 years old. At that very moment, he was woken from his reminiscence by the sudden words of his wife, "Did I keep you waiting too long?" said W/ro Brkti, with the coffee pot delicately poised on her hands. They started drinking their coffee and enjoying their time together. The heated argument they had a few minutes ago was totally forgotten.

Grazmach and W/ro Brkti did not know then, but at that very hour, Bashay and W/ro Lemlem were also talking about their doubts and fears concerning the imminent partnership.

* 7 *

Bashay and W/ro Lemlem were deep into a serious discussion. W/ro Lemlem had expressed her disappointment at the decision to sell the shop. Since its purchase, the shop had taken care of all her grocery needs. She further expressed her displeasure at buying a bakery in partnership with the Grazmach family.

Bashay pointed out to her that they wouldn't have been able to buy the bakery, had they not collected cash from the shop's sale and had Grazmach not loaned them the money. He assured her that regarding success, the bakery was a business he knew very well and that within a short time, it was going to be much more profitable than the shop.

"Habtom and I will work from within the bakery, while Grazmach and Tesfom will help us from the outside. We will jointly be successful in no time," said Bashay, expressing his confidence and optimism.

"I doubt that Tesfom will help you much, especially in the setting of a bakery. As you very well know, he is extremely arrogant and full of pride. He focuses so much on his appearance; he wants nothing to touch his impeccable clothing and shoes."

"Why is that an issue? We do not expect him to assist us in handling the flour and baking bread. Both father and son are going to assist us only in administration and finance," said Bashay, without directly responding to her harsh and abrasive comments about Tesfom.

W/ro Lemlem was not done. "Do you think they will be able to work peacefully with Habtom? We both remember, how the boys were always at each other's throats when they were children. Tesfom is also extravagant and excessive, while our son is hard working, thrifty and responsible."

He still decided to ignore her other comments and instead respond to her reasonable concern. "Are you talking about their rivalry when they were children? They are not children anymore. That was then, now they go along very well," said Bashay, with slight impatience in his voice.

Although W/ro Lemlem had realized that her husband was getting upset, she still decided to push her luck. So, she said, "It is also not fair that you and Habtom perform the hardest part of the job, while they only help with paperwork and then share the profits equally with you."

Bashay was now clearly upset and angry. "Holy Mother! *Madonna!*" shouted Grazmach. "Listen woman! I told you, if it was not for them, we wouldn't even be co-owners now! I also told you, that Habtom and I will be remunerated for our work! Above all, please be thankful that God has given us this unique opportunity! Instead of thanking God, why do you have to scramble so far ahead and throw irresponsible comments right and left?!"

He paused for a while, breathing heavily and then continued with more fury, "Be careful, *Guarda!* Don't ever utter such poisonous comments in front of Habtom!" he growled at her making gestures with his hands, the veins in his forehead clearly visible.

"Ok, Ok, don't get upset. I was only expressing my worries

and concerns for you," said W/ro Brkti, very aware that she had extremely angered her husband. She wanted to normalize the situation and decided to change the subject. She said, "Would you like tea or coffee?"

"Prepare tea! I have no time for coffee! I have an appointment," he snapped tersely, with anger in his voice.

When his wife went to prepare tea, Bashay went into deep thought. He remembered how his son had initially opposed the idea of working in partnership with the Grazmach family, especially with Tesfom. He had also vehemently opposed the sale of the shop and getting a loan from Grazmach. Habtom had reluctantly accepted the whole decision, after Bashay explained to him that they had no other viable option. Now Bashay's worry and concern was that his wife might arouse Habtom's feelings anew, thus complicating the new partnership in its infancy.

While reflecting deeply on the subject, Bashay was continuously pulling at his goatee on his chin. Whenever he was in deep thought, that was his habit. While reflecting, he was awakened from his daydreaming by the clattering of beakers. His wife had come in, delicately balancing a tea kettle on one hand and beakers in the other.

W/ro Brkti noticed that her husband was still angry and growling and wanted to calm him down, so she said, "Please enjoy the tea now. I have also brought you bread *(Hmbasha)* as a snack."

"I will only drink one cup, take the kettle away! I also don't need the bread!" he said curtly, growling at his wife. He added again, with a menacing expression, "Be careful, *Guarda*! Don't ever mention anything about the shop or this partnership to Habtom."

"I won't mention anything to him. Don't worry about it." she said, hoping to appease and assure him.

Bashay was still angry. He drank his tea in silence, stood up and immediately went out without uttering another word.

On the one hand, here were two worried mothers siding with their own first-borns, while on the other hand, there were two fathers optimistically hoping for the same two sons. This reminds us of the Tigrinya proverb, '*Aboyn Adeyn Bebeynu Tselotom,*' meaning, 'My father and mother have differing aspirations and prayers.'

Whether the worries of the mothers or the hopes of the fathers would come to pass was a question that should only be left to time and to life itself. Although the youngsters did not fathom this, the elders understood it perfectly, because life and experience had given them unforgettable life lessons.

* 8 *

The bakery which the Bashay and Grazmach families bought was in the center of the city, located in front of the main large Mosque, in an area called *Merkato.* It was a well-established business, with adequate parking and many Italian and Eritrean customers.

As a first call of duty, Bashay and Habtom decided to refurbish their flour stock. They bought the flour and then finalized agreement with Yemeni transporters, who transported the flour in a four-wheeled horse cart (popularly known then, as Arebia Jebelli. At the time, Eritrean natives were not generally involved in the commercial life of the country.

Thanks to Bashay's bakery experience, Habtom's strong work ethic, and Grazmach's and Tesfom's impeccable financial handling, the bakery made outstanding progress in a short time. The fact that they were now running their own private business, was the other secret of their success; they knew success or failure depended on them. The zeal that came with that knowledge gave them an added incentive. Thus, Bashay and Habtom were able to pay off the 2,000-Krshi that had been loaned to them by Grazmach in only two years.

On top of having lived for many years together as neighbors, the two families now were also business partners, which made them much closer. Tesfom and Habtom's immediate families also became very close, due to their business collaboration and the christening of the twins.

* 9 *

The two new families continued to grow not only in terms of business but also numerically. When Alganesh was 24-years-old, she gave birth to a third child. The new baby boy was named Hadsh. The twins Kbret and Samson continued to make good progress.

When Medhn was 22 years old, she gave birth to a baby boy. They named the new baby Legesse. The twins, Bruk and Timnit, who were now four years old, continued to make good progress.

The State Bank where Tesfom worked, was closed on Saturday afternoons and Sundays. On Saturday afternoons, Tesfom took all the children of the two households for treats. The children enjoyed the ride and the treats immensely. Tesfom was very much loved and adored by the children of both families. Alganesh appreciated and cherished Tesfom's thoughtfulness and care for her children.

Tesfom went to the bakery from Monday to Friday. He wouldn't go to the bakery on weekends, claiming Saturday afternoons and Sundays for himself. Medhn also appreciated and valued what Tesfom was doing for the children. However, there was one aspect of it she didn't like. After passing time with the children, Tesfom would immediately run off to his friends, returning by midnight, intoxicated and with a strong stink of alcohol on his breath.

As always, Medhn was patiently waiting for Tesfom to come back home from his weekend entertainment. Since it was Saturday, she knew the wait would be long. She patiently sat down, dozing frequently. Tesfom arrived a few minutes before midnight, filled to capacity.

When she saw his condition, she couldn't stand it and immediately said, "What is wrong with you Tesfom? This is not your usual self. How can you allow yourself to come home every weekend, looking like someone else?"

"Come on! Who told you I look like someone else?" He asked, dragging every word.

"I don't need to be told by anyone. I can see it for myself!"

"Listen, listen!" he said threateningly, pointing his finger at her. Medhn slightly moved backwards. When he noticed that, he brought his hand back and continued from where he thought he had stopped and said, "I work at the Bank from Monday to Saturday and after six, I go to the bakery for accounts every day. I never see my friends. They meet every night and enjoy themselves. Now just because I go out Saturday evenings and enjoy myself, you want to accuse me of turning into someone else?" he growled at her, accusing her menacingly.

Although she was aware that there could be consequences, Medhn didn't want to let go. Thus, she fearlessly said, "Even on Sundays, we never see you after breakfast. You spend the whole day and night with them drinking and playing cards."

"So now, enjoying myself two days out of the whole week, has become a big deal that you can't tolerate?" he shouted, visibly angry. He got very close to her.

She stepped back again and calmly said, "Please calm down, and keep your voice down, you will wake the children."

"Have you forgotten that you were the one who started this at this ungodly hour?! Now listen! I need to sleep in peace! I don't want any more talk!" he said. Then he turned back and strode towards their bedroom.

"Ok, as you wish. Since we can't understand each other now, we will talk tomorrow."

When he heard her respond, Tesfom stopped and then turned back slowly and menacingly. He hesitated for a short while, then seemed to have changed his mind. Then staring at her, he said, "There will be no need to talk about this tomorrow. Now, let me sleep in peace!"

Medhn decided to keep her mouth shut. When he saw there was no response from her, he turned back and went into their bedroom. She went to check the children and after about 15 minutes, she went to their bedroom. Tesfom had already slept soundly, snoring loudly. She shook her head several times, saying under her breath, "My God Tesfom, what is happening to you?" She shook her head again and climbed into bed. It took her a while to sleep.

* 10 *

Before going to bed, Medhn had resolved to talk to Tesfom in the morning. She got up early and gave the children breakfast. As a result of the previous night's drinking, Tesfom slept late into the morning.

When he got up, as was his custom, he went straight to the children. They were happy to see their father. He started to make them laugh, and they were enjoying their time with their father immensely. Tesfom loved and enjoyed playing with children. Medhn watched the proceedings from afar. As the enjoyment of the father and children rose in intensity, her resolve to talk to him started to weaken.

She felt that it wouldn't be fair to ruin such a joyous atmosphere. She began leaning towards dropping the idea of confronting Tesfom. Her love for her children and her motherly instinct kicked in and prevailed. Bringing further logic and rationale against talking to him that day, she told herself, "I think I am being too harsh and strict. It is obvious that Tesfom has great love for his children and his family. What more do I need?"

Fortified with that logic and attitude, she firmly decided to drop the matter. She then went and joined the children and Tesfom, who were having a great time and enjoying every minute of it. After an hour, Tesfom told the children that he had an appointment and must go. They begged him to stay, but to no avail.

Medhn knew that she had failed to do what she had resolved. She knew that Tesfom would be gone for the whole day and into the night. Still, she had no heart to do otherwise. She thus bid him farewell and watched him go without further comment.

* 11 *

Two years after the birth of their third child Hadsh, Alganesh and Habtom had another child. They named her Rahwa. The twins were now five years old. Habtom at 30 and Alganesh at 26, had already become responsible for a family of four children.

It was now already four years, since they had bought the bakery. Habtom had hoped that the load and work hours of the bakery would be lighter than that of running a shop, but he soon learned that was not the case. In fact, in some regards, the bakery was a job that demanded more time and intensity.

Habtom was by nature a workaholic, so the new workload did not pose any problem to him. He never took time off work and had no interest in any form of entertainment or pastime. Any time free from work was spent for meals and sleep.

On top of his dedication to work, Habtom also never liked spending time with his wife or children at home. This did not seem to bother the children, since they were used to not spending time with their father. But Alganesh, on the other hand, was bothered and worried about it, because she understood its consequences.

One Sunday morning Habtom was eating his breakfast in haste, anxious because he was already late for work. Alganesh, who followed his every movement, couldn't stand it anymore. "Listen Habtom, why don't you at least occasionally try to sit down and spend time with your children? Don't you understand that, though they might not say it, they miss your love and this might eventually hurt them?"

"What? What are you saying? Why should they be hurt? They have everything! They lack nothing!" said Habtom, incredulous at her complaint.

"Well, materially they might have everything, but have you ever considered that they might feel envious that they don't get to play and pass time with their father, as other children do?" she said coolly.

"Did you say like other fathers? Are you referring to Tesfom and trying to compare me with him?"

"Why should I compare you with him? I am merely talking about my own family."

"Then if you are talking about your family, I have repeatedly told you that once you provide children with everything they need, there is nothing else required. The rest merely spoils them and will do nothing good for them." Then as an after-thought he added, "You also know very well, that I don't have time."

"I know that you don't have much time, and I am also aware that you don't spend time outside of your work and that you are working hard to improve our livelihood."

"Then if you know all this, why do you have to raise such an unnecessary topic?" said Habtom, somewhat calmer, happy that Alganesh finally understood his situation.

But Alganesh was not finished. "Children are easily pleased and contented. If you would allocate for them half an hour or an hour a week of your time, it would be adequate," she persisted.

"It is not only about finding and allocating an hour a week. I could easily do that, but as my father used to say, a child should not be too close to his father. Anything can happen to a man at any time. Children who are very close to their fathers suffer the most when they lose their father. It permanently affects them emotionally. So, it is not only about finding time. It is about principle," he said, confident in his logic and principle.

"Who is better off, a child who loses his father after having been fulfilled with his love while alive, or a child who is hungry for his father's love all the time his father is still alive and then loses him?" said Alganesh, throwing a question laden with impenetrable logic.

"Don't you listen at all? I am telling you it hurts them," repeated Habtom, with no conviction in his logic, somewhat irritably.

"It is true that the child who has been used to a father's love, will suffer more intensely when he loses his parent." said Alganesh.

Habtom was happy and relieved that she had finally understood his point of view. He thus quickly added, "Exactly, that is what I have been trying to tell you!"

"Wait a moment. The child, full of his father's love, suffers and misses his father more, because his life had been filled with love. The one who really missed out, and the one who needs sympathy, is the child who didn't enjoy his father's love while his father was alive."

Habtom had started to fume and was furious by the time she finished. "Why are you suddenly trying to be a philosopher?" he said sarcastically and bitterly.

"Believe me Habtom, I am not trying to philosophize. I know you are not working this hard only to provide our daily bread. You are working hard so that we will be secure in the future. Am I right?"

"Of course. Then when you clearly understand all this, why do you have to engage me in this wasteful argument?" said Tesfom calmly, seeming relieved.

"What I am trying to tell you is that, in like manner, the fatherly love you would give them now, will serve them as a provision and security for the future, if and when they lose their parent," said Alganesh, very intent on driving her point home before the conversation was done.

Habtom was now clearly irritated and frustrated. "That comparison is totally inappropriate. The two examples have no correlation at all. Don't try to blabber your seemingly sensible nonsense to me," said Habtom, gritting his teeth threateningly.

Habtom's aggressive pose did not perturb Alganesh. She decided to press on, whatever the consequences, and thus added, "If you want the truth, what I am talking about is not just about passing time with the children," she said, unaware that she was pouring fuel over fire.

"What else do you want to bring up?!" Said Habtom, his face contorted, his nerves and muscles taut, moving slightly forward.

Something inside her was warning her against the next point.

Yet she ignored the feeling and decided to press on. She thus bluntly said, "On top of spending time with their children, other fathers buy things that their children desire, to make them happy. But you always believe nothing should be spent, except for extremely essential and indispensable things. As a result, the children feel envious of other children and this is definitely not good for them," said Alganesh firmly and fearlessly.

"Holy God! *Dio grande*! Incredible! What madness? *Wey Tsigaaaab!* Listen, and listen carefully! I will not repeat this again. The life you and your children are living now, is a life we never even dreamt to ever see! We grew up with enormous problems and difficulties. Because we learned that lesson, we are doing ok now. With hard work and thrift, we are improving, although we are not there yet."

Alganesh started to say, "Yes, but" ...

Habtom did not let her finish. He stopped her with his voice and his movements. He suddenly stood up threateningly over her and said, "Shut up! that is enough! *Basta!* I don't have time to waste on such nonsense! More importantly, I also have no patience to listen to such impertinence!" He stood over her, closing his fists. The veins on his face were clearly visible, his eyes were wide open and his eyes red hot. He looked like a monster ready to jump on her at any sign of movement or sound.

Alganesh quickly assessed the situation and realized the physical danger she was in. She desisted from uttering a single sound or making any sign with body language. When he failed to get any response, Habtom quickly turned around, shaking his head and gritting his teeth and after kicking the table in front of him, he stormed out.

Alganesh decided to keep her mouth shut, because she knew her husband's violent nature and character. Despite this, she repeatedly tried to talk to Habtom, hoping that one day, he might understand. And whenever their conversations ended in such a manner, she always felt hurt and sad.

* 12 *

While Alganesh was hurt and sad, Habtom was nearly exploding with anger. He was talking to himself under his breath, "Bewildering! Incredible! Shocking! *Wey Tsigaaaab!"* This Tigrinya expression is used to describe a person you feel has been too spoiled!

After such repeated mutterings, he slowly calmed down. Soon after, he slipped into memory lane, remembering his childhood years. He thought about the house they grew up in. They had no wardrobe for their clothes which were all kept in a box. His dad's special occasion clothing was hung on the wall, so it wouldn't be crumpled. They had only one chair, where his father sat. For all the rest, including their mother, they had very low stools known as *Duqa.*

He smiled, when he remembered how each child had his own stool and how there was much infighting about someone taking one's stool. The big circular communal plate from which they all ate - the *Meadi* - was itself placed on a higher stool. Oftentimes, the meals prepared were not enough to satisfy everyone. Thus, at meal times, each child would choose a strategic position from which he/she could take as large a handful as possible, before everything was gone. When the food on the plate was depleted, that was the end of the meal. Everyone would say thanks to the Lord and stand up. There will be nothing more — no snack, no nothing, until the next meal.

He shook his head and said, "Now, when there is plenty to eat, we have gotten to a time when parents worry about a child losing his desire to eat! Wow!" The more he thought about the idea, the more he couldn't believe it. Habtom was sure that his children had all the bread they needed from the bakery and were eating at will, at any hour of the day. He shook his head again and thought, "Wow! And now, Alganesh and a few like her, complain about trivialities like passing time with children and giving them attention," he said loudly, shaking his head once more.

After thinking about food and meals, he passed to another memory. When he was growing up, the family didn't have enough beds. He remembered that at first, before his sisters were born, he and his brother used to sleep on the only single bed they had. Later they had to sleep three in one single bed. Two on the upper-side and one on the lower-side. Although as children, they could sleep through the discomfort, there were other consequences as well. The punching or crushing of your sibling's head or nose with one's feet was a natural and common consequence; it was considered part of the deal and arrangement of sleeping together. Thus, the resulting damages were never a concern for grudge or complaint.

He then remembered and shook his head and said, "Actually, we were the lucky ones who were blessed to sleep on a bed!" He remembered many families, including his uncle's, who hadn't any beds because the house was either too small with no space for beds, or the family could not afford a bed. In such cases, families slept on mats (*Tenkobet*), which they would spread on the floor at night. The mats would be rolled up at daybreak and put against the wall. He shook his head again and said, "And now, Alganesh and her kind have everything, and yet they complain!"

His memory shifted from children's bedding and meals to adult meals. At the time, children were not allowed to sit and eat with their parents or other adults. It was frowned upon as lack of discipline, and only spoiled children ate with adults. Children had to wait until the adults finished their meals and only then where they allowed to eat from the left-overs of the adult meal, with some additional sauce and *Injera (Taita).*

There was no running water or wash basins then. It was the children's duty to bring water and a pan for adults, so they could wash their hands before and after meals. Habtom as the eldest, was the one who took the responsibility first. When his siblings were old enough, they took over the job Habtom hated most. In certain areas, kissing the hands of your parents, and standing up whenever they came into the room, to give them your seat was a common sign of respect and family protocol. Habtom reminisced with sadness, that unlike the present, parents and elders were far more respected and feared in his childhood years. He was thus shocked at the unreasonable expectations Alganesh and her contemporaries held today.

Over the years, Habtom's opinions had remained completely unchanged, not moving an inch, which is why he was finding it extremely difficult to comprehend such demands and even harder to remotely understand Alganesh's logic. Thus, he not only detested her complaint, but was deeply revolted by it. He arrived at work, shaking his head for the nth time and repeatedly exclaiming, "Astounding! Unbelievable! Shocking! *Wey Tsigaaaaab*?!"

* 13 *

Five years had passed, since they bought the bakery. Habtom had managed to install a telephone in both his and his parent's house. He had also managed to buy a small old car, which would serve the whole family.

Grazmach was now nearly 56 years old and was due to be retired into pension. Bashay was 61 years old. Grazmach and Bashay were gratified by the efficiency and dedication shown by their two eldest children, who were running the bakery impeccably. They agreed that they were both advancing in age. At that time, the mortality rate for men in Eritrea was normally not more than 55-60 years. They realized that from then on, there was not much more they could contribute to help their children.

The two partners sat down and discussed their options seriously, eventually agreeing to hand over the administration and day-to-day running of the bakery to Tesfom and Habtom. Thereafter, the two parents stopped going to the bakery daily, remaining on the sidelines and acting as observers, providing only advice and direction to their children.

Soon enough, Tesfom and Habtom made even greater progress, and both families reaped greater benefits from the income of the bakery that improved their lifestyles. Habtom had now mastered the whole workings of the bakery. Under the former Italian owner, the bakery only baked bread. Now, in addition to bread, they started making and selling bread sticks and a traditional flat bread called *Hmbasha*.

The employees contributed significantly to the success of the bakery. All workers were exerting themselves with extreme interest and care. Tesfom played an important role in the encouragement and maintenance of this goodwill, as he gave the workers a sense of belonging and satisfied most of their needs and demands.

Habtom did not like spending money. The employees knew this, so whenever they had problems or needs, they would approach Tesfom and he would help them instantly. He usually did this without even informing Habtom. When he realized what was happening, Habtom was not happy. Although he was content that Tesfom worked well with the employees and he recognized the benefits of this compatibility, he also felt Tesfom was wasting too much money.

One Monday at 6 pm, Tesfom went straight from the bank to the bakery. After greeting everyone, he went into the second room, where he did the accounting. Habtom followed him, and before he even sat down said, "Listen Tesfom, I feel you are making it a habit to bend to every demand the workers are making. It is not fair or right that you do whatever they ask. You are squandering too much money on them."

The suddenness of Habtom's complaint took Tesfom by surprise. He looked up confused and asked, "What do you mean 'squandering' money?"

Habtom smiled and said, "I am sure you know perfectly well that I am referring to bending to the worker's demands. If everything was up to you, we would be bankrupt by now! But thanks to Habtom, who is always vigilant, we are still ok," he added, smiling sarcastically.

"Of course, I have no doubt that nothing escapes Habtom," said Tesfom smiling back. Then he instantly became serious and said, "Well honestly, I strongly believe that, in order to get the most from your workers, you need to earn their trust and faith. If you do not satisfy their needs and help them with their problems, it is almost impossible to do that. This is of course, on top of my firm belief, that it's also part of everyone's responsibility to be as fair and as just as possible to your fellow workers."

"Oh, come on, please, *per favore Tesfom*! You should understand that commerce and humanity and commerce and philosophy do not go together! You should never forget that we earned our money after much toil and immense sacrifice. Not all of us are as lucky as you," Habtom smiled wryly. Then he added "You were born with a golden spoon in your mouth, thanks to Grazmach! So, you can spend money easily, because you do not truly understand how it was earned! Even in your daily life, you don't think twice about spending money right and left!"

"My God Habtom, how you always love to rub this in. You have made this statement several times! You should understand that money is earned, so we can spend it and enjoy life. When are you ever going to be convinced that you are ok now? Thanks to the bakery, you are now not only stable but also at par with most of your peers."

"Well, you can say and do that, because thanks to Grazmach, you have a reliably firm solid back-up. On the other hand, people like us need to move cautiously, lest we falter and fall. If we ever fall, we have no one to back us up or lift us up! And by the way, it is not enough to be at par with most of your peers. To be 100% secure, you should be above all of your peers," replied Habtom.

"Wow Habtom! You'd better slow down my friend! This is a very dangerous ambition. As they say, you seem to have "a hunger you will never be able to satisfy and a thirst you will never quench!"

Habtom instantly responded, "You wouldn't be saying that, if you were the one who had to go through our childhood years. I don't think you remember clearly our childhood and how we were raised. We are where we are now, because we worked hard and saved every cent we earned. That is why, unlike you, we've learned to move cautiously all the time."

"Habtom, don't forget that we lived our childhood years in one compound. I was there," said Tesfom.

"Although we were in the same space and time, our lives were very far apart," replied Habtom and then quickly added, "*Don't forget that knowing about it and living it, are two diametrically opposite things and experiences.*"

"Habtom, don't live your life in yesterday or in the fear of yesterday. That was then, this is now! Bashay had limited income then, that was why it was important to move cautiously. But now your situation is not the same!"

"Are you trying to teach me by quoting high sounding words and philosophies or subtly trying to remind me of your educational superiority?"

As Tesfom was about to air his resentment at that statement, they were interrupted by an important supplier who had come to meet them. By the time they had finished, it was already too late, and they decided to go home.

While driving home, Tesfom thought about his conversation with Habtom. For some time, he had been postponing a topic he wanted to raise with him, because he was afraid it might cause some friction. Habtom's decision to talk to him over a small matter gave him the incentive and courage to act. He resolved to make an appointment with Habtom in the next few days and talk to him.

* 14 *

Tesfom and Habtom fixed a new date for their meeting, but, on the day of their appointment, a big demonstration took place in Asmara. The participants were primarily workers and students, along with people from other sectors of the population. At the time, Ethiopia was abrogating many of the rights granted to the new Eritrean Administration by a new federal agreement. The demonstration was conducted in Asmara, the capital of Eritrea, in December 1958.

People across the city stopped work to oppose the systematic abrogation of the statutes of the Federation. The demonstration started from the St. Mary Coptic church and then moved to the center of the city called *Combishtato* or in Italian, *Campo Cintato.* (It was so called because during Italian colonialism, Eritreans were legally forbidden in this area. It was segregated only for whites.)

Even though the sounds of gunfire and bombs could be heard in both areas, the opposition continued unabated. Businesses and houses were burned down. It was reported that 50 people died and about 300 were wounded. A state of emergency was declared, and the workers union and its offices were permanently closed and disbanded. The newspapers reported that Asmara was paralyzed for five days, after which the opposition and demonstration cooled down. Tesfom and Habtom waited to set up a convenient time to meet and talk, and finally, decided to meet after work at Habtom's house.

When Tesfom arrived at Habtom's house, Alganesh — and especially the children — came and welcomed him enthusiastically. They asked him if he had brought anything for them or if he was there to take them out.

Habtom shook his head and told them. "He didn't come to see you; he is here, because he has an appointment with me. Since we will need privacy, you must go to your rooms," he told them sternly. The children were disappointed. Their smiles turned into frowns; their eyes signaled their disappointment. They bowed their heads and went out dejectedly.

After the children left, Tesfom felt bad and said, "I am so sorry; I have disappointed the children. It is my fault. As children, they have every right to expect what they have been used to," said Tesfom shaking his head.

Habtom hastily expressed his disagreement. "It is not because they are children. It is only because you have practically spoiled them by always succumbing to their wishes. The correct approach is to distance yourself from children, so they don't get too close to you and expect things from you!" said Habtom, confident of the correctness of his logic and principle.

"I don't think we will be able to see eye to eye on this subject. Let's postpone the topic for another day. If we start arguing about it now, we will not find time to discuss the issues I want to raise with you," said Tesfom, without hiding his disappointment at Habtom's views.

"Ok, *va bene,* agreed. What is it that you want us to discuss today?" asked Habtom.

Tesfom delved straight into the subject, "I have heard reports that we are not adding enough yeast in our bread and *Hmbasha*. As a result, some customers are complaining about its quality. Some are also questioning the weight of the bread. They feel the quality and the weight do not look the same as it used to be."

"You will always find fault finders and irresponsible persons, who purposely distort the truth to ruin other people's reputations," said Habtom hurriedly.

"I agree that there are indeed some people like that. However, I am not talking about those kinds of people. *I am talking about people who do not judge hastily, who collect all facts and then instead of talking about you, talk to you and advise you, because they care!* Anyway, the important question is, are we doing that?"

"The weight of the bread we are selling is the same as before. As for yeast, you know that the price of yeast has recently gone up. We can't increase our prices at will, just because of the increase in the price of yeast. But we also need to maintain the profits we were making before. So, to compensate for that loss, we had to reduce the amount of yeast we add. Otherwise, we would lose a part of our profits. Why should we be the ones to bear the loss?"

"If we do that before any of our competitors, we will lose customers. It is better to endure a little longer and accept the loss for a while. Why not wait for a while?"

"We are new in the business, and we don't have as much leverage as our competitors. They have amassed profits for years. It won't hurt them much, but it will hurt us. It will especially hurt me most."

"Hurt you most? What are you trying to say?!" shouted Tesfom, slightly irritated.

"Well, you and your family have, beside the bakery, other additional income. If the bakery is not enough and you encounter a problem, you additionally have a dependable backup in Grazmach."

Though he was irritated, Tesfom calmly said, "You and your family are also now in a strong and stable financial position. But if you always say and believe that you are paupers, then you might feel and become one. Haven't you heard of the wise saying, '*A man is what he feels,*' or something along that line?"

It was Habtom's turn to be irritated. "Come on Tesfom, please, *per favore*, spare me such quotations and keep the philosophy to yourself," he said, not hiding his irritation. Then he quickly added, "Do you have any other issues you want to bring up?"

Tesfom hesitated slightly and looked like he had something else he wanted to bring up. He looked uncertain and hesitated again. Then almost instantly, he showed signs of changing his mind. His body language said it all. Finally, he decided to say no more and shook his head, saying, "No, nothing more."

The employees of the bakery had told Tesfom, that Habtom was indeed reducing the weight of the bread and *Hmbasha*. He knew if he brought that straight up front, Habtom would be annoyed and that such a confrontation would bring friction and conflict. To avoid this, he had decided to keep the information to himself.

Habtom had noticed Tesfom's hesitation and became relieved that the subject was over. In a much-relaxed mood, he said, "Since you have finished, I have one or two new proposals. I have thought of some new additional products we can introduce to the bakery.

There are small hand machines, with which one can make small amounts of pasta spaghetti, tagliatelle and lasagna. I know someone who has three such machines, and he is asking a reasonable price. We could buy them and make and sell pasta and some biscuits to a few selected customers. It would be an additional source of income."

"That is a great idea Habtom. Let's do it. You know, you are really very good in commerce and at discovering new sources of income," said Tesfom smiling.

"Yes, but still, you and your kind do not give much credit to people like us, who possess only experience. Your judgement is always based on education."

"Come on Habtom, isn't that what I am just doing? I was just expressing my belief in you! The problem however, is that it seems you still do not believe in yourself," said Tesfom, laughing heartily.

"Have you forgotten how you used to look down upon us? I am sure there could be some lack of respect leftover even now! When we were children, you were impossible and hard on us. You made sure all of us lacked confidence in ourselves by flaunting your looks, hair, elegance, school, house and parents. There was nothing you didn't hold up against us! You were all over us!" said Habtom sourly, putting Tesfom on the defensive and releasing pent up emotions.

"No, no, Come on Habtom! That was childish stuff and the folly of childhood. I still remember though, that it was especially you and I, who were at each other's throats. That was why I was harder on you, because you were so competitive and stubborn!"

"Of course, I never gave up. I fought and struggled against your dominance because you came at me with full force. Everyone else was ready to accept and bow to your dominance!"

"I don't know how you still remember every detail. I don't remember most of it."

"How can you remember? Don't you know the saying, 'The one who inflicted pain might forget, but the one who was on the receiving end will never forget.'"

'Wow Habtom, today you have become completely invincible. I am thus raising my hands and giving up. I think it is time that I go," said Tesfom, standing up. Then he added, "If the children have not yet slept, I would like to see them before I go. If they are asleep, then let me bid Alganesh good night."

Alganesh heard their movements and came. She told him that the children had tried their utmost to wait for him, but they were engulfed by sleep. She insisted that he stay a while and eat dinner with them. Tesfom explained that he had to go, since Medhn and the children were also waiting for him. He bid them good night and left.

While driving home, Tesfom was in deep thought. He marveled at Habtom's work ethic and natural brilliance in commerce and business. On the other hand, he also started to worry about Habtom's greed and willingness to make money at all costs.

He felt the child he knew as Habtom was still unchanged, still residing inside the man Habtom, with all his competitiveness, obduracy and obstinacy. He remembered something his father always repeated, '*As we advance in age, most of us only become bigger in size, older in age, more cunning, mischievous and malicious; yet though we count the years, we still remain unchanged, without attaining maturity, insight and wisdom.'*

While still reflecting on his father's thoughts, he suddenly realized something and whistled to himself. He found himself saying, "My father is right, it is amazing. *As we continue to grow up, we don't really change much. We think we are changing, but only the games we play and the playthings we use really change. We continue the same behavior by playing adult games with adult playthings.*"

Steeped deep in such philosophical reflections, Tesfom arrived home in no time.

CHAPTER 3
PASTA FACTORY

THE BAKERY CONTINUED to make steady progress. On top of bread, *Hmbasha* and *grissini* (bread sticks), they were now producing and selling biscuits and pasta. They had become so successful, that they were now even looking for an appropriate house to open a pastry shop. However, despite their concerted effort, they couldn't find the kind of house they wanted in the general area of their choice.

Although they didn't succeed in establishing a pastry shop, Tesfom and Habtom did succeed in another venture. With the permission and blessing of their parents, they managed to buy two twin houses for their residences. The houses were built in front of the *Collegio Lassale*, near the Catholic church of St Francis, within the area known as *Alfa Romeo.*

The identical twin houses sat side by side, separated only by a short wall. Each house had three rooms, a kitchen and a bathroom. Each had a very small courtyard, which also served as a garage. The houses were built slightly elevated and thus had stairs that led up to the door.

When the houses were bought, both Medhn and Alganesh were

again pregnant. Soon after moving into the new houses, both gave birth consecutively. First Medhn gave birth to a baby girl named Hirieti, and Tesfom at 31 and Medhn at 26 became the parents of four children.

Two months later, Alganesh gave birth to a baby boy who was named Negassi. Habtom at 33 and Alganesh at 29 became the parents of five children. The twins of both families were now eight years old and were already going to school.

After moving to the new house, the children, the parents and the grandparents became much closer to one another. The proximity of the twin houses especially helped the two mothers and their children to be much closer than the rest.

It was now seven years since the bakery was bought. Habtom, who was thrifty and careful with money, had by now managed to set aside a large amount of savings. Unknown to everyone else, he had also managed to establish another secret source of income, which further augmented his savings.

Tesfom, on the other hand, was careless and wasteful. Although he used to live a comfortable life, he was not saving much. Medhn and Grazmach were very much aware of this condition. But, even if he was not saving much, they were satisfied that at least he had managed to buy the residential house.

Habtom by now was well aware that he was becoming wealthier than Tesfom, which gave him immense pride and satisfaction. However, he was careful not to flaunt his wealth in front of the Grazmach family. But, whenever he was in the company of his own family, he made constant reference to his accomplishments.

* 2 *

A year after they had bought their residences, Tesfom learned about a small pasta factory that was for sale. The owners of the factory were Italians, and they had gone to Tesfom to seek approval for a bank loan, because they wanted to open a new and bigger factory.

They filled out all the required application forms. Tesfom reviewed their application and gave them an appointment when they could come back to receive the bank's final decision on the loan. After the loan was approved, Tesfom asked them their plans for the old factory. They told him that they intended to sell it.

As soon as he heard their plans, a new thought came to Tesfom, which he kept it to himself. The whole afternoon, he remained in deep thought, until the evening, when he went to the bakery. He immediately called Habtom from the front of the shop and when he came in, he went straight to the subject that was bothering him. "Listen Habtom," he said, "The limited amount of pasta we sell, has a large demand, right?"

"Are you kidding me?! There is so much demand, even if we produced a hundred times as much, it wouldn't be enough!" said Habtom with emphasis.

"Why don't we start producing a 100-fold then?!" said Tesfom sarcastically.

"What do you mean? How can we do that?" growled Habtom. Then he added, "Remember, we merely have a bakery, not a pasta factory! As things stand, there is no way we can increase our output."

"Yes, you are right. We don't have a factory. We are just working on and on by hand," he said, shaking his head. Then he looked at Habtom and asked, "Then why don't we buy a factory to produce a 100-fold?"

"Are you ok today? Are you crazy? How can we do that?" asked Habtom, with astonishment and doubt. Habtom had started to wonder whether Tesfom had come straight from the bank or had passed through one or two of the bars he frequented.

Tesfom then went on to recount his encounter with the Italians, finishing his report by sharing with Habtom the thoughts that went through his mind.

When he was done, Habtom said, "Well as an idea, it would be great. But beyond that, how can we ever buy such a factory? We can't raise the cash required to buy such an enterprise."

"If we agree in principle that is a viable idea, then allow me to tell you, my proposal."

"Sure, go ahead," said Habtom, with interest in his voice.

"First, we collect whatever cash we can raise. For the rest, we put the bakery and our two houses up as collateral and apply to the bank for a loan," said Tesfom with conviction.

"Well," said Habtom. "Generally, putting all your assets up as collateral to open a new business is risky. But in this case, from our little experience, we have proved that producing pasta is a safe and profitable business. Therefore, I have no objection to your suggestion. Concerning the loan, I am sure you can take care of it, since you know the business inside out."

"Of course, that is obvious. I can take care of that myself."

"You will also have to ask the Italians, if they will agree to accept part of the cost on an installment basis. Did you let them know that you were interested?"

"No, I didn't even give them a hint. We have a very good business relationship and, since they have applied for a loan, I am sure they will be more than favorable towards me. As far as price and other details are concerned, I am positive they will give me precedence over anyone else," said Tesfom with full confidence.

"Very good, then go ahead."

"Ok, good. Since we have agreed on this, it will be important to inform my father and *Aboy* Bashay of our plans, since we will need their approval and support."

"Do you think we need to tell them at this point? They removed themselves from active participation, gave us power of attorney and full freedom to take decisions because they have full confidence on us."

"Yes, but still, we need to tell them," Said Tesfom firmly.

Habtom finally agreed with the idea. They then finalized their meeting harmoniously and in full agreement.

* 3 *

Tesfom and his father agreed to meet after work hours. He chose to meet his father at his home, because he wanted to discuss the issue with both Grazmach and Medhn. Grazmach was warmly received by Medhn and his grandchildren.

After a while, Tesfom told the children to go to their rooms, assuring them that he would call them as soon as they finished their conversation. When all three sat down, Tesfom recounted the idea and plans concerning the pasta factory in detail.

In Eritrea, it is customary for men, starting with the eldest, to speak before women express their views. Hence, after Tesfom finished, it was Grazmach's turn. However, Grazmach gave Medhn his permission to express her views before him. She was not comfortable to speak before him, but after an initial reluctance, she bowed to his wish.

Medhn agreed that the idea Tesfom proposed was, in principle, very good and beneficial to all of them. But buying a factory on loan by putting up all the capital they had was risky. Instead of improving and progressing, they might lose everything they had already saved, or they could even end up drowning in debt. She further noted that Habtom was extremely careful and thrifty, while Tesfom was kind, giving and carefree about spending. In conclusion, she confessed that after considering all the angles of the proposal, she felt more unease and apprehension than hope and optimism.

Tesfom was infuriated by her last statement. He said it was not fair to compare him with Habtom based only on spending habits. He said that she knew very well that Habtom was a miser who didn't even spend money on his wife and family. He finally pointed out that, let alone all the ways in which they differed, had it been Habtom, she would not even have been given the right to sit with them to express her point of view.

Medhn hastily apologized for having inadvertently hurt Tesfom's feelings. She immediately and emphatically agreed with everything he said and assured him that she knew Habtom very well. She had no doubt that Habtom did not even come close to him in most things. She explained that she had pointed to their spending habits only to show that the inherent natural difference might have an impact in their future undertakings.

Tesfom felt slightly appeased and reassured by her explanation. When he was about to open his mouth, "May I say something?" Grazmach said smiling. "I think it is my turn now." Both Tesfom and Medhn immediately nodded their heads and sat back in deference.

"You and Habtom are now planning and thinking big. Bashay and I merely established a small business for our families. You deserve our admiration and congratulations for your vision. This gives us immense pride and satisfaction. Therefore, in principle, you will have my full support in everything," said Grazmach seriously.

Tesfom was ecstatic, "Thank you, that is really great!"

"Wait Tesfom, I haven't finished. There are still other important points and considerations we need to address. First, let me go back to the points Medhn raised, which are valid. This is a big undertaking that requires decisiveness, hard work, sacrifice and strength of character. If you are to succeed, then you need to be ready to change. The question is, are you ready for this? If you are not, then I will not also be part of it!" said Grazmach emphatically.

Tesfom's expression changed instantly. He quickly blurted, "I assure you father, I am ready!"

"My dear son, readiness to succeed in this undertaking is not only about making promises and declarations. It requires decisiveness and determination to make changes in your character. To be fair, you don't have many problems except in a few areas. For instance, spending too much money on friends and spending lavishly beyond your means are problems. And sometimes your lack of interest borders on carelessness. These are Medhn's worries, which I also share."

"Ok father, I completely understand your worries and I am ready to address them. I promise, I will try my best to overcome these problems!"

"Very good. We can only ask for your word on it. We all can only do our best. If we truly do our best, then God will also help us! We will also stand by your side, checking on you and helping you in any way we can. God be with you," said Grazmach and sat back in the chair, indicating that was his final word on the matter.

"Amen father; Amen father," said both Tesfom and Medhn.

After they finished their discussion, Medhn called the children who came running and started to play with their father and grandfather, while Medhn prepared tea and *Hmbasha.*

After they finished their snack, Grazmach stood up and said, "It is getting late. Allow me to go now. I hope and pray that God will make this venture successful and, most importantly, that this will bring love, peace, and health to our families."

Tesfom and Medhn again said, "Amen father; Amen father."

Soon after, Grazmach bid them farewell and left.

* 4 *

Habtom had asked Bashay to wait for him at home. When he arrived, he greeted his mother and informed her that he had a business affair to discuss with his father in private. He closed the door and, without going into much detail, he told his father the basic facts of the proposed plan.

"Listen son. Thanks to the bakery, our family is doing fine now. We have made much progress. But, the idea of taking out a loan to buy a factory by risking your house and the bakery makes me very uncomfortable. Both you and I have worked hard for years. The Bakery and your house are now the two foundations we can fall back on for security. Bank loans are dangerous affairs. They have bankrupted many people."

"You are right, many people may have gone into trouble because of bank loans. However, you know very well that I am not like other people. Don't you have confidence in me?" asked Habtom.

"Of course, I have full confidence in you, why wouldn't I?" replied his father. Then he added, "But this is not about you. Loans in general and bank loans in particular are worrisome affairs. Tesfom knows the inside out about loans, because it is his job. But you are merely a hard-working person and wouldn't know the ins and outs of it all. I am worried lest we sink into something we did not envision."

"Don't worry about it, father" said Habtom confidently. "I have thought about it in depth. As you rightly said, Tesfom knows the loan business more than anybody else. I am sure he will take care, because it will affect both of our families. As far as the pasta business is concerned, I am sure that in the long run, it will be even more profitable to our family than theirs. Even though he is more educated than I am, in the world of business, I have more experience than he does. So, rest assured, there will be no problems".

"If you say so and feel very strongly about it, then ok, *va bene* son. You should know that I never doubt your abilities and work ethic. So, go ahead. God be with us."

"Amen, father. I am in a hurry. I have to go now. Until we finish this, don't mention it to mother or Alganesh.".

"No, why should I? You can tell them yourself when the time is right."

"Ok, father," said Habtom and departed immediately.

* **5** *

The next day, Tesfom started serious talks with the Italians. The owners were pleased that he was interested in acquiring the factory. They considered it an opportunity that would streamline their loan application. They thus decided to cooperate with Tesfom and grant him all the assistance they could.

The owners had already determined a price for the factory

at 90,000.00 *Krshi*. However, they offered Tesfom a discount of 10,000.00 Krshi, proposing to take 60,000.00 Krshi as an initial payment and to receive the remaining 20,000.00 Krshi within a year.

Tesfom and Habtom had already made their own assessment of the value of the factory, and they recognized that the price and terms they were being offered were very generous. When they first went to see the factory, they had been very impressed with its machinery, set-up, workings and its location. The factory was in the area of Asmara known as *Amba Gagliano*, 500 meters after the *Sitawian* Seminary, turning right off the *Keren*-road.

They agreed to raise 10,000.00 *Krshi* in cash and to apply for a loan for the remaining 50,000.00 Krshi. Tesfom compiled all the necessary loan documents and submitted an application, which was quickly approved. They then finalized all sales agreements with the Italian owners. Since the end of the tax year was only one month away, they agreed to undertake the hand over in a month's time. They also agreed that Tesfom and Habtom would spend the month getting acquainted with the daily workings of the factory.

Tesfom and Habtom began visiting the pasta factory every day to observe its workings. They compiled notes about the source and purchase of raw materials, the stocks required, sales of products, the regular customers, the personnel and their monthly salaries, as well as other monthly expenses and pertinent details.

The month went by very fast and it was soon time to take over the factory. The handover went smoothly, which was when they both realized the wisdom of spending a month becoming familiar with the details, before taking control. Thereafter, they didn't encounter any problem running the factory smoothly.

They bought the pasta factory eight years after acquiring the bakery and at the same time their twins celebrated their ninth birthday.

* 6 *

The new owners took over the pasta factory on a Saturday. That afternoon, Habtom and Tesfom were sitting in the office, discussing the division of responsibilities.

"We have agreed that I will be responsible for the technical and day to day running of the factory and that you will be responsible for administration and finance, right?" asked Habtom. When Tesfom nodded his head, Habtom continued, "Good. However, we are still going to need help. It would be inconvenient and difficult for the two of us to constantly run back and forth between the bakery and the factory. The best thing would be to bring in, our brothers, Dermas and Araya to help us."

"That is a good idea. Let's assign my brother Araya to help in the factory and your brother Dermas could help in the bakery," said Tesfom.

"No, that is not what I had planned," blurted out Habtom hastily. He immediately realized that he had used the word planned and instantly said, "Sorry, I meant to say, thought. Anyway, I strongly feel it is better if we assign Dermas to the factory and Araya to the bakery."

"I hope you will not misunderstand or misinterpret why I am proposing Araya for the factory," said Tesfom cautiously, knowing well how Habtom was extremely sensitive about education and status.

"No, no problem, go ahead," said Habtom at ease.

"It is simply because Araya has a stronger educational background than Dermas, so he has greater ability in the larger enterprise with higher revenue," said Tesfom confidently.

"That is the exact reason why I am proposing Araya for the bakery," said Habtom.

"Then why are we not on the same page?" asked Tesfom slightly confused.

"I am proposing that Araya help us in the bakery, because, though it has comparatively much less monthly revenue, it has far more transactions than the factory. Araya could handle the more complex monetary traffic better than Dermas. While here at the factory, as far as finance and accounts are concerned, you are going to handle those yourself. Dermas could then help me here, with the day-to-day technical aspects."

Habtom seemed like he had already envisioned the conversation and planned it every step. Tesfom was not aware of any other ulterior motive that Habtom might have. Thus, he sarcastically said, "Well you have a point there. I hope that is your only reason, because a lot of times, you also have a habit of insisting only on your own point of view."

"No, it is not anything like that. I just told you my reasons for it. And don't forget that I will be the one who will be at the factory full time!" said Habtom smiling.

"You are right about that. Ok then, let it be," said Tesfom putting the matter to rest.

Habtom started to feel a great sense of self-satisfaction. He was gratified because he had succeeded in putting in place, the arrangement he had wanted and planned for so long. Moreover, he also felt pride that he could twist Tesfom as he wished, despite his educational superiority. His internal gratification became evident in his facial features.

Tesfom noticed that Habtom's mind was drifting somewhere else. "Hey Habtom, you are far away, where did you go?" said Tesfom with sarcasm.

Habtom looked embarrassed. He felt as if he had been caught red handed, thinking aloud. He quickly took control of himself and, with renewed composure said, "Yes you are right, I had completely drifted. I was reflecting on how we are working in complete understanding and dreaming about a great future together."

"Ok great! That is a nice dream," said Tesfom, laughing heartily.

Habtom joined him in laughter. Agreeing that they had nothing else to discuss, they departed.

* 7 *

Almaz was a 22-year-old girl who worked at the factory. She had been employed by the previous owners. The Italians liked her very much, and she had become one of their favorite employees. Although they had no evidence to prove their case, her girl companions used to suspect her of an amorous relationship with the owners. When word reached her, she vehemently rejected the allegation. She maintained that the source of all the backbiting was because the other girls were envious of her beauty.

Almaz was of medium stature, with a light complexion, large round eyes, straight nose, and black long hair that adorned her shoulders and back. She possessed perfect weight for her height. The parts of her body which seemed to carry extra weight were her ankles, thighs, buttocks, and to a certain degree her breasts. No one could detect an extra inch on any other part of her body. Her waist was so slim, it could practically be encircled with one hand. It looked like it was created not to carry weight, but only to serve as a joint to give beauty to the top and bottom parts of her body.

Her teeth seemed to have been placed in perfect rows, each in its own place, in accordance to its size and weight. It looked like an immense amount of time and patience was spent, not only in creating all parts of her face in perfect proportion, but also in fitting each part in its perfect position commensurate with the others. Hence her eyes, mouth, nose, ears, cheeks, chin and forehead were all positioned in their assigned places to create a perfectly beautiful and mesmerizing face.

Whenever she smiled or laughed, Almaz always looked like she was solely created to provide joy and happiness to the observer. Whenever her gaze fell on anyone, that person would feel that she was specifically born to be of service to his eternal happiness. In short, Almaz was not only a stunningly beautiful young girl, but was also endowed with an inherent ability to captivate and capture anyone's attention.

* 8 *

In Highland Eritrea, there is a traditional celebration called *Hoye Hoye* that ushers in the *Geez* New year by lighting torches. When Tesfom and Habtom were children, they used to go to neighboring houses, singing traditional songs of good wishes for the New Year. Every household would offer them between a few dollars to a few pennies, and the children spent the money on whatever treats they chose. Back then, children were not given pocket money. The only time they were permitted to spend money was whenever they collected any in such a fashion.

When Tesfom and Habtom became neighbors and started to live side by side, the love between their children flourished. The children went to school together and after school, played together every day. Their proximity also enabled the mothers to become very close to each other. They were chatting and drinking coffee together daily.

One day, while Alganesh and Medhn were drinking their daily coffee, their conversation drifted to the time when the factory was bought. "Since the day he called me and his father, to get our points of view on the viability of buying the factory, Tesfom has become extremely busy. So much so, he has practically forgotten to take the children out," said Medhn.

"Lucky you, Habtom does not tell me anything about his work, let alone seek my opinion. He says a woman should only be concerned about her house work," said Alganesh bitterly, with disappointment in her voice.

"Well, that is not right, but it is ok. At least Habtom does not have other vices and shortcomings," said Medhn.

"Yes, you are right there, though he really irritates me when he repeatedly says, 'If a child is provided with food and clothing, then he doesn't need anything else,'' said Alganesh sourly, mimicking Habtom's voice and tone.

"That is not right at all. Many parents fail to understand that more than anything else, a child needs love and time with his parents. Food and clothing can differ according to the wealth of each family. In the end, lack of good food and clothing does not hurt a child much. But the lack of love and time with his parents adversely affects a child for life. While growing up, our families didn't have much to provide us materially, but we had their love and their time," Medhn said, with emotion.

"Absolutely true," said Alganesh.

"Anyway, that is how life is. You get some and learn to live with the rest. After all, no one is perfect."

"Yes, you are right. No one is perfect except the All mighty. Since we are not perfect ourselves, neither should we expect perfection."

As soon as Alganesh said that, they heard a voice calling, "Hello, is anybody home?"

Alganesh stood up and went to meet the guest. She was a relative who had come to visit. They greeted each other and Alganesh went to prepare tea for the guest. Medhn reminded her to prepare enough tea for the children as well, to drink with their snack. When everything was ready, Alganesh went out and called the children.

Bruk, Timnit, Kbret and Samson never liked to be interrupted from play. They came in reluctantly, because they were ordered to take their snacks. As soon as the children filed in, the woman said, "Wow your children have indeed grown up. How old are they now? All four are not your children, am I right?"

"They are nearly ten years old now. Medhn and I gave birth to our twins on the same day. Two of them are ours and the other two are our friend's children. Can you tell by their looks, which ones look like Habtom and me?" asked Alganesh, smiling.

"I can surely try, let me see. Come nearer my children, so auntie could give you a kiss and see you closely," said the guest, gesturing to the children.

The children came and kissed the woman one by one. Then she made all four, stand in front of her. They looked like a guard of honor waiting to be inspected. She looked them over closely and finally made her decision. Holding one boy and one girl on her right and another boy and girl on her left, she said with near certainty, pointing to Bruk and Kbret, "These two are yours," and then pointing to Timnit and Samson, "These ones are your neighbor's children."

As soon as she spoke the words, the children roared with laughter. The guest held her head and said laughing, "Oh my God, I must have made a mistake, the children are laughing at me."

"You are ok, you got at least 50%. You have correctly identified the girls. Your mistake was in the identity of the boys. These two, Kbret and Samson are my children, while these two, Bruk and Timnit are my friend's."

All of them laughed heartily. The children took their snacks and the women drank their tea. When the children finished their snacks, Medhn stood up, bid them farewell, and went home with her children.

* 9 *

Both Tesfom and Habtom noticed Almaz's beauty, from the moment they first saw her. It would have been unusual, if they hadn't noticed her mesmerizing beauty, because that was evident to everyone.

In the first weeks, their whole attention and focus was on organizing, streamlining and managing the factory. Even so, whenever they saw her, they couldn't avoid being amazed by her beauty and the aura that emanated from her. However, despite Almaz, they continued to focus their undivided attention on their work.

Almaz was very much aware of her exclusive beauty and body.

The only thing that would amaze and sometimes exasperate Almaz was, if men failed to notice her and her unique endowments. If that happened, she would be very offended and, whether she wanted the man or not, she would do everything she could, to make him kneel down on her altar. Once the man succumbed, then she would move on, and never notice him again.

Tesfom's exclusive weaknesses were only drinking and playing cards. As a married man, he had no interest in other women, whatsoever. He was now 33 years old, and whenever he noticed Almaz, he merely admired her beauty as an amazing creation of nature. Other than that, he never considered her as someone that had anything to do with him.

Despite that, after streamlining the workings of the factory, it was Tesfom who started to be attracted and bothered by her beauty. Habtom had no time for anything, other than work and money.

It did not take much time for Almaz to notice, that every time she visited the office, Tesfom eyed her with interest. She was already attracted by his handsomeness and elegance, so she started creating small excuses to go to the office repeatedly, to get a chance to see him and be seen by him.

She knew Tesfom was married and the father of four children and also that Tesfom was much older than she was. But, none of that discouraged her from pursuing and desiring Tesfom. Almaz was a girl who knew very well what she wanted to be, how far she wanted to climb, and how to achieve her goals. As long as she achieved her goals, she never cared much about what people said.

Tesfom became engulfed with feelings he had never felt for any other person. This was completely new to him and his nature. He started thinking about her and visualizing her even while he was at the bank. The more he tried to control his emotions, the more he felt entrapped and falling down further and deeper. He was sure that if he wanted, the prey his body was desiring was his for the taking.

By this time, Almaz was almost sure that Tesfom had developed similar, if not stronger feelings for her. She explained their mutual feelings by telling herself, "Our stars have met." Despite his inclinations, Tesfom did not make a move. She felt he needed more encouragement and a delicate nudge.

She began to devise a strategy to achieve her goal and heart's desire. Though certain of his feelings for her, she also knew that something was still preventing him from making the initial move. From that day on, she took it upon herself to use every armament in her possession to trap and capture Tesfom for good.

* 10 *

As a matter of principle, Tesfom always shared whatever serious problems or challenges he faced with Medhn, his brother Araya or his father. In other less serious matters, he had a multitude of friends with whom he shared both his problems and joys. The trap Almaz had entangled him in and the emotional impasse he faced was completely different from anything he had encountered in his entire life.

He couldn't master enough courage to bring the subject up with anyone of his family or his multitude of friends. As much as he was extremely well liked and loved by many and was very gregarious and affable, Tesfom now felt alone and lonely. Thus, for several weeks he began to spend his time alone, in deep anguish, sinking in a deep well of loneliness. For several days, he felt like a lone prisoner, all by himself.

Almaz began to use all the means at her disposal to nudge and push Tesfom into action. Without the use of language, she started using her body to send clear messages about her feelings and desires. Every part of her body spoke without words. Sometimes her flickering eyes, along with her mouth and teeth would send a well-orchestrated strong message that no words could express. At other times, she would send an unmistakable message with her breasts and buttocks. They seemed to tell him how hungry they were for his touch and how they were ready to be enslaved by him. All of these actions seemed to penetrate Tesfom's body and soul. The urgency and ferocity with which she transmitted her incessant messages clearly showed that Almaz too was desperate and on edge.

Tesfom was continuously bombarded with these relentless messages. He had clearly understood for weeks what Almaz was trying to tell him and what she urgently wanted. That was not his problem. Nor did he fail to clearly understand the choice he had in front of him. His only problem was that he couldn't find the courage to decide either way. He was trapped between two swords. He smiled wryly when he remembered a Tigrinya proverb, "*Bezi Inte Kedkn Wedkn Yimotekn; Beti Intekedkn Sebaykn Yimotekn,*" meaning, "If you proceed in one direction, your son will die; if you proceed in the other direction, your husband will die." It was a choice between a hard place and a rock.

Despite her desperate attempts, Tesfom was still not making a move. Almaz started to have serious doubts. In her entire life, she had never had an experience like this. She was used to men flocking to her and buzzing around her like bees around flowers with pollen. That happened even without her making any advances or showing signs of interest. If she exhibited the slightest interest, men's reactions and haste would normally increase a hundred-fold.

Almaz was comfortable with men who adored and worshipped her but not with those whom she adored or worshiped. She was only comfortable with men she was sure of controlling and not men who would control her. Almaz felt uneasy and was worried that she had let herself fall deeply in love with Tesfom. Her worries were doubled, because she had allowed herself to be vulnerable, without any sort of assurance of his love and devotion.

At this point, Tesfom was hanging over a cliff. A lot of emotional conflict was going on within him. On the one hand, he had fallen deeply in love with Almaz. His entire body, senses and mind wanted and desperately desired her. He started to reason that the only way out was to accept the inevitable.

He told himself, *"I am just in love with her. There is no other meaning to this. This is love. I have just become a victim of love. This is something that came over me and overpowered me. I had nothing to do with it. I didn't bring this willingly on myself. Every part of my body including all my nerves, sinews and senses in unison are crying out for her. They are crying out to be enslaved by her. There is nothing I can do in such a situation,"* he said, thus freeing and absolving himself from any responsibility.

Tesfom was encouraged by the arguments he had laid down to prove he was on the right path. He reinforced his train of logic and supported his position with further points, continuing as if he had not stopped. *"Love is something good and sweet. Love is never bad. In fact, that is why my whole body wants and desires her and expresses its ardent wish to possess her. I can't fight against myself and my true feelings. It is impossible!"* he said, forcefully.

He patted himself on the back for having created an array of reasonable unassailable arguments to overcome his present predicament and validate the way his body and desire were leaning. In the meantime, his inner voice, with the help of his spirit and conscience, continuously clamored to be heard. Finally, Tesfom grew tired of the clamor and agreed to listen for a while.

Spirit and conscience quickly took control and started their counter argument by saying, "*Come on Tesfom, don't fool yourself. When all of your faculties that are pushing you to achieve their carnal gratification have had their fun, they will not remain there to support you. You will have no one to help get you out of the complicated quagmire that will inevitably be your fate. You will be all alone.*"

Tesfom didn't want to hear such rationalizations. He was thus repeatedly ignoring and belittling them, while reinforcing his physical and emotional desire. He was sliding fast and was near to succumbing to Almaz's wishes.

Part of Tesfom's conscience was well aware that he was nearing defeat. He was at a very critical stage and if he didn't make the right move now, he might not get another chance. Thus, his soul and conscience clamored to be heard. *"Please give us another chance,"* *they pleaded. "Up to now, you have not heard us out properly. We have not been able to present all of our arguments and points. Please, please, hear us out."*

When they had his attention, they began their argument from where Tesfom had stopped them, saying, *"We completely agree with you that love is indeed good and sweet and that genuinely true love brings only goodness and sweetness."*

When Tesfom heard this initial argument, he was happy that they were close to his views and was thus encouraged to listen attentively. When spirit and conscience noticed this, they moved quickly to the rest of their argument, saying, *"If love's fruits and results are not goodness and sweetness, then it is not true love. The feelings that are pulling you along blindly are not love, because nothing good can come out of this. You are wrongly considering temporary physical gratification as a permanent advantage. But, don't fool yourself Tesfom, this temporary gratification is as transient as smoke and will eventually vaporize and disappear. After you have had your fun, don't doubt for a moment that many tears, agony, suffering, separation and break-ups will follow, affecting everyone in the family you love."*

Gradually, Tesfom's defenses began to crumble and he was not far from coming back to his senses. Spirit and conscience decided to use the last ace in their armament, against which they knew Tesfom was vulnerable. They said, *"You only possess one body and one soul, but don't forget that the home you have established and nurtured has five additional bodies and souls - your wife and four innocent children. You may satisfy one body and soul, but you will condemn many innocent bodies and souls to suffering and breaking apart. In your selfish pursuit to satisfy only your own body, how can you sanely condemn so many innocent souls and bodies to suffering? Such a painful and destructive act can't be called love! So please, be caring and thoughtful and come back to your senses!"*

After this last point, the internal voice stopped, resting its case.

Tesfom was torn between the desires of his body and the strong argument of his spirit and conscience. Whenever he wanted to slide towards Almaz, his conscience would bring his dear sweet innocent wife Medhn before his eyes until he shuddered. After a while, Almaz would come into his mind in all her mesmerizing beauty, and Tesfom would start to swing back towards her. Then his conscience would bring back the children he loved more than life itself, and he would freeze.

Tesfom was trapped between his sensual desire and the red warning lights of his conscience. After a long struggle, he moved near to a decision. He was by nature a very just and fair person. Since early childhood, his father had instilled in him the golden rule, "Don't do unto others, as you wouldn't want others to do unto you." Because of that guidance, he couldn't put himself and his desires above those of Medhn and his children. He couldn't bring himself to be unjust and cruel to his wife and his innocent children.

He was now near to a decision. But no matter what he finally decided, he couldn't forget how greatly he had been tempted. He understood he would never forgive himself for how close he had come to burying the golden rule according to which he had been raised. In the end, this was what saved Tesfom; it was not his courage, valor or decisiveness – it was his sense of guilt!

Tesfom then spoke aloud to himself, "*My God! How very true that love is often considered blind. Although some may say, 'love is blind,' the real saying should be, "Love makes everyone blind!" I became completely blind. It was not love, but actually pure madness. I was basking and wallowing in a dream world without a compass. This is like driving downhill without brakes. My conscience was right to tell me, love is something that should spread goodness and love to many, not destroy it. It was right to tell me that the power of love should bring people and families closer together, not break up and destroy the very fabric of their lives. Love should bring warmth not cold; laughter and merriment for everyone, not anguish and agony to many. Love should expand and spread to many and all, rather than withdraw and be limited to a couple."*

Tesfom while still talking to himself, suddenly stood up. He put his hands behind his back, put his head down, furrowed his forehead, squinted his eyes and started to pace right and left for a few minutes. He then suddenly lifted his head, as if he had reached a decision.

His face was now completely relaxed. He brought his hands forward in a fist and shouted, *"I was about to throw away into a precipice, my wife, my children and my family, just so my body and my senses could have their momentary joy and gratification! I am sorry Tesfom, that you have stooped that low! I pity you that you have desired and considered this for weeks!"*

He stood still for a few seconds and then said, "*Now enough madness!*" Then he knelt down, closed his eyes, bowed his head and said, *"I thank you dear Lord for saving me from this madness! I promise in the name of my children to never look back on this decision, so help me God!"*

He stood up slowly, confident in his resolution and final decision. He felt his head clear, his nerves and muscles relax, and his body lighten. Nothing was tearing him apart anymore. He had no more worries.

He knew Almaz would be devastated by his decision, but he realized that it was going to be her problem. He knew how he would handle her. From that day forward, Tesfom changed his body language toward Almaz and became the embodiment of seriousness. He completely stopped showing any signs of desire or interest in her.

Almaz was confused by Tesfom's sudden change. She did not understand its meaning and she didn't want to judge him hastily. But when things did not improve, she began to boil with anger and frustration. Almaz had never encountered anything like this before; let alone by an older married man, even with other younger unmarried men. She became angry, bitter and desperate. Wanting him at any cost, she refused to go down without a fight or before she got her vengeance.

* 11 *

Habtom did not spend money for clothes, shoes, drinks or entertainment, and was extremely thrifty with money. In fact, his thriftiness bordered on miserliness, and he was well known for it among his family and friends. Whenever the question of money arose, the family used to tell each other, don't even hope of getting a cent from Habtom. Even his wife and children spoke to each other in the same fashion.

Such talk was also common among his friends, relatives and their employees. Most frequently they would say: "Habtom has not yet realized that he has become rich; he still believes he is poor. Poor Habtom, he should be spending sleepless nights counting his money." The inevitable question posed after such comments was: "If he doesn't use his money to enjoy life now, when is he going to use it for himself?"

Most of these remarks eventually reached his ears, so he was well aware of the details of such murmurs and backbiting. Habtom was not bothered by such small talk, so, he stuck to his beliefs and principles. He still continued not spending money for anything he did not consider essential.

* 12 *

In the beginning, Habtom had not noticed Almaz at all, but as the days went by, he slowly started to notice her mesmerizing beauty. He noticed the way she carried her immaculate body and the smile that adorned her beautiful face. He felt like he was truly seeing her for the first time.

As far as Almaz was concerned, Habtom was only a co-owner

and an employer. Nothing more, nothing less. She had no personal designs for him and had not taken any steps to try to attract him.

But, at the time when she was facing Tesfom's change of heart, she began to notice that Habtom was eyeing her with interest. When she was certain this was happening, she decided to use him for her own ends. She began to feign slight interest in him, throwing little crumbs of attention towards him, making sure that Tesfom noticed. She wanted to arouse Tesfom's envy, hoping that he might resume his interest in her.

At first, Habtom didn't notice Almaz's attentions to Tesfom, but when he saw it repeatedly, he became envious. The more he noticed her flirtation, the more he felt jealous and competitive. Meanwhile, Tesfom had already made his own decisions about how to handle Almaz, though Habtom obviously had no knowledge of it.

It did not take long for Tesfom to notice Habtom's interest in Almaz. When he first saw it, he was surprised and incredulous. Soon after, he also observed that Almaz was showing interest in Habtom. The suddenness of it amazed and perplexed him. Tesfom had already made his decision. However, his body was still raw and hurting and his senses were still rebelling. In reality, he was still fighting his desire for her. Witnessing this flirtation between Habtom and Almaz provoked his competitive and combative spirit.

When Tesfom's feelings and desires awoke anew, he told himself, "No, no way, Habtom should not take her." For a few days, he struggled with himself, caught between his solemn promise and this newly awakened emotion. But having determined to stay away from Almaz, he caught himself and his emotions in time and was finally able to stand firm by his decision and the promises he had made.

Habtom was not aware of Tesfom's turmoil and final decision. He realized that if he was to possess Almaz, the silent war that would be waged between them would be long and fierce. He accordingly started to draft a strategy for the bitter struggle ahead.

Habtom knew if he was to compete with Tesfom, looks, clothing, elegance, charm and similar attributes were not going to be on his side. He resolved to concentrate on his areas of strength and to study other means of capturing Almaz's heart.

Since she had desired Tesfom, he knew that she did not have any problem having a relationship with an older married man. Almaz could have any younger single man she desired, so, her decision to have a love affair with a married man showed that she had important interests other than love.

Habtom suspected that one of those other interests might be money and future financial stability. If that was the case, he knew he could be a serious contender, and he also knew that if he acquired enough information about her weaknesses, the coming battles would be easier to handle and win.

He started to enquire discretely about her past life and activities. He particularly sought details about her tendencies, desires, dreams and her ambition in life. He looked for details about the real relationship she had with the previous Italian owners of the factory.

With a good deal of background information, he drew up a plan designed to trap and bring Almaz to his bosom. At first, he approached her with considerable anxiety, lest she reject him outright. So, before showing her any intimate interest, he started to shower her with money and expensive gifts.

* 13 *

At this time, Habtom's interest in Almaz was growing in leaps and bounds. Almaz was still not doing anything to encourage Habtom's advances, even after she realized that there was no more hope for Tesfom. Meanwhile, Habtom's unending flow of gifts continued unabated. Though she remained non-committal, Almaz made no effort to discourage him. She decided not to reject his advances outright, because she thought a rich man, with co-ownership in two businesses, who would continually shower a woman with precious gifts was a rare combination.

Habtom noticed that Almaz neither actively discouraged him nor rejected him outright. This, for him, was encouraging and positive and his desire and longing for Almaz grew. He wanted her more desperately than ever before. He began throwing away large chunks of money on expensive gifts. Such behavior was completely new to Habtom. He showered her with precious gifts of gold and ivory. Almaz who loved power and money, finally succumbed to his repeated advances and accepted Habtom as her lover.

* 14 *

Throughout his life, Habtom had never been interested in his appearance or his attire. He never wore even the few dressy clothes he had, but rather wore his work clothes (coveralls) for practically all occasions. But now, he became extremely interested in his attire, making drastic changes. He not only stopped wearing work clothes, but started buying extremely expensive shoes and clothes. He used to abhor and criticize people like Tesfom, who wasted money on nonessential expenses. Now it became his turn to spend heavily on what he previously called unnecessary expenses.

Habtom's transformation was not restricted to clothes and his appearance. The hours he came home for lunch and dinner, as well as his eating habits started to dramatically change. When Alganesh noticed these changes, she was happy that her husband had started to dress decently and was taking care of himself. Alganesh also noticed another positive change in Habtom. He had become more generous with money towards her and their children.

Despite these positive changes, she still found other changes a little peculiar. He started coming home at irregular hours, and most of the time barely ate or just tasted the food she prepared. Alganesh decided to follow these new developments and events with patience, hoping the new behavior would be temporary.

Though she waited patiently, nothing changed. With time, it even got worse.

On a Saturday evening, Habtom came home at 11.30 pm. This was a little later than his recent habit. "Are you going to eat? should I prepare dinner?" Alganesh asked.

"I am too tired now, I don't feel like eating," said Habtom.

"It has now been some time since you changed your hours and eating habits. I am amazed and can't understand the new habit you have recently embraced."

"What new changes and habits are you talking about? You know that I work day and night. So, If I change my usual hours, what are you trying to insinuate?" asked Habtom, acting like he was the injured party.

"That's not the only thing I am talking about. Most of the time, you barely taste or eat the food I prepare," she said firmly.

"Listen, I meet with clients and businessmen, and sometimes we go out for a bite or a snack. As a result, and because I'm often very tired, sometimes I don't feel like eating. That is all there is to it, or are you intending to feed me by force?" Habtom shouted angrily.

"Of course, no one can force you to eat. In the past, you ate with regularity without anyone forcing you. So, you know what I am talking about," said Alganesh, unperturbed by his shouting.

"Anyway, whatever! I am not going to eat when I don't feel like it."

"I am not asking you to eat if you don't feel like it," Alganesh responded calmly.

"Then what are you asking me to do?" he shouted again.

"I am simply asking what is the real reason for this sudden change?" asked Alganesh, point blank.

"That is what I have been trying to get through your thick skull. But because you are stupid and ignorant, you can never understand or accept the explanation provided. I have been through so much the whole day and when I come home, this what I get from you! You are getting on my nerves now. I don't want to hear another word from you. Watch out or else you will be responsible for the consequences," said Habtom furiously. He stood up, growling at her. He kicked the small table in front of him and strode towards the bedroom.

Alganesh knew well her husband's violent nature. She was terrified of the consequences that could arise, not having imagined the subject would be so sensitive.

Thus, a sense of self-doubt crept into Alganesh. She asked herself if she had hastily misinterpreted his latest changes or was misjudging his deeds. She knelt down and started saying her prayers, asking God for forgiveness. "Forgive me God, you have clearly instructed us not to judge. Tonight, I have sinned, God. I have hastily judged." After her prayers, she went to bed, taking a long time to get to sleep.

Unknown to Alganesh, her husband had been taking significant steps in his relationship with Almaz. The recent weeks, Habtom had been looking for an apartment to rent for Almaz, and he had found one that same day. If Alganesh knew of this, instead of censuring herself for judging prematurely, she would have damned Habtom and his betrayal in the strongest terms.

* 15 *

Habtom bought brand new and exquisite furniture for Almaz, and soon she moved from her old place to the new larger house in *Geza Kensha,* near St. Mary cemetery. Soon after, he made her resign from her job at the factory, and she started living like a regular house wife.

Tesfom did not know of the swift steps Habtom was taking concerning his love life with Almaz. When he started hearing rumors, he rejected them outright as exaggerated hearsay. His reaction was based on what he knew about Habtom, as he was sure Habtom would never spend that kind of money on anyone. Tesfom wasn't yet aware that Habtom was diving much deeper into his relationship with Almaz.

After a while, Habtom established a construction materials sales shop *(Ferramenta)*, under his name and that of Almaz. It was situated in the main street of Menelik the 1st, near the St. Mary Coptic church. He began giving his whole attention and time to Almaz. Any free time he had outside the factory was spent with her, either at home or at their new shop.

Asmara was a small city, and everything that was happening with Habtom and Almaz quickly became common knowledge. Soon the whole Bashay family heard of Habtom's affair, but none of them had the courage to talk to him about the matter. On the contrary, many - including his parents - did not even consider Habtom's affair as unjust or wrong.

* 16 *

Tesfom had by now nearly forgotten the subject of Almaz. Although slight remnants of her memory resided in his subconscious, he was now freed from any emotional attachment to her.

Habtom had a well-built muscular body, which made up for what he lacked in facial features. Above the neck, he was far from handsome, but his chest, back, and the muscles in his arms and thighs were made to perfection. Although Almaz first was drawn to Habtom for his money, she later came to love him as a man. Whether it was out of spite or she believed it, she often told herself, "A man should look and be like Habtom! It was a blessing in disguise that I got Habtom, instead of that good looking but good-for- nothing Tesfom!"

Months had passed since Almaz accepted Habtom as her lover. He was now secure and comfortable, having achieved what he most desired. His measure of success and achievement was to get and own whatever one desired and wanted by any means. There was nothing in his conscience that would prick him and make him doubt his actions or their consequences.

For Habtom, the principle of talking and arguing with oneself, challenging one's desires courageously and contemplating the consequences of one's actions, was foreign and had no place in his personality. If he got what he desired by any means, Habtom would sleep happily like a log, unconcerned with the pain his actions would cause to others. For Habtom, any means was fair and just, because the end justified the means.

As a result, Habtom's love for Almaz tripled and quadrupled in the months that followed. In contrast, the care and feelings he had for Alganesh and her children diminished dramatically. He almost completely stopped eating dinner with Alganesh and the children, although he still occasionally ate lunch.

Being a woman and a wife, Alganesh started to notice Habtom's changes before anyone else. Since Habtom had no previous history of infidelity, she had doubts in case she was misjudging him hastily. When her repeated conversations with him lead nowhere, she decided to talk to her father-in-law about the matter.

However, Bashay was not receptive to her concerns. He asked if there was anything that she lacked in terms of money and provisions for her and her children. When she told him that was not a problem, he sternly advised her that if everything was provided, she shouldn't complain about anything else. As a final word of wisdom, he said she should understand that is how men are and should accept that as a fact of life.

Alganesh talked to her father-in-law knowing full well that she wouldn't get much sympathy or help from the Bashay family. She knew that the whole family not only worshipped him, but also feared his wrath; thus, she lost all hope of getting sympathy or help from the Bashay family.

* 17 *

No matter what she said or did, Alganesh couldn't bring any change in Habtom. On the contrary, his habits even worsened. He had by now completely stopped eating dinner at home, although he still came home to sleep, no matter how late it was. Finally, the day came when Habtom for the first time ever, did not come home to sleep. He came the next morning, going directly to the wardrobe and changing his clothes, as if there was nothing inappropriate.

It had been weeks since Alganesh had promised herself that, no matter what, she would not complain about his behavior. When she saw his utter disregard and audacity, her resolve to stay silent began to crumble. Habtom finished changing his clothes and strode towards the door, ready to leave without saying a single word. That was the last stroke for Alganesh. She was enraged by his boldness! She said, "My God, how people change! You have now made it official. You have even started to sleep out!"

"I have told you several times, that there is no one who can prevent me from eating out and staying out whenever I wish," snapped her husband.

"It has been a long time since you ate or spent time at home during the day or evenings, but I am now talking about this brand-new habit of sleeping out."

"You'd better understand that there is also no one who can prevent me from sleeping out, whenever and wherever I want. I am a man! I can do anything I please." He said firmly.

"A man?! So now, to deserve to be called a man, you have to forsake your home and sleep out! Is that what you are trying to tell me? Well, my dear, on the contrary, if anyone deserves to be called a man, he first and foremost should respect and protect the very family he established and attend to the children he begot!"

"What are you trying to say? There is nothing that is amiss as far as my family and children are concerned. I still provide everything for my family," he said with an air of confidence.

"Don't you understand that children and families need more than bread and provisions?" said Alganesh firmly.

"As usual, it is only because you want to exaggerate, otherwise there is nothing that my children don't have or miss."

"Well for one, your children miss the father they should have."

"I have not thrown away my children or my family. I am still with my family."

"What more can you do to disrespect your marriage vows? Do you think you can respect your vows and responsibilities only through material supplies and provisions?"

"I am still at my home with my children; I am respecting my vows! Aren't they teaching you anything in the church you run to every morning? Or have you completely switched religion to some of these new fancy ones?" said Habtom, shifting the subject from himself to Alganesh.

Alganesh immediately understood the game her husband was trying to play. She courageously said, "You are unbelievable! If you think you can wiggle out of your responsibilities by switching the subject to be about me, instead of you, then you are only fooling yourself!"

Habtom was furious. He couldn't match the logic she was expounding. So, he turned to the only way he knew to stop it. He shouted, "Enough! *Basta*! You are now trying my patience. No other man would have lived with such a nagging and annoying woman as you. I don't want to hear another word from you now, or you will bear the consequences of your insolence and disrespect!"

He stood up noisily, kicking the table in front of him. He growled at her, heaving and breathing heavily. When he was sure there was no response from her, he strode out.

Alganesh remained frozen where she was. She struggled to stop her tears. After a while, she couldn't and the tears came streaming down. She let her emotions out the only way she knew and her face was completely awash with tears. She became very sad and miserable, pitying her bad luck and destiny.

After a long time, Alganesh gained control of her emotions. "I should remain strong. There are worse things happening to many women and children around the world. I should be thankful for what I have. If nothing else, I am healthy and my children are healthy. Forgive me God for pitying myself. Even if Habtom, in his madness, foolishly decides to throw away his children and family, I solemnly promise not to lend him a hand. Whatever happens, I will take care of my children by myself!" She then proceeded to say her prayers. After that, she dried her eyes and went to her children.

Habtom stayed out the whole day and did not come home to sleep that night as well. Alganesh was deeply troubled and shocked at Habtom's extreme sudden changes. But she said her prayers with her children and went to bed without bothering to wait for him.

She got up the next day and moved her bedroom. Habtom eventually noticed the change, but made no comment about it. His silence sent Alganesh a message to the effect that her decision meant nothing to him.

* 18 *

Alganesh was now certain that Habtom was having an affair, but she didn't know with whom, or where or the depth of his involvement. While she was trying to understand what was going on, Medhn came to see her.

"How have you been Alganesh?" asked Medhn.

"I am ok and how have you been yourself? What good timing Medhn *Habtey,*" she said with an air of sadness. "You came at the right time, when I needed a good friend like you."

"I couldn't stop thinking about you," said Medhn, worried for her friend. "I came to see you, even if it was for a minute. You look upset and troubled. Are you ok?"

"You know what I am going through. I don't even know how I

am enduring it. Habtom's behavior has worsened further. He has made it official now. He has even started to sleep out!"

"That is actually why I am here," said Medhn. "I have received reliable information, which I thought you deserved to know. Is there any specific information you have been able to gather on your own?" she asked.

"No, nothing. You know me. I barely see or meet anyone," replied Alganesh. "You know my routine; I only venture from my house to the church and back. I never go anywhere else or have contact with anyone else."

"I do know that Alganesh *Habtey*. I am asking, just in case."

"No, I know nothing. You are the only one I have *Medhney"*, replied Alganesh.

"Anyway, you know that Tesfom does not have interest in hearsay and information which does not concern him. Even when he possesses such information, he never likes to talk or share uncorroborated hearsay," offered Medhn.

"I know that very well. Tesfom does not involve himself in things that do not concern him," said Alganesh emphatically.

"That is right. Anyway, when I heard the rumors that are circulating around, I decided to first learn the truth before telling you anything. I asked my brother-in-law, Araya, and he had also heard about it. He agreed to ask around and confirm the veracity of the rumors. He came yesterday evening and told me the full story."

"Oh my God, poor me! Please tell me about it," said Alganesh, wringing her hands, scared to hear the harsh and unpleasant truth.

"Habtom is seeing a young girl. She is very much younger than himself. Her name is Almaz."

"My senses had been telling me that something of that sort had been going on," said Alganesh hurriedly, interrupting Medhn.

"Wait, Alganesh *Habtey*, that is not the worst. The worst is that the girl is now in an advanced stage of pregnancy," said Alganesh.

"Oh my God?! What am I going to do now? What is going to

happen to me and my children? Oh God!" said Alganesh totally broken, not sure about her options.

"What can you do Alganesh *Habtey*? When some *Habesha* men become suddenly successful and rich, their first step is to trap younger girls into love affairs, give birth to children from two to three women and eventually establish second and third families. For them, that is a sign of development and growth. They don't care about infidelity or the fate of their children. It is very sad!" said Medhn sadly, shaking her head.

"I don't merit and deserve any of this!" cried Alganesh. "I have given him five children. I have single handedly cleaned, scrubbed, washed, cooked for years without any help. I have tolerated his ugly and violent nature and character for years, without any complaint. After all this and more, for Habtom to repay me in this manner is totally deplorable and unbearable," she said bitterly.

"Absolutely, Alganesh Habtey," said Medhn, extremely saddened by the whole affair.

Alganesh acknowledged Medhn's sympathy with a nod and continued from where she had stopped, "But it is ok, Habtom has done what he believes is right," she said bitterly, shaking her head, and then added, "I will wait with patience to see what God will do. God never forgets his children. I am sure all the tears I shed, the suffering and the sleepless nights I endured, will not be for nothing. God will not forget me and my innocent children. I am being widowed and my children orphaned, while my husband and their father is still alive," she said bravely, with extreme sadness in her voice.

"Habtom and his kind do not deserve women like you Alganesh *Habtey*. Men like him deserve women who are gold diggers. The kind who first collect all their money and then throw them away for other younger men. But I guess that does not happen to men like him. It happens to the nice ones," said Medhn with sadness.

"Yes, that is right. That rarely happens to the ones who deserve it. Anyway, I need your advice now. What should I do?"

"Whatever you do, you should not be hasty. You should think about all your options slowly and thoroughly. On the one hand, it is infuriating to leave your husband of many years to such an opportunistic woman. On the other hand, once your husband starts to sleep around, then it is debasing and demoralizing and even worrying to let him touch you," said Medhn with disgust in her voice.

"Don't worry about that. I have already moved out of the bedroom and I will never let him touch me," said Alganesh quickly, with certainty in her voice.

"That is very good. You should also consult your family about this. When you decide, you should not only decide for yourself. You should make the children the center of your decision," said Medhn

"Thank you very much Medhn *Habtey*. I am always indebted to you."

It was Alganesh's turn to ask, "How is Tesfom doing?"

"There is no change up to now. As I told you, he is still the same," said Medhn, shaking her head.

"Poor Tesfom *Hawey*. Tesfom is a very kind and compassionate person. This shouldn't have befallen him."

"You shouldn't sympathize with him Alganesh. After all, he is the one who is bringing this drinking problem upon himself."

"Don't say that Medhn. Tesfom's is a temporary aliment. He will overcome it in time. Irresponsible and callous men like Habtom, who bring destruction to their families and children are the ones who should be condemned."

"Well," said Medhn, not convinced by Alganesh's line of thinking.

"Tesfom at least admits and accepts and knows his problem and his weakness. After staying out late with friends, at least he always comes home to his wife and children. You should understand that Habtom has practically sold me and my children to another," said Alganesh sourly, emphasizing the stark difference between the two men.

"I understand what you are trying to say, and I admit that there is a difference."

"It is not a simple difference my dear Medhn. It is like day and night. Habtom's sin is infidelity of the highest order! Don't worry, you will see, Tesfom will soon correct his ways,"

"I hope so Alganesh *Habtey*. You also take care. Be brave. Don't worry; God will look after you and your children. Allow me to go now," said Medhn. She stood up and after bidding Alganesh farewell, went home.

After Medhn left, Alganesh sat frozen for several minutes, astonished and frustrated by what she had just heard from her friend. Her tears started to pour down her cheeks. She then remembered that she had to consult with her family members as soon as possible and chart a course of action. She started to think about the various options before her. After thoroughly pondering the subject in depth, she was finally able to come to a decision.

* 19 *

Everyone concerned was now aware of Habtom's new love life. After realizing that it was already public knowledge, he stopped bothering to make his affair discreet. He spent even less time at home, passing all his days and most nights at Almaz's place.

For the first time ever, Habtom failed to come home for three consecutive days and nights. On the third day, Medhn went to see Alganesh. After greeting her, she said she was in a hurry and would not stay for long, explaining that she was there, because she had some critical information.

When they sat down, Medhn said, "There is an important development that you need to know. Habtom's lover was admitted to the hospital three days ago, and she gave birth to a baby boy yesterday. I am sorry Alganeshey, that I had to be the one to bring you such unpleasant news; but I had to do it, since no one else would. I will come back in the afternoon and we will talk then. But for the moment, please be strong Alganesh *Habtey*. The children need you to be strong."

"Thank you very much Medhn *Habtey*.," Alganesh said softly. "I don't know what I would do without you."

When Medhn left, Alganesh locked the door. She didn't want the children to see her in that condition. She poured out her sadness and frustration, crying and sobbing, her breasts heaving heavily. The flow from her eyes and nose became unstoppable. After about an hour, she began to get her emotions under control and stopped crying.

The next day Habtom came home. He went and saw the children for a minute and then went straight to the wardrobe and started changing his clothes. Alganesh watched him with amazement. She marveled at the recent drastic changes in this man and repeatedly asked herself, "How can a person change so much, in such a short period of time?"

She decided against talking to him about what she knew, feeling that it would only make it easier for him, and she didn't want to give him the satisfaction of seeing her anger and frustration. Habtom finished changing his clothes. The more she thought about what was happening, the more she became upset. However hard she tried; she couldn't hold it anymore.

As he was about to leave, she heard herself say, "May I be the first to congratulate you, for fathering a child out of wedlock?!"

"I see that you have established an army of spies who feed you information by following me day and night," he said, trying to change the subject.

"No one needs spies to know what is common knowledge and obvious to the whole world. Now that you have a second wife on the side, you have become a full man, right? What a pity!" said Alganesh with rancor, shaking her head.

"Don't try to make it seem as if I committed something that is out of the ordinary. I have only done what many other men like me do!" he said, unapologetically.

"It is ok, you have done what you had to do. With the guidance of God, I will do what I need to do soon," she said firmly.

"You can do whatever you want to. I am not the kind who is threatened easily," he said defiantly.

"I will make a decision after properly consulting with my family," said Alganesh, equally defiant.

"Go ahead. If you want, you can even leave now. But understand that you will not find anyone like me, who will enable you to live in such great comfort," he said with pride.

"Did I hear you right? Did you say, comfort? Do you honestly believe that what you are putting me through is comfort? You can't be serious! Don't you realize that you are practically roasting me alive? Of course, you can't understand that, because you do not possess a conscience which confronts itself and asks, how about if this was done to me or to my sister or to my mother? Since you don't possess such a conscience, you can still sleep at night without being bothered by your selfish and unjust actions, irrespective of their consequences. But don't worry, it won't be long until I am freed from all of this."

"You can leave even right away!" shouted Habtom.

"You'd better understand that my decision will not be based on contention or rivalry with you. Unlike you, I will not make a decision based on what is best for me, but it will be based on what is best for our children. Sorry, I shouldn't even say 'our children'. I should say 'my children', since you have abdicated your responsibility of fatherhood. I don't want my children to be motherless, now that they have become fatherless. Unlike you, I have a parental responsibility. My children need me to care for them, since they don't have a father who cares for them!"

"Ha! Ha! Ha! Don't make me laugh. Your caring or loving won't provide anything for the children. I am the only one who can provide them with everything they need. If called upon, you wouldn't even be able to feed them for a week!" he said with sarcasm, feeling triumphant.

"Can't you comprehend that everything that you possess has not been earned only by you?"

Habtom roared with laughter again. "Ha! Ha! Ha! Then please tell me by whose effort it was earned. Every single cent is a result of my efforts and hard work. You haven't contributed even a single cent to this family," he said with absolute conviction.

"Unlike you, I might not go around sleeping with others and destroying my family, but that does not mean I don't know anything! Every single cent that has been earned so far has been earned by both of us. You, working out of the house and I working from home!" said Alganesh defiantly.

"Is that right?! My, I didn't know that it was so! Ha! Ha! Ha!" he laughed sarcastically.

"Of course, it is right! It is a hundred times right! I carried five babies for nine months. I gave birth to them by shedding my blood and putting my life on the line. I breastfed and washed them and their clothes. I raised them by loving and caring for them. On top of all that, I also took care of all your needs and took care of this house from morning till night for over 16 hours a day! Now look at me in the eyes and tell me if this is not work! If you say this is not work or contributing my share, then tell me what it is! Or do you want to dismiss it, just because all this was never calculated monetarily. Well, wake up my dear! If we start calculating, then my contribution would greatly outweigh yours, not only monetarily but in every other respect!" said Alganesh with passion and certitude.

Habtom had no answer to such logic. Instead of responding to the argument, he chose to go on a tangent. "I see that you have employed people who have coached and prepared you on how to be nasty and argumentative. Anyway, together with those who are putting you up to this, you can do whatever you want. I wonder if they will be there for you tomorrow. I have to go now, because unlike you, I have a job to do. I don't have time to waste on useless squabbling," said Habtom, making a strategic face-saving withdrawal.

Alganesh was not willing to give him an edge. She wanted to throw the last punch and say the last word. So, she said, "Of course, you have to go. Even if you don't have work to do, you have a second family to attend to!"

Habtom did not let her finish. He strode out with blood shot eyes, breathing heavily, the veins on his forehead clearly visible.

Although Alganesh knew that she was not going to make any difference, she was satisfied that she had given voice to everything she felt and that he needed to hear. She knew that she needed to reach a decision soon and finalize her next steps.

When Habtom fathered a baby out of wedlock, he was 36 and Alganesh was 32 years old. The twins Kbret and Samson were 11 years old, while Hadsh was eight. Rahwa was six and the youngest Negassi was just four years old.

* 20 *

Alganesh's family lived in an inaccessible village, about 100 kilometers away from Asmara. They therefore had no knowledge of what was going on in her marital life. Alganesh's father was a very devoted priest - part of a line of priests in his family tree. She had two uncles; one from her father's side and the second from her mother's side. Both lived in Asmara.

When her uncles heard that Habtom had fathered a child out of wedlock, they were indignant and came to talk to her. Alganesh welcomed them. After taking a snack of tea and bread (*kitcha*), she told them that she had planned to send for them. They then asked her the truth about all the things they had heard.

Alganesh confirmed to them, that most of what was being said was the truth. She explained that although she had been having doubts, she never expected it would go that far. She told them that she had only received confirmation of Habtom's full infidelity three days ago.

Her uncles talked about the issues and started presenting their viewpoints. Immediately interrupting their discussion, Alganesh told them that it would be best if they first sent for her father; then after her father arrived, the four of them could discuss the matter in detail and come to a decision.

Her uncles agreed and promised to send for her father as soon as possible. In the meantime, they encouraged her to remain strong. Giving her some advice and encouragement, they bid her farewell.

* 21 *

Alganesh's father arrived three days later. She gave him enough time to rest from his journey, and then sent for her uncles. All four sat down to discuss the matter.

They first discussed all the details thoroughly. After gaining full understanding of the background and the present condition of the affair, they asked her what her plans were. She said she would prefer to hear their suggestions first.

The three men took identical positions and offered the same opinions. They believed that Habtom's case was not a case of simple infidelity; it was not a one-time case of adultery or a mistake. It was a calculated step to establish a second family. Since there was no worse way of repaying her sacrifice, the only option she had was to officially ask for a divorce. There they rested their case.

Alganesh listened patiently until they were finished and thanked them for their love and care. She expressed her great appreciation for their thorough analysis and the clear points they presented. She then humbly asked them to hear her out until she was finished.

She started by saying, "As you are aware, I have been thinking about this without respite for days and nights. We have one basic difference. You are approaching the subject from the standpoint of what is best for me. Obviously, I understand why you would do that. After all, I am your daughter," she said and smiled at all of them.

She then became serious and continued, "I, on the other hand, am approaching the subject, not from the standpoint of what is best for me, but what is best for my children! Remember, as I am your daughter, so are they my children," she said and smiled again.

She became serious again and continued, "Allow me to explain what I mean. In the beginning, when I was extremely angry and frustrated and thinking only about myself and about how to get at Habtom, I reached the same conclusion as you. But you know better than I, that any decision taken in haste and with emotion is not bound to be the right one. So, I decided to cool down and examine the subject without much emotion. I told myself that whatever I do, I should put the interest of my children before mine. I resolved that for every step I took, I would first consider how it would negatively affect my children. It should be enough that I have suffered. I do not want my children to suffer as well," she said firmly.

After saying that, she became emotional. Her eyes welled with tears. She bent her head and waited for a few seconds. Mustering all the strength she had to control her emotions, she raised her head and gave them her final decision.

She said, "Starting from this day, as far as I am concerned and for all practical purposes, marriage with Habtom is over. I will never allow him to touch me. Furthermore, from now on, I have decided not to look at another man. I will devote myself to my children and my God. I want to follow the virgin Mary's example and live a life of chastity. I hope the Virgin Mary will help me. That is my final decision," she said, with tears rolling down her cheeks.

"What? What are you saying? Are you in possession of your senses? Why shouldn't you care about yourself? You yourself are barely a child," said her first uncle with disbelief.

"Why should you talk about a life of chastity, when you are so young yourself?" said her second uncle. "If you want to do that, you will have time in the future. Now is the time to think about yourself. Don't forget that you also have rights and deserve to enjoy life," he added.

"I am young but I also have five children. My age is not the only consideration that is important here. I only have one body and one soul. My children have five bodies and five souls. The future life and destiny of five innocent children is far more important than one life. I don't want to sacrifice the lives of five children so I can satisfy myself and enjoy life's gratifications," said Alganesh with determination.

"What you are saying and trying to do is indeed very noble and admirable. However, you also need to take into consideration your age, your life and your circumstances," said her first uncle.

"My main concern is to prevent my children from going through emotional turmoil and scars. I don't want to go through the rancor of court proceedings and expose them to their destructive effects," said Alganesh resolutely.

"If you don't go to court, there is no way you can ever get your rights!" shouted her second uncle.

"I understand the ramifications and repercussions of all of that uncle. But if I go to court to get my rights, the court rulings might hurt my children. I can't bear to see the court ordering custody of some of my children to him. What would be an even worse nightmare would be to see some of my children being taken care of by this woman. Rather than see that while I am alive, it will be easier for me to bear the pain and keep my children with me, by pretending to be a married woman with a husband," said Alganesh bitterly but firmly.

The men could not understand or accept her rationale and decision. They vigorously tried to point out the enormity of the blunder she would be committing, if she went ahead with her decision; warning her that she would realize that she had made a huge mistake when it was too late to do anything about it.

They concluded their final attempt by saying, "Why would

you want to make your life like hell by pretending you have a real marriage? If you make this decision now, you will regret it for the rest of your life."

Alganesh didn't agree with them. She repeatedly underlined that the life of her children was more important than hers. During the whole exchange her father barely spoke, but followed the argument calmly, deep in thought. He was impressed by his daughter's firm stand. Knowing her very well, he knew that once she made a decision, she would see it through with conviction and determination.

He cleared his throat he said, "I think it is now my turn to express my view and stand on the matter. At the outset, I had the same opinion as my two honorable and caring brothers. But the more I listened to what Alganesh said and felt her passion, the more I wavered in my stand. What she is proposing to do will not be easy. It will require fortitude and sacrifice. She wants to sacrifice herself for her children. This is very commendable. God and our religion order us to encourage anyone who tries to follow the way of the Lord. So, I say, let her go ahead with her decision. Let us support her with our prayers. Let us pray that she finds the strength and stamina to put into action her resolve and her stand. Since she is planning to sacrifice herself for her children, I am positive that God will also be on her side. That is my last word," he said with finality.

Her uncles unsuccessfully tried to convince her father, but he stood firm. Alganesh thanked her uncles, appreciating their concern for her well-being. She thanked and assured them that, with their moral support, she would not fail in her resolve.

Her uncles had to finally give in. With their discussion over, Alganesh brought dinner. After the meal was over, her uncles bid them good night and left. Her father was very tired and soon went to bed.

After making her final decision, Alganesh felt a sense of relief. The pressure she had been feeling the last few days was lifted from her shoulders. Since she did not need to wait for Habtom anymore, she went to bed early and fell into deep sleep.

Since her father had decided to leave for his village the next day, she got up early to prepare breakfast for him, and they ate together before he left.

After the confrontation with Alganesh and her threats, Habtom was very worried. While she was taking courageous and selfless decisions, Habtom became concerned about what steps she was going to take and decided to take his own steps as a cautionary move.

* 22 *

Habtom was extremely satisfied and gratified with both his business and private life and was enjoying the happiest and greatest time of his entire life. The main reason for this new found overall joy was Almaz.

Almaz's attractiveness was not restricted to her beauty and gorgeous body. Even as a person, Almaz was a refined and lovable woman. She knew how to please and gratify a person. In conversations and discussions, she knew exactly what to say, to whom, where, and when.

Habtom's parents started to admire and worship her from the moment they were introduced to her. Whenever they came to visit, she would welcome them with open arms and would go to great lengths to make their stay comfortable. She would always address them as my sweet dad and mom (*Aboy Mearey, Adey Mearey*), and never with their names.

She started to brew their favorite home-made traditional light-bear (*Swa)* for them. When she didn't have the time, she would buy a commercially brewed one and take it to them, claiming she made it herself. Every now and then, she would cook dishes they liked and would take it to them. Bashay and W/ro Lemlem felt that Almaz was doing too much and would occasionally object, but she would emphatically assure them that what she was doing was nothing, compared to what they deserved as parents. She would humbly add, that "Her hope was that this small gesture would give some relief to her beloved mother-in-law from cooking constantly."

During holidays, she would take money from Habtom and buy them gifts, clothes and shoes. She would never claim credit for any of what she was doing. She would always tell them, we have been blessed with all this, thanks to your efforts. With words that touched their cores, she would repeatedly tell them, "All this is yours, more than it is ours. We will continue to be blessed with more, only if we receive your blessings."

Bashay and W/ro Lemlem were totally captivated by Almaz's words, mannerisms and actions. They started thanking the lord for blessing them with such a blessed daughter-in-law. They continuously showered her with unending blessings.

Before long, Bashay and W/ro Lemlem began to depend completely on Almaz for everything they needed; if they wanted something, they wouldn't go to Habtom. Soon, they began to feel that Almaz was closer to them than their own children, including Habtom, as if she was their first born, their own blood and bones.

* 23 *

Habtom was extremely satisfied by how Almaz cared for his parents. That was of course, only one of the many great attributes Almaz possessed. When it came to him, Almaz tripled and quadrupled her efforts and care many times over. She was a woman who possessed not only the art of capturing men, but she also knew the art of satisfying, gratifying and keeping men happy. She knew what men's egos wanted, and she fed that ego day and night. She would never call him by his name, but rather always called him, "My Habtom, My *Habti, Habti* of my soul", etc.

She would cook the most delicious dishes Habtom loved and then wash and feed her child and put him to bed early. She would then shower, dress and wait for him. When he arrived, she would welcome him with open arms, often telling him, "When you come home after a hard and rough day, I only want you to rest, relax and enjoy your time. The hard day you have at work is already too much!"

At first Habtom was ill at ease with all that Almaz was doing for him, because he had never been used to such royal treatment. He didn't expect it to continue. When Almaz continued to shower him with not only sweet words, but also sweet and thoughtful deeds, he couldn't believe his luck. His love for Almaz tripled and quadrupled as he became totally captivated and conquered by her. She started to become his whole life and world.

Soon there was no one else closer to him in the world, and she became the only one with whom he would share his secrets. For all intents and purposes, Almaz became Habtom's God mother as well. He had only one major worry. He was dreading the day when Almaz would confront him and ask him to officially divorce Alganesh. Habtom didn't want formal divorce from Alganesh, not because he cared about his family, but because of the consequences of divorce on his finances and capital. If she asked him, he knew that he wouldn't hesitate for a moment. Still, he was silently thankful that, so far, she hadn't put him in that situation.

Almaz knew that she had Habtom wrapped around her fingers. She was certain that she had nothing to worry about in the way of competition from Alganesh. She knew that if she wanted it, she would get her way any time she wished. Almaz had her own plans and timeline and had already charted a path. She was certain that the reins of the when, the how and the what were firmly in her control.

* 24 *

Although Habtom and his family were worshipping Almaz, there were other parties who disapproved of her actions. In the beginning, Almaz had kept her relationship with Habtom a secret, and her family members were unaware of her activities.

When they eventually knew, they expressed their strong disapproval. They knew that, due to her natural endowments, she would have no problem getting any young man she wanted. Since the sky was the limit for her, they couldn't understand why she would settle for a much older married man with five children. They therefore tried to convince her to untangle herself from Habtom.

Almaz, on the other hand, had started to feel comfortable and secure. She knew she had Habtom's wealth and his devotion at her disposal, and she was happy and gratified that Habtom was constantly showering her with gold, ivory and other expensive ornaments. She therefore declined to accept her family's demands. They tried to increase the pressure, but she still rejected their demands. When she completely refused to bend, they condemned her and started ostracizing her from the family circle.

Not long after, Almaz gave birth to her first son. When her family heard of the birth, they understood that she had reached a point of no return. Slowly and reluctantly, they started to accept the status quo and eventually pardoned her and accepted her back into the family fold.

In this manner, the newly established house and family of Almaz and Habtom blossomed. On the contrary, the original family of Alganesh and her children started to shrink and shrivel and became a distant second family for Habtom. Alganesh and her children began to feel the physical and emotional emptiness of the house.

* 25 *

Alganesh was no less than Almaz in all-natural endowments and beauty. Even in intelligence, character and wisdom, she was no less, if not better than Almaz. Moreover, as far as care, responsibility, thoughtfulness and sacrifice for family and children were concerned, Alganesh was far superior to most people, including Almaz.

Nevertheless, in terms of socially correct words and behavior, Alganesh was no comparison to Almaz. In this area, Almaz was a professional. Her words and tactics were always meant to please, especially in handling men and their egos. Alganesh was no match to Almaz in this area.

Whenever she had an objective, Almaz knew how to make other people feel happy and important, never hesitating to use a word or expression to manipulate people to win them over. These were learned behaviors she used on people when she had ulterior motives, and she used different strategies and tactics for different people. However, her careful handling skills were not for everyone; when a situation called for toughness, she could be mean and harsh.

Alganesh on the other hand, was nice with everyone and to everyone. She was a deeply caring and loving person. Whenever she saw a mistake, or witnessed an unfair act from someone close, she would consider it her responsibility to comment, give advice and correct. She firmly believed that not facing that task was an abdication of one's responsibility and unfaithfulness to a loved person. Despite that, she was not the kind who would interfere in other people's affairs, nor would she express her opinion on matters which were not her concern.

Whenever Alganesh volunteered to give advice, she never doubted or feared that her words and actions might be misunderstood or create friction. What she felt and believed and considered important was the fact that she was talking and advising out of care and love. She felt this couldn't and shouldn't be misinterpreted or misrepresented, since the motive was obvious and clear. For her, it was an act of love and responsibility.

Habtom had never liked Alganesh's attempt to correct and advise him. He felt it as an affront to his manhood and to the respect he deserved as a man. He believed she was doing all that to satisfy her ego and put him down. He deeply resented her actions, considering them a lack of respect and failure to recognize his business successes. He wrongly assumed, like many other people like him, that success in business or education or other endeavors meant you were perfect as a person in every aspect of life. He couldn't accept being talked to by a woman, whom he believed was naturally inferior to him. He never understood that Alganesh was talking to him out of love and thoughtfulness.

He frequently thought, "How can she dare to point out my weaknesses, when I have none and am far superior to her? How dare she advise me, when I don't need any?" People like Habtom, who think of themselves as complete and infallible, not only reject advice from others, but really resent them. They prefer listening to people who sing their praises, even while they're hanging over a cliff.

Alganesh on the other hand, had not grasped an important aspect of the nature of human beings. She had never realized that most people love only those people who praise them and repeat words they want to hear. Most of us love only people who agree with us all the time, even when we are wrong, rather than those who, out of love, try to correct and advise us. So, Alganesh had a problem here; although in reality, Alganesh was not the one who had a problem here – it was us human beings and the ways of our world!

Alganesh never understood that it is mostly advice givers like her who are resented. Still, even when this began to dawn on her, she persisted in her old ways, because for her, it was a matter of principle and loyalty.

* 26 *

In a short time, the pasta factory made good progress. Habtom's brother, Dermas, assisted Habtom in purchase and sales. A huge amount of flour was needed for both the bakery and the factory. Being able to buy in bulk allowed them to acquire higher grade flour at lower cost and to maintain a stable amount of stock.

It did not take much time for Tesfom's brother, Araya, to get used to the workings of the bakery, and they soon started reaping good profits from both businesses. They made their monthly loan payments without any problem. The partnership, collaboration and success of the two families reached its pinnacle. It was now two years since they had bought the pasta factory and ten years since they bought the bakery. The twins were now eleven years old and were attending 4th grade.

People started to express their admiration at the exemplary and successful partnership of Tesfom and Habtom. Many began flocking to their sides. Some wanted to establish close friendships with them, but most were there for their own personal gains. A few were the type who come around at the time of success and disappear at the sign of any problem. Most were buzzing around Tesfom, because of his reputation for benevolence and extravagant ways.

* 27 *

For a very long time, Tesfom had his nights out with his friends only on Saturdays and Sundays. They played cards and drank late into the night. This continued for a long time. But, after the workings of the factory were organized and properly streamlined, he changed his routine and started staying out and drinking even on week days.

Medhn, who had never accepted his weekend getaways and overindulgences, could not accept this new change in Tesfom. She decided to have a serious talk with him. She thought the best time would be to talk to him when he was completely sober. She started giving the children early dinner and putting them into bed early. She waited for the right time. On Wednesday, Tesfom came home early.

Whenever Tesfom came home early, he always looked forward to passing time with his children. When he walked in and couldn't see or hear them, his face changed. "Have the children already gone to bed?" he asked, with disappointment in his voice.

"They all looked tired, and after eating dinner, they went straight to bed," said Medhn, not giving away her motives.

She hurried to the kitchen to bring dinner. As he did most days, Tesfom went to the children's bedroom. Seeing that they were all sleeping peacefully, he kissed each one on the forehead. Medhn came with dinner and they ate peacefully. When they finished, she put the plates away and didn't bother washing them, but instead immediately came back with tea.

While drinking tea, Medhn said, "Listen Tesfom, I want to talk to you."

Tesfom was taken aback. "What about? Is everything ok?" he asked, a little worried.

"To tell you the truth, there are things that are not ok!" said Medhn, without hesitation. She quickly added, "You are not aware of it, because for the most part, you are the cause of it. I want to talk to you about this new habit that you have adopted lately," said Medhn firmly.

"You can talk, but there is nothing new in my habit that you don't know about," said Tesfom a little uncomfortable.

"I have been meaning to talk to you for a long time now. I am sure you have been noticing that I haven't been happy about it. I have been postponing it, hoping you would change. When you are sober, your character, your personality and thoughtfulness are extremely adorable and admirable. But once you start drinking, you completely change and become a different person."

"I have told you before that with the work pressure I have, I need to relax with my friends now and then."

"I can understand and accept that only up to a point. It would be understandable if you went out with your friends occasionally, and even sometimes drink. But you and most of your friends are now going directly from your offices and work places to bars, where you drink to 11 pm or midnight and then go home, eat dinner and sleep. This is not only unacceptable but is also outright irresponsible. In fact, ..."

"Come on, Medhn," said Tesfom, abruptly interrupting her.

She did not let him continue. Before he finished his sentence, she said, "Yes, I am right Tesfom! This is irresponsible. In fact, it looks like you have converted the bars into your night offices and your homes into restaurants and hotels. Such behavior, coming from a person who calls himself a responsible husband and father, is not acceptable in any circumstance."

"Please Medhn, you have to understand that life without occasional entertainment and fun has no meaning at all," was the only weak argument Tesfom could pose.

"Do you want to tell me, that the only source of entertainment anyone has is going to bars and drinking? If that is so, then the so-called fun you are having is not yours. It is not coming from you; you are borrowing it from bars and alcoholic beverages!" said Medhn emphatically.

"No, no, what I meant was...," said Tesfom.

"You can't say no, no, Tesfom. You can entertain yourself in various other ways, without drinking and endangering your health and suffering from the harmful consequences of alcohol," said Medhn, pressing her advantage.

"I understand and accept your logic Medhn. But you also need to understand that for men, drinking is part of the entertainment," he replied.

"Drinking one or two glasses could be considered fun or entertainment. But drinking until you are no longer in control of your senses is definitely not entertainment," said Medhn strongly.

"Come on Medhn, don't exaggerate. You know that I am not that kind of a person. You know that I am not a drunkard or an alcoholic. I just drink for fun."

"How do you think all the alcoholics in the world became addicted? Don't you know that it happened while they were telling themselves, "I am not an alcoholic. I am just drinking for fun!"

"There is another aspect you also need to understand Medhn. Business dealings require inviting or being invited for drinks to discuss business. It is in a way, a small part of any businessman's duty," said Tesfom, hoping to steer the subject in another direction.

"At the end of the day, what is the measure of success in business? Isn't all the hustle and effort for the benefit of your children, your wife and family?" asked Medhn, preparing a trap for him.

"Of course, it is! All the effort I put in is for you guys?" said Tesfom, falling into the trap.

"Well dear Tesfom, the time you are spending away from your children, in their name, is their time. You are practically stealing their time from them. Your children need time with their father now, not tomorrow. Once they grow up, they will not need you and will not even want you. It is going to be too late for you and for them," she said, presenting an unassailable argument with impenetrable logic.

"You are absolutely right Medhn. You know that I love my children very much. I don't want to be a bad example. I remember very well how my father raised us. He was always exemplary. In all the years, I can't remember a day when I saw him act or behave in an unpleasant manner. I don't want my children and my father to see any major weakness in me. Please have patience with me and, if you can, help me."

"I want to help you. That is why I wanted to have this talk."

"Don't worry. This is not difficult. I will take care of it. But if you truly love me, then have patience with me."

"Of course, I love you. I don't only love you, but I also respect you in many other aspects. Let me remind you what *Aboy* Grazmach repeatedly says about health, 'Health is like money that we have deposited in our savings accounts. If we fail to keep and save money during our youth, then we will have none when we get old. The same is true of health. If we don't keep and guard our health when we are still young and strong, then when we grow old, we will have none.' I have been repeatedly talking to you about your drinking, because I don't want to lose you. I love you and care too much not to try my best to correct your ways to save you," said Medhn, emotion creeping into her voice.

"You are so loving, wise and adorable Medhney."

"You yourself are loving, thoughtful and adorable Tesfom. The only problem you have is this drinking habit. That is why I am fighting to save my Tesfom, before alcohol snatches him away from me."

"Don't worry Medhney, nothing will take me away from you. You will see, I will change. Ok now, I think we have talked enough. It is late now, let us retire."

"Ok, go ahead. I will first go see the children and then I will join you."

Medhn went to see the children. On her way, she started thinking and talking to herself. "There aren't many men who would allow you to sit down with them, listen to you and have a conversation with you. He also understands and accepts his mistakes and weaknesses. I should also understand that he has immense peer pressure from his friends and coworkers. I need to understand his problems and be patient. He is a husband who loves his children and family very much. I should also be thankful for what I have."

These thoughts and words calmed and reassured Medhn. She had an ability and the blessing of talking and confronting herself without mercy. Furthermore, she was also blessed with the ability to look at issues from the other person's perspective. More importantly, she understood her blessings. After re-examining the problem from every angle, Medhn was ready to go to bed and sleep heartily.

* 28 *

Dermas was five years younger than Habtom. He had dropped out of school at the elementary level, because he could not progress beyond the fourth grade. The family was forced to find him a job as an apprentice. But he somehow failed to do well at every job he tried. He was lazy and liked hanging around doing nothing. He started drinking early and became quite a vagabond.

The family was exasperated with him. When he was in his early twenties, Bashay and W/ro Lemlem begged him to get married, hoping that once married, he might change and become responsible. Habtom did not agree with his parents' proposition. His argument was that anyone who could not even take care of himself, was not fit for marriage.

Dermas continued to drink, doing nothing and wasting away his youth. He was now 31 years old. Although he had become good-for-nothing in taking on life's challenges; as a human being, he was good-natured and never hurt anyone.

Habtom had tried several times to help his brother get on his feet. All his past efforts had not born fruit, but his latest attempt was a crowning success. It came about after Habtom convinced Tesfom to assign Dermas to the pasta factory. When Dermas started working at the factory, he became extremely committed and serious at his job.

Habtom was delighted to see such real change in his brother. When Habtom insisted on putting Dermas in the factory instead of the bakery, he had two distinct goals, and he deliberately failed to explain to Tesfom the second goal he had in mind. His brother now was a changed man. Habtom thus became confident, that nothing would prevent him from achieving both of his initial goals.

Dermas continued to make positive strides in his character and habits. At first his parents and family did not believe these changes would be permanent. They expected him to revert to his old habits. But, as time went by, the family saw that Dermas' changes were indeed permanent.

It was after all this, that the parents felt it might be a good time to ask Dermas to get married. This time, even Habtom agreed with his parents' proposal. They all sat down with Dermas and put their suggestion to him. He had previously never accepted the idea of his marrying, so they were all pleasantly surprised when Dermas assured them that he had been thinking about it and had decided it was time to settle down.

They agreed to give Dermas three months to look for and

choose a bride. They further agreed that, if he failed to find a bride within that time limit, the family would find him a bride from a reputable and respectable family.

After a month, Dermas informed his family that he had made his choice. He explained that his eyes had fallen on Selam, Grazmach's daughter. Both his father and brother were taken aback by his suggestion. It was an unexpected choice.

Habtom was the first to recover from astonishment and shock, "What do you say, father?" he asked, looking intently at his father.

"I don't see any problem at all. After all, we are from the same village; we are neighbors, friends and partners. There is nothing in our blood relationship that would prevent us from the bond of marriage. On top of everything, we also know, that Grazmach's children are very well behaved and decent," said Bashay with utmost confidence.

"The points you just enumerated are all valid. However, everything you just stated is from the point of view of our family. We also need to examine the proposal from their family's standpoint. My concern is would they be willing to give their daughter's hand to us?" said Habtom.

"What do you mean? Let alone now, when we have become close partners, even much earlier, they wouldn't have hesitated to give us their daughter's hand!" said Bashay, with extreme confidence.

"Come on father, don't fool yourself! If it was some years back, they wouldn't even have looked at us twice, let alone accepted our request!" said Habtom, slightly irritated.

It was Bashay's turn to get irritated, "Don't say that son. Grazmach is a very decent and righteous man!"

"I am not talking about Grazmach", said Habtom. "I am talking about W/ro Brkti, her children and especially Tesfom. I am talking about their feelings of superiority towards us. I understand that things are different now. We are partners, Godfathers, and we are now on a par with them in every respect. Hence, I don't also imagine we would encounter much opposition at this point," he added with measured confidence.

"Very good. We are in agreement then. Habtom and I will decide as to when and how to go and ask Grazmach's family for Selam's hand. God be with us," said Bashay, concluding the discussion.

"Amen, Amen," said Habtom and Dermas. Soon after, the brothers left together.

* 29 *

The large majority of marriages in Eritrea at the time, were arranged. In the highlands, certain traditional rules governed marriage. The family of the groom would select a bride from a family they knew and respected. After making an initial assessment, they would send a delegation composed of close family members to the chosen family and ask for the hand of the bride.

Later on, slowly, a few youngsters began to select their own mates. Even then, the family had to send a delegation to formally ask for the hand of the bride. Bashay and Habtom decided to go to Grazmach's family alone, without taking along other family members.

They made an appointment with Grazmach and Tesfom for Saturday, without actually specifying the exact motive of their visit. They just said told them; they were coming to discuss an issue important to the future of the two families. Grazmach and Tesfom assumed they were going to talk about their partnership.

When Bashay and Habtom arrived, Tesfom led them to his parents. They greeted each other warmly. W/ro Brkti went to the kitchen and came back with *Hmbasha (flat bread)*. She asked them what they would prefer to drink. Grazmach suggested *Swa* (light local beer); everyone agreed. Tesfom got up to help his mother.

Grazmach handed over the *Hmbasha* to Bashay. Custom demands that it is the eldest man who blesses and cuts the bread. Bashay received the bread, prayed and then cut the *Hmbasha* by hand. He finished his prayer by begging God to make their discussion successful and fruitful. W/ro Brkti asked them to help themselves. After a while she went to the kitchen, leaving the men to themselves.

As soon as W/ro Brkti left, Bashay cleared his throat. He started by asking forgiveness for their failure of not clarifying the purpose of their visit ahead of time. He then said, "As we all know, thanks to God, we have come a long way from being mere neighbors, to being partners and close confidants and family. We are here today, because of our desire to fortify and cement this relationship further," he said, looking at both.

Grazmach and Tesfom didn't understand the direction of Bashay's train of thought. Nevertheless, they acknowledged his statement by nodding vigorously. They waited attentively to hear his next statement.

Bashay continued, "We are therefore here today, to ask for the hand of your daughter Selam, for our son Dermas," he said, clarifying the real purpose of their visit.

Grazmach was taken by surprise. He had not expected this. He noticed that his son, Tesfom, was even more astonished than he was. Nevertheless, neither of them showed any outward reaction.

"We thank you very much for your wish and desire to further strengthen our relationship and love. To be frank with you, we hadn't expected this request at all. Nowadays, some youngsters get to know each other and when they decide to live together, then they inform their parents and the families meet and give blessing to their wishes," said Grazmach calmly, looking at both.

Bashay and Habtom nodded their heads up and down in agreement. Grazmach continued, "The second traditional way is something we all know very well. You do not directly approach the concerned family. You first send a friend of both families to enquire and ask the disposition of the girl's family to the idea. Then if the family agrees, you send a family delegation to officially ask for the hand of their daughter. Both of you are aware of this procedure. I am therefore assuming you decided to forego the procedure, because you believed we do not need to include a third party, since we are very close. Am I right?" asked Grazmach.

"Exactly Grazmach, that is why we didn't follow the normal procedure," said Bashay hurriedly.

"May I ask one question? asked Tesfom. "Has Dermas in any way approached my sister prior to now? If so, is there some kind of agreement between them that we are not aware of, or is this the first attempt?".

Habtom who had been listening to the exchange without interruption said, "No, Dermas has not contacted Selam. He told us of his choice and we are here to ask for her hand in his name. Of course, we do not expect you to respond to our request today."

When Grazmach was in deep thought, he had a habit of coiling his mustache with his hands. He was following the conversation, coiling his mustache with concentration and, when Habtom finished, he said, "You are right Habtom *Wedey*. We will first need to ask our daughter's wishes. We need to move forward with the times. We will also need to talk with her mother and our family members, after which we will inform you of our response."

"Very good, thank you," said Bashay, expressing his satisfaction at how the discussion had progressed.

"That is good. Ok then, please gentlemen help yourselves," said Grazmach.

After finalizing the discussion for the day, they moved to other subjects of work and current events. After finishing their conversation and drinking the *swa*, Bashay and Habtom stood up to leave. Grazmach and Tesfom saw them to the door.

* 30 *

As soon as they saw their guests off, Grazmach asked his wife, if Selam was at home. W/ro Brkti informed him that she was due within the next 15-20 minutes.

W/ro Brkti's feminine and motherly instincts and curiosity were immediately aroused by her husband's question, "Why do you want her? What was the purpose of Bashay and Habtom's visit? Was their visit only about work and the partnership?", she fired consecutive questions.

"They came in peace, there is nothing to worry about. Let's wait for Selam and then we will inform you together," said Grazmach.

"Why, what was it about?" asked W/ro Brkti, her curiosity aroused further.

"Please be patient Brkti. Let Selam come and we will then properly explain to both of you," snapped Grazmach slightly irritated.

It was W/ro Brkti's turn to be angered, "I don't understand why it should be such a mystery, but it is ok, as you wish," she said, with clear annoyance and disappointment written all over her face.

Tesfom was following his parent's conversation with interest. Grazmach turned towards Tesfom and said, "Rather than postponing this, I thought it would better to wait for Selam and finish this issue today. Is that ok with you?"

"That is a good idea father. After all, she will be coming soon."

He turned to his mother and asked her, "Mother, can you in the meantime brew for me that delicious tea of yours?"

"My pleasure son," said his mother, brightening her facial expression. She got up and went to the kitchen.

Grazmach noticed the change in his wife. He started thinking, "Did Tesfom really want tea or did he ask his mother for tea to diffuse the situation?" He couldn't be sure either way. Continuing his thoughts, he told himself, "Well, if he did it to diffuse the situation, then that is really good insight and wisdom."

Thereafter, both Grazmach and Tesfom took the task of waiting for Selam. They were sitting together side by side. Though sitting together, they were both immersed deep in their individual thoughts, analyzing the pros and cons of the serious issue facing them.

At that time in Eritrea, it was rare for girls to attend school.

Only the very few like Selam, who were privileged, were able to go to school. Because they were a small minority, all of them were extremely self-conscious and shy. In every aspect of life, including clothing and hairdo, they were exactly like other girls. The only thing that separated them from the others was that they were attending schools.

As was the norm then, Selam came wearing long clothes and a scarf on her head. W/ro Brkti told her that her brother and father were waiting for her and then rushed to inform them that Selam had arrived.

Selam came in and greeted her father and brother. "Did you want to talk to me?' she asked with humility and shyness.

"Yes, Selam *Gualey*, have a seat," said Grazmach.

She sat on the edge of the chair, and W/ro Brkti sat beside her. Grazmach started to explain the purpose of the visit of Bashay's family. After he finished his report, he asked them if they had any questions or required any clarification.

Both mother and daughter shook their heads. Grazmach continued, "As is the culture in this family, whenever we have to make a serious decision, we always come together and discuss the issue thoroughly. We reach a decision after proper consultation. This is a matter that is more pertinent to your future life than to anyone else, so we want you to think about this and tell us your thoughts and desires, without worrying or fearing anything or anyone. We will do what is best for you and we will respect and uphold your wishes," Grazmach assured Selam.

"Whenever the issue of marriage arises, I have heard so many horrifying stories about how many girls face much anguish and desperation at the hands of their parents. But here in our family, we are lucky and blessed to have parents like you, who give us the chance to express our opinions," said Selam with confidence.

W/ro Brkti was proud of her daughter and beamed with pleasure. She said, "I am so proud of you Selam *Gualey*! God bless you."

"I am so glad to hear that. Now let's proceed and hear your opinion," said Grazmach.

First Selam explained her stand on the matter. After that Grazmach, W/ro Brkti and Tesfom expressed their opinion. Thereafter, the family started to discuss the issue thoroughly, assessing the subject from every angle. They finally arrived at a decision. They agreed on the response to give Bashay's family.

"I think that was a very good and thorough discussion. We pray to God that this be the right decision. Tesfom and I, along with Bashay and Habtom, will fix a date when they could come to hear our response. We will tell you the date ahead of time, so you can have enough time to prepare," said Grazmach.

The discussion was concluded. He turned to Tesfom and asked him to stay and eat dinner with them. Tesfom declined, explaining that Medhn and the children would be waiting for him. They accepted his excuse and Tesfom left.

Soon after, Grazmach's family ate their dinner somberly. All were still immersed in thought. More than with anyone else, the subject matter stayed with Grazmach for the whole night and the days that followed.

Chapter 4
Massawa-Pearl of the Red Sea

Grazmach extended a lunch invitation to Bashay and Habtom, which they accepted with gratitude. They all agreed the best day would be on a Sunday, so they could have adequate time for their lunch and discussion.

As is the tradition on such occasions, Bashay and Habtom wanted to bring along three or four additional close family members. They asked Grazmach for permission, but he maintained that there was no need for additional people from either side. He argued that four of them could adequately handle the matter. Bashay had desperately wanted to include his close relatives and was disappointed. Grazmach saw his friend's disappointment but he still stuck to his decision.

W/ro Brkti prepared delicious chicken sauce (*Tsebhi-Derho)*, meat sauce (*Tsebhi Sga* or *Zgni*), a vegetable combo (*Alicha*) and injera and *Hmbasha*. She brewed excellent *Swa*. While eating lunch, Bashay and Habtom frequently expressed their appreciation and admiration for the delicious dishes and fine *Swa*. After lunch, they held a traditional coffee ceremony with popcorn and *Hmbasha*.

Bashay and Habtom thanked W/ro Brkti profusely. Bashay kept repeating, "What a great cuisine! Great hosting. Thank you Brkti!"

Grazmach, who did not like compliments or flattery, was eying the whole conversation with particular unease. When all was over, Grazmach said, "Let's give Brkti a few minutes to clear the table and then we will proceed to the issue of the day." W/ro Brkti cleared everything and left the men alone.

As soon as his wife left, Grazmach cleared his throat, "Thank the lord that so far, we have had a good and peaceful afternoon. Our two families have come a long way together. This has not come about without commitment or intense dedication to love and friendship. The friendship between Bashay and me has blossomed for years and now we are seeing its fruits. The understanding with which our children are working in partnership is a testament to that. We are even witnessing this friendship trickling down to our grand-children. Whenever there is love and understanding, God multiplies even the few blessings we possess. But where there is discord and hatred, God takes away his blessings and even whatever love, peace or wealth we own," he said and then paused for a while.

"That is correct. *Ee vero, e vero*," said Bashay, nodding his head vigorously.

Grazmach acknowledged Bashay with his eyes and continued, "But enduring friendships are not usually tested during smooth times of understanding, and peace. They are tried and tested to a greater extent when we face misunderstanding and discord." Finally, Grazmach concluded, "Small disagreements that test our devotion to each other are part of life and that is when we should prove our faithfulness to our love for each other."

Even though he did not specifically understand where his friend was going with his statement, Bashay nodded his head and said, "Well said Grazmach."

Bashay had comprehended only the general outline of Grazmach's comments. But he had not understood why Grazmach was stressing these points right then. Instead of being encouraged by Bashay's supportive comments, Grazmach felt more uneasy. He noticed that all of them were looking at him intently, waiting for his next words. He felt indecisive about what to say and hesitated for a while.

Finally, he bowed his head, took a deep breath and, looking up, said, "I don't even know how or where to start. This is not easy to say, but, since there is no other way, I have to tell you as it is." After hesitating again, Grazmach finally said, "I want to assure you that we have done all that we could to satisfy your demands and bring happiness to you and to all of us. Unfortunately, I'm sad to say that we are unable to grant your request. I know and understand how disappointing this is and I am really sorry!" His body language was clear evidence of Grazmach's uneasiness and discomfort.

"Whaaat?! Did you say that you couldn't accommodate our request?", said Bashay nearly getting up from his seat.

"We have all tried our best to convince Selam, to accept the proposal, but she is totally adamant. She flatly told us, "I don't want to hear about marriage or to marry any time soon," said Grazmach, leaving no doubt about the finality of the decision.

"Madonna! Holy Mary! What kind of disappointing and devastating news are you telling us Grazmach?"

"What can we say, we are as disappointed as you!" said Grazmach.

"This is not the response we expected from you Grazmach", said Bashay angrily. "You know that we could easily find a multitude of families that would gladly give us their daughters' hand. But we didn't want other families. We wanted your daughter, because we desired and wanted your kinship. That is why we came to you. Our ultimate desire and wish were to cement the love between our two families with matrimony."

"You are absolutely right, Bashay," said Grazmach.

Habtom had been following the conversation with utter disappointment and abhorrence. The moment Grazmach uttered the words of rejection, Habtom's eyes had narrowed, his forehead was furrowed and the veins on his forehead visibly bulged. Habtom moved forward in his chair and said, "*Aboy* Grazmach, if what my father is saying is correct, then the right thing to do is not to absolve yourselves of any responsibility by giving up easily. The right thing is to continue doing everything possible until she accepts the proposal!" said Habtom, not hiding his disappointment and frustration.

"Let me assure you Habtom that my father, mother and I have done our utmost to convince her, but she completely refused," said Tesfom, who had not said anything up to that point.

"I am not sure about that. I find that very hard to accept. We came to you based on the premise that we were and are neighbors, business partners and even Godfather's to each other's children. We wrongly concluded that if we were good enough for all the rest, we would also be good enough to merit being welcomed and accepted into your family fold! Obviously, we are not!" said Habtom bitterly, with much resentment.

"Don't say that Habtom *Wedey*!" said Grazmach.

Bashay interrupted him by saying, "Listen Grazmach, how about if we do this. We will give you more time to think about this and discuss further with your daughter. We have no problem waiting. We can give you as much time as you wish."

"The whole of last week we have done nothing but try to convince her to accept but she has flatly refused. There was nothing more we could do, except force her, which we can't do. There is no sense in giving us more time," said Grazmach with finality.

"Let them be, father. Everything is clear and obvious. Let's go!" said Habtom with bloodshot eyes and fury in his voice.

Bashay was not finished, "Listen Grazmach, you know better than I do that you approach parents beforehand with the firm belief that they can convince and command their children. We know very well how obedient your children are. So, it is difficult to believe that in this particular instance, you couldn't make your daughter abide by your wish!"

"Listen Bashay," said Grazmach. "It is true our children are born from us, but they are not ours. They have their own lives, their own calling and their own world. We can't expect them to live their lives for us to gratify our wishes and desires."

Bashay was confused, so, he asked, "What are you trying to say Grazmach?"

"What I am saying is, our children are not merely born for the benefit of our satisfaction," asserted Grazmach firmly. Then he continued, "When it comes to choosing their path of life, we have never tried to force our children to satisfy our wishes. What good would it be if we force them into marriage now? How about if after begetting children, they disagree and fight and separate? When that happens, they will fight, we will fight, and the children will be separated. So, we will not try to force our daughter against her will. We have never done it before, and we will never do it henceforth!", said Grazmach irritably, dropping the tact and diplomacy he had been using to handle the delicate issue.

"Grazmach, please understand that I am desperately trying to make you reconsider only because we fiercely desire and want your kinship. After you extended to us such a great invitation and after we had such a great day, it will be a pity that we go back empty-handed," Bashay pleaded.

"Don't say that Bashay! You should be an example to the youngsters. If we still uphold the love and friendship we have, we will not be empty-handed. Despite this setback, our relationship, partnership and love can still blossom. If we do that, we will all prosper in every sense. Especially you two have a great responsibility in this regard," he said, looking at Habtom and Tesfom. He then added, "You have to watch out that nothing bad spills over and creeps into your relationship at home and at work. You should help us to surmount this temporary setback without any negative consequences to our lifetime relationship and love."

Habtom wanted to show he was not impressed with Grazmach's words. So, he sarcastically said, "Nice words Aboy Grazmach...,"

His father saw where Habtom was going and abruptly interrupted him. "If that is your final word Grazmach, I think it is better if we go," said Bashay getting up, clearly disappointed and saddened.

"Why don't you stay for a while? Tesfom, why don't you bring us more *Swa*," said Grazmach.

Habtom, who had not said much for several minutes, stood up. He was breathing heavily and gritting his teeth. His face was burning, his eyes bloodshot and the veins in his forehead were bulging. Although his body language said it all, he stood up and merely said, "It is ok, we will go!"

Grazmach and Tesfom immediately stood up. They went up to the gate to see them off. Nobody said a word. Bashay and Habtom left. Grazmach and his father returned to the house. W/ro Brkti met them at the door and before they even had a chance to sit, asked, "So, how did it go? How did they take it?"

"It went exactly as we feared it would," said Grazmach. He then began to explain to his wife how the whole event proceeded. Grazmach was tired, disappointed and sad. He wanted to rest for a while, so he excused himself and soon after, Tesfom left.

Grazmach and Tesfom had expected Bashay and Habtom to be reasonably disappointed. But the reaction and disappointment they saw was beyond their expectations. At the time, none of them understood or realized the flood gates they had opened or the monster they had let loose. They had awakened a 30-year grudge that Habtom had carried since his early childhood.

* 2 *

Habtom was fuming. The moment they got out of the house, he started venting his frustration and anger. "Damn this family! They still feel they are superior to us! They will never accept us as equals or stop looking down at us. What a blunder we committed to come and ask for their daughter. We have now become their laughing stock!"

When Habtom was annoyed or angry, he never listened to reason. Bashay knew this very well and decided it was best to let Habtom cool down before trying to talk it over with him. He continued to listen to his son's angry tirade without response.

W/ro Lemlem and Dermas were anxiously waiting for them. When they arrived home, they noticed that Habtom was breathing heavily, his face contorted, and his eyes bloodshot. Before he sat down, he banged the door heavily. They feared the worst. They decided to wait for Bashay to sit down before asking anything, knowing that Habtom when angered was difficult to deal with. Dermas looked at his father and brother with apprehension, shifting his eyes from one to the other.

When they were both seated, W/ro Lemlem spoke cautiously, "Your condition and body language don't look good. Did they reject our request?"

Habtom leaned forward and said, "You can succeed only if you approach a family that respects and wants you! We made a great blunder by going to people who don't accept us as their equals. With such people, nothing can succeed, whether you equal them or even surpass them!" he shouted in fury.

"Oh my God! How can they do this?" said W/ro Lemlem clutching her head with both hands. "But let's first hear the details of exactly how they responded to your request."

"Details! Why would you want to hear details, mother? It will not do you any good! It will only sadden you more!" shouted Habtom.

"They deserve to hear all the details of what transpired," said Grazmach. Without waiting for Habtom to respond, he started to recount the afternoon's proceeding in detail.

While his father was talking, Habtom did not attempt to offer any further explanation or participate in the account. He kept looking at the ceiling or the floor with a furrowed brow and blood shot eyes. He was repeatedly breathing heavily.

When Bashay was finished, Dermas, who had been following his father's explanation without any interruption said, "Well, it is possible they are telling the truth. Selam might have completely refused to marry at all."

"If you were not my brother, I would punch you until you passed out! How can you say that? In such a case, it is the family that should decide, not her!" shouted Habtom, glaring at his brother.

"Habtom is absolutely right. I am not surprised that Tesfom and his mother took such a decision. Both have a feeling of superiority. What I can't understand is Grazmach's position. I had confidence at least in him," said W/ro Lemlem, siding with Habtom.

"I had serious doubts about them from the very start. These people's sense of superiority has no end. I tried to tell you that father, but you wouldn't listen," said Habtom, pointing his gaze towards his father.

W/ro Lemlem immediately added, "I had my doubts about the family from the very start, even before you entered into partnership. I warned you, but you wouldn't listen to me either. I expressed my strong opposition to working in partnership with Tesfom," said W/ro Lemlem.

"Why do you have to bring up the subject of partnership now? Don't try to take us on a tangent by diverting the subject," shouted Bashay with irritation.

"She is right. She is not diverting the subject. This is part of the subject. You know that from the start I didn't like the idea of selling the shop. I accepted your decision with reluctance," said Habtom supporting his mother.

"They agreed to work with us in partnership, not because they liked us or accepted us as equals, but because they knew that they would reap profits through Habtom's hard work," said W/ro Lemlem, adding fuel to the fire.

"Holy Mary! Madonna! Woman! Why can't you just shut up!" said Bashay furiously.

"Don't tell her to shut up father! Isn't what she just said, right? You know very well that they are taking advantage of our hard work. They are laughing at us, while we are spoon-feeding them. But it is ok. There will soon come a day when they will regret this. One way or the other, they will pay for this!" Habtom said threateningly.

"What is wrong with you two?", said Bashay. "All of us have benefitted from this partnership. They profited because they had the money, and we gained because we worked hard. Don't forget that this partnership has benefited us greatly. If it were not for this partnership, Habtom would still be closed in that kiosk and I would still be laboring as an employee in the bakery. Please, let's not forget our blessings, lest we sadden God. Let us be grateful!" said Bashay sternly.

W/ro Lemlem did not accept Grazmach's point of view. She uttered a sound and showed through body language that she was not impressed by her husband's argument. When Bashay saw and heard this, he turned towards her and looked at her sternly. However, as he was about to respond to her reaction, he seemed to change his mind and turned towards Habtom and Dermas.

Then he said, "Listen my dear children. I am saddened even much more than you about what Grazmach's family has done today. Nevertheless, let us not mix two different things that have no relationship to each other. The business partnership we have and the unfortunate incident of today are not related. If the partnership we have established is jeopardized, the disadvantage and loss will affect us all. Today Grazmach talked in detail about this, because he was worried that you youngsters would mix up things and risk our partnership. So please, don't try expand this misunderstanding more than it deserves," concluded Bashay with an appeal.

None of them spoke after that. After a moment's silence, Habtom said, "Don't be disappointed and don't worry about this Dermas Hawey. Soon, we will make sure that you marry any girl of your choice. They can keep their daughter to themselves. Such women do not become obedient wives; they end up becoming your superiors and bosses. As for her, trust me that she will remain a spinster to the end of her life. Although what they did is extremely irritating, I think in the end, you will be better off without her," said Habtom.

"Habtom is right. Don't worry son. This might even be for the best. God has put aside for you the girl that will be your bride," said Bashay.

"The Grazmach family have today shown us clearly that they do not consider us to be their equals. That is very good to know. Knowing where they place us will help us show them that we are not people to be looked down upon!" said Habtom standing up, still immensely angry.

Dermas also stood up and the two brothers left together.

Bashay family's expectations were dashed to the ground. This was clearly evident in their mood and body language. The family had expected a memorable Sunday of success, triumph and happiness. Instead, it turned out to be a day of anger, frustration and sadness.

Bashay was especially saddened by the turn of events. He knew that Habtom would never forget a grudge and that he had a habit of not giving up until he got back at the people who hurt him. This made Bashay very anxious and troubled for the future of the two families.

* 3 *

From his parent's place, Habtom went directly home to Almaz. She quickly read Habtom's body language and understood that things had not gone right. Habtom was still fuming with anger.

She listened to Habtom's account patiently, giving him her undivided attention and absorbing every word he uttered. When he finished, she vehemently expressed her anger, fury and disappointment in the strongest possible words and body language. She went on to condemn the Grazmach family's unacceptable behavior, specifically condemning Tesfom and calling him the very embodiment of Satan himself. By the time Almaz was finished, Habtom was all worked up. When she felt she had expressed her feelings adequately, she decided it was time to unwind and cool Habtom down, so she used all her talents and soon succeeded in smoothing his feathers and calming his mood.

In the days that followed, she continued to show her anger and express her sympathy to her parents-in-law and Dermas about the abhorrent behavior of the Grazmach family. She used one expression of sympathy with Dermas and a different tune and approach with her parents-in-law. Almaz had the ability to adopt a different tune and approach to each person and each situation. In this manner, she successfully managed to show the whole family how she truly was saddened and angered by the actions of the Grazmach family.

Bashay, W/ro Lemlem and Dermas appreciated her sympathy and were touched by how she was genuinely affected and saddened. Their love and admiration for Almaz soared. They were impressed by the positive role she was playing in the family in times of joy and adversity. Almaz was especially able to build an unassailable rapport with W/ro Lemlem. In her eyes, Almaz became the brightest star among all other stars.

* 4 *

From Monday to Friday, Tesfom used to go from the bank to the bakery and Pasta factory regularly. But, in the last few months, he started slackening this regular routine. He was regularly absenting himself from his duties, and as a consequence, he started failing to perform his administrative and accounting responsibilities. Habtom and Dermas were the first to notice, but eventually, all the workers of the factory were aware of Tesfom's absences.

Habtom had discreetly asked and found out that Tesfom's absences were solely due to his drinking. In the beginning, these absences disappointed and irritated Habtom, but after a while, he started to accept them as normal. Later on, he even started to see them as a blessing in disguise, because they allowed Habtom and Dermas to take full control of the factory.

Habtom was a disciplined hard worker. He also had an instinct for business and making money. However, he did not possess any administrative or financial skills for running a factory. Nevertheless, the factory had capable staff and a well-established working system in place, which was entirely due to Tesfom's effort.

Habtom did not acknowledge or accept Tesfom's contribution. He began to repeatedly say, "Tesfom and his kind are born lucky and blessed. They don't have to work like we do. They have people like us to spoon feed them!" He firmly believed that the success of the factory was only due to his contributions and hard work.

* **5** *

Tesfom's incessant drinking began to extremely worry Medhn. She complained bitterly and nagged him incessantly. Although he continually assured her that he would change, his assurances and promises came to nothing. He was making resolutions and promises every morning, only to blow it in the evening. He began blaming himself for his weakness and his lack of self-control; he soon realized that he was becoming an addict.

This cycle of failure and regrets, made him increasingly angry and frustrated. His health and good nature started to take a dive, as he became a victim of a double-edged sword. Under normal conditions, Tesfom was a happy and a good-natured person, but now his good nature started slipping away as he became increasingly irritable and sullen.

Medhn increasingly worried about Tesfom's change of character and mood and she wrestled with telling Grazmach what was happening. After considering the pros and cons, she decided against it, fearing it would hurt both of them. She also did not want to be the cause of misunderstanding and friction between father and son.

By now, Medhn was certain that Tesfom had fallen into an

addiction he could not control. The more she thought about it, the more she was convinced that Tesfom's brother, Araya, was the right person to ask for help.

* 6 *

Grazmach had wished his younger son would continue his education, but Araya did not proceed beyond middle school. Nevertheless, he was very well read and a very perceptive and intelligent person. Apart from his decision to not pursue higher education, Grazmach was extremely satisfied and gratified with his younger son's general disposition and personality.

Araya was a teacher. He was married at 20, in the same ceremony along with Tesfom. Araya and his wife Embaba had become close friends when they were classmates in middle school. They had a very close relationship, which was uncommon in those days, and eventually, they fell deeply in love and were married after four years of friendship.

Though they were married ten years ago, they were still childless. They had tried all modern and traditional means to conceive a child recommended to Embaba, but nothing came of it. There were varying degrees of disappointment within the family. W/ro Brkti was especially saddened by this. She even expressed to Araya, that it would not be wrong to try to have a baby out of wedlock. Araya did not accept his mother's recommendation, and she didn't push the idea any further, because she was afraid of the wrath of her husband, who was vehemently opposed to such a suggestion.

Grazmach on the other hand, loved and respected Embaba very much. Since the case was none of her fault or doing, he stood by his belief that it was not fair to judge her. He also firmly believed and repeatedly said, "It is God that denies or blesses us with children. We should accept his verdict and wish. We don't even know for certain if what happens is for our benefit or not."

At times, he even went further and raised critical questions like,

"What if Araya had been responsible? What would we have said and done? What if she asked us for permission to go to someone else to try to conceive? Would we have allowed her graciously and still loved and respected her as our daughter in law?"

Whenever Grazmach raised such unorthodox questions, W/ro Brkti would be shocked at the enormity of his ideas. For her, such utterances were practically heresy and anathema. Whenever she heard him utter such 'nonsense,' she would say, "No one has ever heard of such ideas. How can you even think and say something that no one else would even think of?"

Grazmach was someone who was born a little before his time. He possessed the courage and audacity to question and challenge anything and everything. He would raise questions about life that none of his contemporaries would ever dare contemplate. His values were not based on, "This is an idea no one has ever raised before, so it can't be right to think or talk about." His yardstick was always, "Is it correct? Is it just? Could it bring goodwill to most? Is it possible and practicable to implement? Might it hurt people?"

Grazmach was a man who preferred to step ahead of the times, rather than walk abreast of his own generation. He was thus known by his close friends as unique and different. People who knew him very little described him as eccentric and odd. The most conservative among his peers would even openly criticize and condemn him for his nonconformity.

W/ro Brkti was often exasperated with her husband's viewpoints. Especially when it came to the subject of Araya and Embaba, she would vehemently say, "Instead of throwing out ideas that do not reflect your age and status, why don't you try to think responsibly? You should try to give advice worthy of an elder and a father."

Grazmach would retort back saying, "If you really want the truth, your suggestion is the one that is extremely irresponsible. Your kind of suggestion will most likely destroy the family they have established. Rather than that, it would be more reasonable for them to adopt a child."

This was something W/ro Brkti never wanted to hear. She would immediately respond with anger, "As a father, how can you possibly think that would be better?" she would explode.

Grazmach would calmly say, "Adoption would have a double advantage. On one hand, they would give an innocent and helpless orphan the chance to be loved and raised by them. On the other hand, they would also experience the joy and love of parenthood, exactly as they would get from their own biological child. Parenthood is not about giving birth, Brkti! Parenthood is about raising a child with love, care and responsibility!"

"Oh, come on! Parenthood is basically about raising your own biological children! Everyone would benefit from my recommendation, but nothing can be done, since both father and son are not ready to listen to reason and logic!", she would shout angrily and storm to her kitchen, sighing heavily.

* 7 *

Medhn decided to talk with Araya about Tesfom's drinking because she knew the fine qualities he possessed. Araya was two years younger than Tesfom. Whenever Medhn described Araya, she used a Tigrinya expression, "*Kab Mhros Aemro,*" meaning "Better to possess wisdom and intelligence rather than just education."

Medhn called Araya over the phone and told him that she wanted to talk to him alone. She didn't explain why she wanted to talk to him in private, so he was a bit worried by her uncharacteristic request. He came on time and before sitting down, asked hastily, "Did you tell me you wanted to talk to me alone? Is everything ok with you?"

"Yes, I am ok. Please have a seat. Can I bring you something?" she asked.

"Don't worry about that. After all, I am not a guest in this house. I am also in a hurry, so I would prefer if we directly go into the subject of your call," said Araya, still curious and apprehensive.

"If you were any other person and a guest, I wouldn't drag you here to talk about my marriage. There is no one closer to me than you," said Medhn, smiling slightly.

"About your marriage? Has anything happened?" asked Araya, with worry in his voice.

"Yes and no. Tesfom up to now, is not directly hurting me or his children."

"Then what?" asked Araya, with a slight relief in his voice.

"He is destroying his health and shortening his life. How much do you know about your brother's drinking habits?" It was Medhn's turn to ask.

"Well, I know that Tesfom has a lot of friends. He likes to enjoy life by going out with friends, drinking and playing cards. Nowadays, that is what most men do. I have never worried about it, since he is not different from almost all men."

"Well, my dear Araya, your information is correct to a certain extent but it is not current. That is what Tesfom was in the past. But, in the past months he has come home drunk practically every day. I also suspect he might be losing a lot of money on his card games. I have talked to him several times without any success. Every morning he promises that he will stop; then he goes back to it the same evening. I am especially worried now because I am noticing a new dangerous trend."

"What dangerous trend?" asked Araya apprehensively. His forehead was furrowed, and he instinctively moved slightly forward in his chair.

"I strongly believe he has now become dependent on alcohol. In short, Tesfom is not in control of his life. It is the other way around. It is the alcohol that is driving Tesfom. What is becoming worse now is that the following day he starts regretting his actions and that drives him to further frustration and depression. He then becomes sullen and withdrawn. He does not talk, smile or laugh with anyone, including the children. On top of his drinking, that is what is really troubling me."

Araya was now extremely worried. "My God! I didn't know it had gone this far. There were people who tried to mention stuff, but I didn't give it importance. You know how people are. So, I never imagined it was this bad."

"Well Araya, I am sorry, but your brother is in a very bad situation."

'Oh man!" said Araya, shaking his head worriedly. Then he looked up pensively, as if he had remembered something and added, "Now that I think of it, Tesfom has not been coming regularly and following the accounts in the bakery. He has thrown all the responsibility to me. He assured me that he was not coming regularly because he had full confidence in me and I believed him. If this is the case, then there is a strong possibility that he might not be following properly even the factory accounts!" said Araya, with concern and apprehension written all over his face.

"Wake up Araya. Let alone not following the details of work, your brother is not even in control of himself!" said Medhn with emphasis.

"So, what do you suggest we do?" asked Araya, accepting the reality his brother was in and shifting his priority to finding a solution.

"I have thought about it long and hard. At one point, I had even contemplated telling *Aboy* Grazmach. Once, when I threatened him with that, he went berserk. He went even as far as threatening me. I had never seen him like that."

"How?" asked Araya.

Medhn recounted the story. When she finished, Araya shook his head gravely and said, "Poor Tesfom *Hawey*. Honestly, I wouldn't support the idea of telling my father. He strongly believes in Tesfom and has huge expectations of him. Telling him would greatly hurt and harm both."

"That is actually why I dropped the idea. I didn't want to hurt Aboy Grazmach and Tesfom for nothing. I also know that Tesfom would never forgive me," said Medhn.

"You are right there. So, what do you suggest we do?" he asked for the second time.

"Since he wouldn't listen to me, I thought he might feel shame about his younger brother coming to advise and correct him. Hopefully that might pinch him and serve as a trigger to change. If you have a better suggestion, I am ready to listen," said Medhn.

"For the moment, I can't think of anything better. So, let's do it. When is the best day and time?" asked Araya, all business like.

"The best is Sunday morning. He sleeps late and gets up around 8 am. It would be best if you come around that time."

"Ok, good. In the meantime, I will also try to find out as much as I can about this dependency. Is there anything else we need to discuss," Araya asked?

Medhn shook her head. "Ok then, let me go now," said Araya standing up.

"Ok Araya *Hawey*, thank you," said Medhn and stood up to see him off.

When Araya left, Medhn felt a big relief. She understood that whatever weight was lifted off her back, it was now weighing on Araya. She could clearly see that Araya was leaving her with a heavy heart and huge concern for his brother. Although she had no option, she felt sorry that she had to put Araya through all that.

After leaving Medhn, Araya was immediately immersed in deep thought and anguish. He made a resolution that starting from the next day, he would seriously follow up his brother's situation.

* **8** *

Araya started collecting information about his brother's night life. Everything that he heard fully corroborated Medhn's account. In certain aspects, it was even worse than what she imagined. Araya was extremely disappointed and saddened by all the information he gathered.

On Sunday morning, Araya went to his brother's house.

Medhn quickly opened the door and welcomed him. She told him that Tesfom was already up and washing. She went to Tesfom and informed him of Araya's arrival.

Tesfom changed his clothes and came to greet Araya. "Hi Araya, welcome! What a pleasure to see you!" said Tesfom, with genuine pleasure written all over his face on seeing his younger brother.

Araya tried his best to respond warmly to his brother's welcome, even though he was torn and uneasy on the inside. Medhn heard the two brothers welcoming each other and joined them quickly.

"I am sorry that I haven't been able to come and assist you at the bakery. Lately, I have been too busy at the Bank. How is business at the bakery?" asked Tesfom.

"Business is ok. There is no problem there, though I don't understand why you had to totally disappear from the bakery," said Araya, indicating that he didn't accept his brother's excuse.

"I am relieved to hear that there is no problem at the bakery. I was worried when Medhn told me you were here so early in the morning." Then Tesfom paused and smiled slightly and said, "Concerning disappearing, it is because I have complete confidence in you!" concluded Tesfom, smiling profusely.

"Well, if that was the only reason for your disappearance, then there wouldn't have been a problem," said Araya firmly.

"What? What do you mean? What other reason can there be?" asked Tesfom, his exuberance and good mood immediately changing and his face becoming somber.

"Wouldn't it be better if I bring breakfast first," said Medhn, who was following the exchange closely.

"It is ok Medhn. It is better if we talk first," said Araya seriously, taking control of the situation.

"Oh, is there something we need to talk about? Then he is right, we better talk first." Tesfom turned to Medhn and asked, "Can you please leave us for a moment?"

"I am part of the conversation," said Medhn and sat down.

Tesfom immediately understood what the conversation was

going to be about. His face became flushed and drained. He shifted his gaze from one to the other. He looked like a prisoner that was ready to hear his verdict.

Araya at first recounted everything he had heard from Medhn and then told him his own findings in detail. Tesfom listened to his younger brother quietly, without any interruption. Araya sat back and turning to Medhn said, "Your turn Medhn. Do you have anything to add to what I just said?"

Medhn acknowledged Araya's invitation with a nod. Then she turned to Tesfom and said, "Listen Tesfom. I am sure you are wondering why I had to talk to Araya about our marriage. But I am scared Tesfom. I am not scared of you, but for you! I am also scared for myself and for our children! I can't stand by and see you destroy yourself. I love you and respect you too much for that. I decided not to talk to *Aboy* Grazmach, because that would hurt you and him. I didn't want to talk to any other family member. I chose Araya, because he is closest to you and to me and because he has the capacity to help us," said Medhn looking at Araya and indicating that she had finished.

Leaning toward his brother, Araya spoke softly. "Listen Tesfom Hawey. You are my elder brother. You are superior to me in everything - including education, intellect, character and experience. Most of what I know is due to you and I thank you. Throughout our lives, you have been my mentor. You have taught me, advised me and guided me. Since early childhood, you have prodded us to be worthy of our parents, not to disappoint them and work hard to make them proud. What I am seeing now is difficult for me to accept. I find myself repeatedly asking, 'Is this you and who is doing this?' I have to accept this bitter fact only because it is the truth. Even now, you are far better than me, but your actions do not indicate that reality. Please help me to understand what is happening to you!" Araya implored desperately.

While Araya was talking, Tesfom bowed his head down. He could not bear the fact that his younger brother was talking to him in this manner and under these conditions. Medhn watched their exchange closely. She noticed that Tesfom even lacked the courage to look his younger brother in the eye. She was saddened by the sight. She told herself, "Poor Tesfom. It really eats my heart to see him reduced to this."

Tesfom took several deep breaths and then looked up and said, "Oh my God! Oh my God!" several times. He bent his head again and shook his head several times, breathing heavily.

Finally, he looked up, locking his eyes with those of his brother. He cleared his throat and said, "Listen Araya Hawey. Listen Medhn, my beloved wife, adviser, sister and mother of the children I love beyond my life. I don't even know what to tell you! I don't even understand what has come over me! I have become a weakling with no self-control. Without realizing it, I have become a victim of alcohol dependency. Every morning I make a promise, but in the evening, when I want to go home, my body forces me back to the bottle."

He was overwhelmed with emotion and had to stop for a moment. He forced himself to continue and, with broken words, said, "I know that I need help! But since I can't help you, I don't know how you two can help me!" He had to stop again. Leaning down and holding his head with both hands, he fought to stop the emotion that was welling up inside him.

"It is ok Tesfom *Hawey*. We will help you in any manner we can, with every strength we possess!", said Medhn, trying her utmost to express her sympathy. She was hurt and saddened by her husband's condition.

Araya had never seen his brother in such a condition of hopelessness. He had never seen him admit to such a gross weakness. He was worried and saddened by what he was seeing. "Don't worry Tesfom *Hawey*. We will face and solve this temporary setback together. If you were not courageously admitting your weakness, then it would be impossible to resolve. But, after all, admitting and accepting one's problem is half way to finding the solution to the problem. So, don't worry and don't lose hope!", Araya said, expressing his empathy and proclaiming his determination to stand by his brother.

Medhn wanted to shift the conversation from expressions of emotion, to a discussion of real solutions to the problem. So, she quickly said, "We have agreed that there is indeed a serious problem. Let's us now talk about a common strategy, on how to face and fight this common enemy."

"Since what I have is a disease, the practical thing to do would be to admit me to hospital. But there are no hospitals for rehabilitating alcoholics in our country. Honestly speaking, even if there were, I wouldn't agree to be admitted to one," said Tesfom dejectedly, with hopelessness written all over his face.

"There is no reason for you to go that far," said Araya. "This is not a problem that arrived overnight. Your dependency has grown to this proportion gradually, and the only way it can be resolved is by taking it down one step at a time," he continued, before becoming pensive for a few seconds. Suddenly, he looked like he was struck by a new idea. His eyes brightened and he quickly added, "The statement you just made about being admitted to the hospital, has given me an idea!"

"What idea?" enquired Medhn hurriedly.

"Although alcohol is the main culprit in this dependency, there are two other contributing factors — friends and bars," Araya pointed out. It is not wise to tackle all three at once. If you agree Tesfom, let's first take on the two outside enemies - the friends and bars — before confronting the main enemy, alcohol," Araya stated firmly.

"How?" asked Medhn, again hurriedly, with anticipation in her voice.

"Let Tesfom make an arrangement with the bank, to take a 15-30-day leave," proposed Araya. "We will also make temporary arrangements to relieve him from his responsibilities in the bakery and the factory. Then you two could go for vacation, to Keren or Massawa or both," he said with conviction.

This time it was Tesfom who hurried to interject, "Ok, and then?"

"This way, you will be far from your friends and the bars you frequent, and in the meantime, you can go ahead and drink moderately in the company of Medhn. If we succeed in separating you from your friends and the bars you frequent, it will be easier for you to confront your alcohol dependency," said Araya with confidence.

"How about the children? What can we do with them?" asked Medhn seeming to like Araya's suggestion.

"We can take care of the children," said Araya. "Since you have never been on vacation together, it will be easy to explain to the family that you two need to go for a vacation. What do you think?" he asked, looking at each of them.

"Amazing! It is a brilliant suggestion," said Medhn. "Wow Araya! It has only been a few days since I told you. How did you come up with such a solution in such a short period?" she said, not hiding her pleasure and admiration.

"What do you say Tesfom?" Araya asked his brother.

"I am ready to try anything you ask of me. But you are going to be swamped with responsibility. On top of all other things, you will also have to take over responsibility for the accounts of the factory. The irony is, I haven't been following the factory accounts as I used to," said Tesfom.

For a split second, Araya and Medhn looked at each other. Tesfom had just confirmed their suspicions. Araya was worried that his brother might notice their body language and hence quickly said, "Don't worry about work. I can handle everything. After we finalize every arrangement, you will need to inform Habtom that I will be following the factory's accounts."

"No problem with that. Ok, that is very good then. If we have finished, can you please bring us some breakfast? I am thirsty and famished," said Tesfom yawning and looking at each of them.

"We have nothing more. We will hammer out the rest of the details in the coming few days," said Araya.

"Ok thank you. God help us and God be with us. Give me a few minutes and I will come back with breakfast." Saying that, Medhn got up and rushed to the kitchen.

When Medhn left, Araya said, "Listen Tesfom *Hawey*. You have an extremely amazing, loving, caring, patient and intelligent wife. Be careful, take care of her! If you lose her, you will hurt not only yourself but also your children!"

"You are right Araya. I understand how blessed I am to have her by my side. I also understand that the problem lies squarely with me. Let's hope God helps me to help myself."

* **9** *

After seeing his brother off, Tesfom went directly to his children and told them to change their clothes. The children were confused and looked bewildered. He knew why they were confused and so, quickly said, "I am going to take you out."

At first, the children could not believe their ears. Their father never took them out on a Sunday. After they realized that he was serious, they couldn't control their delight. Some jumped up and kissed their father repeatedly; while the others ran to their mother to tell her the unbelievable news.

Medhn did not believe what the children were telling her. She knew very well that family time was Saturday morning only and that Saturday afternoon and Sunday was Daddy's time. She went to Tesfom to learn if what the children were saying was true. Tesfom assured her that it was true. She did not comment. She just said, "Oh ok," and went to change. On her way, she told herself, "This is a good beginning, let's hope it continues."

They went out and enjoyed their time together. For the first time ever, Tesfom took his wife and children out on a Sunday. Moreover, for the first time ever, Tesfom stayed away from his friends on a Sunday and stayed at home with his wife and children. The children were delighted and happy. As far as they were concerned, there was nothing more to it. They couldn't fathom the decisive underlying currents that were afloat and the threatening issues that were affecting their home.

Medhn had mixed feelings. On the one hand, she was delighted that Tesfom showed determination to make a small gesture and take a small step. On the other, she felt a little guilt and remorse. She knew how difficult it must be for Tesfom to take these steps. She also knew how lonely and miserable he must have been, despite being surrounded by his wife and children. She felt pity for him and more than once, she was on the verge of asking him to go to his friends for a while and come back. But then she knew what would happen, once he went out, so, she decided to keep her mouth shut.

The children were ecstatic and enjoyed their outing immensely. Both Tesfom and Medhn also enjoyed the day, despite their inner thoughts and doubts. They came home and had a good evening together, eating dinner together at a decent hour. They slept happily and peacefully.

The next day, when Tesfom went to the bank, Medhn told Araya of Sunday's developments. He was pleasantly surprised and happy. Both agreed that helping and saving Tesfom was going to be a long, hard, and bumpy road, with a lot of ups and downs. They further agreed that despite the difficulties they might encounter, if they handled him with care and love, they would in the end succeed to save him. They ended their telephone conversation on a high note of enthusiasm and hope.

In their hope for the future, both Araya and Medhn were overlooking the important fact that we human beings can only shape our destinies to a limited extent and also forgot that we have no way of knowing and predicting the future. At this point, no one knew what Tesfom's fate was going to be; whether it would end up as they honestly and deeply wished for him or something totally different. Still, they were on the right track, since wishing and hoping for the best is the right way forward.

* 10 *

In the past few months, the relationship and closeness between the two families had gradually and substantially cooled down. The major reason for this was the rejection the Bashay family felt, after they were denied the hand of Selam. Habtom, and to a limited extent Dermas, didn't try to hide their feelings. Tesfom immediately noticed the changes, but he continued to act as if there was nothing wrong. But despite his efforts, their working relationship started to deteriorate.

Habtom wanted to show the Grazmach family, that it wouldn't take long to find a bride for Dermas. He relentlessly tried his best to make this happen and in a short while, they found a family who granted them the hand of their daughter. The two families agreed on a wedding day.

When Dermas's wedding preparation began in earnest, Almaz was given a significant responsibility and decisive role. But while she took center stage, Alganesh became a distant onlooker in the whole process. Although Almaz came into the household much later than Alganesh, it was evident to everyone that she was now firmly in the front seat.

During the joyous event, Alganesh and her children were not the only ones who realized and understood where things stood. The whole family had a chance to see the pecking order and how exactly things were lined up. It was a time when the family hierarchy was announced both silently and loudly to the whole clan. From that day on, everyone near and far had no doubt about the importance of Almaz within the family structure.

Dermas's wedding was held in the month of January. Habtom wanted to hold a very large lavish wedding, not because he was an extravagant spender, but because he wanted to dangle that fact in the face of Grazmach and Tesfom. Almaz was against the massive spending. She opposed the idea, especially because she knew why Habtom was doing it. Habtom stuck to his guns and wouldn't budge from his decision. When Almaz realized that there was no way to dissuade him, she dropped her opposition and joined him as if that was her wish as well.

Bashay was also against the idea of overspending lavishly. He talked to his son, but Habtom wouldn't listen. Dermas also raised his opposition to the idea of spending that much money on a one-day ceremony. When his brother wouldn't listen, Dermas proposed an alternative idea. If Habtom was intent on spending that much money, then he suggested that he give him and his bride half of the amount, so they could use the money to establish their new life.

Habtom who was bent on a mission of vendetta, refused to listen. So, despite their reservations, the wedding was celebrated in a grandiose manner. Habtom felt he had his day over the Grazmach family. He felt slightly vindicated and while it lasted, savored his victory.

When Dermas's wedding day was announced, Grazmach gathered his family. He instructed everyone to participate and help in the coming preparations, as if nothing had happened. He explained that no one should be affected by what they might see or hear. Though everyone knew what Habtom was up to, he urged all of them to act as if they didn't understand the message Habtom was trying to convey. Accordingly, Grazmach started to accompany Bashay everywhere, from start to finish. Tesfom, Medhn, Araya, Embaba and W/ro Brkti were also doing their best to comply with Grazmach's instructions.

Bashay and Dermas immediately acknowledged and appreciated their support. They showed their gratitude for what the Grazmach family was doing. Habtom, W/ro Lemlem and Almaz on the other hand, were not impressed with what they were seeing. It was as if they were literally saying, "Don't even try it. If you expect us to forget what you did to us by this gesture, then you must consider us little children." In reality, that was the exact message they were trying to transmit through their body language.

What Habtom, his mother and his second wife failed to understand was that no one was being asked to forget. Even The Almighty God does not ask us to forget but to merely forgive. They were especially failing to understand that forgiving was possible without forgetting.

Dermas's wedding was finalized joyously and happily. Though, they understood that Habtom, Almaz and W/ro Lemlem were not placated by their support, Grazmach was satisfied with how his whole family conducted their civic and neighborly duty. After the wedding was over and the Grazmach family returned home, he told them, "What all of you have done in the past few days has been admirable and exemplary. Despite the reactions portrayed by some of them, we should be satisfied that we had done our duty responsibly. If nothing else, at least we have saved these two families from further exacerbation of the existing misunderstanding. That is a success by itself. So, thank you all."

* 11 *

Whenever Tesfom saw Almaz and Habtom together, he would always wonder what it would have been like, if he had been in Habtom's place. He would immediately shudder at the idea and thank God for saving him from an abyss.

Tesfom was not surprised that Habtom took in Almaz and eventually fathered a son from her. That was in line with who he was; everything was about him and what was best for him, irrespective of the consequences. What was hard to accept was how he had changed so much, when it came to spending. When Tesfom first heard that Habtom had opened a household-materials shop for Almaz, he found it hard to believe.

Whenever possible, Habtom would do everything in his power not to spend money for anyone, including himself. Yet here he was, acting the opposite of the person he was supposed to be. He was not surprised that Habtom was able to afford to buy a household materials shop. When compared to him, he knew how thrifty and careful Habtom was.

Habtom had recently opened a second household materials shop near the *Kidane Mehret* Catholic church, just on the side street of Emperor *Menelik's* Avenue. Tesfom was not aware of this. If he knew that he had indeed bought a second ferramenta, which Dermas would administer, he wouldn't have believed it at all.

The second shop Habtom opened was not something that was long planned. He took the step after he had the last fiery argument with Alganesh, when he fathered a son with Almaz. The threats Alganesh made then forced him to hurriedly withdraw the money in the bank. He bought the Materials shop and put it under Almaz's name. He was taking such a step out of caution, in case Alganesh decided to go to court.

It was uncharacteristic of Tesfom to spend so much time occupied with the affairs of others. When he realized how much time he was wasting thinking about Habtom's affairs, he scolded himself, "How can you waste valuable time and concentration on other people's troubles, when you have tons of your own?"

The scolding brought him back to reality and he soon started thinking about the impending trip they had planned. According to their agreement, the plan was to go first to Massawa, for two weeks; if that trip became successful, then they were to return and stay in Asmara for a week; after which, they would then go to Keren for two weeks. He was not sure if he would be able to handle it all. He shuddered at the thought.

After lunch, Tesfom went to the factory and met Habtom. He told him of their planned trip to Massawa. Habtom immediately accepted the idea without any reservation. Tesfom then told him, that Araya would be taking care of the accounts of the factory on his behalf.

Habtom did not like the proposal at all; he immediately

objected in the strongest terms. He pointed out that whenever Tesfom had been unable to make it, he and Dermas had taken care of the accounts. He insisted that there was no need at all for Araya to come and help in the factory.

Tesfom did not understand why Habtom objected so strongly. He explained that Araya had already taken leave of absence from his job for the occasion. Habtom continued to object, though without providing a good reason. Although Tesfom knew that Habtom was stubborn, he had not anticipated such strong objection concerning Araya. He was finally forced to say, "I don't understand your objection. Can you please explain what the problem would be, if Araya comes to help? You will only be getting extra help!"

Habtom was finally forced to accept the arrangement, because he could not provide a rational response.

* 12 *

While driving to work that morning, Tesfom's thoughts went to their upcoming trip to Massawa. He began contemplating and day dreaming about their impending trip. He visualized the amazing fog that starts from the outskirts of Asmara and engulfs the road to Massawa. Whenever he had driven to and from the port of Massawa, the view had always amazed and mesmerized him.

At first, he remembered the huge chain of mountains that seemed to stand guard on both sides of the road. He visualized the slopes, valleys and plateaus that lay beyond them. For the first 16 kilometers from Asmara, whenever there were clouds, one practically drove above the clouds. It always gave him a sensation of floating on air. The feeling came back to him and he smiled to himself. Tesfom had never flown in an airplane, but if he had, he would have understood that driving those few kilometers to Massawa, in those particular seasons, was exactly like flying over clouds.

He then remembered the snow-white fog that engulfed and covered the area from November to February. In those months, drivers can barely see a few meters ahead. He remembered the fog rushing right and left between the innumerable valleys and the famous mountains of *Arberobue* and *Shegrni.* He remembered fog ploughing in through various directions seeming to compete, over which would arrive first at the top of the plateau and the city of Asmara. All this passed through Tesfom's mind in a flash, as if he was watching a film in his mind. Immersed in such reminiscence, he arrived at the Bank in no time.

* 13 *

Tesfom and Medhn finalized preparations for their upcoming trip to Massawa. They received everyone's blessings and good wishes, for a safe trip. Only Araya knew the real purpose for their trip.

Asmara city sits at an elevation of 2325 meters or 7628 feet above sea level and enjoys a temperate climate all-year-round. Massawa is a port city on the Red Sea, and at its peak season, is one of the hottest ports in the world. Between the two cities, one travels through three different seasons in two to three hours.

About half of the 110 kms Asmara-Massawa-road curves around huge mountain chains. It is very narrow, bordered on one or both sides with treacherous precipices and tall cliffs. When maneuvering corners, it is difficult for opposing drivers to see each other. The road requires the utmost caution and concentration.

When thick fog is added to this equation, the dangers of driving multiply exponentially. It is difficult to judge where the side road ends and the precipice begins. Drivers can barely see a few meters ahead, in front or to their sides. When it rains, visibility is even more difficult as drivers can't be sure if the road is turning or going straight. Such dangerous driving conditions become even more risky at night, making it extremely dangerous to maneuver with a very thin line, between life and death.

In such a situation, drivers can barely drive more than 5-10 kilometers an hour. Tailgating big trucks that move slowly up the steep slope, helps drivers stay centered on the road. Drivers also rely on the small zebra stones planted along the edge of the pavement to indicate where the road ends and the cliff begins. These stones have adorned the road since the Italian occupation. The whole road system was built by Italian technicians and Eritrean laborers.

Luckily, Tesfom and Medhn were going to Massawa in the month of April, when there was no fog and the skies were clear and blue. They started their trip early in the morning. As they drove to the outskirts of Asmara, they passed through *Biet Giorghis*, passing the Indian burial site on their left and the British cemetery on their right.

After passing the Asmara city limit, they drove down the escarpment and were soon able to see on their right, the huge magnificent railway bridge, known locally as *Dldl Arbaete Igru* (the four-legged bridge.) They passed it and continued through the village of Shegrni, marveling at the naturally growing cactus fruit (*Beles*) that covered adjacent mountains. These delicious wild cactus fruit provide free nutrition and income to many for several months each year.

At *Arbe Robue*, the road and railroad converge. After a few kilometers, the railroad they had crossed was now, way below them. They could see the steam driven locomotive spewing dark thick smoke to the atmosphere, from burning charcoal in an open furnace. The train kept appearing and disappearing in and out of the multitude of tunnels along its route.

When they arrived at the spot known as the *Siedicissimo,* meaning the 16th kilometer spot, they got out of their car, and were greeted by a mesmerizing view of unending valleys and vast plains, that stretched nearly all the way to the Red Sea. To the left and right, they saw unending chains of majestic mountains, plateaus, escarpments and valleys.

Continuing their descent, they stopped their car right on top of the small town of Nefasit. They got out of the car and were able to see the majestic Monastery of Debre Bizen, perched on top of the highest mountain in front of them. The foot-trail winding upwards is the only means of reaching the monastery. On their right, they saw the fertile plateau and plains of Mai Habar and Ala. Upon leaving the town, the roadway became comparatively flat and they drove comparatively faster, completing the ten-kilometer road to Embatkala in a short while and speeding on to the town of Ghinda.

At Ghinda, about half way to Massawa, the altitude decreased significantly, while the temperature increased considerably. Ghinda was known for its oranges, mandarins and watermelons (*Birchik*). It was home to a large railway station where trains and *Litorinas* (a bus-like one-coach-train) converged and stopped. Most people going to Massawa or coming back would stop in Ghinda for refreshments, rest and to acclimatize their bodies to the oncoming increased heat, humidity and zero elevation of Massawa.

Tesfom and Medhn stopped in Ghinda, ate a breakfast of *Shehanifull* (a traditional bean skillet recipe popularized by Yemenis), drank tea and relaxed for an hour. They then tackled another round of winding roads passing the very small towns of Dongollo Laelay and Dongollo Tahtay and soon arrived at Gahtelay. After which the road to Massawa is mostly on a flat plain. Tesfom increased his speed and raced towards Massawa.

After Gahtelay, they passed the large Gahtelay bridge which was built by the Italian General Menabria. It was an engineering feat at the time it was constructed, with no support from machineries; most things had to be done by hand. The bridge construction required resolve and sacrifice and its supervision became a personal challenge for the Italian General. Upon its completion, he posted an inscription in Latin, bearing the General's name which read, '*Ca custa, lon ca custa,*' meaning 'Let it cost, whatever it costs, the bridge will be built.' The bridge, his name and the inscription remain standing to this day.

They sped past the bridge and could now feel the hot air rushing towards them. They passed the famous historic war site of

Dogali, where the Italians were decimated by Ras Alula. The places they passed were now totally devoid of vegetation and the soil and rocks seemed burned. The air was hot and was only slightly cooling them. If not for that, their bodies would have been drenched in sweat. The temperature range of that area is between 38 and 42 degrees Celsius.

They soon approached Forto Batsie (the Massawa fortress), which signaled their imminent arrival in Massawa, where they drove past the Humtublo and Amatere zones of the city to the Market area (*Idaga)* and continued straight to the edge of the sea. They were immediately confronted by Sigalet Ketan, a one-kilometer straight causeway that joins the mainland with the island of Twualet, that was constructed by reclaiming the sea. They stopped at the entrance to the causeway, overwhelmed by the sight of the gleaming beautiful Red Sea (known as the Virgin Red Sea). Straight ahead, they saw the old city of Massawa, gleaming in the light.

Massawa has long been known affectionately by its admirers as the Pearl of the Red Sea. Their nostrils and lungs filled with the characteristic scent of the Red Sea, which immediately lifted their spirits and made them feel one with the sea and the land. Passing the causeway, they arrived at Twualet, passing the Red Sea Hotel, the St. Mary church, the railway station and finally arrived at the entrance to another causeway (.......). This much shorter causeway joins Tualet with the Island of Massawa, and the main port area. On their left, they could see the majestic golden domed Turkish palace, which eventually became Emperor Haile Selassie's Imperial palace (Gbi).

Driving straight from the port area, they passed the famous Savoia and Torino edifices to the left and continued to the right, towards Riesi Mdri, where the Massawa Light House stands. They drove through the excursion boat club, the famous cabaret and night club Dance Maria, and the open-air Red Sea Cinema until they came to a small pension by the sea.

After being shown to their room, they took showers. In Massawa, the hotel rooms are not equipped with warm water, as the water from the ground pipes is always naturally warm. At times, it is even too warm. Tesfom and Medhn were lodged in a very small modest pension, known as Asmara Pension that overlooked the Great Gedem mountain and the Sheik Said Island (Green Island) on one side and the Massawa Light House on the other. The sea was a few meters away from the pension building. From within their room, they could hear the natural music of the sea waves splashing onto the land.

Tesfom and Medhn did not feel at ease and couldn't relax for the first two days. They were worried about their children, whom they had left alone for the first time ever. Araya was taking the children from and to school while their grandmother Brkti stayed day and night with them, taking care of all their needs. Grazmach was staying with the children during the day time. Tesfom and Medhn relaxed and took it easy after being assured that the arrangement, they had set up were working perfectly.

The months of March and April come after the relatively 'cold & rainy' season of Massawa and right before the hot season of May to August. These are the months with perfect climate for a visitor who wants to enjoy Massawa. During the day, the climate and the temperature of the sea is such a perfection that it beckons and pulls everyone to come right in and take a long dip. Swimming in the Red Sea is like taking a bath in a personalized self-adjusting bathtub. The water temperature is as if it was warmed to the exactly right temperature.

During the evenings, the fresh evening air with moist breeze beckons you to go out for a stroll and invites you to breath in the clean mild moist air. Tesfom and Medhn started enjoying this temperate and perfect climate in unison, with love, peace, common purpose and a common goal. They were enjoying it so much; they couldn't believe their blessings. They firmly believed that this was a grace they were blessed with, not something they deserved.

Every day they went to the sea and passed the day swimming

and relaxing. After eating their dinner, they would go out for a long walk to enjoy the beautiful climate. Sometimes, they would go to the open-air Red Sea cinema house nearby and enjoy a movie.

Anyone who saw them in that condition would only conclude that they were newly-weds enjoying their honeymoon. The reality was Tesfom and Medhn were now 36 and 31 years old respectively and were parents of four children. The twins Bruk and Timnit were now 13 years old, Legesse was nine and Hiriyti was six years old.

The couple continued to enjoy their vacation. They were having the time of their lives. Medhn was additionally gratified that Tesfom was behaving himself and working hard to control his dependency.

* 14 *

On top of his Bakery duty, Araya started to go daily to check the accounts of the pasta factory. It did not take long for him to notice that Habtom and Dermas were not happy to see him. After a while, they even started to clearly and actively show him that he was not welcome. Araya was not perturbed by this reception. He told himself, "As long as I have been delegated by my brother to do this task, nothing will stop me from fulfilling my responsibility."

Araya and Medhn were constantly in touch, sharing information about Tesfom's progress. Medhn assured Araya that Tesfom was doing very well. She further told him that if the success held, then she would love to also go ahead with the Keren trip. Araya was encouraged by Medhn's report.

Araya, on his part, assured Tesfom and Medhn that there was no problem at home or at the factory. He asked his brother not to worry about work and concentrate on his vacation. They were relieved and happy to hear that. They thus continued to enjoy their second 'honeymoon' without any anxiety.

Araya had now become used to the workings of the factory accounts. He encountered no problems and became confident that he had things under control and could take it easy. However, on the 8th day after Tesfom and Medhn left, he noticed an irregularity. He found that Dermas had made two to three sales but failed to hand over the transactions to the cashier. He found that strange. Before coming to any hasty conclusion, he decided to wait and watch closely.

On the third day, Dermas repeated the same action. Araya was alarmed. He decided to compare the pasta produced, the sales and the stock. After the comparison, he found out that there was indeed a discrepancy. He was now certain that Dermas was skimming cash from the factory.

He didn't know what to do. If Dermas was any regular employee, he could have dealt with the issue easily and swiftly. But since Dermas was Habtom's brother, he understood that handling the matter would be complicated. On top of that, he also remembered that their relationship was at an all-time low. He thus decided to keep the matter to himself and wait until Tesfom returned.

Araya continued to assure Tesfom that everything at work was fine. Tesfom and Medhn enjoyed their two weeks in Massawa and arrived back the last day. Araya went home to welcome them back, but decided to postpone sharing his discovery with Tesfom until the next day. He wanted them to enjoy the day in peace with their children.

* 15 *

Although Araya wanted to meet with his brother as soon as possible, Tesfom was reluctant to talk about work so soon. Araya insisted that he needed to give him a report as soon as possible. They met the next day and Araya explained the details of what he had found. Tesfom refused to accept the findings. Without providing any contra arguments or refuting the findings, he just kept repeating, "No, this is impossible! No, this can't be!"

Araya begged his brother to listen to him with an open mind.

He reminded Tesfom that he himself had admitted that he had not been following the accounts properly. Finally, Araya quoted the Arabic proverb their father often used, "*Wana Zeyblu Mal, Seraki Yetri,*" meaning, "A property without an owner, attracts thieves."

Finally, Tesfom agreed to see the documents which allegedly showed discrepancies. After he had checked all the documents himself, he was finally forced to accept the validity of his brother's findings. Araya was relieved that he was finally able to convince his brother. Tesfom wanted time to think about their next move. Araya left his brother to consider their next steps.

After Araya left, Tesfom started talking to himself, "It is amazing that this can happen. It is actually not surprising that something like this happened, because I haven't been following the accounts regularly for quite some time. What is surprising is though, how Habtom was unable to see this. After all, Habtom is always at the factory," he said and shook his head several times.

Tesfom continued talking to himself, "If this is true, it will be incredulous; especially because no one can believe that Dermas could pull this off. Dermas seems like a good natured and harmless person with average intelligence. How could he even come up with this?" he asked himself. He shook his head again.

He scolded himself for trying to avoid accountability by attempting to analyze Dermas's personality and capacity. He realized that he needed to admit his weakness and squarely accept his responsibility. He remembered that he knew full well that ultimately, "It is actually those whom we look down upon, that take advantage of us and use us!"

He shook his head again remembering something his father used to say, "When it comes to doing something bad, or to cheating and swindling, nearly all people are clever and intelligent. It is when it comes to doing good things that the trait becomes rare!"

He finished his internal monologue and stood up. He went directly to the factory where he began comparing and re-checking the discrepancies in the documents that Araya had found. By the time he finished, he had no doubt that the documents substantiated Araya's findings. He went to Habtom and told him that there was an urgent matter they needed to talk about. Since it was already lunch time, they agreed to meet in the afternoon.

* 16 *

Although Tesfom greeted Habtom warmly, Habtom did not reciprocate. Tesfom ignored Habtom's cool reception and without further ado, delved straight into the issue, "Listen Habtom," he said. The matter I want to talk to you about is delicate. Since you are still annoyed and upset, it could complicate our rapport further. So, for the sake of our relationship and partnership, I beg your patience and understanding."

"What kind of issue are you talking about?" said Habtom coolly, not hiding his displeasure to even sit down and talk with Tesfom.

"There are some irregularities that Araya noticed while I was away on vacation."

"What kind of irregularities?" asked Habtom hurriedly, interrupting Tesfom.

"I will get to that in a minute. I believe, it should have been something you were not even able to notice," said Tesfom.

"Something I was not able to notice? What do you mean?" Habtom again hurriedly interrupted Tesfom.

Tesfom hesitated, then took a deep breath and finally said, "Your brother, Dermas, has been making several sales and pocketing the transactions."

'Whaat? What are you saying! This is a false allegation your brother is concocting to destroy Dermas's reputation! When are you guys going to stop treating us like dirt?" exploded Habtom furiously.

"Please Habtom, let's not take this somewhere else," said Tesfom patiently.

"Why shouldn't I? You guys are accusing my brother of theft!" exploded Habtom again.

"Well, would you have kept quiet, if you had found my brother in the same act? But now, please first hear me out. I will enumerate all of Araya's findings, one by one."

"Go ahead, enumerate as much as you want, but you will not find anything," said Habtom in a more subdued tone. It was clearly visible that he was shaken. The veins on his forehead were bulging and traces of sweat could clearly be seen on his face.

Tesfom started producing the sales documents, the daily cash sales, purchases, and stock cards, and started to explain the discrepancies. The proof Tesfom presented was air-tight. Habtom had no means of counteracting Tesfom's accusations.

Habtom's perspiration and unease increased. Finally, all he managed to say was, "I can't accept any of this. There should be an explanation. If you had suspected Dermas of such acts from the beginning, why didn't you tell me? Why did you have to bring Araya in? Or was this vacation thing a cover-up for a carefully considered plan from the beginning?" Habtom asked.

Tesfom in his haste to affirm his innocence, did not understand that Habtom was cross examining him. "Never, I had no suspicion or any sort of a plan. I earnestly brought Araya to help you with the accounts," said Tesfom

"If that is the truth, I will accept it," said Habtom, seeming slightly relieved. He quickly added, "Anyway, I want to closely examine the documents myself. I need to make my own assessment about the accusations you are throwing at Dermas. Moreover, I will also need to question Dermas about this," said Habtom firmly.

"Ok, no problem. Can we meet tomorrow then?"

"I will need more time. Let us meet after tomorrow," said Habtom.

"That is fine," said Tesfom, standing up. Habtom also stood up and both left without another word.

* 17 *

On the third day, Tesfom went to the factory and met Habtom. Although Tesfom again tried to greet him warmly, Habtom did not choose to respond to his greetings. He acknowledged him with a cool undefined grunt. Tesfom noticed the cool reception, but decided to ignore it, and said, "Ok then, let's get down to business; please go ahead."

"I have talked with Dermas about the allegations and he strongly rejects all accusations. We have also closely examined the alleged documents in great detail. As you know, Dermas is not cautious and meticulous. The discrepancies can only be a result of human error. I am therefore satisfied and I have accepted his innocence," said Habtom very cautiously, as if he was reading from a prepared, well-rehearsed text.

"You should know that I don't easily throw out uncorroborated accusations. I have presented solid evidence of discrepancies to you. If you are going to claim that Dermas did not commit any of this, then you will have to present to me or any other professional, concrete evidence and documentation. Only one of us could be right; so, we have to settle this either way," said Tesfom firmly and strongly.

Habtom was taken aback by Tesfom's strong stance. He seemed to hesitate for a moment and then said, "Can we, for a moment, put aside our opposing positions on the issue and instead discuss about the resolution of this problem. I mean, either way, have you thought about how you want to eventually settle this issue? Do you have a proposal in that regard?" asked Habtom, still probing and wanting to examine all avenues ahead of time.

Again, Tesfom did not stop to think about the depth of Habtom's investigative probing questioning and hurried to sincerely respond, "I have no objection to proceeding to the next stage, provided that we don't forget that we have a substantial disagreement that requires a decision. Having said that, my response to your question is simple. If Dermas was an outsider, we would have filed charges and brought him to justice. But Dermas is a member of this family. So, there is nothing we can do in that regard. But there is one thing that needs to be done. Dermas has to immediately resign and cease all participation in company operations," said Tesfom firmly.

"Resign? Come on! How can go that far? Can't you come up with something fairer?" asked Habtom, feigning to be shocked with Tesfom's proposition. Unlike his words, his body language however, seemed to display relief.

"Yes, resign! I have thought about this and that is the only way out of this!" said Tesfom firmly.

"This is not fair or just. To take such a decision, when we still have diametrically opposite positions on the discrepancies is not right. But if you insist and you become adamant about it, then for the sake of our partnership, Dermas could leave," said Habtom with a sign of hopelessness.

"It is not about insistence or obstinacy. That is the only practical and sensible way out of this situation," said Tesfom, and as an after-thought added, "I suggest you talk to him and finish this with him yourself. I feel it will be more painful for him, if both of us talk to him," he said, thoughtfully.

"Wow! Amazing! This is so unfair and unbelievable!" said Habtom shaking his head. Then he added, "Anyway, ok I will talk to him," said Habtom, shaking his head again and trying to show signs of unhappiness and discontent.

Although Habtom was trying to wear a face of discontent, Tesfom's senses told him otherwise. He felt he saw signs of relief and being at ease. When Tesfom noticed this, he was pleased with himself. He was happy that he managed to make Habtom accept his proposition, without much acrimony and bitterness.

Encouraged by his success thus far, Tesfom said, "I have one additional suggestion."

Habtom looked suspicious and genuinely fearful. "What additional suggestion?" he asked anxiously.

"Since we are relieving Dermas of his duties here, it would be better if Araya continues to help here in the factory."

Habtom looked shocked and quickly asked, "Why do we need to bring Araya here? You and I can perform the task adequately."

"Simply because we need help. We had Dermas here because we needed help," said Tesfom firmly.

"I will never agree to this proposal!" shouted Habtom furiously.

It was Tesfom's turn to be shocked. He was surprised by Habtom's overreaction and asked, "Why? What is the problem?"

"Do you want me to tell you the truth? We are now at odds with each other because of Dermas. I don't want to face that tomorrow because of Araya. We can adequately perform the tasks ourselves. That is my final decision!"

Tesfom immediately went into internal dialogue and thought, "Wow! I see that Habtom is suspicious, lest Araya pocket funds like Dermas. If that is his concern, I think it is legitimate." He was satisfied with his deductions and thus said, "Well, if you have such serious reservations, then ok, we will do without Araya."

"Ok, good. We have finished, right?" said Habtom standing up.

"Yes, we have," said Tesfom and stood up. Habtom went to the factory and Tesfom remained at their administrative office.

After their talk, Tesfom had an uneasy feeling about something he couldn't put his finger on; something illusive about his conversation with Habtom, stuck with him. He tried hard to identify the uneasy feeling, but to no avail. Finally, he decided there was nothing there and he was just needlessly wracking his brain. He had to force himself to stop thinking about it.

* 18 *

Though Tesfom tried his best to avoid thinking about it, the nagging sensation he felt about his conversation with Habtom, refused to go away. The more he tried to forget it, the more it stuck with him. But after a long struggle, he finally grasped what his subconscious had been trying to communicate with him.

After the accusation, Tesfom had expected Habtom to fume, rant and create an ugly scene, but instead, his reaction was nothing like that. He had shown only a very mild and meek reaction, but that was not the real Habtom he knew. In retrospect, he realized that Habtom's mild reaction was staged rather than real. He looked like someone who had prior knowledge of what was going on.

This new realization begged many questions. Could Habtom have known beforehand about Dermas's cheating? If he had, was this done with his cooperation and support? If so, then the scamming could be much greater than what Araya had discovered and this might only be the tip of the iceberg. These were the possibilities that hovered in his mind.

The reality of its possibility scared Tesfom profoundly. If it was the case, it would lead to far greater complications and even the possibility of dissolving the partnership. He hoped with all his heart and prayed that this wouldn't be so.

He knew that the in last few months, he hadn't been following the accounts regularly and properly. This was, of course, due to his incessant drinking and weakness. At first, he tried to convince himself that, though his weakness played a part, what happened was primarily because he put too much faith in Dermas and Habtom; it was not his fault that they failed to uphold their trust and promises. After a while, however, he rebuked himself for making meek excuses to cover up his weakness and absolve himself. He resolved to at least be courageous enough, to accept blame and responsibility.

In the end, he collected enough courage to fully accept his failure and responsibility. He knew that henceforth; he had to open his eyes and ears and check every entry himself and not just sign what was presented to him. Then he started thinking about his next move. What he had surmised so far about a larger cheating conspiracy, was just conjectures and possibilities. The only way to find out the truth was to roll up one's sleeves and get to work. He knew that he had to go back months and trace every step from A to Z, which meant going back many months and checking every purchase, production entry, sales and stock records at every level.

He knew the work was massive, but it was not beyond his capacity, if he upheld his discipline and behaved. He decided to take a vow right there and then, in the name of his children, that he wouldn't go anywhere before accomplishing the projected plan. After making this promise, he was confident that he would see his promise through.

Tesfom could only be sure that he had taken a vow and made a promise. Whether he will see through his promise, was another matter. He needed someone to remind him, that judgement time would come and although his words would be forgotten, his deeds would be recorded for eternity, because time is eventually the ultimate witness.

* 19 *

He arrived home reiterating his vow and promise. He recounted to Medhn everything that had occurred between himself and Habtom, explaining to her his resolve and promise. He explained why their vacation plan for Keren had to be postponed and replaced by this new unplanned challenge. Medhn had no objection to the suspension of their vacation. She assured Tesfom that she would give him all the support he needed, if he stuck to his promise and controlled his drinking and dependency. Tesfom was encouraged by her support and confidence.

The next day, Tesfom reported to Araya the conversation he had had with Habtom and informed him of his plan and the promise he made. Araya assured his brother that he fully supported his plan and expressed his willingness to help Tesfom sort the previous months' documents. Tesfom was elated by his brother's support.

The support of his wife and brother gave Tesfom a much-needed boost. He started his task with great optimism and resolve. After sustained work, within a week, he observed that he had already made great progress. He could already see that the scamming and cheating was not restricted to Dermas. But he was not satisfied with the proof he had managed to collect up to that point and continued his effort to collect full-proof evidence of the theft. Habtom could not understand Tesfom's new-found discipline and work ethic. He eyed him with suspicion. He did not hide his feelings and clearly signaled his disapproval. But, Tesfom was not perturbed by any of it.

The more evidence Tesfom found, the more he was saddened by his weakness. This began to affect him negatively and hurt his pride and morale. But he was determined to stop pitying himself and his weakness. Instead, he forced himself to stick to and concentrate on the work before him.

In this manner, Tesfom was able to collect ample evidence, that showed Habtom had been the mastermind behind the cheating and theft. He had sufficient evidence to conclude, that the cheating and scamming had been carried out on a large scale, for a very long time. After collecting all the paper-work he needed, he started questioning some employees he trusted.

The next step was to carefully think out his next move. In deeply thinking about his next move, Tesfom knew he needed to consult with the people he trusted most and whose judgement he valued. The first on that list was, of course, his father, Grazmach Seltene. There was no major decision he ever took, without seeking the advice of his father. But this case was different. This was a case that he brought upon himself by his own weakness. He felt that it would eventually be inevitable, but at this point, he didn't want to sadden his father prematurely. He decided to take the advice of Medhn and Araya and get legal advice from a friend he trusted.

After taking a firm decision about his next move, the time for confrontation was at hand. Tesfom told Habtom, he needed to talk to him about an important matter, that would affect the future of their work and partnership. They made an appointment and to have complete privacy, they agreed to meet after work hours. He suggested that both Dermas and Araya attend the meeting, because they were going to be important contributors to the plan. Habtom accepted the proposal with slight uneasiness and apprehension.

Tesfom had worked long and tiresome hours for weeks. He used to go home very late from the factory and would eat his dinner in haste and go to bed immediately. But as soon as he got into bed, sleep would evade him. So much self-blame and regret would creep in and he would spend the night tossing and turning.

Medhn was aware of this and was much worried that he might be hurting his health. More than once, she contemplated talking to him, but then thought otherwise. She told herself, "Leave him be, he was nearly drinking himself to death." She thus resisted the urge to talk to him.

* 20 *

Four of them arrived at the factory on time. They sat in the room that Habtom and Tesfom used as their administrative office. Tesfom sat behind a large table in front of them, while Habtom and Dermas sat to his left and Araya sat to his right. On both sides of the table, there were multiple files and folders.

Tesfom's eyes were visibly blood shot and his whole demeanor showed lack of sleep and fatigue. Anyone who didn't know what he had been through the last few weeks, would have attributed his physical features to his habitual drinking.

When all of them were seated comfortably, Tesfom cleared his throat and said, "Today's meeting is going to be different from any that we have held in the past. It is going to have a huge impact on our future working relationship. I beg you all to listen to me patiently. I will ask both Araya and Dermas to write the minutes of our meeting. At the end of our discussion, all of us will sign the minutes."

Habtom and Dermas looked at each other with anxiety and apprehension.

"Since when do we write and sign minutes of our meetings? What is the exact nature of our talk? Why don't you first inform us of the meeting's agenda?" asked Habtom with distrust and suspicion.

"I will soon come to that," said Tesfom firmly and seriously, handing over sheets of paper and carbon papers to Araya and Dermas.

Habtom and Dermas again looked at each other. Tesfom and Araya noticed their discomfort and bewilderment.

Tesfom cleared his throat again and seemed to hesitate and then said, "I don't know how to say this or where to start. I guess there is no other diplomatic way to saying this, except stating it bluntly," he said, looking at the two brothers.

Habtom was already on edge and anxious, and Tesfom's procrastination irritated him further. He was forced to interrupt him, "What do you think you are doing? Don't you understand that you are still going in circles and procrastinating?! Why don't you simply tell us the agenda of this meeting?" demanded Habtom impatiently.

"You are absolutely right Habtom, I am indeed procrastinating. Then let me put it straight to you. Over the last two weeks, I have been checking and rechecking the factory accounts day and night. What I have unequivocally found out is that you, Habtom, have for a long time been scamming income due to the factory and pocketing it!"

"Whaat? Whaat did you say? Do you know what you are saying?" shouted Habtom, rising from his chair menacingly. His eyes were immediately blood shot and his veins bulged on his forehead.

"Please sit down and listen carefully. I have documentation that corroborates the statement I just made," said Tesfom firmly, locking his eyes on Habtom.

"It is now very obvious, why you rejected our request for your sister's hand and later accused Dermas baselessly! Your strategy is now very clear! From the very beginning, we were so trustful and naïve that we were blind to your schemes and intentions." said Habtom furiously, slowly sitting back in his chair.

"It is interesting that you brought up the subject of Selam. What is amazing and unbelievable is that, while you were asking for our sister's hand with your right hand, you were robbing us with your left! Anyway, I don't want to be diverted to another subject and a side issue," said Tesfom and started opening a folder.

"You'd better watch your language! I am not diverting you to another topic. It is the same issue. It is clear now that you are fabricating accusations because you want to dissolve this partnership!" shouted Habtom.

"The matter you are raising now is an issue that will come later in the discussion. Please be patient and hear me out. At least allow me to explain why I arrived at this conclusion," said Tesfom coolly and patiently.

"You can continue; but your end game and goal are definitely not different from what I just said," said Habtom firmly.

Tesfom ignored Habtom's comment and decided to continue. "I have ascertained that you were purchasing flour from outside sources without my knowledge and without registering the purchases to our stock," he said.

"Of course, I was purchasing! If we were to wait for you to sober up, the factory wouldn't function at all!" shouted Habtom.

"Yes, you are right there. It was all due to my weakness and my lack of regular follow-up that led to this. But what I was trying to say before you interrupted me is that you were producing and selling pasta from the flour purchased secretly and siphoning and pocketing the proceeds!" said Tesfom firmly.

"If I had been pocketing the revenue, how do you think we managed to pay our loans to the bank? I will never accept any of these false accusations! You are just trying to ruin my reputation! Don't ever doubt for a moment that I will take serious issue with your attempts to undermine my name!" shouted Habtom.

"If my intention had been to destroy your name, I wouldn't

have warned you and informed you here privately and informally. I would have sued you and taken you to court. I have adequate documentary evidence to prove my case. I also have witnesses that can attest to this, and I even have a list of the persons you were purchasing flour from and selling to. Most of them believed that you were doing it with my knowledge!" said Tesfom furiously.

"Anyone bent on destroying another person's reputation can line up false witnesses and write false testimonies!", said Habtom, without much conviction in his voice.

"I don't have any reason to accuse you of something you didn't do. Even If I had, I am not foolish enough to try it without evidence. I have shown the evidence and documents that I have collected to law professionals and accountants. I have been advised as to the avenues that are legally open to me. If I decide to, I can proceed in that direction," said Tesfom firmly and angrily.

"Are you trying to threaten me?" Habtom shouted, by bringing his body and face nearer to Tesfom.

"I am not threatening you," Tesfom said calmly.

"Then what are you doing?" asked Habtom.

"I am merely trying to explain to you, that it would be better for you if we conclude this peacefully between ourselves. Otherwise, if we go down the legal route, the whole world will come to know of this. If you want to prevent this, then hear me out," said Tesfom calmly.

"Ok, I can hear out what you have to say," said Habtom meekly. By now, Habtom seemed like a broken and defeated man.

Tesfom understood that he had Habtom in his grips. He continued confidently by saying, "All right. After such gross dishonest and untrustworthy acts, we can't work together anymore...,"

Habtom did not let him finish, "I don't care if we don't work together anymore. From the very beginning, it was not because you wanted us or saw us as equals that you wanted to work with us in partnership. It was because you understood that you would benefit from our hard work ethic and discipline!" shouted Habtom again.

"Come on Habtom, don't take us on a tangent again. I am not going to give credence to your statement or adorn it with a response. If I do, it is going to divert us from our main topic. If you will allow me again, let me finish what I started," said Tesfom calmly.

"Ok, you can continue, but I am positive you have nothing important to say," said Habtom, much more subdued.

Tesfom ignored the last statement and continued from where he had left. "As I said before, even now, my intention is not to take you to court. This is because we are practically family. We have been bound for years as neighbors and friends through our parents, our wives and our children. Therefore…,"

Habtom could not control himself and again interrupted Tesfom. "How could you take me to court when I haven't done anything? It is unbelievable that you want to act as the accuser, the investigator and the judge all at once! You are more educated than me but don't try to underestimate me. I am not a newborn baby frightened by false accusations. It is better that you understand that I will never accept any of this at all!" shouted Habtom again.

"Ok, then let's do this. I will give you copies of the documents I have. You can examine and closely study them yourself or with the help of any professional. Let's meet after you do that. Is one week enough for you?" asked Tesfom.

"Yes, one week is enough for me. Let's do that," said Habtom, fuming and shaking his head.

"All right, very good. Then let's sign the minutes Araya and Dermas have written and then we are finished for today."

They began signing and exchanging the minutes of their meeting. There was no other sound in the room, except the sound of shuffling paper and the sound of pen on paper. When they finished, four of them stood up and went out, without another word.

Chapter 5
Confrontation

Since early childhood, Habtom had felt chronic jealousy and held a grudge against Tesfom. This latent grudge lurked within Habtom's subconscious long after childhood. Even after they became Godfathers to one another's children and became partners, this dormant grudge had hibernated remaining intact. Habtom was also a very stubborn and ruthless person, always led by blind emotions.

Generally, Almaz was not led by her emotions, but rather by what was practical and best for her. She had the strength of character to steer away from her emotions and think clearly and rationally. However, when it came to Tesfom, she was incapable of doing that. She had never been rejected by any man, except Tesfom. And he was also the only man she had ever truly loved and wanted. She was never able to forgive him for rejecting her and thus developed blind loathing and hatred against him.

Tesfom's recent allegations added fuel to the fire that was burning within both Habtom and Almaz. They fumed and expressed their anger and hatred of Tesfom in the most extreme manner.

Habtom was impressed by Almaz's genuine expressions of hatred. He acknowledged her support and expressed his appreciation for her unflinching love and concern for him. Habtom did not know the real reason or rationale for her hatred. Their common feelings of disgust and hatred of Tesfom did not only emanate from their conscious rational minds. It also arose from their deep emotional subconscious, which was beyond their say and control. Habtom had full confidence in Almaz's abilities and judgement. He would thus share with her everything that went on in his life and his work.

The Grazmach family's rejection of the marriage proposition and the subsequent accusations against their children totally dominated the conversations between Bashay and W/ro Lemlem. The events completely clouded their judgement and their discussions always ended up with condemnation and demonization of the so-called satanical Tesfom. They both wished and prayed for the worst things to befall him.

* **2** *

Habtom realized that the partnership with the Grazmach family was at a point of no return. He thought it was the right time to inform his parents about what was going on. He didn't think it was necessary to inform his first wife, Alganesh. He felt it was none of her concern and was certain that she would eventually come to know of it through what he called her, "agents and spies."

Habtom told his mother that he and Dermas would be coming the next day for lunch and asked her to inform his father that they would be coming to discuss something important. After lunch and tea, they sat down to talk. Since they had arrived, W/ro Lemlem had been eying them closely. Her feminine sixth sense had told her that things with her children were not ok. Before anyone said anything, she asked, "Are you guys, ok? Is everything ok?"

"Well, you can say we are ok. Though, in another sense, we are also not ok," said Habtom solemnly.

"What? Is anything the matter?" asked Bashay, leaning forward. His body language showed that he had not suspected anything unpleasant, up to that point.

"Oh my God! So, there is definitely something wrong!" said W/ro Brkti, already wringing her hands.

"It is not anything that should unduly worry you mother. The Grazmach family, especially Tesfom is giving us a hard time," said Habtom coolly.

"How?" asked Bashay, again leaning forward.

"Oh my God! So, finally, Tesfom's good-for-nothing pride has caught up with you!" said W/ro Brkti, shaking her head.

"*Madonna!* Holy Mary! Before jumping to conclusions, can't you wait until they tell us what it is?" Bashay shouted at his wife, and then turned back to his son and said, "Continue, son."

"About a month ago, he went to Massawa with his wife. Before he left, he asked me if Araya could come to help in the factory in his absence. I didn't think there was anything to it and I agreed. As soon as he came back from Massawa, he leveled a preposterous allegation against Dermas. He told me, "Araya has found out that your brother Dermas has been selling pasta from the factory and pocketing it!"

It was Bashay's turn to be shocked and to interrupt, "Whaaat? What kind of a wild accusation is this?"

"Yes, absolutely! He used those exact words. I told him straight out that my brother is not that kind of person. He insisted that they had documentary evidence to prove their case. I told him that was a false accusation and a total fabrication. Then he told me he had no intention of suing Dermas, but he wanted Dermas removed from his position at the factory. I told him if that was his intention from the beginning, he could have demanded Dermas's removal without falsely accusing him."

"My God! What kind of insanity is this? His pride and spiteful absolute disregard for other people is unbelievable!" said W/ro Lemlem, shaken and fuming with anger.

"Anyway, after that, I told him that Dermas was doing us a favor by coming and helping in the factory. I said, "If you feel we don't need his help, neither Dermas nor I would have a problem with it." As soon as we finished Dermas's issue, he had the audacity and rudeness to ask me if he could bring his brother Araya to help in the factory. I was shocked by his impudence, insensitivity and blindness. I didn't even feel like talking or explaining why, I just told him point blank, "No! No! and No!"

"I am extremely dismayed and distressed that my beloved son Dermas had to be dragged through this dirt. They have not been satisfied enough to have shamed us by denying their daughter's hand. They now want to add another victory to it, by accusing Dermas of robbery and shaming him!" said W/ro Lemlem, her face flushed with anger.

"It is ok mother, don't be unduly saddened," said Dermas.

W/ro Lemlem glared at her son, "What more do you want them to do to you and to us?" She looked disappointed with her son's weak reaction and lack of combative anger.

Habtom calculated it was the right time to feed his parents further inflaming and enraging information. "This was not the end of the saddening saga. There is more to it!" said Habtom quietly, pushing his parents into further worry and anguish.

"What can be worse than this?" said Bashay sadly.

"Don't tell me they went further than this!" said his mother apprehensively, her motherly instinct kicking in.

"When he finished with Dermas, he had the audacity to come at me!" said Habtom, continuing his carefully choreographed delivery.

'Come at you? How? Why?" asked Bashay apprehensively.

"What can they say against you? After all, you are spoon feeding them by working day and night!" said W/ro Lemlem confidently, as always wary of anyone who attempts anything against her favorite son.

"Three days ago, he came and leveled a new accusation against me. He told me that the cheating was conducted with my full knowledge and cooperation. I was extremely mad. I wanted to kill him. After I cooled down a bit, I told him, 'After such an allegation against me and my brother, I don't want to work in partnership with you or your family!'"

"You did the right thing!" shouted W/ro Lemlem.

Habtom was now certain that the well thought-out story-line he had prepared for his parents' consumption was on the verge of success. He didn't want to lose his timing and momentum and before letting anyone else speak, he quickly added, "In the end, I told him I was going to decide how I plan to proceed forward. I parted from him by telling him that henceforth I don't want to see him or talk to him again!"

Habtom was thus able to simultaneously close the story-line he had prepared for his parents and his delicately rehearsed report with one final touch. Dermas by nature was not prone to talking much. He said nothing and kept his observation to himself. However, he marveled at how his elder brother had spun the whole affair to perfection.

It was Bashay's turn to be shocked and offended. "Oh my God! So, Tesfom had the nerve to level such a horrible accusation? On top of everything they have inflicted on us, he is now branding us thieves and robbers?" He shook his head repeatedly and added, "Ok! ok! We will see about this! Tomorrow I will go and confront Grazmach. I will tell him why he is not controlling his children's offenses and transgressions. I will ask him "Are you waiting until they kill each other?" said Bashay, breathing heavily, his face ashen and grave.

"Habtom and I did not want to work in partnership with these people from the very beginning. It was you who insisted and imposed the decision on us!" said W/ro Lemlem, accusing her husband by opening up an old wound.

'*Madonna!* Holy Mary! How you love to point out things in hindsight! Why didn't you raise this issue when they were working in agreement for all these years and changing their lives and our lives? Everyone is wise in hindsight!", said Bashay furiously.

"What is wrong with saying that what we feared has come to pass! I still believe we shouldn't have gone into partnership with these people!" repeated W/ro Lemlem, sticking to her guns.

"All of you know very well that we didn't have enough hard cash to start on our own. They were our only option. You also know very well that Grazmach is a very nice and decent human being. We come from the same village, they were our friends and neighbors for years and they have been with us through thick and thin. What more could I have done?" said Bashay, suddenly feeling slight liability and responsibility for the debacle.

"Don't worry about it, father. None of this was your fault. If a person decides to change and act out of faith, there is not much you can do!" said Habtom, acting innocent and 'graciously' giving moral support to his father.

W/ro Lemlem was not finished. "I think this has been part of their agenda and plan all along, even when they denied us their daughter!" said W/ro Lemlem.

"What would they gain from sinking that low?" said Bashay, shocked by the prospect.

"Evidently, it gives them pleasure and satisfaction to destroy our family's name and reputation. That is what they think they are achieving. But let them beware. They will soon feel the full weight of my son's fury!" said W/ro Lemlem bitterly and threateningly.

"Listen, father. Listen, mother. We didn't tell you all this to merely worry and sadden you. We told you about this, to inform you about what is going on. We will see how things proceed from here on. Meanwhile, you don't have to worry about anything. Now, allow us to go," said Habtom and stood up.

Dermas also stood up with him. When they were leaving, both were aware that they were leaving their parents with a heavy heart.

* 3 *

Habtom and Dermas walked silently for a few minutes. Then Habtom turned towards Dermas and said, "I purposely told our parents an abridged version of the events. I strongly believe details will not help them; in fact, they might even confuse them further."

"Yes, I understand. You did well," was all that Dermas could say.

"The details of the case have to remain between you and me, forever," Habtom underlined.

"Ok, no problem. I understand," repeated Dermas.

"Ok then, I have to leave you now. I have an important appointment. See you." Said Habtom.

Habtom and Dermas went their separate ways, with their separate internal monologues and thoughts.

* 4 *

In the Grazmach household, whenever important family issues arose, there was a long-standing tradition of seeking advice and consultation. When faced with such circumstances, they were used to conducting serious discussions, after which they would finally reach a common consensus. When they couldn't arrive at a common consensus, then it fell on the individual concerned to make the final call and decision.

Tesfom had, up to that point, purposely not informed his father about Habtom's cheating. He knew the problem was mostly self-inflicted and was a result of his own weakness. Thus, he wanted to take responsibility and first see it through up to a crucial stage.

Since the case was now at that crucial stage, he decided it was time to inform his father. Tesfom and Araya arrived at their parent's house at 7.30 pm. They knew that by that time; their parents would be winding up dinner. After appropriate greetings, their mother said, "We have just finished dinner. Go wash your hands and I will bring you something."

"There is an important business affair that we first need to discuss with father. In the meantime, it would be great if you could quickly prepare us your special *Shro*," said Tesfom.

"My pleasure, son. Shiro will not take me much time," said W/ro Brkti with pleasure written all over her face.

When his mother left, Tesfom recounted the details of the case from A to Z. He went on to explain where things stood and finished by explaining why they had chosen to keep it to themselves up to that point.

Grazmach listened intently, with both hands under his chin, fingers locked together. He continued to listen to his son's account without interrupting until Tesfom was finished. He understood very well that the case was grave, and he was very concerned.

"My God! Lord the Almighty! What is this? We human beings are pitiful! The situation you have described is very serious, with a lot of grave consequences. You are accusing them of a serious crime. How sure are you of this? This is something you should never level at them, if you are not 100% certain. It would not be fair and I, for one, would not permit it!" said Grazmach firmly, with serious concern written all over his face.

"When Tesfom was on vacation, I was the one who first caught Dermas in the act. When I told Tesfom upon his return, he flatly refused to accept my findings. He only reluctantly accepted it after repeatedly examining the documents I presented," said Araya.

Tesfom stepped in and said, "When I informed Habtom about Dermas's theft, his reaction was extremely mild. With his temperament and personality, I had expected him to go wild and his mild reaction nagged me. That was when I decided to double-check all the documents for the past year. My nightly check-ups clearly showed a pattern of a systematic and concerted scamming. After I was satisfied, I gave the documents to Araya and he examined them carefully and reached the same conclusion. So, as far as certainty is concerned, we are indeed 100% certain," said Tesfom confidently.

Grazmach asked some questions and when satisfied said, "I could have spoken a lot about what should not have been done and why certain things were not done in a certain way. And it wouldn't have been improper to do so. However, simple recriminations and finger-pointing will not do any good. We can't change the past. We should talk about the past only when it enables us to correct our mistakes and learn lessons from them. Therefore, if you learn lessons from this and use this experience so you don't repeat the same mistake again, then I don't need to dwell further on this topic," said Grazmach seriously.

He stopped for a while and looked at his sons and continued. "There is one crucially important element I want you to implement. I want this case to be finished peacefully. As you very well know, both of our families have come together a very long way. God did not permit it, but maybe we would have even become family, if we had accepted their request. So, I want you to promise me that you will finalize this peacefully!"

"We know your beliefs and principles. So, we will do our best to finalize this peacefully," said Tesfom, assuring his father of their willingness to comply.

"We will do our best is not good enough for me, Tesfom. You need to not only promise but also to exert yourselves to the utmost to finish this peacefully. Don't forget that this partnership was started out of love, caring, and hope. It was built with goodwill and trust. It is a pity and sad that it couldn't continue to flourish. Therefore, the least you can do is to finish this in a civilized manner, peacefully. We don't want any animosity and enmity to be fomented between you and our two families!", said Grazmach, underlining his priorities and worries.

"What is disconcerting and saddening is the fact that, on the one hand, they ask for the hand of our sister, and on the other they scheme to cheat us," said Tesfom.

Grazmach's body language showed that he didn't approve of Tesfom's remark. He said, "That is ok. When we scheme to do harm to others, we always end up harming ourselves. That will not bring any good to Habtom and Dermas. What is important though is why this came to be. I didn't want to dwell on this, because, as I explained earlier, it is useless. Otherwise, it was because of your lack of control and follow up that this came to be. Even now, it is thanks to Araya that you have become aware of this before further damage occurred."

"You are right, father. It is my weakness that led to this. I accept full responsibility," said Tesfom bowing his head.

"Anyway, we can't go backwards. We should only focus forwards. So, although we shouldn't forget the past, you should now concentrate on your plans. What is your plan going forward?" asked Grazmach.

"Our plan is to first prepare an estimate of the value of both businesses. Each family must take one business. Then, based on the costs and on who took which, we will settle the accounts by paying the difference in cash," explained Tesfom.

"Ok, fair enough. As I said, just finish whatever you need to do peacefully. Update me on developments regularly. You don't have to worry about your mother; I will provide her myself with the information she needs. Now call your mother and eat dinner."

Araya got up and called his mother. They ate dinner and soon after, left together.

* **5** *

After her children left, W/ro Brkti asked her husband, "What was that about? You took a very long time. Are they ok?"

"Well, they are ok. Have a seat, let me tell you what has happened," said Grazmach.

W/ro Brkti sat down. As soon as Grazmach began his narrative and started telling her about the cheating, W/ro Brkti became angry. She did not let him finish. She said that, if it were not for him, she would never have supported the idea of partnership from the very beginning. Grazmach did not want to be dragged into an argument about hindsight, so he decided to ignore her comments and continued his narrative. He went on to tell her that it was partially Tesfom's fault that this happened; he was not following the accounts closely and regularly. He added if it was not for Araya, they wouldn't have known until much later and further damage.

W/ro Brkti didn't accept the criticism leveled against her eldest son. "Well, I told you beforehand that you were giving him too much responsibility. What can he do? Two jobs and responsibility for a wife and children is too much to handle for any one person. What could he have done? Poor him, as if what he had in his plate was not enough, he even had to go to Massawa to take his wife for vacation. So, don't lay blame only on him."

"Come on, Brkti. You know that he went to Massawa as much for himself as for her. Moreover, it was partially thanks to their vacation, that Araya was able to detect the scamming."

Although she was not satisfied with his explanation, she let it go and instead said, "Anyway, I don't want my son to go into rivalry with that crazy Habtom. So please, follow the matter closely lest they fall into deep conflict and enmity."

"Don't worry, I will give it my full attention." He said, getting up and adding, "It has been a long day, let's retire."

They both retired with uncertainties and worries about the future of the two families.

* 6 *

In the days following the confrontation, Almaz continued to fan the flames. She approached everyone differently and developed her messages individually. She built on the story-line that Habtom had already started by adding her own twists. This added to the anguish and agony of the elders. As the days went by, Bashay and W/ro Lemlem became more infuriated and frustrated.

Grazmach and Bashay had agreed to meet and talk. As the day of their appointment approached, Bashay became very impatient. He started counting the hours. On his way to the appointment, his mind was totally preoccupied with going through the points he had prepared. He arrived at Grazmach's residence without even realizing it.

W/ro Brkti opened the door. Before even greeting her properly, he asked, "Is Grazmach in?"

W/ro Brkti was quick to notice his mood and coldness. Without much enthusiasm and in the same tone, she answered back, "Yes, come in. He is waiting for you."

Grazmach, who had been waiting for him, came out of his room and greeted him profusely. "Welcome Bashay, please come in."

Bashay greeted his friend slightly cooler than normal. Although Grazmach noticed the change, he did not acknowledge it. He had decided to still show him that he was very happy to see him.

When they were both seated, Grazmach asked Bashay, "What would you like to have?'

"It is ok. I am in a hurry. Let's just proceed to the matter at hand," said Bashay, with an air of seriousness.

Soon W/ro Brkti came and asked Bashay if he would prefer tea or coffee. Grazmach thanked his wife and told her that Bashay was in a hurry and would not take anything at this point. "If we need anything later, we will call you," he said.

W/ro Brkti left the two men and Bashay immediately said, "Listen Grazmach. You know me. I don't like to beat around the bush. I speak my mind and my feelings without any reservation. I am really angry, hurt and saddened. What your son is doing to my sons is unacceptable and unjust!"

"You have every right to be saddened. It is a disappointing and distressing incident," said Grazmach.

"As if what you had done to us in regard to your daughter was not enough, adding this on top of it, is totally unfair and unjust!"

"Come on Bashay, don't mix up two incidents that don't have any connection at all."

"Why not? Of course, they are interconnected. First you showed us you didn't want to accept us as family and now you are indicating to us that you don't also want our partnership!" said Bashay bitterly.

"Please Bashay, for the moment let us agree to keep each issue separate. If we don't handle each issue separately, instead of a discussion, we will have an argument and, instead of attaining agreement, we will end up in discord. Now if you will permit me, let me first say a few words regarding the misunderstanding that occurred because of Selam. May I?"

"Ok, go ahead," said Bashay reluctantly, with a body language that showed his discontent and displeasure.

"I have never been able to forget the disappointment and hurt you felt at the time. What happened was unfortunate and regrettable. However, what occurred was not because we didn't want you to be part of our family. It came to be only because the case was beyond our control. That was why at the time, I warned and begged everyone to take care, that the incident does not spill over and poison our relationship and partnership. Now, allow me to ask you a favor. Can you please agree to shelve the old case until we discuss and deal with this present issue? Do I have your promise?"

Bashay was not happy. Despite his feelings, he granted Grazmach's wish by saying, "Ok, I will defer the old case for the moment."

"Thank you so much. Now go ahead, please proceed," said Grazmach, showing his readiness to listen.

"Your son is accusing my children one by one. First, he accused Dermas and now he is hurling allegations against Habtom. Both of them have been working day and night for the success of the factory and the bakery. This is not what they deserve! This is unfair and unjust. This could escalate into a situation where they could hurt and harm each other. If that happens, who is going to take responsibility? How can you sit by and let this happen without doing something about it?", Bashay fumed and raged.

Grazmach listened without interruption. When Bashay was finished, he calmly said, "When we initiated this partnership, we started it out of our friendship, neighborliness and love. I therefore completely understand and sympathize with your anger and frustration at what is happening. Because age has educated us, we both know that such incidents happen among friends and families. When they do happen, it is right that both parents should put our weight on them and tell them they are in the wrong," Grazmach summarized.

"You are the one who should put your weight on your children and tell them they are wrong. It is your children who are in the wrong and who are responsible for all this," shouted Bashay hurriedly.

"My dear friend, your children say my children are in the wrong and my children say your children are to blame. They are the ones who can truly prove who is in the wrong, because the accounts and documents are in their hands. If you and I blindly support only our own children, we will not resolve anything. We will only end up fighting like them. This will not be helpful to us or to them."

"So, should we just become bystanders and watch them butcher each other?" said Bashay angrily.

"No, we should not become bystanders. We should calm them down and push each of them to see reason and reach an understanding."

"What about if they refuse? What then?" asked Bashay.

"Well, if they refuse, there will not be much we can do, except to accept the inevitable and advise them to dissolve the partnership peacefully, without bitterness and enmity."

"What good will that bring? We will be gaining nothing!" asked Bashay, again.

"The question is not about what we will gain? It is about saving ourselves and our families from further damage!" said Grazmach.

Bashay was confused by what Grazmach meant. He hurriedly asked, "What do you mean?"

"If we save them from a bitter fight, drawn out legal battles and courts and convince them to settle it peacefully, that will be an accomplishment in itself. There is one thing I want to beg you to do, Bashay Hawey."

Bashay was confused by Grazmach's last statement, "Beg me to do? To do what?"

"This friendship and love were established by both of us. We hoped this friendship and partnership would pass to our children and their children. Up to this point we have been successful. Even if we do not succeed to convince them to forgive and forget and regain their friendship and partnership, we should at least not allow the situation to get out of hand. We should do our utmost so they don't hold serious grudges and become mortal enemies."

"Grazmach, if this partnership is dissolved, grudges and enmity are inevitable. You know better than I how Habtom and Tesfom are!"

"Well, if we can't prevent them from enmity, then there is also something else we can salvage."

"After that, everything is over Grazmach! What is there to salvage?" said Bashay hurriedly.

"That is a very important question. If they refuse to make peace, then you and I should also refuse to take sides with our children. Let us not be drawn into the fight. Let us keep our friendship and love. *You and I are not children who become friends when our children are friendly and fight when our children disagree!"*

"Well, Grazmach…," said Bashay, who had become calmer and was by now, listening carefully.

"Allow me to finish my point, Bashay Hawey. If you and I maintain our friendship and love, we can eventually patch up their grudge and bring peace. If we can't do that, we will at least prevent this enmity from permeating our two families, including their wives and children. Only if we do this, will we merit to be called elders and heads of the two families. But to succeed in this, you and I must desist from bias and emotions and resist the pressures of women and children. Do you follow me, Bashay?" said Grazmach with emotion and conviction in his voice.

Bashay had been listening with a furrowed forehead, very much absorbed, all the time pulling at his goatee. He seemed to have quickly grasped the ramifications of what his friend was trying to say. He nodded his head and said, "I am following your points and your concerns Grazmach."

"In short, Bashay Hawey, this is the responsibility and challenge that is before both of us!"

"I perfectly understand your fears Grazmach and appreciate your emphasis on our greater responsibility. I will try my best, though it will not be easy. Whatever happens, I will make sure that at least you and I will remain friends. That is the only promise I can give you at this moment," said Bashay solemnly.

"That is fair enough. Each of us can only do what is possible. That is the only thing required of us, the rest is up to God. We have discussed the issues adequately and we have arrived at a mutual understanding. This is great progress. Thank you, Bashay," said Grazmach, concluding their fruitful discussion. Then he quickly changed the subject and said, "Let me call Brkti. What will you have?"

"As I said, I am in a hurry. I have an appointment. I have to leave you," said Bashay and stood up. Grazmach stood up and called his wife to come see off Bashay.

"Why don't you take something. I could make coffee or tea. I was just waiting for you to finish," said W/ro Brkti.

"Thank you Brkti. I was just telling Grazmach. I am in a hurry," said Bashay.

Then W/ro Brkti opened the door and saw Bashay off. When Bashay was leaving, W/ro Brkti noticed a substantial difference in

Bashay's disposition and mood. She was curious, and as soon as he left, she asked her husband. Grazmach explained what he felt were pertinent and relevant points without going into great detail.

At the end of his narrative, he repeated the important points they should adhere to in order to protect the two families from hostility and antagonism. "I beg you Brkti; you should also be very careful and wary about the points I have just raised. If we are to save these two families, we have to move maturely and responsibly," he said, concluding the subject.

* 7 *

Tesfom was completely preoccupied with the upcoming meeting. While going to the encounter, he was thinking about how the confrontation would proceed. He had no doubt that Habtom was indeed guilty of the concerted cheating and scamming. He was also certain that all the actions and moves Habtom was performing were all an act to make it look as if he was the injured party. Tesfom was sure of all of this, but he was not certain what Habtom would decide to do.

Habtom was extremely competitive and stubborn, so Tesfom was apprehensive, lest he drag them into unending dispute and rancor. When it came to holding your ground and obduracy, Tesfom knew he was Habtom's equal in every sense. The only problem he had was his father's decency and principles, as well as his specific recommendation and request. Tesfom always upheld his father's reasonable wishes and, as much as possible, complied with his requests. His problem was with his own father's values, not Habtom's obduracy.

They all arrived on time. As they sat down for their meeting, there was an awkward silence in the room. Tesfom broke the silence. "The last time we met, we parted by agreeing to give you time to examine the documents and deliberate on the case. Since we are here today to listen to your response, the floor is yours," he said, nodding at Habtom.

"We were totally unaware and unsuspecting of exactly what your motives were for leveling all the unfounded allegations against us. However, when we look back and examine the train of events which led to this, it is very clear that you were purposely working to destroy this partnership from the very beginning!" said Habtom.

"Come on Habtom, we already delt with that in detail in our last meeting. Now, don't take us backwards!" said Tesfom.

"I am not taking you backwards. I am taking you forward to where you are rushing to arrive. Since your whole plan has been to avoid working with us, we also don't ever want to work with you. So, I have no objection if we move to the next stage. That is my answer!" shouted Habtom.

"Good! Great! Since the consensus is to dissolve the partnership, the next issue to discuss is how to proceed with it. The two establishments we share are the bakery and this factory. So, do you have any proposal as to how we should divide them?" asked Tesfom.

"Since you are the one who had been planning to do this for a long time, I guess we should listen to what you have to say," said Habtom with a mixture of sarcasm and an underbelly jab.

Tesfom decided to ignore the sarcasm and jab and instead said, "Ok, good. First, we bring in professionals who can assess the value of the two establishments. Once we have the figures, we take one establishment each. Then the family who got the more valuable establishment will pay the difference to the other. In this manner, both families receive an equal amount of assets."

"Wow! Amazing! That makes it even clearer how you had thought out every detail for a long time. Unbelievable! Anyway, does it also mean you have already thought out about who should take which establishment?" asked Habtom sourly, again with a tint of sarcasm.

"Of course! I have thought about what the best scheme would be, as to who takes what. Let me explain it to you. From the very beginning, the bakery was Bashay's idea, although father had advanced the major part of the financing. Since Aboy Bashay has worked his life-time there, the bakery is also part of your lives and your heritage. On the other hand, from the very beginning, the whole idea of buying the factory and securing the loan was my initiative and doing."

Habtom did not wait to let him finish. "Instead of beating around the bush, why don't you tell us in short where you are going?"

"Well, in short, it will be only fair that you take the bakery and we take the factory."

Habtom instantly stood up, his eyes burning with fury, "Don't you possess any sense of decency and justice? You should be embarrassed to even make such a preposterous suggestion! I know all this going around was not out of concern for us and our families, so we wouldn't lose an emotional and historic attachment. Unbelievable! Have you forgotten that I developed and built this factory to what it is now, with my blood and sweat?"

"You should say, 'I was slowly eating up the factory with my blood and sweat!' That is why you have managed to open other establishments in such a short time!" said Tesfom angrily.

"I was able to do that, because unlike you, I haven't been throwing away my money around bars and booze!" said Habtom.

Tesfom was mad. He was about to stand up, but then controlled himself and instead said, "Listen! Your family's beginning capital was the money you initially paid up. You had no other capital. You will need to prove with adequate documentation that you used solely your share of the profit from the bakery and the factory to buy the establishments you have recently opened. I have enough documentation with me to prove otherwise. In the end, either you have to admit to the scamming or you will be forced to prove that you bought what you have with what you have legally earned."

"Did you say, I will be forced?"

"Yes! You will be forced. You have to understand that if we go that route, you will be openly labeled, ridiculed and liable. You will also be scrutinized as to whether you paid due taxes for all that you were selling under the table. If we don't agree to settle this peacefully, then I will sue you openly and take you to court. At the end, if all this doesn't add up, you will not only lose everything you have, but you might even be imprisoned!" said Tesfom, furiously.

"*Midispiacce!* What a pity! Are you trying to threaten me?" said Habtom, moving his head up and down as a warning to Tesfom. The body language he was trying to transmit failed to impress. Though he was trying his best to stay calm and composed, it was evident that he was shaken and scared. His eyes and face gave him away. Signs of sweat had started to appear on his forehead.

"Of course! If you don't understand the consequences, I have to threaten you. Now, listen to me. We have adequately discussed the issue. I will give you another week to seriously think about my proposal. If you agree, we will end this quietly and peacefully. If you don't, I will take you to court and the whole world will laugh at you. The choice is yours!" said Tesfom with finality.

"Is this your final say?" asked Habtom weakly, though he was still trying to look defiant.

"Yes, that is my final say and decision!"

"Then, let me tell you this. I will never ever accept this!" shouted Habtom.

"That will be your choice, but it will be better for you, if you think about this very carefully and seriously!" said Tesfom.

"You can't tell me what is best for me! I know what is best!"

"Ok, suit yourself. I have finished here." He looked at Araya and Dermas and said, "Let us sign today's minutes and we will call it a day," said Tesfom.

They signed the minutes in silence and took their copies. Tesfom stood up and said, "We will meet in the same place and same time, exactly a week from today."

All of them stood up. Araya went out with Tesfom, while Dermas went with Habtom.

* 8 *

As soon as they were alone, Araya asked Tesfom, "Have you forgotten father's recommendation and request?"

"Which part?" asked Tesfom.

"The part where he explicitly warned us that we should finish this peacefully."

"No, I haven't forgotten it. Why? Are you worried?" asked Tesfom.

"Yes, because I thought you were too harsh and a bit aggressive in your approach."

"No, don't worry. If I didn't want to finish this peacefully, I wouldn't have warned him about the consequences. I would have simply sued him and hanged him by the neck. I don't want to do that for his family's and our family's sake. I acted tough on purpose. He is also bluffing. He knows that is the best option he has."

"I hope so. I am not as optimistic as you, but ok," said Araya, seeming unconvinced with Tesfom's optimism.

"It would be better if we don't tell father the details of our talks. He might get worried as you are. If he asks, we can tell him that we are talking and that we are in the preliminary stages," said Tesfom.

"Ok, as you wish," said Araya. They then parted company.

* 9 *

After their talk, Habtom stopped even responding to Tesfom's greetings. Tesfom noticed it, but he didn't care much as he was thinking, "How can that surprise or shock me, that is typical of him." He smiled, because he remembered a Tigrinya saying that put in a nutshell what he was thinking, "Aashas Kitselie, Selamta Yikelie." Meaning, "When a fool hates, he denies and withholds greetings."

In their next crucial meeting, all of them were on time, except Habtom. After waiting for a few minutes, Tesfom turned to Dermas and asked him, "Habtom is late, is he on his way?"

"Habtom is not coming," said Dermas quietly.

"How? Why?" asked Tesfom with astonishment and disbelief in his voice.

"He has given me a note to convey. I will read you his response to your proposal," said Dermas, again quietly.

"Ok." was the only thing Tesfom could say. He was confused and bewildered by Habtom's unexpected move.

Dermas started pulling out from his coat pocket a carefully folded paper. He slowly unfolded it and put it on the table before him. Then he started reading it in a low voice.

1st. All the false accusations you have leveled against us are unwarranted and totally unacceptable. I, therefore, categorically reject every aspect of it. If, as you threatened, you go to a court of law, nothing of that will hold and stick, because it doesn't have substance. I am confident of that. However, I am not like you, I am a hard-working person. Since I don't have time to waste in a long-drawn-out court proceeding, I will not accept your bait to waste my time in court. I will therefore accept the terms you presented last time, not because of your threats, but because I want to go back to work, to recuperate the assets you are unfairly and unjustly grabbing and acquiring.

2nd. Prepare the necessary paperwork and I will examine it.

3rd. I don't ever want to sit with you at the same table or talk to you at any moment whatsoever. Therefore, henceforth, all our communications and contacts will be through Dermas.

4th. I don't want you to ever approach or talk to my wife and my children. I therefore don't ever want you to come near my house.

5th. Don't you ever forget that I will come after you until my last breath. I will never rest until I get my revenge one way or the other.

They were waiting for Dermas to continue, but suddenly Dermas stopped. Then he folded the paper and put it into his pocket.

They were not sure if that was the end of Habtom's note. So, Tesfom asked, "Is that the whole message?"

"Yes, it is," said Dermas quietly.

Dermas by nature was a very quiet person. This was for him the longest message he had ever delivered in his lifetime. He was therefore very uncomfortable, which was evident in the perspiration on his forehead and his uneven voice tone and breathing.

"Ok, good. We have heard Habtom's response. I will not dwell much on the uncalled for, unnecessary and unfortunate points he raised. The good thing is that he has agreed to the terms I proposed last week. This will enable us to move ahead to settle this smoothly and peacefully," said Tesfom with an air of seriousness.

He paused for a while to digest the contents of Habtom's message and collect his thoughts. After hesitating for a while, he seemed to have made a decision. He cleared his throat. "It is unfortunate that Habtom wants to extend this misunderstanding to personal and family issues and escalate the incident. It saddens me that he wants to embroil even our children and wives. However, if he doesn't want me as a neighbor and friend, obviously, I wouldn't also want him," said Tesfom sadly and somberly.

He looked down for a few seconds and then looked up and said, "His last threat about getting revenge is strange and totally unwarranted. If there is anyone who should seek revenge, it would be me, not him. After all, I am the injured party, not him. However, if he is thinking about revenge, tell him I am not the kind of person who is easily frightened by threats of any kind!"

When Tesfom finished his response, Araya remembered something important. He said, "Sorry, Dermas, I had almost forgotten. Could you give me the note? I want to copy it and hold it with the minutes we are keeping."

Dermas immediately handed over the note without a word. As Araya was registering the note, there was complete silence. Tesfom took out documents from his bag and laid them on the table before him.

When he was finished, he looked at Dermas. "This is the first agreement we have written about who will take which company and how we will compensate each other. Show it to Habtom and see if he agrees with the wording; then four of us will sign it and we will proceed to action."

He handed over the copies of the agreements to both Dermas and Araya. Taking out a new set of documents, he said, "Moreover, these are sample letters we have to write to the accounting offices, entrusting them to calculate the assets and capital of both establishments and hand us over their final findings. Ask your brother to choose one of the two accounting firms that has assisted us in the past. When you bring me his response, we will write them an official letter."

Dermas said, "Ok," and accepted the letters.

Tesfom was finished. Araya then said, "Let's sign today's minutes," and handed them the minutes. Three of them signed the papers in silence, keeping their own copies.

When they were done, Tesfom said, "Since we have nothing else, I think this is it for today. I will wait for you tomorrow," he told Dermas and stood up.

Araya and Dermas stood up and went out.

Chapter 6
Break-Up

Tesfom and Habtom had worked in partnership for 13 years at the bakery and for five years at the Pasta factory. They had become the subject and envy of many for their exemplary and successful partnership. They had become neighbors and God-fathers to one-another's children and their wives and children were very close to each other. Despite all these benefits and successes at their disposal, they were still heading towards an unpleasant and rancorous separation full of enmity. Tesfom and Habtom were now in their forties. Grazmach was in his mid-sixties and Bashay was near seventy.

It was under such circumstances that Dermas went the next day, and handed Tesfom the documents of the agreement signed by Habtom. In addition, he informed him that his brother had no objection to the assignment of anyone of the firms. Tesfom immediately wrote an official letter to the accounting firm, awarding it power and responsibility to carry on the assessment. They thus began the real work of dissolving the partnership in earnest. All this was happening in September 1966.

After the agreements were signed, Tesfom and Araya went

to update their father. Before offering any explanation, Tesfom handed over the signed documents to his father. Grazmach read them slowly and thoroughly. When he finished, he looked up at his children and said, "It is really admirable that all of you were able to reach an agreement to finalize this nasty business peacefully. I hope you will maintain this up to the end."

"Don't worry father, we will do that," said Tesfom with confidence in his voice and manner.

"Good. I pray the Lord will be on your side," said Grazmach.

"Amen. Amen," muttered both brothers.

Tesfom cleared his throat and said, "The second important point we want to discuss with you and get your advice and blessing is about our plans going forward. Since we are taking the factory, it is obvious that we are going to be the ones who will pay the difference in asset size between our two businesses. We will thus need a loan for a large sum of money. The original bank loan on the factory has been fully settled. My house will not be adequate collateral for a large loan, so on top of mine, we will need your house as well. Hence, we need your permission and your blessing, to use it as additional collateral," concluded Tesfom.

"I have no objection to the use of our house for collateral. I will also be able to help you with some extra cash that you may require for stocks and other purchases," said Grazmach.

"Thank you, father. In truth, we asked your permission only for the sake of decency. Otherwise, let alone cash and property, you have been sacrificing your whole being for us for your entire life," said Tesfom with a voice and emotion that showed his appreciation and gratitude.

Grazmach did not choose to respond to Tesfom; he merely acknowledged his comment with a nod. Grazmach by nature, was a person who was very uncomfortable with compliments. Since Tesfom knew this, he did not dwell on it for long or wait for further acknowledgement. He continued, "As far as administration is concerned, Araya and I can adequately administer and run the factory satisfactorily," said Tesfom with confidence.

"Actually, that is one of the important points I want to raise today," continued Grazmach. "I have reservations concerning administration. We have to make changes in administration before we proceed further," he said firmly.

"What kind of change?" asked Tesfom bewildered, his body language showing he had not anticipated the request.

"Since Bashay and I withdrew from active participation, primarily you and Habtom have been responsible for the whole administration. Since we are going to have full ownership of the factory henceforth, all three of us should oversee and be responsible for the administration of the establishment. We are putting every asset we have on the line, so it would not be wise or prudent that you or one person alone makes all decisions," said Grazmach.

"Sure, no problem. That is a good idea. We can do that," said Tesfom, trying his best to hide his discomfort. He knew that his father was talking about the damage that occurred, as a result of his not following and doing his job properly.

"Very good, it is settled then. There is another important point I want to raise. I don't think both of you can run the factory appropriately on a part-time basis. I strongly recommend that one of you resigns from your position and attend to the factory on a full-time basis," said Grazmach.

"That is a good idea. I can resign from my position," said Tesfom hurriedly.

"Actually, I would prefer that you stay in your job and Araya resign from his teaching position. The precondition for this is of course, Araya has to not only receive appropriate salary and remuneration as a full-time worker, but also get a shareholders stake." He turned to his son and asked, "What do you say Araya Wedey?"

Araya had been following the discussion with utmost concentration. He had not said a word up to that point. His father's suggestion had been unexpected. He only had seconds to think and respond. He raised his head and looking at his father said, "As you rightly said, if we are to run the factory appropriately, then it is imperative that at least one of us work there full-time. As for your next suggestion, if Tesfom *Hawey* does not object, I am ready to comply with your proposition."

Grazmach instantly turned to his eldest son and asked, "What do you say Tesfom Wedey?"

"Why would I have any objection to such a brilliant idea? I am all for it," said Tesfom without any reservation.

Grazmach was not finished. He immediately said, "One more thing. Since Araya will be the one working full-time at the factory, I would further suggest that the power of attorney that you hold be transferred from your name to Araya."

"Why do we need to do that? I don't think we need to change that at all," said Araya strongly.

It was Tesfom's turn to oppose his brother. "No, Araya. I think what father is suggesting is very important. Since you will be a full-timer at the factory, it is only appropriate and more prudent that the power of attorney be in your name," he said firmly.

"Great! God loves and extends his support and blessings whenever families sit down together, discuss peacefully and reach decisions unanimously. We've had a good discussion and have taken important decisions. Let's pray that God will bless our decisions and grant you long healthy lives," said Grazmach, his satisfaction and happiness clearly visible in his voice and body language.

"Amen Aboy! Amen Aboy!" said both Tesfom and Araya.

The brothers were both satisfied with the overall fruitful discussion they had with their father. After a while, Tesfom and Araya departed.

* **2** *

After signing the agreement, Habtom and Dermas went to inform their parents of the new developments. Habtom presented a very well-thought-out description and explanation. He put it in such a way that his parents - and especially his father - would consider it the most practical and forward-looking viable decision.

He told them how Tesfom and Araya, out of greed, had insisted that they had a right to the factory. There was an option to decide who got what by casting a lot, Habtom continued; that however, he and Dermas did not want the factory, because they knew that the machines were all old and out of date. He also told them why they believed, it was more prudent and economically sound for the moment, to run the bakery and the two construction material shops; because if they were to take the factory, they would have to pay the difference in value to the Grazmach family in cash and explained how such a decision would put a strain on their liquidity and be cumbersome on their establishments' cash and stock requirements. He concluded by sharing with his parents that when they were ready, they planned to import machinery and set up a new pasta factory.

Habtom thus spun his story by highlighting the benefits of giving the factory to the Grazmach family. In this manner, Habtom was able to convince his parents of the correctness of their decision.

The parents were satisfied with Habtom's explanation, and he was happy that his parents accepted his presentation without question. However, he did not want them to forget that the enmity and grudge were still intact. So, he said, "At the end of the signing, I told Tesfom that, even if we have made this agreement, we will never forget what you have done to me, my brother and my family, and that we will never rest until we take our revenge!"

Thus, Habtom's mission was accomplished according to plan. All his points, including the one about not forgetting their grudge, had hit home. His parents, especially his mother, thus sank into further resentment and hatred.

* **3** *

Habtom always believed that Alganesh did not deserve to know about his business affairs. This belief deepened after Almaz came into his life. As a result, he had no plans to tell Alganesh about the new developments with the Grazmach family. However, he felt he needed to make an exception just this once, so he could warn them not to go near Tesfom.

He went to Alganesh at 5.30 pm and, without going into any detail, told her, "We have broken up with that Tesfom. After taking advantage and benefiting from my hard work, he has betrayed my trust. Anyway, since I don't ever want to see him or work with him, we are going to dissolve the partnership."

"Betrayed? My God! When did this happen? I didn't know that Tesfom was capable of such an act!" said Alganesh, incredulous at the one-sided story she was receiving.

"You always have only good words and praise for him. You don't know that he is an angelic-looking Satan! Anyway, I don't want to talk much about it. I have told him and I am telling you now, that from today on, I don't want him to come near my house or my children. I also don't want my children to go to his house or his children to come to my house," said Habtom, firmly.

"Well, I can understand what you are trying to say concerning Tesfom. What I can't understand is what this has to do with the children. They have been neighbors, playmates and friends for years. How can we tell them to suddenly distance themselves from them?" said Alganesh firmly.

"I am telling you; I don't want my children to be friends with them or play with them. Don't you understand?" said Habtom, irritation and anger creeping into his voice.

"Since the contradiction is between you and Tesfom, why do you want to involve the children? They have no part or fault in this. The children of both houses are innocent!" said Alganesh courageously.

"Don't talk to me about innocence! It is a subject that is beyond your capacity to understand and comprehend. If my children knew what he did to me, and if they were much older, they themselves would have decided not to have anything to do with them," said Habtom, happy with himself that he was able to come up with a "logical" explanation.

"In that case, why don't you give them time, until they come of age to understand and decide for themselves? Why do you want to confuse them at such a tender age?" said Alganesh defiantly.

"You are the one who is confused and muddled! The children will not be confused. As a parent, I have responsibility to tell my children, to befriend those who are good to them and stay away from those that are not," said Habtom, again confident of his "logic and rationale."

"Wow! How can you call this parental responsibility? What kind of parental responsibility is telling children, "When I clash with someone, be hostile to them; when I make peace, be at peace with them?" Parental responsibility would have been to commit to your vows and execute your obligation and responsibility to your first wife and children!" said Alganesh, hitting him hard with a double-edged sword.

Habtom was mad. He instantly stood up. He clenched his fists and said, "Woman! You'd better behave yourself or else!" He threatened her menacingly.

Alganesh immediately went into protective mode. Her body prepared itself for the worst. She stiffened her body and protected her head. His fists still clenched, he stood over her breathing heavily. He hesitated for a while, then he said, "AHH! AHH! AHH!" banged the table and sat down.

Alganesh realized the storm had passed. As she began to relax, she heard him say, "Now! Are you going to do what I told you or not?" he shouted, putting his blood shot eyes and his fists closer to hers. He growled at her. Although his demeanor and body language appeared as if he was about to crush her, his spirit looked defeated - defeated by a far superior intelligence and strength of character.

Alganesh understood that, irrespective of the consequences and what befell her, she had the upper hand, not in brute physical strength but rather in moral justice and strength of logic. She thus decided to stand her ground; for the sake of her children and the truth.

Hence, with courage and determination, she said, "Let alone when I am in my right mind and in possession of my faculties, I wouldn't even think of doing what you are demanding in my dreams. I will never make myself tell innocent children, 'Because your father has broken up with Babba Tesfom, you should also break up with his children.' Never! If you want, you can tell them yourself!"

"Stupid! Ignorant! Since you don't possess an intellect that comprehends and grasps complex issues, you can never understand that anyone who tries to hurt me is also indirectly trying to hurt my children!" shouted Habtom.

"I consider myself fortunate, that I don't possess a brain that rationalizes in that manner and even luckier and more blessed that I am not capable of understanding such twisted logic!" said Alganesh, showing him that he had the muscles but she had the grey matter.

'Oh, Wow! Unbelievable! So, I guess I should congratulate you for becoming like those so-called philosophers, whose job is just to twist words. Actually, what else can you be? After all, you have nothing better to do!" was all that Habtom could say.

No matter what he said, he had finally clearly understood that all the posturing and show of strength was not going to take him anywhere. Habtom, who was always used to getting his way, was extremely frustrated and irritated. He was ready to explode. He started banging the table repeatedly while uttering the sound, "AHH! AHH! AHH!"

He then seemed to have made up his mind and immediately stood up. He wanted to look as if he was still calling the shots, so he sought to have the last say. He said, "Call the children, I will tell them myself!"

Alganesh went to call the children. Habtom was furious. He looked like a wounded animal, ready to fight and trounce anyone. His blood shot eyes were bulging, the veins in his temples were throbbing and he was breathing heavily. He started pacing up and down the room. The minutes he waited for the children seemed to him like hours. He started muttering to himself and continued his pacing with fury.

* 4 *

Alganesh didn't waste much time. She instantly came back with her children. When he saw his children filing in, he stopped his pacing and sat down, greeting them one by one.

"Have a seat, I want to talk to you about something important," said Habtom. For a moment, he looked as if he had remembered something. He kept quiet for a moment and then seemed to have reached a decision. Then he turned his face towards Alganesh, and said "Leave us, I want to talk to the children alone!"

Alganesh didn't make any response. She looked as if she hadn't heard him. The children were confused. They were not sure whether their mother had heard their father or not. They looked at each other and kept quiet. After a few uncomfortable seconds, Habtom again turned to Alganesh, "I am talking to you. Didn't you listen? I said, leave us! I want to talk to the children alone," said Habtom, in a comparatively milder tone in consideration for the children who were in front of him.

"I have heard you, but since I am their mother, I have every right to be with them when you talk to them," said Alganesh defiantly.

The children were taken aback by their mother's uncharacteristic defiance. They started looking sideways, first at one and then the other. Signs of fear and apprehension were evident in their faces. They knew that after a few seconds, their father's inevitable fury was going to be unleashed.

Habtom was surprised at Alganesh's defiance. He couldn't understand where it was coming from or why and was a little uncomfortable and wary. After few seconds, he came to a decision. "You can stay, but I warn you, I don't want any interruption or interference," he said, trying to make it look as if he had graciously given her permission to stay.

The twins, Kbret and Samson and their younger brother Hadsh, realized that the subject their father was going to raise must be very serious. This added to their apprehension about what was happening and about their future as a family. They thus mentally prepared themselves for the worst and waited with apprehension. Negassi and his younger sister Rahwa did not understand what was going on. They were confused and looked back and forth between their siblings to get a clue.

Habtom's words brought them back from their internal monologues. "Listen, children. Since you are now young, there are many adult issues you can't understand at this age. Until you are able to understand them on your own, you have to follow whatever we tell you. Do you understand? Is that clear?" he asked them repeatedly.

Although none of them understood the subject or the direction of their father's talk, all of them nodded their heads and repeated "Yes, Ok," one by one.

"Many times, a lot of adults seem nice and kind on the outside, while on the inside they are bad and rotten. Do you understand what I am saying?". Habtom repeated his question.

The children still did not understand what their father was talking about. Nevertheless, they were forced to acknowledge his command by nodding their heads and by replying, "Yes," in unison.

"Our neighbor Tesfom, looks and seems like a nice person on the outside. Tesfom has recently done so many bad things to hurt me. Anyone who tries to hurt your father, is indirectly trying to hurt you too. Right? Do you understand?" he asked looking directly into their eyes.

All the children nodded their heads in unison and said, "Yes, you are right."

"Therefore, starting from today, I don't want you to go near him and I don't want him to come near you. Is that clear? Do you understand what I am saying?"

All the children again nodded their heads in agreement. They all seemed relieved, that the subject matter they had feared so much, was not after all that serious and frightening. This soon became evident in their faces and body language. They all heaved a sigh of relief and their breathing returned to normal and they began to relax.

However, their father was not finished. When he said, "Moreover," the children again went into fear and stress mode. This was instantly visible in their body language.

Their father continued, "Moreover, I also don't want his children to come to my house or my children to go to his house. From now on, there will be no companionship or friendship with his children," he said firmly.

The children became instantly alarmed by this sudden change of events. They had to reassess the situation and began to conclude that the problem must indeed be very serious. Confused and bewildered, they tried to uncover an explanation by looking at each other. Habtom repeated his question more forcefully, "Is that clear? Do you understand?"

The two younger children immediately nodded their heads. However, the faces, eyes and body language of the eldest children showed apprehension and distress. Habtom noticed the lack of clear response from his elder children and, looking at them, repeated, "Is that clear?"

His eldest daughter, 14-year-old Kbret, gathered her courage and decided to risk asking, "Have Babba Tesfom's children also tried to hurt you, father?" It was a question that was already bothering each child. Each of them moved slightly in their seats, eager to hear his answer to the most important question that was bothering them.

"No, they did not. How can they? They are children. But...,"

At that very moment, Kbret's twin brother, Samson decided to emulate his sister's courage. He didn't let his father finish his next sentence but instead asked the next logical question. "Then why are you also breaking up with Bruk and his siblings?" he asked, naming his best friend, the person who as far as he was concerned, was his utmost concern.

"I have repeatedly told you I broke up with Tesfom, not his children. This is simple, why can't you understand it?!" said Habtom firmly.

"Then why are you asking us to break-up with Babba Tesfom's children?" asked Kbret courageously, encouraged by her twin brother's support.

"It is complicated. As I said earlier, you can't understand it now, because you are children. Just do what I am telling you to do!" said Habtom, his patience dwindling.

"But Babba, they have been our friends and playmates forever!" said Samson.

"Offa! That is enough!" shouted Habtom. With a stern voice, he added, "I don't want to hear another word now! Just do what you have been told!" he fumed, his eyes glaring.

The twins felt the situation was getting dangerous and decided not to say anything further. They instantly bowed their heads and kept silent. The youngest, 7-year-old Rahwa, opened her mouth. Without realizing the depth of the question, she was posing, she innocently asked, "Babba, when you and Babba Tesfom become friends again, can we also become friends with his children?"

Habtom's mood changed. His face and body relaxed. He smiled at his little girl, and without understanding the depth of her question, responded confidently, "My child, when adults break up and fight, it is forever! They never make peace again!" Satisfied with his "correct" answer and with himself, Habtom smiled again.

Although Rahwa heard her father's response and saw his smile, his response confused her further. *In her world, breaking up and becoming opponents and then, after a short while, patching-up and becoming friends again was a very important part of life. Now her father was telling her the most hideous thing in the world. Once you fight, you never become friends again!*

Rahwa started to think and talk to herself. *'Oh wow, what kind of people are these adults? Once they fight, they remain enemies forever! Once they break up, they do not forget or forgive. Nothing is erased.*

That is heartbreaking and sad. I really pity them. They are not even capable of doing what we do. We are much better than them. I am happy I am not an adult. Anyway, if that is what they want, let them be. In the end, they will end up without friends.'

The voice of her father woke Rahwa from her internal monologue. "Ok. We have finished. As I told you, I don't want you to go near any of them!" said Habtom and stood up, satisfied that he performed his duty as a responsible father. When he was leaving, Habtom was in a great mood.

* **5** *

As soon as Habtom left, the children immediately surrounded their mother. Her older children shouted, "Mamma, Mamma, Mamma." Alganesh instantly understood their urgency and what they wanted.

"We will not talk about this now. Negassi and Rahwa are hungry. They need to eat their snack now," she said firmly. She asked her eldest daughter Kbret to help her.

As soon as they were alone, Alganesh explained to Kbret that it was not right to talk about such a sensitive matter in front of the young children. She assured her that once the children started eating their snacks, she would talk to them in private. Kbret was overjoyed.

As soon as Alganesh sat with her three eldest children, all of them started to shout at her at once. They told her it was not fair that she kept quiet against the monstrous steps their father was commanding them to commit. They told her it was not fair that they break-up with their best friends.

Alganesh quietly explained what exactly had transpired between her and her husband, before they met their father. She concluded by telling them, that he had ordered her to take the responsibility of informing them and that it was after she flatly refused, that he talked to them himself. She was near to tears when she finished.

She controlled herself in time and assured them that she hadn't betrayed them and had stood her ground for them.

The children were satisfied that their mother had stood firm on their behalf, and Alganesh was pleased that her stand meant so much to them. Before diving straight into the explanation and guidance that they deserved, she wanted to formulate an appropriate explanation that would be appropriate to their age. Alganesh hesitated for a few seconds, not sure of how to begin, while the children waited with anticipation. All of them were staring at her eyes.

Finally, she took a deep breath and said, "I know how much you fear your father. This is not your fault. This is only because he has not been close to you and hasn't given you the self-confidence you deserve. He does that, not because he doesn't love you, but because he wrongly believes that it is not good for children to be too close to their father. Despite that, the way you courageously confronted him was amazing. I am happy and proud of you!"

The children were pleased that their mother was proud of them. Their faces were glowing with confidence and pride. Alganesh was happy to see that. This gave her encouragement. She paused for a while, trying to organize her thoughts and then said, "This misunderstanding and break-up is between Tesfom and Habtom. As long as Tesfom has not hurt you or me, let alone his wife and children, there is no reason why we should be at odds even with Tesfom himself. The same would be true with Medhn and Tesfom's children. That is the right and correct thing to do. However, adults many times commit gross errors and end up making blind decisions. When such situations arise, they can only be improved or solved if we patiently follow the right strategy."

"I am sorry mother. I don't understand what you mean by strategy," said 12-year-old Hadsh. His elder siblings nodded their heads in unison.

"It is my fault that you don't understand what I mean. Let me try to explain it further. If you have an open relationship with Babba Tesfom's children that everyone sees, your father will not allow it and he will clash with you and me. In fact, the whole Bashay family should not see your continued friendship. However, I, Babba Tesfom and Mamma Medhn will have no objection to your playing together and continuing your friendship."

"Well, mother, if we don't show them our friendship openly, they will feel we are ignoring them and might break up with us," said Samson with worry in his face. The others nodded.

"Yes, you are right Izi Wedey. I have already thought about that. I will talk with Medhn as soon as possible and will make sure that she explains the situation properly to them, so that they don't misunderstand you. Is that clear?" she asked.

All the children nodded their heads affirmatively and, in unison said, "Yes, Mamma, it is clear."

"Ok. Now you go and eat your snacks." They kissed their mother and went out with their heads up and their morale strengthened.

Alganesh understood that she had to talk to Medhn urgently. She started talking to herself, *"Wow, it is unfortunate what children are sometimes forced to go through. It is unforgivable that we adults become blind with hatred and push little children to be involved in our despicable cruel games of hatred. While the so-called children pose incisive and bold reservations against hatred, the so-called adults try to force them to hate. We push them to go against their conscience and their good hearts. Ultimately, the innocent children learn evil ideas from the adults who are supposed to teach them and guide them in the right direction. It is a pity! Sometimes it is difficult to differentiate between who the adult is and who the child is!"*

While Alganesh was pondering thus, she heard her youngest child scream, "Mamma! Mamma!" Alarmed, she woke from her reverie and rushed to see what was wrong. As soon as she arrived, Rahwa said, "Look Mamma, Negassi is giving me a hard time." She breathed a sigh of relief that there was nothing to it. She soon forgot her thoughts and proceeded to settle their quarrel.

* 6 *

Early the next day, Alganesh went to talk to Medhn. Since Alganesh had still no idea of the details of what had happened between Tesfom and Habtom, she asked Medhn about it. When Medhn explained the whole situation in detail, Alganesh was struck with disbelief at what she heard. Then it was her turn to report what had transpired between her, the children and Habtom. She explained with pride the hair-splitting questions the children raised and the courage they showed in front of their father.

"My dear Medhn, if you had witnessed their readiness to pay whatever it takes for their friendship, it would have amazed and saddened you," said Alganesh, shaking her head.

"Poor children. They are absolutely right. I can feel their pain. They have been friends, neighbors and playmates for their entire lives. After all that, to be told out of the blue, to forsake each other is monstrous." said Medhn.

"Well, what can we do?" sighed Alganesh with sadness.

"Well, as you said, there is not much that can be done. The enormity and complexity of problems children face from either of their parents is often beyond comprehension. When I think about it, I wonder if there was something that can be done to minimize or prevent it. *I often wonder, if it would have helped, if all prospective parents were required to pass certain tests and possess certain qualifications that proved their ability and worthiness to carry out the responsibility of raising children. For example, what if all prospective parents were forced to possess licenses before being allowed to marry,"* said Medhn pensively.

Alganesh was confused. She wrinkled her forehead and asked, "Licenses? What do you mean?"

"I mean since everyone is asked to possess certain qualifications, degrees and years of experience just to perform a job, why not pose similar requirements for the bigger task of raising the citizens of tomorrow?" said Medhn seriously.

"Wow, Medhn! You are amazing! How did you come up with this idea?" asked Alganesh, with incredulity and admiration.

"The idea crossed my mind when I was reading job descriptions for newspaper job openings and the various qualifications required. That got me thinking. We go to so much length to hire qualified and responsible persons who would be qualified employees who perform optimally. Yet, we allow unprepared, unqualified and irresponsible individuals to misguide and destroy innocent children and families!" said Medhn forcefully.

"Wow, when you see it from that perspective, it is truly contradictory and tragic. It basically boils down to how much precedence and importance we are giving to work and business, rather than to human beings and life!" said Alganesh.

"Exactly, Alganesh Habtey, but sometimes it is very difficult to comprehend the ways of this world and life itself," said Medhn.

"Yes, absolutely," said Alganesh. She remembered the main purpose of her visit. She immediately changed the subject and asked, "So, what is the best way of handling this issue about the children?"

They went on to discuss the various options in detail and finally reached a common understanding. Medhn promised that she would explain the situation to their children as soon as possible. Satisfied with their strategy, Alganesh departed.

* 7 *

Medhn couldn't wait to tell Tesfom about her discussion with Alganesh. After lunch, Medhn explained everything that had happened. They immediately agreed that it was imperative that they explain the situation to their children soonest. They decided to do it that evening.

After dinner, all of them sat down and Tesfom said, "During everyone's life-time, love, companionship and sometimes break-ups happen and are part of life. As you children fight and break-up with each other, so do we also adults fight and break-up."

As soon as he uttered those words, a sign of apprehension and anxiety was clearly visible on the faces of the twins. 14-year-old Timnit interrupted Tesfom, "What's wrong? Are you and Mamma breaking-up?"

"Oh, my poor child. What made you think of that? Tesfom and I haven't clashed and we will never fight or break-up!" said Medhn hurriedly.

"It is my fault. It is my lack of clarity and the wrong words I chose that scared them. I am so sorry!" said Tesfom, feeling bad that he had put his children through needless apprehension and anxiety.

'It is ok, father. We were alarmed only because many of our friends constantly tell us that their parents have clashed and broken up," said Bruk.

"I understand Bruk Wedey. Anyway, the topic we want to talk to you about is not about us. It is about Habtom and myself. We have a disagreement concerning our partnership in the bakery and factory. Mind you, we are not fighting, we have merely disagreed," he said. Without getting into much detail, he gave them enough information about the break-up that was commensurate with their age.

After Tesfom finished, it was Medhn's turn to inform them about the discussion of Habtom and his children. The children were shocked. They condemned what Habtom was demanding in the strongest terms. They fervently stated that what was being asked of their friends was totally unfair and illogical. Both parents took their time and were finally able to adequately explain the complexity of the issue to the children's satisfaction.

Finally, Tesfom cautioned them, "From now on, you should not go to Habtom's house, because if Habtom finds out, the children are going to suffer the consequences. They can come here and play. Even that will have to be done with utmost care and discretion. In addition, none of Habtom's family members should see you together."

Tesfom and Medhn gave the children detailed tips on how to navigate the problems ahead of them. The children were finally satisfied. Then Medhn and the children retired.

When Tesfom was alone, he sank into deep thought, "My God, what a problem. We adults can tolerate and withstand such challenges and obstacles, but it will definitely not be easy for these poor children to handle such impediments. I hope other additional unforeseen complications do not arise as a result of the children. If they do, the conflict is going to be aggravated and might expand. I hope God the Almighty will protect us from further complications and conflict." After that, he stood up and retired with a heavy heart.

* **8** *

Tesfom wanted to get a rough estimate of the cash needed to pay the Bashay family. He didn't want to wait until the accountants finished their report; he wanted to avoid the possibility of facing Habtom's immediate cash demands. With the help of Araya, they started computing the assets of the two establishments based on the documents they had. After a few days, they were able to arrive at a rough estimate of the amount of money they would owe Habtom. Based on this estimate, they immediately initiated the application for a loan.

As soon as the loan process was on the verge of being finalized, the accountants presented their reports. Tesfom and Habtom individually and independently studied the reports. Then they both accepted the accountant's assessment and put their signatures on the documents. They now knew the exact amount of money the Grazmach family owed. Thereafter, the handing-over of each establishment was conducted smoothly. They agreed that the final payment would be made within two weeks after the signings. They further agreed that the official and final transfer would be conducted after the finalization of all payments. True to his word, during all these agreements and signatures, Habtom did not meet Tesfom. Everything was completed with Dermas shuttling from one to the other.

The bank loan came through on the third day, after the accountant's report. Tesfom and Araya were prepared to pay the difference, and on the appointed day, they paid the full amount and took official control of the factory. All necessary documents for the dissolution of the partnership were signed and the delicate and messy affair was concluded peacefully.

Araya officially resigned from his teaching post and started working at the factory full-time. In a short while, both brothers were able to organize and streamline the workings of the factory. Both Medhn and Araya noticed with amazement and satisfaction that Tesfom's drinking problem seemed to have receded.

One day, when Medhn and Araya were sitting alone, she said, "Since we came back from Massawa and after this incident with Habtom, your brother has made immense progress. Have you noticed?"

"Of course, how couldn't I? It is not only progress, Medhn. He has changed," said Araya.

"Well Araya, you know the going out with his friends and drinking moderately is still there," she said, smiling.

"Well, my dear Medhn, you can't and shouldn't expect a 100% change overnight."

"Yes, you are absolutely right. Seriously, I don't want him to be totally cooped up at home. That might have its own problems. I want him to go out with his friends and relax."

"That is wise Medhn. You are extremely perceptive and thoughtful. It is important that a person always has the freedom to unwind and relax with his friends. Otherwise, as you rightly pointed out, it might backfire."

"Yes, you are right. This reminds me of the wise saying that "Every problem does not necessarily come to harm us." Many times, it turns out to be for our benefit and in our best interest.

You remember that it is since you encountered the problem with Dermas and Habtom that he is holding firm. I hope this lasts," said Medhn with a heartfelt sigh.

"It will! Don't worry. I am confident there will not be any going backwards," said Araya confidently. He stood up to leave. He bid Medhn farewell and left.

* 9 *

While Araya and Medhn were satisfied with Tesfom's improvements, there were other parties who were not. These were primarily his drinking bar-mates and friends. For quite some time, Tesfom had not been joining them as much as he used to. He would disappear the whole week and then appear on a Saturday. As result of their disapproval and disappointment, they would poke fun at him as soon as he joined them.

Their favorite joint was the Lalibela Hotel Bar. Lalibela Hotel was a five-story building, sitting on the right side of the twin road that went to Geza Kensha and Massawa. It was more or less in front of Bar Tre Stelle and had a gas station and enough parking space for customers. It was here that Tesfom and his friends spent their evenings, playing cards, drinking, having fun and when hungry, eating snacks and sandwiches.

Tesfom always preferred and chose the best quality in everything. When drinking, he always started with imported Heineken beer. When shifting to liquor, he would go for either Gin Gordon or Johnny Walker whisky. He never touched any cheaper or local stuff. His friends always used to make fun of him by saying, "As far as Tesfom is concerned, if anything is to be the best, it has to be the most expensive!"

One Saturday, Tesfom went to join his friends after a long absence. As soon as they saw him coming, the humorous and talkative Werede stood up and, smiling broadly, said, "Please everybody, let's stand-up and receive his holiness, the Holy-Water man, (*Beal May Chelot*)!"

Tesfom was bewildered. He looked to both sides and then backwards. He couldn't see any other person that was joining them. Still confused, "Are you talking about me?" he asked.

"Well, since no one else is joining us, I guess I am talking about you!" Werede said, laughing profusely.

"Wow! I didn't know that my friend Tesfom had started using Holy Water," said Zere'.

"I don't know what he is talking about. Let alone visit a Holy Water site, I haven't even gone out of Asmara!" said Tesfom confidently.

Werede threw his arms into the air and shouted, "Why are you guys asking him? I am the one who provided the information!" he said, feigning to be offended and hurt.

"Sorry! You are right Werede *Aerkey*," said Berhe, and turning his face towards Zere', jokingly added, "Instead of asking the source of the information, how can you ask a person who doesn't even know where he has been?"

"Come on guys, what kind of a joke is this? Why don't you stop this and instead order me something? I am thirsty!", said Tesfom seriously.

"Don't worry about that Tesfom Aerkey. As soon as I saw you coming, I ordered your favorite for you. I understood that, although you had been wetting your body on the outside, you are absolutely dry and thirsty on the inside!" said Werede, roaring with laughter. All of them laughed heartily, even Tesfom had to shake his head and laugh at the ingenuity of his friend.

When Tesfom saw his drink coming, he looked at Werede and said, "I have to admit, you have many good qualities, although you own a tongue and a mouth which never stops talking!"

"Werede Aerkey," said Zere' with a laugh, "Do you know why he is admiring and appreciating you? He wants you to forget about the subject you have brought up.

All of them joined in the laughter. It was Berhe who stopped laughing and said, "Yes, Werede, come on. Bring back the Holy Water stuff."

"Are you guys serious? Do you really mean you don't understand what I was talking about?!" said Werede, with an air of exaggeration, looking at each of them for emphasis.

"Come on guys, how can you take this guy seriously? You know how he is. If you let him, he will convince you that from here, he can see the silhouette of a man farming on the moon! If you let him proceed further, he might even claim he can see the man's cap and the cows' ears!" said Tesfom, trying to even the score.

They all laughed again. Then Werede stood up and said, "Ok, let me present my case. For the last two months, Tesfom has stopped joining us except on an occasional weekend, right?" he asked. They all nodded their heads in agreement. "Ok, good. Now please ask yourselves what had occurred about two months ago?" he asked, looking at each of them.

"Two months ago? Two months ago?" asked both his friends bewildered.

When he saw his friends confused, Werede said, "Ok. Allow me to solve the riddle for you. Two months ago, his wife took him to a Holy Water site for the usually prescribed two weeks. If you want to know where, the answer is simple. She took him to the Red Sea. Now let me give the opportunity to our esteemed friend to admit the truth of what I just stated. Is that the truth, or not?" Werede asked, turning his face towards Tesfom.

"My God, come on, Werede. How can you?! You should be ashamed that you had to go all over the place to come up with this nonsense," said Tesfom smiling.

"Very good. Great! Tesfom has not denied that he went for Holy Water for two weeks. If he insists that the Red Sea is not Holy Water, then allow me to prove that it is," said Werede, standing up and bowing to his friends one by one.

"Oh, come on! Since when has the Red Sea or Massawa become a Holy Water site?" Tesfom countered.

Both Zere' and Berhe said in unison, "You got your chance Werede, come on, prove it," they said encouraging their friend.

"Some months ago, when we were all high and having a great time, Tesfom told us how Medhn was against our getting together on weekdays. He told us that she was ok with weekends, but was totally opposed to weekdays and was incessantly telling him as much. Tesfom, as we all know, likes to enjoy life. So, though Medhn talked to him constantly, our friend refused to stop. Do you remember that?" he asked his friends.

Both said, "Yes, yes, we clearly remember!"

"Good! Then Medhn, who was frustrated by his unending promises, came up with another brilliant plan. She decided to take him to Holy Water for the prescribed two weeks. Since then, as she hoped, our friend has started to roost early and stay put at home every evening!" said Werede, with an air of seriousness.

Both Zere' and Berhe couldn't hold their tears with laughter. As soon as they had a chance to say something, Berhe said, "You are absolutely right." Then he stood up, put his right hand up and in all seriousness said, "This is the whole truth, nothing but the truth!" They roared with laughter again. Tesfom was also laughing heartily.

Werede, encouraged by their response, stood up again and waited for their full attention. Then he solemnly said, "For anyone who has doubt whether salt water can be considered a Holy Water, I can explain. Holy Water does not have to necessarily be fresh water that leaks from rocks, that springs from the ground or falls from a high ground. It is a place with water that you believe will help you resolve your physical, mental or social problems!" He bowed at each one of them solemnly and then said, "I rest my case!"

All of them, including Tesfom, roared with laughter until their eyes teared. In between their bouts of laughter, Zere' and Berhe were shouting, "Man! You got him! You really got him!"

Tesfom continued to shake his head and laughed with amazement at his friend's impromptu performance. "You are something else, man! You are in the wrong profession. You should have been a lawyer. Not the serious kind of lawyer, but one of those who create disposable cases in seconds and then patch up stuff in minutes!" said Tesfom.

After all the laughter subsided, the joke-poking at Tesfom was over and they decided to concentrate on their card game. They continued playing cards, drinking and laughing until midnight. When all of them had enough, they called it a night and bid each other farewell. After leaving his friends, Tesfom's mind went back to reality. He arrived home thinking about Habtom.

* 10 *

Within less than a month after separation, Habtom started a campaign of vilification against Tesfom and the pasta factory. He and Araya had thought the Habtom case was a done deal, and they never wanted to talk about him or the case with anyone else. For the few who asked closely about what happened, they would merely say, "We started having small administrative disagreements and decided it was better to split, before the conflicts became more acute."

Habtom on the other hand, had concocted a well-thought-out story, which he presented to different audiences. To those very close, he would tell them that because of his laziness, Tesfom was not helping him at all; that he was sick and tired of spoon feeding him; that he chose to take the bakery, because he knew the factory would not last long; that when he wanted to replace the old machinery, Tesfom had no money to spare, except for his drinks; that while he was working day and night, Tesfom and his brother were bent on cooking the books and falsifying the accounts; that he then decided it was better to terminate the partnership, so he could open a new factory in due time. Finally, he would tell them that he had already initiated an evaluation and assessment towards establishing a new factory.

In addition to the above, Habtom would tell their former clients, (and especially those to whom he was selling pasta on the side), that the main cause of their break-up was that, while he was bent on keeping the quality and standard of the products intact, Tesfom wanted only to maximize profits. Habtom maintained that, as a result, Tesfom wanted us to decrease the ratio of the number of eggs and yeast we used, and he even went as far as insisting that we buy cheaper flour from contraband sources. Finally, Habtom would tell them that, until the last moment, he was able to stand his ground to maintain the quality, but that he had doubts that this would continue after him.

Habtom was not only trying to defame Tesfom and Araya, he was also actively engaged in taking away their customers and destroying the factory's reputation. He then rented a small place, bought hand-operated pasta machines, and tried to increase his pasta output. He took away a few customers with modest demands by convincing them that his product was far superior than that of the factory.

Meanwhile, Araya and Tesfom had started to run the factory more efficiently than before. As a result, they were not only able to maintain their sales, but had also started to register slight growth. Habtom's negative campaign had not affected the pasta factory at all, so when he realized that his attempts had not borne fruit, he was frustrated and started to redouble his defamation efforts

When Habtom's renewed vilification reached Tesfom's ears, he was furious, and he threatened to expose Habtom. "How dare he spread such outright lies, when we are not saying anything, despite the fact that we possess so much solid evidence against him?" Tesfom, fumed.

Araya tried to cool down his brother by saying, "He is doing all this because he is desperate and frustrated. Let him fret and fry, why should we even dignify him with a response?"

But, when Habtom's slander continued unabated, Tesfom couldn't stand it anymore and wanted to retaliate. But, instead of outright retaliation, Araya proposed that they send him a stern warning through Dermas. Tesfom accepted the proposal reluctantly.

They arranged a meeting with Dermas. When he arrived, Tesfom told him, "Please tell your brother to stop defaming us falsely. We have heard everything he has been saying. We have not retaliated so far, not because we don't have the evidence to destroy his name, but because we don't want to escalate this further. Tell him, this is our last warning for him: he must desist from escalating this further and plunging our two families deeper into rancor and enmity.

Dermas promised that he would deliver the message verbatim. When Habtom heard the message, he was even more encouraged. He felt he was succeeding in his scheme by getting under their skin and irritating them. He thus, continued his vilification with even greater vigor.

When Tesfom realized that Habtom was not going to stop, he decided to retaliate. He began divulging Habtom's dishonesty and his scamming and cheating. At this point, the rivalry and hostility of Tesfom and Habtom became extremely malevolent and venomous. Two presumably mature men finally sank back into their childhood rivalry and animosity.

* 11 *

This rivalry and competitive defamation finally reached their family's ears. Grazmach was extremely saddened and disappointed by it. He urgently called both of his children. As soon as they sat down, without even greeting them properly, he said, "Lately, I have overheard a lot of nonsense. What is this absolutely unnecessary denigration that is going on between you and Habtom?"

Tesfom slowly explained the whole story that had led to the current sad circumstances. "We did everything we could to stop it, but Habtom kept going further. In the end, we had no choice but to retaliate.,

"Are you telling me that Habtom is the one who started the whole nasty affair, but that at the end, you had to join him?" asked Grazmach sharply.

"Yes, I mean…," said Tesfom, not very confident of his next response.

Grazmach interrupted him. "Please, wait Tesfom. If you would have told me that you were able to resist his bait without falling into his game, I would have been proud. But now, you are telling me that you tried your best, but finally you failed to prevail and fell into the dirty game along with him. In short, by making you like him, he has prevailed and triumphed over you!"

"Come on Grazmach, what do you mean? While he was falsely defaming them right and left, what could they have done?" said W/ro Brkti, coming to the defense of her children.

"Oh Brkti, please! Before you rush to interrupt, you should first hear me out. Don't forget that they are also my children. It would have been easier for me to dart and sprint to their support." Grazmach looked like he wanted to address his wife further, but after hesitating, he seemed to have changed his mind and instead, turned back to his children.

He took a deep breath and then continued from where he had stopped. "As I was trying to say, it is not unusual to occasionally disagree with people. In such circumstances, despite the disagreement, it is still civilized to at least maintain formal greetings. It is sad and unfortunate, that you are not able to greet each other, as two human beings. I can at least understand why that has happened. I know that Habtom is a rivalry ridden, extremely obdurate person. Still, that level of animosity should have been more than enough and your disagreement should have ended there."

"You know what, father…," Araya started to say, but his father stopped him.

"Please Araya Wedey, allow me to finish," he said. Seeing

Araya's nod, he continued, "If he still tries to take the disagreement to another level, then you try to put a stop to the dangerous traffic coming your way. You stop listening to what he is spewing and you completely push him out of your mind, as if he doesn't exist. You tell the people who peddle such stories, I am not interested. You refuse to give them your ears. After all, these are the same people who are the conduit for all backbiting. You shut off their business and stifle their output. That is the only way!"

"You are absolutely right, father. I completely understand what you are saying. But when he is creating and spreading false fiction to vilify and defame us, what is wrong with expounding the truth and setting the records straight?" said Tesfom.

"My son is right. We all know what kind of a person Habtom is. It is he who is at fault. What else could Tesfom have done than standing his ground to force him to stop?" said W/ro Brkti.

"It does not give me comfort or pride, to see that my children are only comparable to Habtom and his kind. I expect my children to be better than him!" said Grazmach firmly.

"I see where you are coming from, father," said Tesfom.

"You see Tesfom Wedey, if you give your ear to the garbage people spew or, worse still, if you put it inside your head and take it home and finally into your bed, then that is when you will lose and be defeated by Habtom and people like him. But you have to understand that they are not the ones who are putting it into your head and heart. In essence, you are voluntarily relinquishing your sleep, health and peace of mind to them. This is equivalent to surrendering control of your life to others. After that, they will be able to manipulate and control your moods, your peace of mind and thinking, as they wish. Do you follow me?" asked Grazmach, with intensity in his voice.

"Yes, I am following you, father," said Tesfom, pulling himself closer to the edge of the chair. He knew his father had not finished.

"If you let this happen, it is equivalent to being whipped twice over. Once when you were vilified and second when you willingly and voluntarily carried his defamation to bed with you. The only solution to that is, whenever you hear garbage, take it in through one ear, and let it escape through the other. Only then, will that person have no power over you. That is when you have won!" he said, looking at his children one by one. Then he said, "Therefore…,"

His wife cut him short saying, "Come on Grazmach, that is enough. How you love to drag it along!"

Araya, who up to that point was following with intense concentration said, "Please, mother. Father is trying to give us life lessons!"

"It is OK Araya Wedey, she is right. You know your mother. She doesn't tolerate prolonged and deep discussions. Anyway, I was also on the verge of concluding," said Grazmach smiling.

"It is ok, father. Please finish," said Tesfom, showing his displeasure at his mother's comment and interruption.

"I just want to conclude by stressing that when the fight gets ugly, both sides slide into the same abyss. Then there is no winner or loser. Everyone loses and everyone is condemned. So, please my children, see it and examine it from a broader view and perspective. Resist the temptation of being dragged into dirt!" Grazmach concluded.

After concluding their discussion, Tesfom and Araya thanked their parents and left.

*** 12 ***

A year had already passed since Habtom's defamation efforts. Despite his attempts, the pasta factory continued to register growth. Habtom was also doing very well in the bakery and in both shops. Yet, he was not satisfied. He was unhappy to see that the pasta factory was doing well. His apparent failure to thwart and impede the factory irritated and frustrated him. He couldn't find peace of mind. That was why he started leaning towards the idea of establishing another pasta factory to put the brothers out of business. While eating lunch, he told Almaz that he was becoming serious about his plans.

"You always assure me that business at the bakery and the shop where Dermas is are good, right?" asked Almaz.

"Of course, as far as business is concerned, we are not only doing well, we are doing great," responded Habtom.

"You are also aware that the shop I am at, is also doing great, right?" she asked again.

Habtom was confused by her repetitive questions, "Of course, I know all that! Why are you suddenly asking me about something both of us know?" asked Habtom.

"Well, my thinking is, since we are doing great on all fronts, instead of starting a new venture, why not strengthen and fortify the ones we have?!"

"Oh, is that what you were driving at? Well, all three businesses are already stable and do not need any further fortification."

"Even then, wouldn't it be better to run the businesses we have properly, rather than taking the risk of establishing a new business with a bank loan?" countered Almaz.

"What risk? There is no risk involved, my dear."

"Well, putting everything you have as collateral and getting a loan is definitely risky," said Almaz firmly.

"I am not diving into this job blindfolded. I am not planning to go into the business just because others have done it. I know the industry inside out. Moreover, I also love the job."

"Is it only because you truly love the job that you are bent on establishing a pasta factory?" Almaz asked, the answer to which she already knew, but she wanted him to spell it out.

True to his nature, Habtom dived straight in and said, "I also very much want to punish the traitor who betrayed me. I want to teach him a lesson he will never forget, so he will never ever try to confront me again!" said Habtom, grinding his teeth and clinching his fists.

Although she already knew that was his real reason, Almaz was still disappointed. "I don't care what happens to him. My only worry is you. While trying to confront and punish him, I worry lest you fall into unforeseen difficulties and harm," said Almaz.

"Don't worry, *stai tranquila*! Nothing will happen to me. Don't forget, I am the one who helped him take his first steps and brought him up to this level," said Habtom, with an air of pride.

"Well, I know all that. I have seen it all. I am a witness to it!" said Almaz, agreeing with him.

It is a blessing to have people close to us, who care enough to give us their honest opinions and correct our ways and doings. On the contrary, what a damnation it is, when the people close to us, do not care enough to correct us, or worse still, encourage us, while we are falling down into a precipice. The problem and misfortune are, Habtom and his kind do not appreciate and do not want anything to do with people who possess such noble traits. They look at it only as an affront and a criticism. That was his problem with Alganesh. Almaz of course, knew all this. She also knew how to manipulate and maximize it for her benefit and advantage.

That day though, Almaz immediately regretted her previous statement. She found herself thinking and talking to herself, "I shouldn't unduly worry about him, after all, if anything bad befalls him, he will be responsible for bringing it upon himself. My main worry should be, that in his rivalry and obduracy, he doesn't end up destroying me and my children."

After which, she was worried, lest the last statement she made to inflate his ego, push him towards the edge. She decided to backtrack and change course, "It is interesting, that now, when he is alone, Tesfom is actually doing well." she said.

"No, Almaz," said Habtom. "You don't get it at all. As far as Tesfom is concerned, nothing has changed. He still thinks brandishing the diploma he got years ago, is enough and still spends his time with the bottle. It is because of his brother Araya, that they are still doing ok," he concluded.

"Well, still I am not really comfortable with your plan. I know that once you set your mind to it, no one can dissuade you, so, there is nothing more I can say," said Almaz, disappointed that she had been unable to make a dent on the issue.

"Don't forget that he has not only treated me like trash, he has also thrown me out empty-handed. If I can't give this drunkard a lesson he will never forget, then I can't even call myself a man!" shouted Habtom, all worked up.

"Don't you think he will create problems and hinder you, when you ask for a loan at the bank?" asked Almaz, trying from another angle.

"He can try, but he will not succeed. I have people at the bank who will check his every move. If he does anything illegal, they will crucify him!"

"Well, I hope so. People say he is very influential at the bank," said Almaz, trying her last card.

"Don't worry about that. I have more powerful people." Habtom looked at his watch, and added, "I have to leave you now. I have an appointment," he stood up and left. Almaz sat for a very long time, deep in thought.

When Bashay and Dermas heard of the plan, they opposed it vehemently. They tried to talk him out of it. However, let alone listen to them, he wouldn't even let them finish.

Habtom was at the pinnacle of his life. Everything was going beyond his dreams. Yet, because he couldn't bring Tesfom down, he was restless with sleepless nights. He was extremely frustrated and on edge.

CHAPTER 7
THUNDERSTORM

HABTOM HIRED EXPERTS who could study the infrastructure, machineries and finance required to establish a pasta factory. When the study was finalized, Habtom started looking for a place that was adequate for a factory. The places he saw were beyond his budget. He thus reverted to looking for a smaller place to rent. Then against the advice of the experts, he rented a house that was much smaller than they recommended.

Finally, he prepared paperwork and supporting documents to enable him to apply for a loan. After completing everything, Habtom finally submitted a formal application for a loan, by putting everything he had as collateral.

Habtom's loan application reached the loan department of the bank. As head of the department, Tesfom made a preliminary review of the application. Then he put his signature on the file and assigned it to a caseworker. He chose a very meticulous and detail-oriented worker. He called him and handing him the file, told him, "I want you to examine this very carefully."

Tesfom was certain that the worker would understand exactly

what he meant and what he wanted. True to his expectation, the worker said, "I know what you mean. I understand perfectly."

After the worker left, Tesfom sank into deep thought. He was certain that Habtom was doing great in all his businesses and had no need to start a risky new venture. No reason whatsoever, warranted Habtom's new venture. He was not doing this to expand or diversify his businesses, but just to get at him and if possible, hurt him. This extremely disappointed and saddened him.

Habtom's application was studied and scrutinized from every angle. The application fulfilled all requirements. Then they proceeded to examine his past record of loan payment. Tesfom was responsible for paying the Pasta Factory's loan. They found that the loan was paid on time, on every occasion, except for one month. That was the month when Tesfom was on vacation. He had reminded Habtom to pay it on time, but Habtom had failed to do so. Tesfom paid the loan after his return. Tesfom knew that if circumstances don't force him, Habtom will never willingly pay any due payments to anyone. Based on the above, Tesfom informed his colleagues that the record of the pasta factory's loan repayment did not reflect Habtom's record.

Another important information required by the bank was the applicant's past record of misdemeanor, felony or crime. Habtom had no such public record. However, Tesfom knew from his own experience, what Habtom had committed. Habtom's application reached Tesfom's desk for final decision. Tesfom chose not to overlook Habtom's past cheating and scamming acts. Based on his personal knowledge of the applicant's record, Tesfom rejected Habtom's application for a loan.

Habtom could not control himself. He was mad, he said, "He is using the bank as if it is his personal domain. He gives loan to whomever he likes and rejects those he doesn't like."

He went and remonstrated with the people who had promised him full support. They met Tesfom and told him, "Despite Habtom's application being acceptable in every other respect, it will not be fair to reject his application based only on what you personally know. This will not look even good on you; it might look as if you are using your position for your personal vendetta."

Tesfom stood firm. "As head of this department, it is my responsibility not to grant any loan to any person with a record that I know of. I will put my signature of approval, only in a case where I don't happen to have information of a misdemeanor, irrespective of whether that information is public or not."

Habtom decided to lodge an official complaint to the bank's governor. Habtom's friends asked him to wait and give them a last chance to reason out with their colleague. They tried to reason out with Tesfom and told him Habtom's threats to lodge a formal complaint.

Tesfom was furious. He gave them a message for Habtom. "Tell him, "As long as I am sitting in this chair, you will not get a single cent from this bank. I will be keeping your secrets safe with me. When I am no longer in this position, you can apply and you have an ample chance to be approved, because your information is safe with me. If you lodge a formal complaint, then I will be forced to present the documents and the details of your misdeeds. Once it is on record, you will never ever be able to apply or get a loan." So, tell him, "It is better if you keep quiet, rather than destroy your name and your future."

When Habtom was told of Tesfom's message and warning ad verbatim, he went crazy. He was extremely furious and started throwing so many threats. His friends coolly explained to him that in the long run, it would be wise not to take the case further. They further told him that Tesfom could be removed from his position at any time and then it will be easy for him to reapply and be accepted. Habtom was actually posturing. Deep down, he knew, he was trapped. Finally, Habtom took this small window of opportunity and dropped his threat.

The following weeks, Habtom became extremely irritable and hostile. His loan fiasco, in conjunction with all the money he spent on experts and house rent, burned him to the core. His days were filled with anger and frustration. At night, he tossed and turned and passed sleepless nights. Habtom had health, wealth, children, two wives, friends and a family. Despite his being blessed with everything, he started living in hell - a hell which he himself created, nurtured and kept burning.

Although Almaz wouldn't dare saying it, she was happy that the loan application was rejected. Dermas and his parents were not also sad that the application was rejected. If it had been approved, they had feared the worst. In front of Habtom though, they all feigned disappointment and anger at Tesfom.

Tesfom and Araya continued to register further growth and success. Habtom also, despite his frustration at not getting at Tesfom, was doing great in all his businesses. Months passed after the bank incident. It was while the two families were all doing fine, that a tragedy which no one expected struck.

* **2** *

It was July 1968. This is the rainy season in the highlands of Eritrea. That afternoon, an extremely uncharacteristic heavy rain, accompanied with wind, hail, thunder and lightning started to pour down. The lightning was especially ferocious and frightening. It poured the whole evening with more intensity and ferocity, and then continued into the night.

Since it was Sunday, most businesses were closed and most people were at home. The downpour flooded many homes and businesses. Many telephones and electric lines were cut. To make matters worse, the strong winds and the lightning had also caused incidents of fire. Many businesses and establishments which encountered flooding or fire asked for help. No one could respond to their requests for help. The small and inadequate fire department had orders to respond and give priority to requests for help from people in mortal danger only. The fire brigade was not prepared for such a scale of challenge and plea. There were about five fire brigade trucks for the whole city.

There was no power in most parts of the city. Tesfom and his family, as well as Araya and Embaba slept early in the dark. Likewise, in Habtom's two households, there was no power. Alganesh and Almaz tucked their children early to bed. It was while all four households were sleeping peacefully, that the unforeseen terrible accident occurred.

* 3 *

When he arrived at the house, it was already 4.00 am. As he expected, the whole neighborhood and the house were dark and quiet. Since there was no bell, he knocked on the garage door. No one could hear him. He continued knocking using every stone or rock he could find, to no avail. The rain had not stopped completely. His clothes and his whole body were drenched with water. Water was dripping from his clothes and body.

He lost all hope that anyone would hear him. He decided the only other option he had was to climb over the fence. As he was preparing to do so, he thought he heard a voice calling "Who is that?" He knocked more ferociously shouting, "It is me! It is me!"

The voice which had given him hope seemed to have disappeared. That is when he thought, maybe his mind was playing games with him. He concluded he had just imagined the voice. He went back to the task of preparing to jump. He knew it was not only going to be very difficult, but that it was also going to be very dangerous. The rain-soaked wall was going to be slippery and the small glass pieces stuck to the top of the wall were going to take their toll on him.

He had no other alternative. He started pulling up his trousers. As soon as he put his left leg on one brick, he thought he heard a voice which said, "Who is it?" He hoped and prayed that it would be for real, so that it would save him from his ordeal. He instantly shouted, "It is me! It is me!"

For the second time he heard a voice. This time he could clearly discern that the voice was male and then distinctly heard the voice asking, "Who is this?" Araya thanked God and shouted, "It is me, Araya! It is me, Araya," twice in a row.

"Araya Seltene?!" asked the anxious male voice.

"Wait, please, do not open hurriedly before you are 100% certain," said the female voice.

"It is ok. It is me, Araya. Please open," shouted Araya.

"Oh my God! My dear brother. What is wrong?" asked Tesfom, coming to the door and fumbling with the key. They opened the door and then saw Araya totally drenched and shivering.

"What is the matter? Are we ok," Both asked?

"We are ok. At the same time, we are also not ok," said Araya, shaking his drenched head.

"Is it father?" asked Tesfom. At the same time, Medhn asked, "Is it mother?"

"No! No! Nothing has happened to any member of our family. Let's get in and talk," said Araya somberly.

Araya immediately read a sign of relief on the faces of Tesfom and Medhn. Within seconds, after that instant sigh of relief, he saw their faces become pensive again. He assumed they had realized, if it was not something serious, he wouldn't have come at such an ungodly hour, on such a night and in such a condition.

They silently and pensively led him into the house. They lit a candle and saw him properly for the first time. They couldn't believe their eyes. He was drenched from head to foot, water was dripping into the floor like a partially opened faucet. They saw that he was shivering, his lips were shaking and his teeth were rattling.

Their whole attention shifted from the still mysterious issue of the night to Araya. Tesfom urgently told Medhn, "Please Medhn, go grab some warm clothes, while I try to get him something that will warm him up."

Both of them rushed away. Tesfom came back with *Areki* (Absinthe) and poured him a large shot. Araya started to drink the hard-burning liquor sip by sip. "Come on, Araya. This is not the way to drink this, while you are in such a condition. Gulp it at once!" Tesfom shouted an order.

With a grimace in his face, Araya did as he was told. Medhn came back with warm clothes. She handed the clothes to Tesfom and said, "While you change the clothes for him, I will go to the kitchen and make hot tea." She rushed away without waiting for confirmation.

Araya immediately threw away all the clothes he had and put on his brother's warm clothes. The liquor and the warm clothes had an immediate effect. His body stopped shivering. Medhn came back with hot tea.

Both of them were still hovering over him, with worry written all over their faces. Araya asked them to sit down. They both sat at the edge of their chairs. "As I have already told you, there hasn't been any accident or death on any member of our family...," Araya started to say.

Both interrupted him instantly, saying, "Really, then what?"

When Araya started his sentence with, "but," both again instantly reverted to attention. They started to intently observe his eyes and his face to see if they could find the mystery in his body language before he spelled it out. They could only read a seriously troubled face.

Araya continued, "But, we have encountered a very serious accident at the factory. A large section of our factory has burned down!" said Araya somberly shaking his head.

"Fire? What do you mean? What kind of fire?" shouted Medhn.

"My God, fire!" said Tesfom and added, "Has the fire been put out?" Tesfom asked a practical question.

"Well, after a lot of repeated two-hour futile effort and time, finally it went out by the will of God!" said Araya sadly, shaking his head.

"What do you mean by the will of God?" asked Medhn.

"Yes, it was put out by the will of God. Around 1.00 am, the two night-guards were awakened by a loud explosive sound and immediately saw smoke billowing from the southern part of the factory. They ran to the area and saw a large fire burning. They tried to put out the fire with buckets. They soon realized that the fire was getting stronger. One of the guards ran to the office to call and inform us and to call the fire department for help," Araya paused to catch his breath.

Medhn was impatient, she asked, "And then?"

"The fire department told them that all their trucks were out and were concentrating their efforts on saving lives and not properties. They thus told them to try to find people who could help with the fire."

"My God, what is this? And then?" said Tesfom.

"Since they were unable to contact us by phone and since they couldn't find anyone at that hour to help, they doubled their efforts to put out the fire by themselves. However, the fire continued to grow. The only other thing they could think of was to get hold of one us, if we could think or do something. Since my house is nearer than yours, they decided for one of them to come to my house," Araya paused to take a sip from his tea.

Tesfom was impatient, he asked, "And then? "

"He came home on foot and we were able to hear him only after a lot of knocking. Then he told me and we rushed back together to the factory. When I saw that the fire was beyond our capacity, I decided to again try to call the fire department and implore with them. I called them and tried to explain the extent of the fire and damage. Their answer was the same. They were not even able to respond to all calls of help to save lives, let alone property!"

"My God, what kind of a night is this? And then?" asked Tesfom, frustrated and saddened by the turn of the events of that night. At one moment he was grasping his hands together, the next moment he would put his right hand on his forehead and back again.

"Well, after that we agreed that they continue their futile attempts, while I come to inform you. At that very moment, God-sent rain started to fall down. We stood there observing the rain and praying it wouldn't stop. The rain continued without any wind with renewed intensity. We started noticing that the fire was getting smaller. After a downpour of about half an hour, the fire was totally out. That was why, I had earlier said, "With the help of God." If it was not for the rain, the whole factory would have burned down!" said Araya, pointing his hands to the sky and acknowledging his thanks.

"Wow! Truly, God's miracle!" said Medhn.

"What seems to be the initial cause of the fire?" asked Tesfom.

"Well, who can say? Trees, telephone and power lines have fallen; there was a strong wind, stormy downpour, flooding and incessant lightning. Therefore, it can be any one of the above or a combination of all of them. That is something that will require meticulous and thorough examination. At this stage, it is hard to say or determine. Only after a detailed inspection will anyone be able to determine the cause." Then as an after-thought Araya added with finality, "Whether it would be possible to ascertain the cause at all, is even debatable!"

"I am sorry, Araya Hawey. I am unnecessarily giving you a hard time, asking impossible and at this point hard to answer questions. Anyway, what has happened, has happened. It can't be undone!" Tesfom said solemnly and sadly.

"Well, my dear Tesfom, you haven't asked a question which I hadn't already asked myself a hundred times. So, you were right to ask. But as you said and as father continuously says, "Once something has happened, the practical thing to do, is to accept what has happened and proceed from there!" said Araya seriously.

"Yes, you are right. Ok. let's go now. As for the rest, we will talk on the way," said Tesfom standing up.

"Since you will be there the whole day, why don't I bring you something, so you take a bite before you leave?" said Medhn, anxiously worried about their difficult day ahead.

"No, it is ok. That will not be a problem," said both and stood up and left.

* 4 *

By the time they arrived at the factory, it was already 5.00 am. Since it was still partially dark, they used a torchlight to go around, to inspect and get a rough estimate of the damage. Soon after, it was light and they were able to go around a second time, to re-examine the damage that had occurred.

The wall of the Eastern and Southern section of the factory was built attached to the fencing of the establishment. Hence, the fencing and factory wall were one. However, on the Western and Northern section, it was built far away from the fence. The largest part of the factory lay on the Eastern and Southern side.

The administrative offices lay on the Eastern side. Here, they had a very large room which served as an office for Tesfom and Araya. In addition, they had two additional rooms which served the accounts, sales and purchases departments. They also had a small bathroom.

The largest surge of fire seemed to have been concentrated on the Southern section of the factory. This was the section of the wall through which the factory received its high voltage power. As a result, they guessed that the fire could have been caused by rain leaking into the high voltage line and causing a spark.

After their initial inspection, they were able to ascertain that the factory had been extensively damaged. All the circumstances clearly indicated that the fire had started from the southern edge of the factory. The Southern section of the factory housed the machineries which mixed flour, water, eggs, yeast and the kneading machines. The greatest damage had also occurred in this particular area.

The storage section of the factory was also on this southern section and all raw materials in store had been reduced to ashes. The other half of the factory, housing the pasta making and packing machines had not incurred any damage. The administrative offices were also untouched and intact.

At 8.00 am, Araya and Tesfom went to the insurance company and the bank respectively. They formally informed them of the accident. The brothers were told to wait at the factory until the inspectors arrived. As agreed, Tesfom and Araya met back at the factory after an hour.

They had left instructions with the guards that all employees were to wait for them, without touching anything whatsoever. They found the workers in shock and in disbelief. Araya made a list of the heads of departments and other personnel, who could help them in the coming days. They told all others to go on leave, until further notice.

While waiting for the insurance and bank inspectors, the brothers and their workers started registering and itemizing every damage. It was 11.00 am and yet the inspectors had not come. At that point, they called both the Insurance company and the bank. Both institutions informed them that as a result of Sunday's accidents, they still had immense number of accidents to be inspected everywhere. They further told them that they needed to wait patiently until the overstretched inspectors could make it to the factory.

Up to that point, they hadn't told their parents about the accident. They thought it would be best for Tesfom to go personally, explain it mildly, and then bring their father and let him see it for himself. Tesfom went to fetch his father. When his father saw the accident, he couldn't believe his eyes. He held his head and said, "Tesfom! What is this?! You didn't tell me properly the extent of the damage! My God! This is unbelievable!"

"Well, we decided it will be easier on you to come and see it for yourself," said Tesfom.

They took him around and showed him the extent of the damage. Grazmach observed and noted everything, without making any comment. When they went back to the office and sat down, Grazmach asked, "What seems to be the cause of the fire?"

Araya and Tesfom tried to explain what they could so far guess and surmise. Generally speaking, Grazmach does not easily get perturbed or imbalanced easily. This time though, his face looked ashen. Grazmach's focus moved from the accident to another important subject. Thus, he asked, "What about insurance?"

Tesfom hurriedly said, "We went to them early in the morning. We are still waiting for them."

"I am not asking about when they are coming. I am asking if the premium is paid and up to-date," said Grazmach.

While Grazmach was waiting for a response, he saw his sons look at each other and hesitate for a moment. Grazmach was alarmed and hurriedly asked, "We have full insurance coverage, right?"

It was a question the brothers had not expected. Tesfom scratched and dropped his head and said, "The premium is paid, but we don't have full coverage."

"What? What do you mean? What does we don't have full coverage mean?!" asked Grazmach in disbelief.

"The bank requires insurance for the amount of money loaned. The coverage we have is for the amount of the bank's loan. We didn't ensure the rest," Tesfom said with embarrassment.

Grazmach couldn't believe what he was hearing, "What kind of logic are you trying to tell me, Tesfom? Being head of the loan department of the bank; knowing very well the workings of the bank; understanding that the bank demands insurance for the money it lends so as not to take a risk; what logic or rationale could there be for not ensuring your own property? Or do you have another good reason?" asked Grazmach, futilely hoping for a rational motive.

"The premium for fire insurance has recently increased dramatically. Since the probability of fire in a factory like ours is small, we thought we could do without it, at least until we repay our bank loan," said Tesfom, without too much conviction.

"Wow, Tesfom! What kind of rationale is that?! I think you are inverting the logic on its head. I am sure you will agree that you need insurance more when you are not financially secure and when any unforeseen accident could wipe you out. Otherwise, when you are strong and financially sturdy, you can even pay any unforeseen damage yourself!" said Grazmach, disappointed by his son's lack of judgement.

Grazmach turned his face towards Araya and said, "How about you, Araya Wedey? What happened to you? Hadn't your brother consulted you on this matter?"

It was Araya's turn to look down and say, "He had consulted with me, but at the moment, I accepted and agreed with his argument. We have made a huge mistake, father."

"A huge mistake indeed!" said Grazmach. He sighed and added, "Anyway, there is nothing we can undo by criticizing each other and looking backwards. The only correct way is to look forwards at what can be done. So, the only thing I have to say is, look forward and concentrate on the present," said Grazmach, concluding the subject of insurance.

All fell silent. After a few seconds, "Ok father, I think it is better if you now retire and rest. I know you will not be able to relax and rest much now, and that is due to our shortsightedness. Still, it is better if you go home, since there is nothing much you can do here. If there is anything new, we'll let you know," said Tesfom, with an air of frustration and remorse.

"Yes, I think you are right. It is best if I go home now," said Grazmach getting up.

Grazmach paused at the door. He looked pensive. He seemed as if he was collecting his thoughts. He then turned back towards Tesfom and Araya and said, "As human beings, we always tend to say, "This shouldn't have been done or that was not the way," etc. but in reality, in the end, things happen because they are the will of God! So, let's take this as a will of God and accept it and pray that he will help us to surmount this devastation. Therefore, don't worry and fret about it *Izom Dekey*! Be strong and positive! God bless you!" said Grazmach and swung back and left.

When his father left, Tesfom said, "Oh my God! We have disappointed and failed a father, who doesn't deserve any of this!" said Tesfom bitterly, clenching his fists and his teeth.

"I am sure that you know that if it was somebody else, he would have raved about it for hours!" said Araya.

"I completely understand. That is what makes it more heartbreaking and painful!" said Tesfom.

"Well, that he should feel it is only natural. But you know father, when all is said and done, he takes and accepts life and the world as it comes and unfolds. So, don't worry yourself too much about father," said Araya, providing moral support and encouragement to his brother.

The last time Tesfom and Araya had eaten was the previous evening, about 15 hours ago. They didn't even realize their hunger, because their minds and bodies were totally focused on the devastating event. However now, their stomachs began to rumble and complain. "I don't think these people are coming soon. Come on Araya, please, send someone to bring us at least tea and bread," said Tesfom, suddenly yawning.

"You are right. I am also famished," said Araya, standing up immediately.

He went and told the guard. As soon as it arrived, they immediately finished everything without uttering a word. Both looked as if they had not eaten in a week.

The inspectors arrived as soon as they finished eating. They took them around. The inspectors took notes and pictures. They made a thorough investigation. They couldn't exactly pinpoint the cause of the fire.

The inspectors had already visited a large number of locations that had been gutted by fire, due to Sunday's adverse weather condition. Their preliminary investigation pointed towards adverse weather, as the cause of the fire. Still, they felt it was necessary to rule out arson. They asked Tesfom and Araya, if they could think of anyone with enough motive to commit arson. Both brothers unequivocally ruled out the possibility. Despite their assurance, the investigators made every effort to find any clue that could point in that direction. They found none.

However, the inspectors were certain of one thing. They had concluded that the owners could not have been responsible for setting up the fire. They arrived at that conclusion because the factory was only partially insured. They had observed that the damage was far greater than what the owners could collect from the insurance company. If the factory was to return to its original state, on top of the forthcoming insurance money, the owners would need to pay a large chunk of their own money as well.

After concluding their preliminary investigation, the inspectors left. Before leaving, they instructed them not to touch or move anything, until the final investigations were completed. Since they had nothing else to do, Araya and Tesfom left soon after.

* **5** *

Medhn had been fretting and worrying the whole morning. She still had no idea of the extent of the damage the fire had caused. As soon as Tesfom arrived, before he barely even sat, she anxiously asked, "How is it? Are we ok?"

"We are not ok, Medhn. The damage is extensive and devastating," said Tesfom sadly, shaking his head.

Although Medhn desperately wanted to know further details, she thought it wouldn't be fair to make him go through complete narration, before he washed and ate. She thus controlled her urge and asked, "Do you want to eat first or wash?"

"I better wash," said Tesfom, standing up and heading towards the bathroom. When Tesfom came out, the food was ready. He sat down and after finishing his food, Medhn brought tea.

Medhn sat down and said, "Now please tell me the details of the damage and your findings."

Tesfom explained to her everything, including the probable cause of the fire. He further explained the damage to machineries and property incurred. Finally, getting up, he said, "Can you please tell the children about what has happened. You don't need to go into much detail. I am exhausted; I want to take a nap."

"Of course, go ahead. Leave that to me," Medhn said.

When the Grazmach family were wallowing in distress and hopelessness, Habtom was in a celebratory mood.

* 6 *

On Sunday night, something woke her up from her sleep. When she got up to check, she saw that it was Habtom that had come in. Alganesh went back to her room, closed the door and slept. In the morning, Habtom ate breakfast along with his children. He used to come to his children only during day times. It had been a long time since he stopped coming nights, except occasionally.

It was also quite rare of Habtom to have the patience of eating breakfast with his children. However, what was most unbelievable was the fact that he came in the afternoon, carrying a cake. He invited his children to the cake. Alganesh was amazed. His eldest children were extremely surprised and looked at each other with curious eyes. The youngsters were delighted. That was when 8-year-old Negassi asked, "Whose birthday is it daddy?"

"It is not anybody's birthday son. It is because your father is happy about something and wants to celebrate. You don't need to know about it, because it is adult stuff," said Habtom.

None of the children understood what their father meant. The eldest children had already formulated follow-up questions within their heads. However, none of them dared to ask him. While eating their cakes, they furtively looked at their father's and mother's eyes, in case they could discern an answer to the mystery. The younger children however, didn't care or mind that they didn't know; the important thing for them was that they were enjoying their cake.

For Alganesh, the scene before her was even more mysterious. She couldn't understand what was happening or why. After trying to unsuccessfully come up with something, she abandoned the effort. She contented herself by thinking, "There is no secret that remains a secret forever, so sooner or later, we will know what this is all about." As she was reminiscing thus, she heard Habtom say, "Ok then children, I will leave you now." Habtom got up and left.

As soon as he left, all the children surrounded her. She was not surprised, because she had expected it. "Mamma! Mamma! What was the cake about?" everyone shouted.

"I am sorry children; I honestly don't know what it was all about. If I knew, I would tell you. I will eventually know and when I do, I will tell you; I promise. Now while I prepare dinner, go and do your homework," said Alganesh, putting a temporary end to the riddle of the cake.

Although the celebration was a riddle to Alganesh and her children, unknown to them, Habtom had already earlier initiated the celebration elsewhere.

* 7 *

The friendship, closeness and love between all of Tesfom's and Habtom's children, was unique and exemplary. However, particularly the care, intimacy and affection of Kbret and Bruk was extremely unique. Even as little children, they were closer to each other and would come to the rescue of each other, rather than their own siblings.

Since quite some time, Alganesh had started to observe certain changes in her eldest daughter, Kbret. The observation had started to worry her. She had wanted to discuss it with Medhn but was worried, lest her observations were imaginations in her head.

Alganesh had been thinking about Habtom's odd behavior the

whole evening and night. When she got up in the morning, both the Habtom and Kbret issues were still in her head. She decided to discuss both topics with her confidant and friend, Medhn. She went to her and as soon as they sat, "Have you lately observed anything new in Kbret or Bruk?" Asked Alganesh.

Medhn did not understand the direction or essence of Alganesh's question. Bewildered, she asked, "What changes or observations are you talking about?"

"Well, I am not sure, but I am having doubts and qualms about their intimacy and care for each other. I have started to ask myself, is it only merely friendship?" said Alganesh.

"Oh, you mean about their special relationship. Why didn't you directly say so then? You had confused me when you popped the question out of the blue. Anyway, their special relationship and love for each other is not new. It has always been that way. Now that they are getting older, I can understand your worries and apprehension. Who knows, you might have something there, though I feel it might only be because we are women and mothers who don't miss anything. Otherwise, I don't think there is anything to it. The truth is, they are still children." said Medhn confidently.

"Yes, that is true. They are still children. But, on the other hand, we have to understand that the times are now different. While we assume it is just children's friendship, we should beware lest they surprise us. It is always better to be on the safe side," warned Alganesh.

"I still think they are not at that stage. However, as you pointed out, since nothing is impossible, let's just be on the lookout," said Medhn.

"Great! Let's do that then. By the way, the main reason I came is because I want to share with you a riddle - a mystery," said Alganesh.

"Riddle? Mystery?" asked Medhn with bewilderment.

Alganesh told her how Habtom visited the children, mostly during day times; and that only occasionally and very rarely would he spend nights with them; that however, on Sunday night, Habtom came very late and let himself in; that when she heard a sound and got up to check the door, she saw that it was him; that she then turned back to her room and slept; and then went on to explain in detail, how he came home Monday afternoon with a cake and what happened afterwards.

Medhn heard her out, without interrupting her even once. When she finished, she said, "Oh my God! Habtom is really a brute who doesn't have any scruples or ethics!" said Medhn, with extreme anger and sadness in her voice.

"What do you mean? Do you know why he did what he did?!" asked Alganesh curiously.

"I hadn't known what it was, until you told me. I just put two and two together and understood what it is. Alganesh Habtey, a very sad accident and disaster has happened," said Medhn shaking her head.

"Oh my God! What has happened? What kind of accident?" Alganesh asked, alarmed, putting both of her hands to her face.

"Well, you won't believe this, but Sunday night, fire has gutted the pasta factory!"

Aganesh nearly stood up with shock. She put her two hands on her head and shouted, "What?! What kind of a tragedy is this?! Oh! I am so sorry that this had to happen to the kind and gentle Tesfom Hawey! He doesn't deserve this! You don't deserve this! Oh God! How can you? Why them, when wicked people like Habtom are just walking around!"

"Well, Alganesh Habtey, we can only say, it is God's will. We can't say anything else, since we can't judge and comprehend God's actions!" said Medhn courageously, with conviction.

"You are absolutely right Medhn Habtey. In my shock, I hadn't realized that I was trying to judge God. Oh God, I have sinned, pardon me," said Alganesh, making a sign of the cross and adding, "*BesmAab*," meaning "In the Name of the Father."

"Anyway, so, in essence, Habtom is celebrating because our factory has been burned down," said Medhn.

Because Alganesh was so shocked by the tragic news, she hadn't made a connection between the accident and Habtom's actions. When Medhn spilled it out, Alganesh nearly stood up again with shock, "Oh my God! Oh my God! Stupid me! I hadn't realized the connection. How could he do this? Nothing ever prepares you to the extent of his wicked deeds. Oh my God! The worst is that my children and I ate from that forsaken devil's cake!" she said, devastated with sadness and remorse.

At that point, the children came in and Medhn signaled Alganesh and they immediately stopped the conversation. After a while Medhn said, "Ok Alganesh Habtey, you can leave now. We will talk about this some other time."

Alganesh went back home, still unable to process that morning's information and Habtom's deeds.

* 8 *

For most people, polygamy or establishing another family on the side, is not considered something to be proud of. However, Habtom was very proud of it. So proud that when Almaz bore a son, he insisted that they name him Haben, meaning Pride! They named their second daughter, Mekeret, meaning Taste. Haben was now three and Mekeret was one year old.

On Sunday, Habtom did not spend the night with Almaz. He went to the shop the next morning and explained what had happened. He described how he had to go from one facility to the other the whole night; to make sure that all three of their establishments were safe. He further told her, he decided to sleep at Alganesh's, because of the heavy rain and the proximity of the house. Almaz was satisfied with his explanation. She herself was very much aware of Sunday night's weather condition and the damage that ensued.

The same day at noon, Habtom came home carrying a large

wrapped-stuff. When she saw him, she was puzzled? At first, she thought, it was his way of asking forgiveness for the night before. But then, since he had adequately explained it, she knew there wouldn't be any need for that. Confused, Almaz hurriedly asked, "What is all that you are carrying? Since when do you come home carrying stuff?"

"Well, this is a special day my dear. I have brought a cake for celebration," said Habtom smiling profusely.

"Celebration?! What celebration?" asked Almaz bewildered.

"Well, we have to sit down before I can tell you what it is!" said Habtom, with great spirit and pride.

"Wow! I can see you are in great spirits! It should be something big!" Almaz said smiling, her curiosity jumping up a notch. She observed a noticeable difference in mood, compared to his melancholy of the previous months.

"It is indeed big. Very big! Come on now, bring the children," he said, and then when Almaz was about to leave, added, "I will bring Cognac and Vermouth. You fetch soft-drink (*Bibita*) and some forks and a knife."

After everything was ready, they all sat down. "Oh, Thank God! Now give me the knife, let's cut our cake!" said Habtom, stretching his hand towards Almaz.

"No! You have to first tell me what this is all about. I won't give you the knife before you do that," said Almaz, pulling the knife away from him.

Haben's eyes were all on the cake. Like all other children, he loved cakes. "Ok, I promise I will tell you, but please, let's first give the children the cake. They can't wait; you know how children are," he added.

She handed him the knife and he cut the cake. Then they poured drinks and drank to their health and their bright future. Almaz couldn't wait anymore and so said, "Please come on now, tell me what it is. You are killing me with suspense!"

Habtom put the palms of each hand against the other and

started rubbing them together. Then he made a fist with his right hand and punching the air said, "Yesterday, it has been proved that any wrong-doer will not eventually escape punishment and justice!"

"Wrong-doer? Punishment? Justice?" Almaz asked consecutive questions, with bewilderment.

"Yesterday, the pasta factory burned down to the ground!" Habtom said, smiling broadly, with victory written all over his face.

Almaz nearly stood up from her chair, incredulous at what she was hearing, "Tesfom's pasta factory?" she shouted.

Habtom's facial expression instantly changed. His eyes narrowed and his forehead furrowed. With extreme disappointment in his voice, he said, "So, you have started calling it, Tesfom's factory?"

Almaz instantly knew that she had touched a nerve. She tried to retreat by saying, "I am sorry, I referred to it as such, only because you agreed to divide the two establishments."

"Divided? Did you say divided? We didn't divide anything! He took it from me illegally!" shouted Habtom. Then as an afterthought, he added, "Anyway, now he doesn't own a factory anymore, since it has been burned down to the ground!" He laughed heartily.

"The whole factory has completely burned down?" Alganesh asked, just to be sure.

"Yes, more or less!" said Habtom and then quickly added, "Now come on! Pick up your drink, let's again drink and cheer. Let that bastard roast, as he had roasted me!" said Habtom with bitterness and acrimony.

Almaz was amazed and delighted to see him happy. She hadn't seen him that way for months. On the other hand, she was also startled and worried at how Habtom could turn into a dangerous wild beast, once wounded and hurt.

Finally, they ended their celebration. Habtom was gratified. He stood up to leave. As he was leaving, he said, "Ok, let me go back to work. At least those of us who have work, can go to work; while those who don't have work anymore, can stay at home licking their wounds!" Habtom roared out laughing at his own joke.

Habtom continued his celebration outside of his home as well. Accordingly, he organized small celebrations for the workers of the bakery and the two shops. He organized greater celebrations for his friends and acquaintances in bars and restaurants. He kept repeating to everyone, "It was not enough that this traitor stole the factory from me; he also unfairly denied me a loan. All this, so he could be the only one with a factory. Well, justice always prevails!"

All the actions and expressions of Habtom eventually reached Tesfom and Araya. Grazmach and the whole family also started hearing about it. Everyone was extremely saddened by Habtom's additional and unnecessary measures of malice and ill will.

* 9 *

While Habtom was celebrating, Tesfom and Araya were extremely demoralized and disheartened. Tesfom immediately took a month's leave from the bank. Since they had no permission to touch, clean or repair anything, there was not much they could do.

They sat in their office and started registering stuff they needed to get rid of and small items they needed to buy and replace. They computed and came up with a rough estimate of the total amount of money they would need, to return the factory back to normal. The money they would collect from the insurance company was far less than the total amount of money required. They knew there was no way they could get a bank loan in the near future.

They calculated the amount of cash they could raise. They were nowhere near what they needed. They had to accept the bitter fact, that they would have no means and no way of running the factory to full capacity. They concluded, they needed to shut off certain sections of the factory and let it work with much reduced capacity. They also concluded that they needed to lay off workers and let others work with reduced salary.

After the accident, all the workers of the factory expressed their genuine sorrow at what had happened. All of them expressed their willingness to lend a helping hand in whatever capacity they could. This was a testament to Tesfom's compassionate handling of the workers. He was gratified by their show of support and sympathy. None of their workers felt or said, "They got their hand, they deserved it." Though that didn't in any way materially help with their present predicament, it still gave them some measure of moral support.

Despite all this, Tesfom was extremely unhappy and frustrated. He felt total and sole responsibility for their present predicament. He passed exhausting days and sleepless nights. As a result, he started going back to his abode, the bottle, for solace and escape.

* 10 *

After the accident, Araya had started going to the factory early in the morning, before office hours. He would then go around the factory with his head down and his hands behind his back. Since they were still not allowed to touch anything, he used to comb every inch of the damaged area with his eyes. It was easy for anyone who observed Araya's demeanor to conclude, that the accident had affected him deeply. Everyone who saw him, feared for him, lest he fall into a nervous breakdown.

They were given permission to start their cleaning and rehabilitation process, after two weeks. Araya called all the staff and instructed them that the whole process of cleaning and disposal will be conducted, only under his direct supervision. He further told them that nothing he hadn't seen or approved should be thrown away.

Tesfom did not agree with Araya's strategy. "I don't think this is going to be helpful. I think it will slow down our work. Why don't you let them perform the cleaning and disposal without your supervision," said Tesfom.

"I will make sure it doesn't slow us down, by putting in more hours. It is always better to do a good job, rather than sacrifice precision for speed and mess things up. I also want to know exactly what we are recovering and what we are throwing away," said Araya firmly.

"I really don't see any advantage to that strategy," said Tesfom.

"Well, on the one hand, we will at least be certain that we are not throwing away useful stuff and the other hand, who knows, we might even find something that will give us a clue about the real cause of the fire!" said Araya with hope.

"What good will that do? Let alone you and I, even the insurance inspectors failed to find evidence that points towards the real cause of the fire. Anyway, if you are bent on it and if it will really make you happy, then go ahead," said Tesfom, giving his brother the green light to proceed.

During his rounds, unknown to Tesfom, Araya had already salvaged a few seemingly unimportant items that had caught his eye and his imagination. He kept them to himself and did not dare show or tell his brother, lest he laugh at him.

The preparatory work they had done, helped them to make good progress. They were thus able to assess that it was going to take them four to five months, before they could start production. They also understood and knew that during this preparatory work, bank interest, workers' salaries and other overhead costs would keep on mounting.

Tesfom understood that a large measure of the responsibility for all this was his. More than anything else, his lack of judgement on insurance coverage especially bothered and scorched him. Tesfom's lack of sleep, frustration and depression reached a new high. To counteract the pressure building up, he started to increasingly escape to the bottle.

Medhn and Araya were quick to notice this. Medhn strongly suggested that they talk to him before he sank further. Araya did not agree and instead suggested that they give him time. His logic was that since he was already under enormous pressure, talking to him about drinking might push him off the edge. Medhn had to finally concur.

After a hard-concerted effort of six months, finally in February 1969, they were able to start limited production. With extreme care and caution, they juggled their limited finances from one to the other, trying to close every crack that appeared.

All workers of the factory, except a handful, were very sympathetic to Tesfom and Araya. During the partnership, there were two to three workers that were especially too close to Habtom. As soon as they took over the factory, Araya had asked his brother to terminate them. Tesfom didn't approve of the idea; he felt it was not right to judge them circumstantially, without any proof of wrongdoing.

Since the fire accident, an inkling of suspicion had been continuously bothering Araya. Even when he wanted to push it away, the feeling came back to him and nagged him. The long hours and the hard work of the last six months did not decrease the intensity of what was bothering him. Since he didn't have any concrete stuff, he couldn't confide in his brother. He also knew that Tesfom, by nature, never suspected anything. He was certain, that if he was to tell him, he would only laugh at him. So, he kept it to himself, but it was taking its toll on him.

A lot of people, including Tesfom, started to notice his condition. Whenever Tesfom asked him what was bothering him, he would answer, "Nothing more than the difficult times we are going through." Tesfom didn't suspect that his brother was preoccupied with much more.

* 11 *

After the accident, Grazmach Seltene forced himself not to think about what had already happened. His principle was always not to dwell on the past, but to concentrate on the present and future. He understood what his children were going through. He was trying his best to prop them up. Thus, he would tell them, "Listen, my dear children, when an accident of this magnitude strikes, we shouldn't only concentrate on our predicament. If we only concentrate on our plight, then we will only be magnifying and multiplying our problems."

He would pause for a while and add, "We should remind ourselves that such misfortunes happen to many people all the time. In fact, we should remember that many people have it even worse. Instead of asking why did this happen to us? We should ask, why not us? We should also count ourselves lucky, that this accident did not happen while you and all factory workers were present. We wouldn't have done anything, if lives would have been lost. So, we should look at the brighter side and count our blessings, instead of our losses."

Whenever his father spoke to them thus, Tesfom would be ok for a while. After a few hours though, he would revert back to his old self. The idea that was especially nagging and bothering him was the fact that he was responsible for risking everything his father had worked and duly saved for his entire life. No matter how hard he tried, he couldn't get it out of his mind and his system. This pushed and drove him into further frustration and desperation.

Six months had passed since the factory had started limited production. Though Araya and Tesfom did everything they could, they found it very difficult to financially fill every hole that appeared. This had a toll on both brothers. Araya used to surmount this pressure with patience and self-control, while Tesfom would at every opportunity run to his abode.

* 12 *

Both brothers were working in their respective tables with concentration, when Araya turned towards Tesfom and abruptly asked, "When we were dissolving the partnership, I had once told you that

I was continually seeing a worker named Gebreab with Habtom. Do you remember it?"

Tesfom seemed to remember something to that effect, but the suddenness of Araya's question, made him pause and slightly hesitate. He thought for a few seconds and then responded, "Yes, I do recollect that you had told me something to that effect, but I don't remember the person. Which one is he?"

"The short, dark skinned, handsome man, which Habtom had assigned to sales. In fact, at the time, I had suggested that we transfer him to the store, to break the chain, in case there was a possibility of collusion."

"Yes, yes, right! I remember him now. In fact, when we transferred him to the store, he even complained bitterly about how it was not fair; after which, you insisted that we terminate him, since you were not even comfortable with him and didn't like him. However, because of his long service, I didn't feel it was fair and didn't agree with your proposal," said Tesfom.

"Yes, exactly, that is the one. At the time, I had also told you additional reasoning for my gut feeling; do you remember? I had told you, people who know him closely say, he is very obstinate and doesn't forget a grudge," said Araya, showing that he had done his homework on Gebreab.

"I don't exactly remember the arguments you then presented for his termination." said Tesfom, furrowing his forehead trying to remember.

"In addition, I had told you that I never liked the man; that even after our separation, I continuously see him with Habtom; that this might mean he could still be feeding him information; and so, I recommended that we terminate him. You didn't agree, because you felt it was not fair to terminate a man with a family, based on a hunch or a feeling."

"Yes, now I remember the whole case properly. What I still don't understand is though, why you are raising the subject now?" asked Tesfom.

"Well, even now after the accident, my sources tell me that he is regularly meeting with Habtom. I have also personally ascertained the information myself."

"So? What is bothering you?" asked Tesfom innocently.

"Well, I asked myself several questions. What is their relationship exactly? Why do they meet regularly, even though they don't have a work relationship? Could it be anything that pertains to us? Could it be something that could hurt us? Etc." said Araya.

"Well, I don't think it could be anything to do with us. At most, it might be Habtom trying to collect crumbs of gossip about us and our problems," said Tesfom confidently.

"It is wiser and more cautious, to think there could be more to it. It is even said, "It is better to err on the side of caution." An employee who still meets regularly with someone, who is doing his utmost to defame our name and that of our factory is highly suspect!"

"Well, it could be suspect, but how can you take action based on that?" asked Tesfom.

"Come on, Tesfom! Why should we live in worry and suspense in our own establishment? Let us give him his rights and terminate him!" said Araya firmly.

"Well, how about if he hasn't committed anything wrong? We will be wronging him unfairly. It is not right to take such a decision without strong evidence," said Tesfom.

"We are not going to treat him unfairly. We will give him all his rights, but we will also be protecting ourselves. I am sorry Tesfom, I still have not put my finger on it, but even when I see him at work, I have a bad feeling about this person," said Araya with strong conviction.

"I am sorry Araya Hawey, but that is still, just a feeling. A feeling could be right or wrong. It wouldn't be fair to terminate him based on our feelings. However, I would say let's follow him more closely and see if we find anything," said Tesfom.

"Well ok. As I told you before, I have been following him for some time, but now I will redouble my efforts and see if we can come up with something," said Araya, not hiding his disappointment.

"Great! Do that then," said Tesfom, concluding the subject. Since it was already late, the two brothers decided to call it a day and go home.

* 13 *

After their talk, Araya started thinking about who the best person would be to follow Gebreab closely. Finally, after a careful and thorough search, he chose a worker named Tekleab, who was a happy-go-lucky guy who was friendly with everyone, except Habtom. He worked at the store, alongside Gebreab. Araya had also received information that they go out together for drinks, on weekends.

Tekleab was a person who had extreme respect for Tesfom, Araya and the whole family. He always expressed his genuine sorrow at the tragedy that had occurred. He felt very bad that an accident of that magnitude had befallen, to a family that didn't deserve it. He showed his sympathy and support both sentimentally and in the way he exerted himself selflessly, during the rehabilitation process.

At the bakery, there was a worker named Weldeab, who had much respect for the Grazmach family. He always complained about Habtom's treatment. After the separation, he was constantly asking Tesfom, if he could place him in the factory. Tesfom liked the man and would have loved to do so, however, he feared Habtom would gain a talking point and would start exaggerating how they were taking away his workers. Araya chose Weldeab as his other candidate.

Araya met both of them separately. He explained to them exactly what they were looking for; he stressed that they were aware of the relationship between Gebreab and Habtom before the dissolution of the partnership; that they were looking now, for more recent information; and specifically wanted answers to the questions: What common interest do they have? What is it that is still tying and bonding them together? Etc.

He further explained to them that they were at a very critical stage; that if anything untoward happens to them at this stage, they will be beyond redemption; that they want to pre-empt any sabotage that could hurt them; and that they could succeed in this, only if they had prior information about the collusion and design of Gebreab and Habtom. He promised that if they assist them in thwarting any imminent danger, then they will be remunerated appropriately.

He told Weldeab that they required nothing more of him, than opening his eyes and ears and observing and listening to everything that went on in the bakery. On the other hand, he told Tekleab that he wanted him to follow Gebreab's movements outside of work, especially whom he met and where? He encouraged him to increase his nights out with Gebreab and entertain themselves without much care for expenses. He promised he would refund all expenses. He told both that if there was nothing urgent to report, they would meet weekly to exchange information.

Araya put this arrangement exactly a year after the fire accident. In a short while, both informants were able to ascertain that Gebreab and Habtom were indeed meeting regularly. What they still didn't know was the why? After about two months, in November 1969, they were able to get new information from Gebreab at the bakery.

After receiving the information, Araya was impatiently waiting for Tesfom to arrive from work. He didn't want to share the information over the phone. As soon as Tesfom arrived, before he even barely sat, Araya said, "The day before yesterday, Weldeab saw Habtom give Gebreab an envelope with money in it." said Araya, finally happy that he was able to share his information with his brother.

Tesfom was taken by surprise, he shouted, "What? What did you say?"

"Didn't you hear me? Your thoughts must have been somewhere else," said Araya smiling, preparing to repeat his finding.

"No, I heard you all right. I was just taken by surprise," said Tesfom.

"Well, if he is paying him money, I am sure it is not out of charity!" Araya said sourly.

"Of course! that is obvious. Let alone for others, Habtom wouldn't part with his money even for his children and family," said Tesfom, agreeing instantly.

"So, that means he is doing something for him," said Araya.

"Yes, or he is paying him beforehand for something he wants him to do," agreed Tesfom.

"Exactly! Then we should try to find out what it is as soon as possible!" said Araya with urgency.

"Yes, but how could you do that?" Tesfom enquired.

"We have to instruct Tekleab and Weldeab to speed-up and accelerate their follow up," said Araya.

"Rushing also has its own dangers Araya. In their haste, they might flounder things and make Gebreab and Habtom aware of our follow up. So, they should be patient and cautious."

"If we are to pre-empt any designs he might have, we have to know well ahead of time. You know we are now in a very precarious situation, and a small shove is enough to push us off the edge," said Araya with apprehension.

"I understand your worries, however caution is important," said Tesfom and then hesitated for a moment as if a new idea had occurred to him. "Listen Araya, you know the money could even be what Habtom had collected from their conspiratorial scamming and which he hadn't paid Gebreab as of yet," said Tesfom.

"No! It can't be! I don't think so. That was a long time ago. How can he have not paid him his due, up to this moment?" said Araya.

"Come on Araya! You talk as if you don't know him. Don't you know that Habtom gets more satisfaction from scamming 500.00 Krshi rather than legally earning 5.000.00 Krshi. In order to deny him his share, he might be procrastinating and postponing it forever," said Tesfom with near certainty.

'Well, there is definitely a small possibility of that. Despite that, the best policy for us is to assume, that it could be something that relates to us and affects us. We should think only about protecting ourselves," said Araya.

"Yes, I think that is a cautious and prudent strategy. Ok, then let's continue our follow-up with care," said Tesfom.

"Very good, then we will accelerate things with caution. I will tell them how they should proceed," said Araya.

After agreeing on that, Araya had to go to an appointment, leaving his brother at the office.

* 14 *

Tekleab started going out with Gebreab more often. Tekleab soon noticed that Gebreab's spending habits were much more, than what his salary would allow. He also noticed that once they started drinking, Gebreab had no qualm about paying every round.

When Araya received the information, he was not surprised. The information coincided with what he had already heard from Weldeab at the bakery. Gebreab was receiving extra income from Habtom. Nevertheless, this did not still answer the main question of why and for what purpose? The two brothers merely acknowledged the information as helpful, but nothing more.

After about a month, in December 1969, Gebreab came to the bakery and he went straight into Habtom's office. Weldeab was all ears. After five minutes, he heard an argument, whose words he couldn't properly distinguish. Then there was a loud and distinct voice, which said, "You have to give me, all of my money. This is not Alimony payment that you have to throw at me piecemeal."

Weldeab was certain that it was Gebreab's voice. Immediately after, he heard Habtom say, "Hey, speak quietly!" The voices after that were hushed and no substance could be heard.

After a while, he saw Gebreab storming out, breathing heavily, his face contorted with anger. When Habtom came out, he clearly looked angry and frustrated. He read in Habtom's face, a sign of worry and apprehension.

Weldeab gave his report to Araya, which in turn transmitted it to his brother. Tesfom was perplexed, "Wow, this is a strange riddle. This is definitely something we haven't as yet put our hands on. It also looks like they are talking about a large sum of money," said Tesfom, very concerned.

"Exactly! Apart from the amount of money, have you also noticed something else that is important?" asked Araya.

Tesfom was confused, "What do you mean? What something else?"

"Well, the fact that instead of Habtom having the upper-hand, in this case, if he can shout at him, it looks like Gebreab has an upper-hand on Habtom!" said Araya.

"Oh my God! I hadn't completely seen it from that perspective! You are absolutely right! So, the mystery is why and how is Gebreab able to have a clout on Habtom! Right?" asked Tesfom.

"Exactly right! As a rule, you would expect the power to reside with Habtom, not the other way around."

'Then you guys are at a critical stage. Sooner or later this thing might burst at its seams; Gebreab might blow it. If that is so, then you have to follow up much more closely than before. Since both are doing a great job, see to it that they are properly remunerated," said Tesfom.

"No problem with that. I will see to it immediately," Araya assured his brother.

"Great then. Continue as planned," Tesfom said, concluding the discussion.

* 15 *

By now, Tekleab and Gebreab had become very close friends. They were going out together drinking and having a great time every weekend. It was a Saturday in the month of January 1970 and that night, Gebreab had drunk more than his usual. It was when he was in such a condition that he divulged an important piece of information that shocked Tekleab.

Suddenly Gebreab said, "That bastard Habtom thinks he can cheat me out of the money he owes me! I will show him!" he said, shaking his head and slurring his words.

"You mean, Habtom owes you money?" Tekleab grabbed the opportunity and asked an innocent looking probing question.

"Of course, he does! Instead of giving me my money in one go, he keeps throwing it at me in little crumbs. He is really frustrating me!" said Gebreab, with threat in his voice.

"Then he owes you a large amount of money?" asked Tekleab, throwing in another innocent looking question.

"Of course, it is a lot of money!" said Gebreab.

"Wow, that is amazing. He being richer, I would have expected him to lend you money, not the other way around," said Tekleab, again probing but also careful lest Gebreab suspect something.

"No! It was not money that I had lent him. It is part of my share for a business deal we handled together. As you know, you can't manage life with only one source of income. Unlike us, those who only possess one source of income, have already perched and settled at home early, just like chickens!" said Gebreab, roaring with laughter at his own joke.

"Or you have to have sisters like mine, who regularly send you money from abroad," said Tekleab, joining in the laughter heartily.

Tekleab wanted to strike the iron while it was hot, so he quickly added a follow-up question. "So, the money Habtom owes you is from before, when he was still in the factory, right? If that is so, I think you are right to be very angry,"

"No, No. It is much more recent. It is money he owes me since he left the factory. I am positive I will get my money either way, by hook or by crook!" said Tekleab threateningly. Then immediately, he waved at the bartender instructing her to give them another round of beer.

When she arrived with the drinks, Gebreab said, "What is happening with you these days? Are you trying to avoid me? Now allow me to buy you a drink."

That was the end of the subject. Tekleab had wanted to know much more, but he didn't want to push his luck. He didn't want Gebreab to suspect anything, so he didn't raise it again that night. On Monday, Tekleab submitted his report to Araya.

* 16 *

Araya called and asked Tesfom to come straight from the bank, so they could urgently discuss the important information he had received. As soon as Tesfom arrived, Araya recounted Tekleab's full report.

When Araya was finished, Tesfom said, "Oh my God, what kind of a mysterious and complicated riddle is this? From Tekleab's report, what I understand is that Habtom and Gebreab's secret deal is not from the time when we were working together, but rather after we went our separate ways. The second point is that this payment is not for something Gebreab will do in the future; it is payment for something he has already done and delivered. Am I right up to this point?" asked Tesfom.

"Yes, you are right," Araya assured his brother.

"Well, the conclusion we can derive from this information is that, though this deal between them could be something illegal, I don't think it is something that pertains to us. If that's the case, I don't see the need to follow this any further," said Tesfom.

Araya was taken aback by Tesfom's unexpected conclusion, "Come on, Tesfom! Why are you in such a rush to brush this off?

There is a possibility that what you are saying might be correct, but to stop before we are 100% certain what this is all about, is something I will not agree to. Gebreab seems to trust Tekleab 100% and has already started to confess things willingly. We seem to be very close and Habtom and Gebreab seem to be at a breaking point. We have invested immense time and resources and we have high stakes in this. There is no way we can drop and abandon this now!" said Araya firmly.

'Well, why should we invest further time, attention and resources in something that does not pertain to us?" asked Tesfom.

"We can only say that when we are a 100% certain that the issue does not pertain to us. I have also told you repeatedly that even if I couldn't put my finger on it, I have a strong feeling that there is more to this than what we presently know!" said Araya firmly.

"Ok, Ok Araya. I really don't see it that way, but since you feel so strongly about it, go ahead," said Tesfom, standing up and adding, "It is already late, why don't we call it a night?"

"OK, go ahead. I will follow you soon," said Araya.

When Tesfom left, Araya sank into deep thought. A year had already passed since he had the strong feeling that refused to go away. Though his hunch was strong, he kept it only to himself. He couldn't even tell the father he respected and the brother he loved. He was afraid that if he were to tell them, they would consider his theory rubbish and refuse to believe him.

Let alone convince others with his arguments, the truth was that he hadn't even convinced himself with any tangible evidence. The only thing he had was his hunch and gut feeling. It was on this basis that during the cleaning and rehabilitation process, he had insisted that nothing be thrown away without his knowledge.

From early childhood, his father used to tell him, "*We should listen to our feelings and senses very carefully. This does not of course mean we should be guided only by our feelings, but that we should give them time and due attention.*" He told himself that might be the reason why he had faithfully listened to his feelings and followed his hunch up to now.

His attention shifted towards the things that he had salvaged from the ashes and in particular to the one that he had been keeping carefully in his office drawer. He opened his drawer, looked it and asked the inanimate object for the 1000th time, "Might you have a role to play in this mystery?"

He didn't wait for an answer from the inanimate object, but answered his own question with a hope, "Don't worry, it won't be long; in the very near future, we will find out if you had a role or not!"

He became conscious and realized that he was talking to himself. He immediately rose from his table, closed the office and strode from the factory with his head down, immersed in deep thought.

CHAPTER 8
REVELATION

FOUR MONTHS HAD already passed since Tekleab and Weldeab were assigned to follow Habtom and Gebreab. They had already collected much information on what was going on between the two of them, but they still did not possess the vital answer that could crack the case. The remaining unanswered questions were: Why is Habtom paying money to Gebreab? How and why is Habtom allowing Gebreab to have an upper hand? How and why is Habtom uncharacteristically tolerating Gebreab's shouts and abuse?

Tesfom was by this time completely ignoring the issue. He felt it was none of their business and following it was a waste of time and resources. He had stopped asking Araya for new developments, and as far as he was concerned, the case was dead and closed. On the other hand, Araya's waking hours and attention were consumed by the case. His strong feeling that there was more to the case did not diminish. On the contrary, it was getting stronger by the day. He therefore pursued the case with vigor.

On Sunday morning, February 1, 1970, Araya got a call at home. The voice said, "We have to meet today!"

"Why, is it something urgent? Can't it wait until Monday?" asked Araya.

"No! It can't wait until Monday!" said the man, with urgency in his voice.

"If you say so, all right. Why don't you come home, so we can talk in private," said Araya?

"Good. I will be there in an hour," said the voice.

"Great, I will wait for you," said Araya.

As soon as he put down the phone, Araya sank into deep thought. He was certain that if it was not extremely important, he wouldn't call him at home. He prayed and wished that the information Tekleab was carrying would be the key that would finally settle the issue once and for all. He knew that any new crucial information would either bury the issue forever or shed light on the mysterious relationship. Either way, he was sure he would finally have peace of mind and closure.

Tekleab arrived on time. After exchanging greetings and pleasantries, Araya launched the urgent issue. "Initially when you called, I was worried, lest something was wrong. I relaxed after noticing that you were calm, but because you said it is urgent, I am in a hurry to hear what it is," said Araya, not hiding his curiosity.

"If it was not urgent, I wouldn't have called at home and on a Sunday. Yesterday, I barely slept three hours. We were out with Ghebreab the whole night," said Tekleab.

"Aha, ok," said Araya, trying to hide his anxiety.

"Saturday morning at work, Gebreab suggested that we go out that evening. He promised we were going to have a great night. At first, we ate a great dinner, and then we started going from one bar to the next, drinking and having a great time. We started to get high," said Tekleab.

Araya was anxious and thus interrupted him: "And then?" What Araya really wanted to say was, "Come on please, skip the introduction, get on with it."

Tekleab was quick to read Araya's body language and sense of anxiety. As if on que, he plunged straight into the main issue. "At about 2 am, Gebreab was totally drank and started boasting about how smart and great he was. After a while, he changed the subject to Habtom and suddenly said, "You know that in truth, Habtom is much better than the others. At least he shares with you whatever spoils he collects, and he tries to pay for your services. Those people on the other hand are miserly. They are the kind who never allow themselves or others a chance to have something on the side! I hate them with a passion!" reported Tekleab. He paused to catch his breath.

"I wanted to be a 100% certain. So, I asked him, "Who are you referring to?"

"Who else? The devils, Tesfom and Araya! But it is ok, at the end, I got them where it really hurts! I really got them!' boasted Gebreab, clenching his teeth."

Tekleab said, "I immediately asked, 'How'?"

"He said, "When they were looking down on people, because they were factory owners, I blew it up and made sure that they had only a factory in name," he said, as a simple matter of fact.

"Whaat?!" asked Araya, edging closer to the edge of the chair.

"I was shocked too. Still, I wanted to be sure and asked him, "What do you mean?"

"He shouted, "I burnt it down! Yes, I set it in a bonfire!"

"Whaat? Whaat?" asked Araya again, nearly getting up from his chair, incredulous at what he was hearing.

"Yes! That is what he told me! Mind you, I was also high, but that shock immediately sobered me up. I couldn't believe my ears!" said Tekleab, finally feeling better that he was able to share the unbelievable information.

"Are you a 100% certain that he told you, he put fire to the factory?" Araya asked.

"Of course, I am a 100% sure. He didn't say it once, he repeated it many times." He even added, "After doing all this for him, even that bastard Habtom is refusing to give me my money. If he does not behave and pay up, I will also punish him and show him who I am!" he told me.

"Are you also sure that he said, 'After doing all this for him, Habtom is refusing to pay me according to our agreement?'" Araya asked again, hoping that he might finally have an explanation for that gnawing feeling of suspicion that had plagued him for over a year.

"I am not only sure; I am a 100% certain!" said Tekleab confidently.

Araya was not satisfied. He still asked, "Mind you, you were both drunk. How can you be 100% sure?"

"Don't even doubt it for a moment! When I drink, I get high, I become jolly, I laugh and joke a lot, but I am always in control of my senses. I always clearly remember the place, the time and what exactly was said! Gebreab is not like me. I have observed that on many occasions, whenever we drink a lot and Gebreab gets really drank, the next day, he can't remember anything of the previous night. After a certain point, he doesn't even remember which bars we frequented and who we met," said Tekleab.

Araya wanted more information about Gebreab's habits and unique characteristics, so he encouraged Tekleab to continue by saying, "Aha, and then?"

"Whenever we drink in excess, the next day, we talk about it. Where we went, whom we met and what we did. When he is totally drunk, he frankly tells me he remembers nothing. He then asks me to tell him everything. He listens with amazement and incredulity. The interesting thing about him is that, when he is in that state and talking, he completely looks normal. Anyone present on the scene would think he is in total control of his faculties. So, don't worry about this. I know him very well," said Tekleab with certainty.

"Wow! That is incredible! I doubt Tesfom will ever believe this," said Araya.

"Let alone Tesfom, who was not there, at first, it was also difficult for me to process!" said Tekleab.

"I can understand your feelings. To be honest, concerning the fire, even before we started this follow up, I always had a sense of something," said Araya.

It was Tekleab's turn to be surprised, "What? You mean throughout the follow up, you had suspected something like this?"

"No! Not directly! Since we were still reeling from the fire and limping financially, we just wanted to make sure that we wouldn't be hit with any kind of sabotage. Though this was the whole idea of the follow up, I don't know how or why, but my subconscious had other expectations," said Araya.

Araya suddenly changed the subject and asked, "Do you by any chance know Weldeab's shoe size?"

Tekleab was confused. He didn't understand what Araya was talking about. So, he said, "What?"

Araya started to say, "Shoe number...,"

Tekleab interrupted him, "I have heard your question. It is only because you suddenly shifted gear, I was taken aback. Honestly, I really don't know his shoe size. Why are you asking me this?" asked Tekleab with curiosity.

"It has to do with feelings I have had for a long time. I have salvaged a few things from the fire and I have curiosity about some of them. Bring me his size. If it has a relationship, then I will tell you," Araya promised.

"No problem, I will do that. Also, if you don't mind, I want to know what the plan is going forward? I want to know and be clear about what our relationship with Gebreab is going to be," asked Tekleab.

"Wow, I was just about to come to that point. The point you have raised is extremely important. It could positively or negatively affect everything we have been doing up to now. I am sure you understand that if we become certain that this accident could be an arson, then we will definitely go to the law to try to prove it and seek justice," said Araya seriously.

"Yes, I think that is obvious. It is only right that people who have been wronged seek justice," said Tekleab, nodding in agreement.

"You should continue your relationship with Gebreab as if nothing has happened. It is important that he doesn't realize that the information we now possess did not come from you. We will try to pretend that we got the information on our own. Unless circumstances force us, we will try to protect the source of our information up to the end!" said Araya.

"That is very good. I was slightly worried about that issue," said Tekleab, breathing a sigh of relief.

"In the next few days, you will have to ascertain that Weldeab doesn't remember the information he divulged. It will be extremely helpful, if we know that he doesn't remember anything at all. That will mean he will not suspect you at all," said Araya.

"I am actually certain of that. Still, I guess it doesn't hurt to doubly ascertain to establish the incident. After all, he has divulged a crucially huge secret," said Tekleab.

"Absolutely! In addition, I want you to understand that as much as you are looking after our interests, we will also try to look after your welfare and protect you up to the end. Also, you should rest assured that at the right time, you will be remunerated appropriately for your services and dedication," Araya assured Tekleab.

"I have no doubt of that. I have full trust in you and Tesfom," said Tekleab, relieved and assured.

"Now more than ever, we will need extreme patience and caution. We are at a very critical stage - it is a make-or-break point. So, utmost caution will be required. So that no one suspects anything, from now on we will only correspond while we are at work and through work related errands," said Araya.

"I understand, that is a very good idea," said Tekleab.

"Last but not least is the question of secrecy. No one should know about this, apart from you, Tesfom and me. Secrecy is vital to the success of all this," said Araya, and after a while he added, "It is also important for your safety."

"Don't worry at all. I understand everything. Utmost secrecy is important to all of us. I will not try to approach you outside of the factory. Today was an exception, because I felt the information was exceptional and urgent," Tekleab assured Araya.

"Today you made the right decision. I am happy that you insisted," said Araya, indicating that he had finished.

"If we have nothing more, let me leave you," said Tekleab, standing up. He left soon after.

* 2 *

When Tekleab left, Araya sank into deep thought. He started thinking about what the wider ramifications of the information Tekleab brought would mean and what the positive and negative results and consequences would be. He understood that if an allegation of arson could be proved, then that might eventually solve their financial problems. On the other hand, he also knew that this was not going to be an easy feat. It would require immense patience, time, effort and perseverance. Furthermore, he also understood that it was going to be complicated, messy and recriminatory.

This realization slightly dimmed his earlier euphoria and temperament. He knew that nothing would be solved in a stroke. Araya shook his head to clear his mind, but then he reprimanded himself for not enjoying the moment and the success at hand. Talking to himself, he asked, "Why are you doing this to yourself? Why do you have to spoil an important occasion and milestone by your pessimistic scenarios?" he scolded himself. After that, he got up and went out.

Araya wanted to share the new revelation with Tesfom as soon as possible, so he went to their residence straight away. As soon as he arrived, Medhn told him, "You just missed him. He ate breakfast and left a while ago. Since it is Sunday, he will be there the whole day and will not be back until midnight. He has completely slid into his old habits. I pleaded with you many times that we confront him and talk to him, but you refused."

"I didn't refuse Medhn. I just chose to wait. I explained to you at the time that he was already under extreme pressure and strain. I believed talking to him might be counterproductive, since it would place an undue burden on him," said Araya carefully, so Medhn wouldn't notice his anxiety and urgency to meet his brother.

"Oh, how stupid of me! I am just blabbering without even asking if everything is, ok? How come you wanted to see him on a Sunday? You never come on a Sunday," Medhn asked.

"Everything is ok. I just wanted to see him about something important that is work-related," Araya said unconvincingly. He knew how much Medhn was intelligent and perceptive and that she missed nothing. So, he was sure, she would see through his excuses, but would still accept his explanation, so as not to make him uncomfortable.

"I sure hope everything is ok. So, if you need to see him now, you have no other option but go to where 'Mohammed' is," said Medhn smiling.

"Yes, you are right," said Araya, and stood up.

"I wouldn't ask you to sit down and take something, because I can see your condition and of course, you are not just any guest," said Medhn standing up.

He had guessed right, Medhn understood that he had a lot in his mind. Without showing a smile, Araya smiled within himself. He chose to respond to the second part of Medhn's statement, "Of course, if I needed anything, I would ask myself. Ok, I will leave you now," Araya said and left.

When Araya left Medhn, he was immersed in deep thought. He feared that Tesfom would not accept or believe the information Tekleab brought; he knew he was going to give him a hard time. On his way, he tried to line up logical arguments that would convince his brother.

* 3 *

Tesfom and his three friends were already in Lalibela hotel. They had already started playing cards. It is mostly during their card game that they often poke fun at each other, tell jokes and anecdotes. Tesfom was holding an imported Heineken beer, while the rest had the local Melotti beer.

After a while, a person by the name of *Hailom* joined them. Hailom was one of Tesfom's closest school friends, who had remained loyal to his friendship. He was a disciplined person who drank in moderation and who stood fast about the hours he kept. It had already been a while since he was introduced to Tesfom's friends. He used to join them every now and then, because he enjoyed their company and their jokes.

However, he still kept his friendship with them at an arm's length. Whenever he joined them, he loved and enjoyed his time with them, but he couldn't join them as he wished, because he knew that playing cards and drinking into the wee hours of the night was part of the bargain. He decided to forego the so-called 'enjoyment,' a long time ago, after which he stood firm by his principles and decision.

It was Tesfom who saw him first and welcomed him warmly, "Oh Hailom, welcome. Come on, please have a sit. It has been two weeks since we last met at work."

Hailom, while greeting everyone said, "Yes, you are right, it has been a while. Didn't Medhn tell you? I passed through your home one day, but didn't find you," he said, sitting down.

"Oh yes, you are right. She did actually tell me, but I had completely forgotten about it," said Tesfom.

"When I was coming in, I could see that you guys had what seemed like a hot discussion. I think I interrupted an interesting topic. Please continue," said Hailom.

"Please Hailom, don't ask them to continue. These days they

have been directing their stick towards me, without respite. If you encourage them, I will hold you responsible for victimizing me for the second time in one sitting," said Tesfom.

"Man! If Tesfom is so scared of it, then it should definitely be interesting. I want to hear it, come on guys," begged Hailom.

They started recounting the chat and by the time they were finished, Hailom was tearing with laughter. They then continued to club Tesfom for a while. After a while, they began talking about women.

Then out of nowhere, Berhe thrust the conversation into a new direction. He said, "Honestly speaking, I don't like it at all, when women tell me what to do and what not to do. In fact, it always rubs me the wrong way!"

"Well, the important point is whether what the woman is saying is right or wrong. If it is wrong, then you have every right to be annoyed," said Hailom.

"No, the important point is not whether it is right or wrong. The important point is you should do it by yourself and not follow the command of a woman," insisted Berhe.

"If you are doing it by yourself, she will have no reason to talk to you. Secondly, why do you have to consider your wife's request as a command?" asked Hailom.

"How else can I take it? And mind you, once you start accepting their orders, women's tyranny has no limit; you are done forever!" said Berhe.

"He is absolutely right," shouted both Werede and Zere'.

"Well, if what she is saying is correct, instead of considering it as an order, why don't you take as advice or as an attempt to help you see right from wrong? I don't of course mean that you should permit her to push you around, when you are in the right," said Hailom.

Tesfom had been following the exchange without a comment. "Since I have been the target of the stick the whole morning, let me say a few words. I hope these guys won't crucify me again," he said, looking at his friends and smiling.

"I don't think you have to fear anything now, you have your friend by your side," said Werede, smiling back.

"Do you guys remember the answer I give you whenever you repeatedly try to belittle me? I mean whenever you say, 'You are scared of your wife'?" asked Tesfom, looking at each of his three friends.

"Who can always remember Medhn's every word that you quote, ad nauseum?" Then he quickly added, "To which one in particular, are you referring to?" asked Werede wryly.

"I repeatedly tell you that it is not her muscles or strength that frighten me. It is her truthfulness, fairness and clear logical rationale," said Tesfom.

It was Werede who hurriedly said, "Please Tesfom, spare us; give us a break! You have repeated this a thousand times! We are sick and tired of it. Don't deceive yourself; a woman will always be a woman! Once you give her an edge, you are finished. Their tyranny is forever. Don't fool yourself with their logic or brains," and after a little pause added, "I am serious!" as if his seriousness was in any doubt.

"Werede is absolutely right! That is exactly what I was saying. Once they have you in their grips, there is no way out!" said Berhe, encouraged by his friend.

Instead of responding to them directly, Tesfom chose to say, "Whenever she brings waterproof logical arguments, I find it hard to rebut her rationale. I don't know what to say to her."

"Oh, come on, don't be a fool Tesfom. If you give her too much leverage, then you are finished. Whenever she brings up such arguments, just tell her, I don't want to listen to another word," said Werede.

Hailom who had been listening to the exchange with interest and concentration said, "Well dear Werede, if you do that, you are in essence admitting defeat. You are accepting that her argument and logic is water-proof and impenetrable."

"That is not defeat at all; that is actually what brings triumph. Whenever she starts asserting herself and tries to be too smart, she should be told to shut-up!" shouted Werede.

Hailom was displeased and disappointed with Werede's comments. However, he kept his cool and patiently said, *"Well, this is equivalent to bullying her with your brute force, while she is right. Brute force is not an instrument for a person who is confident in himself and his principles. Threatening anyone, including our children and wives with force is a sign of weakness and lack of confidence. In the short run, they might obey us temporarily, because we possess brute strength. But this will not mean they are doing our bidding, because they respect us and want to follow us, but because they are frightened of us. In fact, they even consider us weaklings and look down upon us. If we want to be looked upon as head of a household or be emulated as an exemplary leader, then we should earn respect and not garner fear. Respect is not gained by force and fear. Respect is what other people willingly bestow on us, because we deserve it. It is a reward we earn, because we are loved and respected, not because we are feared!"*

"It looks like our friend Tesfom raised this subject today on purpose. I see that you were confident that your friend attorney Hailom would back you up!" said Zere', laughing and pointing his finger at Tesfom.

"Seriously though Hailom, do you realize that you are painting women as perfect?" said Werede.

"Listen guys, don't misunderstand what I am saying. I am not saying women are perfect or don't have problems. I am not even saying you have to accept or do whatever they say or suggest. Although we have many similarities, it is important to understand that we also have many natural differences in feelings, tendencies, desires and priorities. As much as us, they also have their own inherent shortcomings and weaknesses," said Hailom.

"So, there you go. If that is so, then what are you trying to say?" asked Zere'.

'What I am basically trying to say is, when a woman is making unacceptable and unreasonable demands, don't listen to her, reject her demand outright. However, whenever she is making logical and reasonable demands, accept it with grace. It is not right to oppress her and her outlook and judgment." said Hailom.

"The problem with that is, once they find an opening, they will exploit it without limitation," said Zere'.

"Well, my dear Zere', that is where good judgement is required. You should differentiate when she is right and wrong. Then you will know when to make a stand and when to give in. *Otherwise, if we do not allow and promote justice in our individual small households, the repercussion is huge. We should be conscious and wary of the kind of message we convey to the children and youngsters that will be tomorrow's citizens!*" said Hailom seriously.

"Man, Hailom, slow down!! How did you fast track to the subject of children?" said Werede.

"*Well, to be honest, this is not a subject that is restricted to children and women alone. To tell you the truth, if we can't maintain the tenets of justice and democracy in that little domain of ours, we call home, then how can we expect it to be disseminated and to flourish in communities and within countries? If we think and proceed in this manner, then we should realize that we will have no right to complain about human rights violations or corrupt and autocratic officials and governments!*" said Hailom, trying to remind them what the wider consequences of their actions were.

None of them had the courage to face the challenge Hailom threw. They did not possess the faculty to question and challenge their own actions. Thus, they refrained from debating Hailom's statement. Instead, they chose to thrust their argument at what they envisaged was women's "weak spot."

Werede therefore, ran away from the serious subject and decided to try from another angle. He said, "Listen Hailom, most women are led by emotion rather than logic and rationality. So, don't try to portray them as perfect by putting them on a pedestal."

"Well, where can you get perfection? I agree that even they, just like us, are far from perfect," said Hailom.

"Like us? Come on, Hailom. At least as we grow older, we become calmer, mellower and more peaceful. Women on the other hand, as they grow older, become less calm, more on edge and aggressive!" shouted Zere'.

"I am not sure about that sweeping statement, but even if we assume it is true, there could be an explanation to it. *Women take responsibility for family and children from an early age. They spend their entire lives under dire and oppressive and unjust conditions; always giving, providing and sacrificing for their parents, families and children. They do their jobs in silence, carrying the oppression of men and society and the stress and weight of life on their backs. When they are at the end of their journey, after having given their all to family and society, what is wrong if they start thinking about themselves and their rights?"* said Hailom.

Instead of confronting Hailom's argument head-on, Werede decided to go on a tangent by using his gift of story-telling. "Listen guys," shouted Werede, "Let me tell you a joke I heard very recently, which literally explains the point we are trying to make here!"

They all turned their attention towards him. "It is said that the devil enters a man's body through his head. By devil, I mean the characteristic which makes men impatient, violent, unjust and unfair," said Werede smiling. He continued, "So, when a man is young, because the devil is in his head, he is constantly violent, impatient, unjust and unfair - in short he is a devil. As he advances in age, the devil moves from his head down to his chest, then to his stomach, the buttocks, thighs and by the time he becomes around 50-60 years old, the devil goes out through his feet. So, when men advance in age, they become mellower, calmer, more peaceful and good natured," said Werede.

All of them roared with laughter. They were all amazed at the originality of the joke and laughed heartily. They were still laughing and shaking their heads, when Werede shouted again, "Listen guys, there is more to it!" When he had their whole attention, he said, "When a woman is young, the devil enters into her body through her feet. So, because the devil is only in her extremities, a woman is peaceful, patient and responsible - in short, she is angelic when she is young! That is why she is able to accept and resist men's satanic behavior and uphold her responsibility of taking care of her family and raising her children, despite all the odds against her. As she advances in age, the devil also advances up into her legs, thighs, buttocks, stomach and chest. Finally, by the time she is roughly 45-55 years old, the devil reaches her head. That is when she becomes less patient, less peaceful, but stronger and more assertive and violent. After some years, eventually, the devil escapes out through her head."

Hailom was the first to recover from his laugh and say, "It is an interesting anecdote. However, even if it were true, then I guess we should say it is good for society, that it is that way."

"What are you trying to say?" asked Werede, who did not understand the point Hailom was trying to make.

"Well, I mean when women and men are young and barely starting family responsibility, it is good that women are not as violent and as irresponsible as men. If they were, there would be no one in the family structure to make the sacrifices necessary to hold the family together and raise children responsibly. That they accept their responsibility selflessly under all oppressive conditions and finally hold the family structure together is an extremely admirable human quality. So, we should raise our hats to them for their sacrifice, rather than putting them down. But I will maintain that I am not trying to claim they are perfect," said Hailom.

"Come on, Hailom, how can you even talk about perfection? Don't you know that women are never satisfied with what they have? They always focus on what they don't have!" said Werede.

"Well, I think that is generally human nature, and if it is a weakness, it is human weakness and not confined to women. However, if we want to determine which gender is generally afflicted by this characteristic, we will need a well-represented study," said Hailom.

Again, smart aleck Werede, deciding to use one of his ploys shouted, "Listen guys, I have an anecdote which fits this discussion perfectly!"

"Oh my God, when this guy starts, there is no stopping him," said Tesfom smiling and then added, "Ok, go ahead Werede Aerkey."

All of them again turned their attention to Werede and he began, "It is said, that when men and women were created, they were given two pockets each. One pocket on the right side and the other on the left. The right pocket was supposed to keep and preserve all the good things and memories they encountered in their lives, while the left pocket was for keeping score of all the bad things that happened to them."

"Oh my God, you are impossible," said Hailom smiling, still not sure where Werede was going.

"Wait, wait, the best is yet to come!" shouted Werede and added, "It is said that man's two pockets are full of holes, which means that man does not have a reliable pocket where he can effectively keep and preserve either the bad or the good. Every event, incident and memory fall out through his pockets and is lost forever, with nothing remaining."

He paused for a moment for emphasis, and when he was about to continue, Berhe, who had become impatient, asked, "How about women?"

"I am coming to that, which is the best part. One of women's pockets is also full of holes, but the second is intact!" said Werede.

As soon as he said that, Berhe could not wait and asked, "Which pocket is intact?"

"Come on Berhe, wait, be patient, he is going to tell us soon," said Tesfom.

"I am first going to tell you that it is the right pocket that is full of holes. This means everything good that has happened to her, every blessing, every positive memory is not kept or preserved. However, the left pocket, which stores the memory of every hurt inflicted on her and every bad thing that had happened to her, is intact. This means, in short, a woman never forgets any misfortune, sorrow or harm inflicted! End of story!" shouted Werede.

As soon as Werede finished, most of them started to talk, laugh, joke and comment at the same time. For a moment, there was utter pandemonium and shouting and laughing. As soon it subsided, it was Hailom who said, "Wow, Tesfom, these friends of yours are really impossible. They are armed ahead of time with a joke and an anecdote that goes with every argument!" he said, still laughing heartily.

"Absolutely Hailom, you still don't fully know these guys," said Tesfom smiling.

"Thank you Werede, those were very interesting and entertaining anecdotes", said Hailom smiling. "However, I notice that you also selectively pick up the stories that give men the edge and leave out the rest. I noticed that you didn't comment on the fact that we men squander both of the pockets we were given. Anyway, though the subject we have been discussing is women, there isn't a single woman representative among us. That is not fair; if they were here, they would have defended themselves," Hailom concluded.

"So? What are you driving at? It is always a problem to be a lawyer," said Zere', smiling.

"I just meant to say, since women are not represented in this argument, there is no way they can defend themselves and present their case. So, it is difficult to arrive at any fair conclusion. However, if you are willing, we can invite them and then we will conclude the argument seriously and properly," said Hailom jokingly.

"Listen Hailom, are we missing anything here? Have you, without our knowledge, by any chance been appointed an attorney for a Women's Association?" asked Werede with a smile.

"Wait Werede! Allow me to respond to Hailom's last statement. My dear Hailom, as far as we are concerned, women are already well represented here. Instead of W/ro Medhn, there is W/ro Tesfom here and, as for the rest, they have you as their attorney," said Zere', roaring with laughter.

All of them joined in the laughter. After it subsided, Hailom started to respond, but Berhe interrupted him. "Tesfom, come on, you had better reign in this lawyer friend of yours, otherwise he is going to drown us in unending argument. You know what that will entail, right? It will mean wasting our valuable time intended for our card game and drinks! Even from the very beginning, it was a mistake to engage in argument with a professional lawyer!" said Berhe, smiling widely.

"You guys are better than any lawyer. Actually, I had never intended to stay this long, but the discussion was interesting and entertaining. I have overstayed," said Hailom, standing up.

Tesfom stood up, saying, "Let me see him off." Hailom bid everyone farewell and left.

Tesfom came back and sat down. They ordered new drinks and restarted their card game. They were all relaxed, because they knew it was Sunday and they had all the time in the world to enjoy themselves - the whole day, the whole evening and into the night.

* 4 *

From Tesfom's house, Araya went straight to Lalibela hotel. On arrival, he could see that the whole group was already assembled and that they had already started their card game. As soon as he set foot in the door, one of Tesfom's friends saw him.

He saw the friend talk to his brother. Tesfom instantly turned around and got up and asked, "Are you ok?" with surprise and worry.

Araya said, "I am ok," and then proceeded to greet Tesfom's friends. He noticed they were still on beer, but he knew that, as the day wore on, they would pass on to gin and whiskey. All of them in unison invited him to sit down.

"I am sorry, I have to go. I will need your permission to take Tesfom for a while," said Araya.

"No problem with that, as long as you don't take him away for good. Don't grant him an opportunity to escape, before he pays his due for what he has already lost," said Werede smiling.

"I will make sure he comes back as soon as possible," said Araya, smiling. Araya and Tesfom went out.

* 5 *

As soon as they were out, Tesfom again asked, "Are you Ok? Is everything ok? Has anything come up?"

"There is a new development that pertains to the factory. It is important and urgent. We need to talk about it now. I had passed by your house before coming here but didn't catch you." Araya said seriously.

"Is it that important that it can't wait until Monday? Do we have to necessarily talk about it on a Sunday and now?" asked Tesfom, slightly relieved that it was not something serious and yet not happy about the disruption to his Sunday schedule.

"Yes, it is! If it were not, you know that I wouldn't have come here!" said Araya firmly.

Tesfom knew his brother wouldn't use that tone for nothing, so he didn't question his brother further. Instead, he said, "Ok, if that is the case, then let me tell my friends that I might be detained for a while," and left.

When his brother left, Araya sank deep in thought. He was pondering deeply, looking at the ground with his forehead furrowed. Tesfom's words brought him back, "Ok, then let's go. Where will we go?" asked Tesfom.

"I think it is best if we go to our office," answered Araya quickly.

They went straight to the factory. As soon as they got to their office and before they even sat down, Tesfom asked, "What kind of important information did you get?"

"It is better if you sit down. It is an unbelievable bombshell of information. While drunk, Gebreab has divulged that he set fire to the factory!" said Araya.

"What? What? Come on Araya! What is wrong with you? So, the bombshell information you claim is from the mouth of a drunkard, while drunk?" shouted Tesfom, disappointed.

Araya was taken aback, still he coolly and patiently said, "Please, allow me to first tell you the details of the incident and then you can judge for yourself."

"Ok, go ahead," said Tesfom skeptically. He agreed to listen out of courtesy and respect for his brother, but his mind was nearly already made up.

Araya told him the new information from A to Z. When he was finished, Tesfom's skepticism was clearly shaken. He said, "Wow! What is this thing? This is unbelievable! Have you accepted this information as plausible and reasonable?"

"Well, yes, I am totally convinced, because the information solves the riddle, we have been unable to crack up to this point. It provides answers to the three basic questions we had, namely: What is the reason for their close relationship? Why is Habtom paying money to Gebreab? Why does Gebreab have the upper hand over Habtom and why is Habtom letting him get away with it?"

"I think I can agree with the conclusions you have drawn. The difficult part for me is, how can we accept any information reported by a drunkard as reliable?" said Tesfom.

It was Araya's turn to say, "What is wrong with you Tesfom? Don't you remember the Tigrinya proverb, "*Sekramsi Nay Lbu Yizareb,"* meaning "A drunk speaks from his heart." Another important point is, if Gebreab had blabbered like a drunkard about some nonsense that had no connection with anything we knew, then you would have a point. However, what Gebreab has revealed is not only the missing information we have been seeking for a very long time, but is also an exact key that fits the door we have been trying to unlock!" said Araya on the verge of irritation.

"I really don't know," said Tesfom, shaking his head, still reluctant to accept Araya's argument.

"Let me add something else. Do you remember asking me, a week after the fire, why I looked depressed and sullen?" asked Araya.

"Yes, I do," said Tesfom, not sure about where his brother was going.

"Do you also remember telling me that some of our employees had talked to you about their concerns for me; that they told you I seem to have taken this very badly; that I was going around the burnt part of the factory at least ten times daily and that eventually it might go to my head?"

"Yes, yes, I clearly remember. You had me really worried then," said Tesfom, recalling the condition.

"Well, to tell you the truth, right from the very beginning, I had not believed the fire was as an accident. I had serious doubts. I didn't dare talk to you then, because I had nothing concrete and if I had done so, you would have considered me crazy. Moreover, I pushed you hard that we assign informants to the case, because I had precisely that feeling and suspicion!" said Araya.

"What? You mean, you had serious suspicions since then? Wow, Araya, why didn't you tell me?" said Tesfom.

"Well, I couldn't, because I had nothing concrete. You would have laughed at me. Look at how skeptical you are even now," said Araya. Suddenly he seemed as if he had remembered something. He stood up and strode to his table. Tesfom did not understand what he was doing. He looked at him bewildered.

"I have something else which will amaze you," said Araya. He leaned towards his table and opened the third drawer and brought out a half burnt plastic sandal (*Shida).* He delicately poised the sandal in his left fingers and came back to the table. Then pointing his right finger at the sandal, Araya asked, "Do you see this?"

"What is that thing?" Tesfom asked still, confused.

"I found this half burnt plastic sandal (*Shida*) in the ashes, a few days after the fire. Since then, I have been talking to it and asking it every day, "Might you have some secret role in the fire? Today, I believe it is ready to unveil its secrets," said Araya.

"I don't get it - how? Can you tell me the relationship of this thing with what we are talking about?" asked Tesfom, still puzzled.

"Since I found it from day one, I have been asking myself the same question. I had asked around and made sure that the shoe did not belong to the guards or anyone they knew. If the fire was due to arson, could it have belonged to the perpetrator, and could it have slipped from his foot, half of it burnt by the fire and the other half saved by the rain? I have had this suspicion and theory since the day I found it," said Araya, looking at his brother, trying to decipher what impact his explanation had on his brother.

"Wow, oh my God! Oh my God! Araya, your far-sightedness and your detailed appraisal and assessment of the accident and then finally putting two and two together and coming up with a near perfect explanation is amazing and unbelievable! As your elder brother, I should have been there to lead you or at least assist you. But I was nowhere near you. I am sorry Araya Hawey, that I failed you," said Tesfom, vigorously shaking his head several times and expressing his disappointment at himself.

"Come on, Tesfom Hawey, I didn't follow these leads because I was better than you or anyone else. It is simply a matter of feeling and luck. I had this feeling that I couldn't explain and which refused to go away. That was all, nothing less, nothing more. You know it is something like what some people call the sixth sense!" said Araya, extremely relieved and happy that he had finally succeeded in convincing his brother.

"Great! I hope your sixth sense wins and we finally succeed in this. If we can nail this, it would be like hitting two birds with one stone. On the one hand, we would pay all our loans and solve our financial constraints, and on the other, that bastard Habtom might get what he deserves!" said Tesfom. For the first time, his facial features showed hope and the expectation of success.

"I sure hope so!" said Araya, much relieved.

"Ok, since we have arrived at this stage, what next?" asked Tesfom and then seemed to change his mind. Before Araya could respond, he started admonishing and reprimanding himself, by saying, "Come on Tesfom, how dare you snatch or share your brother's sole victory?" Then looking at Araya straight in the eye said, "I should rephrase my question. I should say, Ok, since YOU have arrived at this stage, what next?" said Tesfom, still feeling bad that he had played no part in the whole affair.

It was Araya's turn to say, "Come on Tesfom, please don't say that!"

"Ok, ok, then, since you seem to think about everything in detail, have you also thought about our next move?" asked Tesfom.

"Yes, I have some ideas about it, but I think it will be best if we could discuss that in detail and then decide the best course together," Araya said.

"Ok, good idea, then I guess it looks like we are going to be here the whole day. In that case, while I call my friends and tell them that I am not coming back, why don't you go ask the guards to order us some pizza and cappuccino?" said Tesfom.

"Ok, great," said Araya, standing up. As he was leaving, his face was clearly shining with a sense of victory and hope.

By the time Araya came back, Tesfom had already finished his call. They sat down. "Why don't you first tell me your initial thoughts and then we will take it from there. And also, since this is a very delicate matter, I think it is best if we keep this finding to ourselves. Neither Medhn nor father nor anyone should know about it," said Tesfom seriously.

"I was just going to say the same thing. I completely agree with you. I have already promised Tekleab that we will protect the source of our information as much as possible. I told him we will try to make it look as if we got our information in another manner," said Araya.

"In what other manner do you mean?" Tesfom asked.

"Well, I am wondering if it is possible to press charges based on circumstantial evidence and without naming our source. Is it lawful for the police to investigate and examine these suspects based on what we have? Since I really don't know much about the law and the workings of the police, I am not sure if my suggestion is viable or not," said Araya.

"Well, I think it will be best to seek professional advice. We can then proceed based on their recommendations. Any other ideas?" asked Tesfom.

"For now, and the next two weeks, let's keep this information between us, without taking any action. Let us use the time to consolidate what we have and collect information from professionals. Let us identify people and professionals who can help us with the case, either directly or indirectly," said Araya.

"I completely agree with everything you say. You are being very careful and thorough. Now let's proceed to the details," said Tesfom.

"Most of the things we have to do on the outside will have to be performed by you, since you are the one who knows important people. I will handle Tekleab and Weldeab with great caution," said Araya.

"Very good. In relation to the legal issue, I will talk to my friend Hailom. Concerning the police, I will go and see my friend Colonel *Habte*," suggested Tesfom.

"Great. As we have already agreed, you will have to inquire discreetly, without getting into details, as though you just wanted some general information," said Araya.

"Yes exactly, that is what I intend to do. Mind you, these are my friends, so when we make it official, they will know. When they find out, they might not like it that I was not forthright with them. So, I will need to tell them that at that point, we were not in possession of any substantial evidence. That should satisfy them," said Tesfom thinking aloud.

"Great, good idea," agreed Araya.

Since their whole focus was on the urgent matter at hand, they hadn't realized the time. It was already 6 pm. They had discussed everything in detail and covered every angle. Since they hadn't eaten anything except the pizza and cappuccino, they both felt extremely hungry.

It was Araya who said, "I have been on my feet since early morning so I am both tired and hungry. If we don't have anything else, I think we should call it a day and retire," he said, yawning and stretching his arms.

"We have nothing else. We can talk about anything else that comes up at any time. Talking about hunger and exhaustion, while it was you who started early this morning, even I am hungry and tired. So, let's go," said Tesfom, and then he seemed to have an idea and added, "Why don't you go home with me. We can eat together."

"No. No, it is not only about hunger. I am also very tired and I want to eat and sleep immediately after. Since I have been out the whole day, Embaba will also be waiting for me. Moreover, if I go with you at this hour, you know that Medhn misses nothing. She might think, how come they are together on a Sunday afternoon?" said Araya.

Although Tesfom only said, "Oh, ok, I guess you are right," he internally suspected that his brother's statement had two hidden meanings. He supposed Araya might be saying, "Since when do we meet on a Sunday? And since when do you go home sober on a Sunday and at this hour?" He was amazed by his brother's sensitivity and intuition, and he smiled to himself.

Araya noticed that his brother had smiled and that he was deep in thought, already far away. He asked, "How come you have already gone away and left me, even before we parted?"

Tesfom could not hold it any more. He suddenly roared with laughter.

Araya was surprised and confused, he asked, "What did I say to merit such laughter?"

Tesfom could not tell his brother the truth that it was his

two-pronged statement that made him laugh. Instead, he chose to say, "I smiled earlier because I remembered something funny my friends had recounted. Then your last statement of "You have gone away before we even parted," made me laugh," said Tesfom.

Araya was satisfied by his brother's explanation, "Oh ok," he said, smiling.

They both stood up, bid each other good night and parted.

* 6 *

It was unnatural for Tesfom to go home at that hour on a Sunday. So, while driving home, he felt uneasy. As soon as he arrived home, he saw in his children's and Medhn's eyes, face and body language something equivalent to Araya's two-pronged statement. He felt as if all of them were telling him without words, *"How come you're here at this hour? What happened? And above all, how come without the usual bulging forehead veins, glazed eyes and slurred tongue?"*

If what he thought they were thinking was true, then he knew he had no one else to blame but himself. Still, that was no consolation and he felt their unspoken words strike his soul like a whip. But also, he saw that within seconds, their body language of surprise, reaction and judgment had instantly changed into welcoming and loving smiles. He immediately matched their expressions of love and welcome, while at the same time acknowledging internally his gratefulness for their love and his blessings.

He quickly told his welcoming children, "If you change your clothes promptly, then I am going to take you out for pizza and cakes."

It was not new for his children to go out with their dad for entertainment on Saturdays, but since it was Sunday, he could see their initial surprise and astonishment. First, he saw traces of doubt, but instantly, their doubts changed to joy. The older ones smiled with happiness, while the younger ones jumped with joy; then they ran away to change.

Medhn observed the exchange silently. When the children went, he expected her to ask him what was going on or what was new. Instead, he heard her say, "Before I change, would you like to eat something quick?"

"Honestly, if it is not a problem, I am really famished and would love to eat something," said Tesfom.

"Ok, give me five minutes. Have a seat and I will bring you something," she said, running into the kitchen.

When she left, Tesfom sank into admiration of how intelligent, perceptive, thoughtful and loving his wife was. His heart felt warmth and he gave thanks for his unending blessings. He told himself, "Will the day ever come, when I will be responsible enough to repay my debts of love to her and warm her heart?"

Medhn's return woke him from his reverie and contemplation. She put the plate in front of him and said, "While you eat, let me go and change quickly, or the children will eat me alive for being late," she said, smiling.

Medhn finished changing and came back. Soon, Tesfom also finished eating. While Medhn was taking the dishes, the children, who were already waiting, begged their mom to leave the unwashed dishes on a plate and promised they would wash them on their return. Alganesh understood their urgency and agreed, so they all went out together. After a cheerful and joyous evening, they arrived back home happy and satisfied.

While changing her clothes, Medhn sank into deep thought. She started talking to herself, "It is amazing how much joy Tesfom gets from the happiness of his children and his wife. His love for me and the children is boundless. However, all that might be impossible to come to fruition with his chronic insurmountable drinking problem. Since his love is genuine though, I hope there will come a day, when we might be able to put all of that behind us. Not only for us, but especially for his sake," said Medhn, expressing her deepest wish.

Continuing her thoughts, she said, "Well, Lord, everything is possible for you!" When she realized that she was solely concentrating only on their problems, Medhn suddenly felt that she was being ungrateful and she admonished herself, "Come on Medhn, don't think only about your problems, think also about the immense other blessings you have been given and thank the Lord for them." She then kneeled down and said prayers of gratitude.

After having a great evening together, Tesfom's family slept peacefully and happily.

* 7 *

When Araya had earlier sat down with Tesfom, he had expected his brother to give him a hard time. He thought he would refuse to accept the facts and reject the findings, so he was extremely happy when his brother agreed with him without much heated argument. Thus, because he was exhausted and satisfied that he had accomplished his mission, he was confident that after eating, he would instantly sink into deep sleep.

However, when he laid down, sleep completely eluded him. The day's events started to replay in his mind and he started making plans about all the meticulous and careful plans they would need to make in the coming two weeks. After a long while, he fell into deep sleep.

In the morning, Araya got up refreshed and in a great mood. He felt as if a large weight had been lifted from his back. As soon as he arrived at work, the first thing on his agenda was to ascertain Gebreab's shoe size. He knew there was nothing he could do, except wait for Tekleab to contact him.

At about 10.00 am, Tekleab came to the office carrying factory documents, and when he left, Araya started eagerly leafing through them. True to his expectations, among the documents, he found a hand written paper with the inscription, "Shoe size 40."

When Araya read the note, he couldn't contain his joy. The half burnt plastic sandal that had been sitting in his drawer for months was size 40. After this finding, he had no doubt about Gebreab's crime.

Though he wanted to immediately transmit the information to Tesfom, he knew he couldn't. They had agreed not to talk about the matter over the phone. He reluctantly decided to wait until his brother came from the bank.

* 8 *

On Monday, February 2, 1970, Tesfom arrived at his office after a good night's rest. When he first heard of Araya's so-called "bombshell information" on Sunday, Tesfom had been very skeptical and dismissive. But after he had heard the details of the case, and after the thorough discussion that followed, he had no doubt that it was indeed a substantial revelation. He told himself, as Araya beautifully expressed it, "it was an exact key, made to unlock a heavily fortified door that they had been trying to unlock for a very long time." This expression and his happy mind-set and great mood made him smile broadly.

That morning, Tesfom didn't attend very much to the bank's tasks. For nearly the whole day he was busy enquiring and collecting information on the viability of their case. Although, there was still much more he needed to know, his first day's inquiries and the information he was able to collect were extremely encouraging. He was in a hurry to report his findings to his younger brother.

Araya was equally in a hurry to transmit his new findings to his elder brother. When they met, they greeted each other profusely, their faces glistening and their eyes smiling. Before they even sat down, Tesfom asked, "How was your day? Anything new on your end?"

Instead of responding, Araya leaned down to his table, opened his drawer and took out the half-burnt sandal with his left hand. Then pointing at it with his right hand, he said, "Well, the new progress is that the *Shida* has started to open its secrets. From now on, I am going to christen it, as the "Historic *Shida*!""

"Really? How?" asked Tesfom with curiosity.

"Gebreab's shoe size is 40. Check the *Shida* for yourself!" said Araya, and handling it like a very fragile and precious relic, handed it over to Tesfom.

Tesfom took the sandal and immediately turned it upside down, to check the number underneath. As soon as he saw the number, he showed his surprise by whistling three times and expressing his satisfaction by saying, "Wow! Wow! My God! My God! So, after all, the sixth sense is on point and is hitting the nail on the head! Congratulations! Give me five!", and he stretched out his hands and his palms and held his brother's hands tightly for several seconds.

Araya couldn't hide his happiness; He spoke with enthusiasm: "I think the case now looks like a very difficult puzzle that you encounter and fail to resolve despite your struggles and perseverance. But finally, you get lucky and find an important element that had been evading you, and from then on, everything falls into place!" He was in a joyous mood that had not been seen in months.

"Well as for me, my findings are not as stunning as yours, but nevertheless, I have found encouraging signs that our case is viable. Mind you, I got the information indirectly, without seeming interested in the issue, except as general knowledge. So, I asked two or three people if information or a confession heard from a person while drunk could be considered to be important evidence, or is it outright dismissed?"

"Aha, ok," said Araya.

"I was told that if the material is inconsequential information that has no relationship with anything, then it can be dismissed simply as a drunkard's blubbering. However, if it has any bearing on something that has happened in the past or present that is pertinent to a relationship between the drunkard and persons he considers enemies, then the drunkard could be interrogated and even accused," said Tesfom.

"Wow, that is very good!" said Araya, his face glowing with hope and satisfaction.

"So, since we are here, what do you suggest we do next?" asked Tesfom.

"Well, honestly, I don't have any good reason to say this, but I would have liked if we waited for a while longer. I feel as if things are mature enough and could soon explode. You can call it a sixth sense, but I feel like in the next few days, we are going to get additional information that will further nail this case. I don't have any specific expectation of a definite event or anything else - it is just a feeling," said Araya.

"Well, we are at this point because you listened to your feelings and senses. However, can you further elaborate on what kind of information you are hoping to get?" asked Tesfom.

"I feel like this Gebreab-Habtom relationship is at a breaking point. If so, before we go and sue, we might soon get further watertight evidence that will make our case stronger."

Tesfom stared at his younger brother, as if he was seeing him for the first time. He looked at him straight in the eye and shook his head and said, "Wow, Araya, I am extremely amazed and impressed by your intelligence, wisdom and long vision. If anyone had been present during our discussion, seeing your maturity and the leadership you provide, they would have assumed you were the eldest brother and head of this family," said Tesfom, expressing his utmost appreciation and admiration.

"I thank you Tesfom Hawey, but that is not true by any means. How can I ever be better than you? You are more educated and more experienced than me in every area and facet," said Araya.

"Well, my dear Araya, you know better than I, that perception and wisdom do not necessarily come from education. Look at our father, who, for obvious reasons only finished fourth grade. However, as far as perception and wisdom are concerned, few university graduates can surpass him! It is true if one is already gifted with perception and wisdom, then education can enhance that gift.

However, in some cases others become even more ignorant and short-sighted after getting an education. This is because once they own a certificate or degree, they think they are superior to most people and soon stop making an effort to learn or improve. Thus, despite their education, they remain ignorant and half-baked," said Tesfom with conviction.

"You know very well that whatever I know and am, is largely because of father and you! As far as perception and wisdom are concerned, you don't have a problem and you are actually much smarter than most men," said Araya.

"Well Araya, you know my weaknesses. That is not a small thing," said Tesfom.

"Well, to be honest, you definitely have a problem there. You love your night life, you have too many friends and drink beyond what is good for you," said Araya honestly but uncomfortably. He hated saying it, but he felt he had to say it, for his brother's sake, for Medhn, for the children and for the family's sake.

Tesfom said, "Exactly, then what more weakness do you want? Or is it because I am your brother, so, you want to absolve me, by minimizing my weaknesses?"

The telephone rang. Tesfom picked up the phone. It was Medhn. "I am with Araya; we are here at the office. We are nearly done, I will come soon," said Tesfom, putting down the telephone.

He turned to Araya and said, "It is Medhn. She is telling me Legesse is feverish. Do we have anything more to discuss?" he asked hurriedly.

"Since we have agreed on everything, we have nothing else. Is Legesse ok? Do you want me to come with you?" asked Araya with concern.

"No, that is not necessary. Besides, he should be ok. I guess it could be something like influenza or cold. It is only because Medhn gets easily worried. We will try to give him something for the fever and observe him," said Tesfom, assuring his brother.

"Ok, then go ahead. I will follow you soon," said Araya. Tesfom left and Araya soon after.

* 9 *

For the next three days, from Tuesday to Thursday, there was nothing new. Tesfom was becoming very impatient. His hatred of Habtom was making the waiting even more unbearable. The only thing holding him back was the agreement he had made with his brother. Though Araya was by nature very patient, he was also finding it difficult to resist the temptation to go on with what they had. Both brothers did not spell their feelings out in words, but for anyone who cared to look closer, the pressure and stress they felt was evident in their body language.

Despite their internal anxiety and impatience, Tesfom and Araya were meeting daily. They were regularly consulting and sharing information and systematically formulating and streamlining their strategies and plans. On Friday at 6 pm, when there was no one at the office, Tekleab came in with a report.

He told Araya, "I have an update about what we discussed concerning Gebreab's memory and recollection," said Tekleab.

"Oh, very good. Go ahead," said Araya, with anticipation.

"I am 100% certain that he doesn't recollect anything at all. I have tried to retrace the places we went and the people we encountered from the very time we met. I probed his recollection deeply, and it ends way before he spilled the secret. We went to many bars and saw many people after that, but he doesn't recall a thing! Let alone what he said, he doesn't even remember the places we went to and the people we encountered. The only thing he repeatedly says is, "We had a really great time on Saturday, right?" So, as far as recollection is concerned, there is nothing to worry about," said Tekleab confidently.

"Very good. That is a great relief. Make sure to go out this Saturday. This time, try to pay all the expenses and make him drink as much as possible. Don't worry about money," said Araya, taking out money and handing it to him.

Tekleab pocketed the money quickly and left.

* 10 *

Pace bakery had one medium-sized room, three other large rooms, and a small bathroom. One of the three large rooms in front was the shop where they sold their products. The two others were the main bakery. The shop was connected to one of the bakery rooms with a door and a small window, which was used as a quick communication point between the shop and the bakery.

On Saturday morning, February 7th, Araya received a call. When he recognized Weldeab's voice, his heart skipped a beat. Weldeab told him there was a new development. They made an appointment to meet at 4:00 pm in the afternoon. Thereafter, Araya could not concentrate on his job; he wished the clock would go faster. Time seems to travel much slower whenever one is anxiously waiting for something. For Araya, 4:00 pm felt like forever.

Finally, it was 4 o'clock and Araya was sitting in front of Weldeab. Araya didn't want to waste time and straight away dived into the subject, "Since I have another appointment right after this, could you tell me briefly the new information you have?"

"As has become customary, yesterday Gebreab came to the bakery. He asked us if Habtom was inside. When he was told that Habtom was out, he was not happy. He said they had an appointment and would wait for him. After waiting for about 30 minutes, he started showing signs of uneasiness and irritation. He started fidgeting, standing up, sitting down, and going in and out of the shop," said Weldeab.

"And then?" asked Araya impatiently wanting to go into the crux of the matter as soon as possible.

Habtom came after an hour. "Oh, you are already here?" he asked, without any apology.

"Our appointment was an hour ago. You have kept me waiting for an hour," said Gebreab, not hiding his discontent and frustration.

"I am sorry, something unexpected came up and I was detained. Come in," said Habtom.

"Aha?" prodded Araya.

"They went inside. The small connector window which is usually closed, was open. For about 15 minutes, we could hear hushed sounds with words we couldn't identify. The only words we could repeatedly discern were, "my money" and "what I earned." Since everybody was curious, everyone was trying to follow what was going on," said Weldeab.

"Ok, continue," said Araya, who was aware that Weldeab was continuing with his report, but because he couldn't stand the suspense, he wanted to push him to go faster.

"Suddenly, the hushed voices turned louder for a few seconds. We clearly heard Gebreab say, "I am not begging you here. I am asking you to give me the money you owe in one go, and not piecemeal like alms!"

"Don't try to threaten me, and keep your voice down!" Habtom retorted. At that point, I think Habtom realized that the window was open and slammed it shut. We all looked at each other with amazement and wonder," said Weldeab.

"And then?" asked Araya.

"After that, we could hear nothing more. We heard sounds for about five minutes after which Gebreab came out, his face flustered, his eyes red and breathing heavily. He slammed the door behind him and walked out of the bakery, visibly irritated and angry. Habtom stayed inside for about 15 minutes, after which he came out with his face contorted with anger and frustration. He immediately went out without saying a word to anyone,"

"Was everyone able to hear distinctly the words Gebreab and Habtom spoke?" asked Araya, wanting to be certain.

"Everyone heard it a 100%. Later on, someone even brought up the subject. He asked, "Did you guys here that? How can Habtom possibly owe money to Gebreab? Did you see how he was shouting at him?" I didn't make any comment except nod my head. So, there is no doubt that everybody heard everything all right!"

'That is very good. Thank you. By the way, rest assured that we are going to handsomely remunerate you appropriately for all your services," said Araya.

"I have no doubt about that. Tesfom and you are decent human beings. I don't need much, as long as you deliver me from this Satan by giving me a job at the factory; that is all I ask," said Weldeab.

"Don't worry about that. At the right time, we will be able to do it without any problem," Araya assured him, standing up.

They soon parted and, Araya headed straight to the factory.

* 11 *

When Tesfom arrived at the factory at 6 pm, Araya reported the results of his encounter with Weldeab. Tesfom was very encouraged by the results; "I think it is time that I go pay a visit to my friends Hailom and Colonel Habte on Monday. What do you say?" asked Tesfom.

"I think it is about time. However, since Tekleab is going to meet Gebreab tonight, and since we will not get his report until Monday, why don't we wait until Tuesday?" suggested Araya.

"No problem with that. One day will not make any difference. We will not proceed before we have your green light," said Tesfom smiling.

"Don't worry, you will be able to hang the bastard Habtom soon enough," said Araya.

"I can't wait Araya Hawey. These days I have barely any other dream," replied Tesfom.

"You are right Tesfom Hawey. There is nothing this evil person hasn't done to completely destroy us!" said Araya yawning.

"Yes, absolutely!" said Tesfom. He was about to continue, but then he seemed to have noticed Araya's exhaustion and said, "Now you go ahead and rest. I will work for a while and then I will head home," said Tesfom.

Araya accepted his brother's recommendation without a second thought, "You are right, I am really exhausted. I will see you then," Araya said and left.

* 12 *

On Monday, Tekleab did not bring anything new. He reported that the only new thing Gebreab said was that he had met Habtom that day and gave him an ultimatum. The rest was just a reiteration of the information he had already divulged. The information Tekleab brought merely confirmed what Weldeab had already reported.

Tesfom and Araya had already agreed that, irrespective of whether they got further information or not, they would proceed with their Tuesday plan. Accordingly, the first thing Tesfom did when he arrived at the office was call and secure an appointment with Colonel Habte and Attorney Hailom respectively.

After putting his signature on urgent and important documents, Tesfom informed his secretary and his co-workers that he was going out and it would be a while before he returned. He walked out of the main headquarters of the bank, to the *Fenili* Bowling Club, where his car was parked in the shade.

He started his car and drove back to the main avenue. He turned left and drove straight past the High Court, the main Municipality building, the Cinema *Impero*, the Cathedral and then turned right and arrived at the Government House (Imperial Palace). He then drove down the road passing the main government offices (formerly *Commando Truppo*) and the Internal Revenue Department and parked his car by the side of the Palace, near the Cinema Capitol.

It didn't take him long to walk the short distance to the Colonel's office. The colonel was expecting him and received him right away. They exchanged pleasantries. Tesfom said, "I know how busy you are; I don't want to waste your precious time. Therefore, let me get into why I am here right away."

"Ever since you called me for an appointment, I have been wondering. I have been asking myself, "since when does Tesfom ever approach and contact the police for information and advice?" said the Colonel, smiling.

"Well, my dear Colonel, you know the famous saying, 'All roads eventually lead to Rome!' said Tesfom laughing, "So, sooner or later, eventually for good or bad, everyone is bound to seek the services of the police!"

The Colonel shook his head and, while laughing, said, "You are never at a loss for words; you always know what to say." Then he turned serious and added, "What can I do for you?"

"I am here today seeking your advice and guidance as a friend. I am not talking to you as an officer occupying this important position. Hence, what I am about to tell you is strictly personal and confidential. We will decide on how to move forward only after you hear me out and provide me with your opinion and your advice," Tesfom said.

"Fair enough. That is clear," said the Colonel, grabbing a pen and a note-book.

"Let me first give you the background," said Tesfom and started explaining about the brotherhood, neighborliness and partnership they had with Habtom; the cause for the dissolution of the partnership and the enmity and rancor that followed; the burning of the factory and Araya's suspicions; the doubts they started to have because of the close relationship of Habtom and one of their workers named Gebreab; the fact that they assigned two persons to follow Gebreab and Habtom and finally related in detail the findings of their informants.

Since Tesfom started his narration, not once did the colonel interrupt him. He was merely taking notes. When Tesfom finished, the Colonel started asking questions and clarifications: "Do you have written evidence of Habtom's scamming and theft?" he asked.

"Yes, we have documentary evidence," said Tesfom.

"During the disagreement and dissolution, what evidence do you have that he in fact threatened you that he was going to take revenge?"

"My brother Araya and his brother Dermas were present. They can testify."

"You don't have any other evidence?"

"Oh, yes, I forgot. We have also signed minutes of the meeting."

"Very good. Anything else you haven't told me?"

"No, nothing else really, I have told you everything," said Tesfom.

While the Colonel was saying, "Ok then, the other thing…," he saw that Tesfom was not with him and was far away. He hesitated and then instead of asking the next question, he asked, "You seem to have something on your mind. Anything else you want to tell me?"

"Well, I just remembered something, although I am not sure if it is important or not," said Tesfom.

"Tesfom, you have to know and understand something. When you report to the police, you have to mention anything you remember, whether you think it is important or not. The police will decide its importance. Sometimes the so called unimportant and trivial information is what solves mysterious cases. Now, go ahead," he told him.

"Ok, I get it. Well, Habtom is generally not a night person; he always goes home early. His first wife said It had been a very long time since he had stopped coming and spending nights in his first house. He only came to visit the children during the day. However, during the night of the accident, he came at 2.00 am and let himself in. She heard sounds and got up to check. The next day, he came back carrying a cake, which was rare for him, and he told the children it was a celebration. On the days that followed, he continued celebrating with his employees at work and with his friends outside."

"Wow, this is a very important piece of information, Tesfom. I am glad you decided to mention it," said the Colonel.

"Wow, I thought such details were like useless bread crumbs that do not help at all," said Tesfom.

"For your information, for the police, above and beyond the main evidence, it is the crumbs that no one notices that are crucial and pivotal. Many hard to crack crimes are solved by finding crumbs around the edges of cases!" said the Colonel.

"Thank you, that is truly enlightening. There are so many things we don't understand because we have been locked down inside the offices of a bank for a lifetime," said Tesfom smiling.

"No problem. Ok, since you have told me everything, let me see, these two people," he consulted his notes and said, "Yes, these Tekleab and Weldeab, will they will be willing to testify?"

"Yes, they are willing to testify," Tesfom said, with confidence.

"Do you know Tekleab very well? I mean do you know him as a person. His truthfulness, integrity and factuality or any habit of exaggeration or falsehood?"

"Well, this is a very difficult question. Generally, it is not right to affirm and swear for the innocence of another adult. However, I can say this: Tekleab has worked with us for many years and we have always found him correct, truthful, honest and full of integrity. We have never seen him exaggerate or double cross anyone."

"I know this is not an easy question and might not even be fair to ask. Nevertheless, I will need to ask you for the sake of completion. Do you know any particular characteristic of his during alcohol consumption and anything about his memory and recollection capacity, after drinking?"

"Well, I really can't say. We have noticed that the information he brings is devoid of exaggeration. Whenever he doesn't have anything to report, he is on point about it. He doesn't try to be creative to satisfy his listeners. That is all I can say," said Tesfom, feeling his response was not adequate.

"That is good enough," said the Colonel. He then consulted his notes and asked, "You still have the half-burnt *Shida* your brother found, right?"

"Has it! Are you kidding me? You wouldn't believe with what reverence he handles it and keeps it honorably in his drawer! He practically talks to it every day!" said Tesfom laughing.

Colonel Habte roared with laughter at Tesfom's description of his brother and his *Shida.* He became serious again and said, "If it was not for him or his obsession with following up leads and not underestimating seemingly unimportant small details, you wouldn't have uncovered such a crime!"

'You are absolutely right about that. I have acknowledged and thanked him over and over again," said Tesfom.

"If we were to be asked to hire potential police officers between you and your brother, we wouldn't even consider you!" said the Colonel with a smile.

"My God, I am that bad, eh?" said Tesfom laughing.

The Colonel again looked at his notes and asked, "This Gebreab, did he have any particular reason or grudge to hurt you or your family?"

"He was one of the persons Habtom was using in his scheme of scamming and theft. I am sure Habtom must have been throwing him small crumbs here and there for his services. After we got rid of Habtom, he might have had a grudge because that side source dried up," said Tesfom.

"Why did you let somebody who was part of the ring continue to work in your factory?" asked the Colonel.

"Araya has asked that question several times. However, I foolishly refused to get rid of him. So, I am not only unfit for police work but I also have poor judgement," said Tesfom sourly, half smiling.

"Well, it is ok. Since you have the bank, you don't need anything else," said the Colonel smiling and then added, "Anything else on Gebreab?"

"Although we did not dismiss him from the job, we had demoted him from the important position of head of purchases to the store. He was also sore about that and complained bitterly, citing his long years of service. In addition, I believe since the income on the side dried up, he was desperate for additional income and must have gladly accepted Habtom's invitation to commit a crime."

"Good. You have given me ample information. If I need further clarification, I can always ask you," said the Colonel satisfied.

"Ok, great. Allow me to ask you the most important question Araya and I have. Based on the information I have given you today, do you think we have a viable case?" asked Tesfom.

"A viable case? You have a solid case! However, it will require careful and serious handling as well as extreme secrecy and caution."

"Wow, thank the Lord! We had been extremely worried. In that case, what is your recommendation on how we should proceed?" asked Tesfom.

"Well, the first thing to do is to submit a formal written accusation. I will then assign one of our best, well-experienced and meticulous investigators to the case. We will call and cross examine both of the accused separately, pitting one against the other. The rest is up to us. I will personally follow and supervise the case. I don't think it is going to be a hard case to crack. If you pass by tomorrow, I can even draft the accusation letter myself, so it is crafted precisely." said Colonel Habte.

"Thank you so much. What a blessing to have a friend like you," said Tesfom profusely.

"Come on Tesfom, not just for a friend like you, I am sitting in this chair to serve everyone. One of the main missions of the police is to uncover crimes and bring the guilty before the law. So, no need to thank me. If and when we succeed in bringing the criminals to justice, then we might celebrate together," said the Colonel smiling.

"Of course, we will!" said Tesfom and then added, "I think I have already taken a lot of your time, let me leave you to your work."

"Ok, good. The draft will be ready tomorrow. I will see you then," said the Colonel standing up. They shook hands and parted.

* 13 *

Tesfom left the Colonel's office in a great mood. The Colonel's assurance that they had a viable case had raised his hopes and his spirit. On his way to Hailom's office, he was very relaxed and whistled while driving.

Hailom's Law office was on the first floor in a building located a few meters after Cinema Croce Rossa, near Bar Torino. As soon as they exchanged pleasantries and sat down, Hailom said, "I was slightly worried when you told me you were coming to consult with me."

"Yes, you are right. We have always met either at home or outside. I have never been to your office," said Tesfom.

"Exactly, that is what got me worried. I knew you wouldn't come to me because you got sick!" said Hailom smiling, jokingly. Tesfom roared with laughter. "But seriously," said Hailom, "I was worried because I thought since when does Tesfom go to any Law office?"

"You have already answered it yourself. When you are sick, you go to a doctor; when you need legal advice, you go to an Attorney," said Tesfom smiling. They both laughed heartily.

Both became serious again, and Tesfom said, "I have now come to you, not as my friend, but as a professional, because I need your professional advice," said Tesfom.

"Ok, it will be my pleasure," said Hailom.

Tesfom went on to narrate the information he had conveyed to the Colonel. He then told him the questions the Colonel raised and the answers he provided. During his narration, Hailom did not interrupt him once. He was encouraging him to continue by nodding his head and once in a while taking notes.

When Tesfom finished, he said, "Wow, Tesfom, how could you

conceal such an intriguing conspiracy from your best friend, for this long?"

"Honestly speaking, until about a week ago, I hadn't given any significance to the information, let alone to the possibility of a crime. It was Araya who had been pursuing it seriously. I had, on many occasions, told him it was a waste of his time but he refused to listen. So, I was just going along with him only to please him. Otherwise, if I had thought it was something serious, you know that the first person I would consult would be you," said Tesfom.

"Ok, at least that is better," said Hailom, smiling and then he became serious and said, "You have a very strong case. As far as winning is concerned, it will greatly depend on the work the police do."

"What exactly does that mean?" asked Tesfom.

"If the police conduct a careful, clever and thorough investigation, and if as a result Gebreab and Habtom admit to their crimes, then the case is a done deal. In that instance, one goes to court not to determine the question of whether they are guilty or not, but just merely to determine the punishment,"

"You have explained what it will mean if the police do a good job. What will not doing a good job mean?" asked Tesfom.

"Sorry Tesfom Hawey. I guess I confused you. My wording was not right. When I said, if they do a good job, I meant if they succeed in their investigations and all their endeavors. Similarly, instead of saying, if they don't do a good job, I should say, if they do not succeed in making them admit to their crimes," said Hailom.

"Oh, ok. I get it now. If they don't succeed in making them admit to their crimes, what will the scenario of the court proceedings look like? And more importantly what will be the chance of our success?" asked Tesfom.

"Well, in that case, it becomes a whole different ball game. The prosecutor will dig out evidence and present witnesses to help him win the case. The defense will try to nullify the evidence presented by the prosecution by presenting its own evidence and witnesses.

This will be gritty and messy. It will involve a lot of back and forth, and it will be a drawn-out process taking a long time. Another extremely important point in any criminal case is, in order to get a guilty verdict, you need to prove 100% guilt. So, if the suspects don't admit to their crimes, it is difficult to predict what the final result could be and even more difficult to predict whether you will win the case or not. I am telling you all these details, so you will know the stakes before proceeding," said Hailom candidly.

"That is very nice of you. I know that you are a dear friend and a professional with integrity. That is why I came to you. Thank you so much," said Tesfom with admiration.

Then Tesfom hesitated for a while, as if collecting his thoughts, and then quickly asked, "So, if that is the case, the role of the Colonel is of utmost importance, right?"

"It is extremely crucial. It is the key. I know you are very close to him, so if he handles it himself as a special case, I don't think you will encounter any problems," said Hailom.

"Thank you, you have made it crystal clear," said Tesfom.

"There is another important matter that you have to understand. The Colonel knows this, so there is no problem. However, it is also good if you understand it," said Hailom.

"Ok, sure," said Tesfom.

"When the perpetrators admit to their crimes, the police should immediately escort them to a judge, so they can stand before the court and establish that they confessed to their crimes without force and duress. If you fail to do that and go to court without a judge's confession papers, then the case could be thrown away. This is because they could claim that they were forced to confess. You should be aware of this, because it is extremely important," said Hailom.

"Wow, ok, very good. Thank you for the enlightenment. I perfectly understand everything now," said Tesfom, nodding his head vigorously.

"Very good. It is very important that you go into this with full understanding of all the possibilities and scenarios. I have the notes you have provided me and if I need any clarifications or have any questions, I will contact you," said Hailom, standing up.

Tesfom heartily thanked his friend and left. Tesfom was gratified by his meeting with Hailom. He looked at his watch and was amazed that it was already close to noon. He headed home, because there wasn't much he could do if he went to the bank at that hour.

* 14 *

After lunch, Tesfom went to the bank. He was aware how much Araya was anxious to hear the results of his talks with his two friends. As he had anticipated, as soon as he arrived at the factory at 6 pm, Araya did not even wait for him to sit down.

"So, how did your meetings go?" asked Araya anxiously.

Tesfom recounted his meeting with the Colonel and Hailom. He then enumerated the questions they raised and the answers he provided. Finally, he recounted the advice they gave him and their assessment of the viability of their case.

By the time Tesfom finished, Araya's spirit was lifted and his face reflected great hope and relief. Araya said, "So, if the Colonel is going to give you the draft tomorrow, then we can immediately proceed to action."

"Yes, I think that is what it looks like. I also want to show the Colonel's draft to my friend Hailom. After that, there will be nothing to hold us from submitting our case before the end of this week. Once we formally submit the accusation, there will be no turning back. After that, we will be in the fight of our lives!" said Tesfom.

"Then before submitting the case, we have to update the family, especially father and Medhn," said Araya.

"Let's first get hold of the draft. The Colonel's draft can help us convince father that we have a solid case. Otherwise, he might think we are rushing to accuse Habtom out of rancor, rivalry and blind emotion," said Tesfom.

"Ok, that is a good idea. So, as a rough estimate, can we plan to talk with the family on Thursday and submit the case on Friday?" asked Araya.

"No problem, we will consider everything and choose the best time," said Tesfom with finality.

After concluding their consultation, they occupied themselves with their daily chores. When they were done, both retired at the same time.

* 15 *

The next morning, Wednesday February 11, Tesfom went to the Colonel's office. He immediately handed him the draft. When the Colonel informed Tesfom that he had an impending meeting, Tesfom understood that he could only take a few minutes of the Colonel's time. He quickly asked him whether it was better to submit the case on Friday or wait until Monday. The Colonel explained that crimes and accidents tend to increase during weekends and since most officers are too busy then, it would be best to submit the case on Monday. Tesfom thanked him and immediately left the Colonel's office. He went back to the bank and called Hailom and they agreed to meet in the afternoon.

In the afternoon, Tesfom handed the draft letter to his friend. Hailom read the letter and approved of its content and form, and he also agreed with the Colonel's recommendation concerning submitting the accusation on Monday. When they were finished, Tesfom thanked his friend and left.

When he arrived at the factory in the afternoon, Tesfom reported everything to his brother. Araya read the draft letter, and he then typed it and put in the necessary signatures and put it in a safe place.

Since they had more time now, they agreed to arrange the

meeting with Grazmach and Medhn for the weekend. They informed Medhn and Grazmach that they would eat lunch together on Saturday.

* 16 *

On Saturday, Medhn prepared a great lunch, and after everyone had finished eating, Medhn told her children to wash the dishes and came back quickly to join the men. The four of them sat down together.

Tesfom started by saying, "What I am about to tell you today will come as a great shock to both of you. Araya and I have been following this case for a long time. Actually, it is Araya who has been following it for a very long time, and it is he who was instrumental in arriving at where we are today. I will go back in time and give you the chain of events starting from the night the factory burned down."

He then went on to describe everything that had happened including the follow up, the leads, the conclusion, the consultation with the police and attorney and the plan forward. Except for Medhn's occasional murmur of, "Wey Gud! Oh, my God!" and Grazmach's facial expression changing from normal to grave, no one interrupted Tesfom.

"If there is anything else, I haven't covered, Araya will help me out," said Tesfom, looking at his brother.

"I think you have said it all." He turned towards Medhn and Grazmach and said, "The only thing I would like to add is that you rightly might be asking, why were we not informed until the case reached this stage? That is a valid question. The problem we had though is, up until two weeks ago, we had no solid evidence to convince or prove to you that we had a viable case," said Araya.

"You don't have to worry about it; no one will blame you for it. It is clear that you yourselves were not even sure of the case. Let alone then, even now, it is very hard for me to accept this as real!" said Grazmach, looking down, with a heavy heart.

"As father has just stated, even for me, it is very difficult to imagine something like this could ever happen!" said Medhn.

Grazmach looked up and said, "I have one important question. The criminal accusation you are raising is a very serious issue. Already the relationship between our two families is at its lowest. Adding this to it will have far wider and deeper implications. The repercussions for our two families are going to be very grave. We have heard everything you have said. However, I still want you to assure me that you are 100% certain about this!"

"Well, when we found out that the fire was not an accident but an arson, we didn't rush right away to accusation. We consulted with reputable professionals of the law and police and asked them if we had a case. They examined everything, they asked us detailed questions and finally both of them told us that we had a solid case. So, we have done everything that we possibly could!" said Tesfom.

"My God, what can I say? I really don't even know what to say! I can't comprehend and understand why we human beings have to revert to harming and destroying each other, when the Lord has abundantly provided for all of us!" said Grazmach, shaking his head, visibly saddened and distressed.

Meanwhile, Medhn was continuously grasping and ungrasping her hands and shaking her head up and down. Grazmach continued from where he left, "Bashay raised his children with a lot of self-discipline and self-sacrifice. Finally, God rewarded his good efforts and they were able to improve their lives. We all know where Habtom was when he started and where he is now. If he has indeed committed this act, what good reason could he have to commit such madness. He has everything. What could he gain from this satanic act?" said Grazmach.

It was Araya who responded, "He wouldn't gain anything, except to sadden and destroy Tesfom as well as me and our family!"

"If there was anything he would gain by this wicked act, then it would be understandable and we would have brushed it aside as the work of a mad man. However, since he doesn't gain anything at all, hurting and destroying you for nothing is indeed satanic. It is correct to wish and pray to God to grant you your wishes and desires and then to work hard to achieve those dreams. But to wish and pray to God to destroy others and feel happy about it, that is pure wickedness and madness. God punishes not only those who do bad things but also those who think and wish bad things on others. God! Where are we? What have we come to? What kind of an era and a generation is this?" said Grazmach, with utmost disappointment and sorrow.

Tesfom felt the disappointment and pain his father was feeling. He felt very sorry for him and said, "Well, it is OK father. Don't take it too much to heart. After all, what has happened to us is something that often happens to many!"

"What has happened to us and to you two, as well as what might happen to Habtom, is not what is angering and frustrating me. What is distressing me is what will happen to the parents, the innocent children and the women who had nothing to do with all this and yet will bear the brunt of the burden. Why should the parents, children and women be forced to bear his madness and guilt?" Grazmach said, clearly deeply hurt and saddened.

"You are absolutely right, father!" said Medhn, vigorously shaking her head.

"Anyway, I am just blubbering trying to express my frustration; otherwise, I am not even being helpful here. There hasn't been an era in our lives when God has given to humans so abundantly; yet, we are living in an era when we humans are becoming increasingly mean and wicked!" said Grazmach.

He paused for a few seconds and suddenly shifting the direction of his focus, abruptly said, "I want you to promise me one thing. I entreat you that out of your anger and grudge, you do not try to hurt him beyond what he deserves. Your goal should only be to get justice, nothing less and nothing more. Otherwise, you and all of us will not be better than him. That is all I have to say," said Grazmach, concluding his remarks and advice.

Understanding that his father had concluded the discussion, Araya said, "Ok, father, before we go, please give us your blessings."

"I will not pray to God asking him to help you win the case. I will only ask God to give everyone justice. I will ask him to show us the truth. Meaning, if Habtom is guilty of this, then let him get his punishment. If, on the other hand, he is innocent and you are accusing him for nothing, then let him embarrass you and punish you appropriately. That is all I can say and that is my blessing," said Grazmach.

"Wow, father! You are amazing! You never bend justice even slightly - not even for your most beloved sons!" said Medhn with admiration.

"My dear Medhn, by bending justice, I will not help my children. I will only be hurting them. After all, there is God above us, who sees everything," said Grazmach, and standing up he said, "I think we have finished. The news I have just heard has really affected me. Let me go and rest and you two can go to work."

"I can go to work after I drop you at home," said Araya, standing up.

"Ok, son. Let's go, bless you all," said Grazmach and left.

* 17 *

Monday, February 16th, at 8.00 am: Tesfom and Araya headed to the police station and were ushered in immediately. They handed the letter to Colonel Habte. He checked it and ascertained its completeness and instructed them to go to the Archives department, register and submit the letter and then to come back to him.

They did as they were told and returned to the Colonel. He then called the Archives department and instructed them to open a file urgently and send it to him immediately. Then he turned to both of them and said, "As soon as they bring me the file, I will hand over the case to the investigator I have chosen. I will give him an order to take concrete steps starting from today."

Both Tesfom and Araya nodded their heads. Then the Colonel turned his head towards Araya and said, "The investigator will now take your statement and, after that, everything will be up to us. Don't worry at all, we will do everything necessary until we get to the bottom of this."

"With you at the helm, we don't have any doubt. We know we have nothing to worry about. We are extremely indebted for everything," said Tesfom.

"You don't have to thank me for this. This is my responsibility. We are not here to merely warm a chair, but to serve people. So, no need for that. Anyway, go ahead now. Then, standing up and looking towards Tesfom he added, "I will call you, if there are any new developments."

They thanked him again profusely and left.

After finalizing their affairs at the police station, they went straight to the factory. On their way, no one spoke a word. Both were immersed in deep thought. When they reached the factory, Tesfom said, "The process is now in motion. There is no stopping it. What will be, will be. We have done everything that can be done. From now on, it is out of our hands, we just have to wait and see!"

"Yes, absolutely! The rest is up to God!" said Araya.

Tesfom dropped Araya off and went to the bank.

Chapter 9

Carscioli Police Station

On Monday at 5.00 pm, Colonel Habte called Tesfom. They exchanged brief pleasantries and the Colonel then hurriedly told him, "We have started the case in earnest. We have already brought in the small fish."

"Oh, wow, thank you so much," responded Tesfom, expressing his appreciation.

"After weighing our progress, we will decide about the big fish. I will call you again when we have something definite. Talk to you then," said Colonel Habte.

"Ok, Colonel, thank you again. Talk to you soon," replied Tesfom.

He immediately called Araya and said, "I had a call from our friend and he told me that they have already started the process in earnest. They have even already brought in the small fish!" said Tesfom excitedly.

"Yes, I am already aware of it. They took the small one from here," said Araya.

"Oh, ok. So, since we won't have anything important to discuss, I will not be coming to the office this evening. I will see you tomorrow," said Tesfom.

"Ok, see you tomorrow," said Araya.

Tesfom had not known that the police had taken Gebreab from the factory at 3.00 pm. Araya had already updated Tekleab about where the case stood, so Tekleab was not very surprised when the police came. On the other hand, Gebreab had no inkling of what was going on, and when they took him, his face didn't show fear or apprehension - only surprise and confusion.

* 2 *

The next day, Tuesday, February 17th, there was nothing new. Tesfom and Araya knew the next two or three days were going to be extremely crucial and decisive. Tesfom had been glued to the telephone the whole morning and afternoon and yet there was no news. He went to the factory nervous and slightly stressed.

Similarly, Araya had been in extreme anxiety and tension. He was looking forward to the arrival of Tesfom, hoping to get some news. The moment his brother walked in; Araya instantly read his body language. He saw that Tesfom was in an even worse mood.

"How awful it is to wait for something you desperately need! It is even far worse when you are alone," said Araya.

Tesfom was not even in the mood to respond or to have small talk. He acknowledged Araya's statement with a nod. Araya continued, "I am starting to have serious doubts whether the case is going well or not. I had expected the police to take Habtom soon after Gebreab. This does not augur well!"

Tesfom took a deep breath and said, "I agree, I too had a similar expectation. At least it shows that up to now, they haven't succeeded in their attempt and that is very worrying," said Tesfom.

Tesfom again took a deep breath and then suddenly stood up and said, "It is better if we go. Although I haven't accomplished a single thing at the office, I feel exhausted. I spent the whole day under immense strain and anxiety, doing nothing."

"You are right, I am also extremely exhausted for the same reason. Work is much better than wasteful stress and anxiety. So, let's go," said Araya. They left without another word.

* **3** *

On Wednesday, February 18th, Tesfom went to the bank at 8 am. Since his arrival, he was looking at the telephone beside him constantly. Whenever it ringed, he would immediately snatch the telephone and respond. However, all the calls he received were not the call he was anxiously expecting. After a while, whenever the phone rang, he started picking it up with exasperation.

After what seemed like a very long wait, he looked at his watch and, to his dismay, it was still 9.00 am. Hoping it would calm his nerves, he had already ordered coffee twice, but it didn't help much. It was now 10.30 am and still nothing. As more time elapsed, Tesfom's impatience and irritation worsened.

He became desperate and thought about calling and asking. He knew it was not a good idea. At that moment the telephone rang. He sprang up and picked it up. He didn't recognize the voice and thus uttered a sound of disappointment, "UHH -UFF," before answering, "Hello,"

"Hi Tesfom, it is me, Colonel Habte. Are you ok? I heard you sigh," asked the Colonel.

"Hi Colonel. I am OK. They have been repeatedly calling me over an insignificant issue and I thought it was them again. Please excuse me," said Tesfom.

"No, no problem. Anyway, we have made good progress," said the Colonel.

"Oh, thank you so much, that is great news," said Tesfom, without giving away the great relief he was feeling.

"In fact, so much so, we are contemplating about our next move concerning the other," said the Colonel.

"This is indeed great progress," said Tesfom, trying hard to conceal his joy and happiness.

"We are hoping to achieve our next objective within the next three-four days. I will update you then. I will let you go now as I have a call waiting on another line. Talk to you soon," said the Colonel hurriedly.

"Ok, thank you, bye," said Tesfom.

Tesfom put down the phone and instantly stood up clenching his fists and then threw punches into the air, saying, "Yes! Yes! Yes!" He thought he heard a knock on the door and sat down instantly. He was relieved that there was no one at the door and reprimanded himself for acting like a child. He told himself, "If anyone saw me do what I did, they would have thought I had lost it. Also, why am I acting as if we have already won everything? We have only climbed up a few stairs; there is still a lot to go," Tesfom tried reigning in his feelings and bringing himself back to reality. Then he suddenly remembered that Araya was waiting for news that would relieve him from stress and anxiety. He picked up the phone and dialed.

"Hello," said Araya with a distinct voice of a man in great distress.

"Hello, Araya, I have great news," said Tesfom.

"Really? Really?" said Araya excitedly.

Tesfom briefly told him what the Colonel had said. Araya could not contain himself. They agreed to discuss in further detail the new development when Tesfom came to the factory in the afternoon.

* 4 *

It was Friday, April 20th. Dermas went to the bakery to see his brother, but Habtom was not there. He did not make much of it. After waiting for his brother for a while, Dermas went home.

On Friday night, Habtom did not come home. No one in the

whole family had any knowledge of this, except Almaz. Though she was not comfortable, given Habtom's unpredictable nature, she was not unduly worried. However, when she got up on Saturday morning, she had an uneasy feeling. When she called the bakery, they told her that he was not there yet. Although she was slightly worried, she still felt he would come for lunch and decided to wait.

When he didn't come for lunch, she was alarmed. That is when she called Dermas. She asked him if he had seen his brother. When he informed her that he hadn't seen him, she told him, "Since he left home after lunch yesterday, Habtom has not come home up to now!"

Dermas did not think much of it. He looked at his watch and saw it was already past 3 pm. He asked, "Have you checked at the bakery?"

"Yes, I asked. They haven't seen him since yesterday afternoon," she said.

Dermas was now worried, "What? Wow, ok. Let me ask around and I will get back to you. Until then, don't call or ask anyone else."

"Ok, I will wait for you then," said Almaz, feeling better that she had shared her worry with Dermas.

Dermas first headed to the bakery. At the bakery, while taking care of some accounts and without seeming obvious, he asked, "Habtom told me he would wait for me here. When did he go out?"

"We haven't seen him the whole day," said one of the workers.

"Actually, he hasn't come back to the bakery since yesterday evening, when he went out with the two men," said the other worker.

"Which two men? Do you know them?" asked Dermas.

"They have never been here before,' said the first worker.

"Yes, they have never been here, but I always see one of them with a policeman I know very well," said the second worker.

Dermas was slightly alarmed when he heard the word police. He decided to push on, "At about what time did they go?"

"It was about 5 pm," said the first worker.

"Habtom always has a problem. He never informs anyone

where he is going or when he is coming back, even when he is going out of town," said Dermas, purposely trying to diffuse the importance of his enquiry.

Dermas didn't want to go out immediately, lest they suspect anything untoward. He waited for a while and then left.

* 5 *

First Dermas went to Alganesh and in a roundabout way tactfully asked and ascertained that his brother hadn't been there for days. He didn't want to ask friends or other family members and unnecessarily create suspicion or panic.

Before his next move, he wanted to be sure just in case so he went to the few hospitals in the city to enquire. When he didn't come up with anything, he decided to go to the police stations. He went and enquired at the police stations of the center of the city (*Maekel Ketema*), *Godaif* and *Idaga Aerbi,* without success. Finally, he went to the largest police station called *Carscioli.*

Carscioli is one of the oldest and most notorious of the police stations. It had secure prisons where the most hardened and dangerous inmates were kept. It was surrounded by an extremely tall and impenetrable hostile wall. Policemen atop the walls stood guard day and night. Under normal conditions, Dermas was not even very comfortable passing nearby, let alone enter its premises.

He gave the policeman on duty Habtom's name, age, home and work address. He also informed him that he hadn't been seen for the last 24 hours. They asked him his name and his relationship and told him to sit and wait until they checked with the responsible department. He waited for 30 minutes.

At about 6.30 pm, a policeman came and took him to an office. At the door, he told him that the captain wanted to see him. He went in and sat down. The captain looked at him and asked, "You are Dermas Goitom, brother to Habtom Goitom, right?"

"Yes, I am his younger brother," said Dermas.

"Ok, then your brother is here with us. He has been accused," said the captain.

"Accused? What kind of accusation? Who accused him?" asked Dermas in succession.

"Those are questions that we will not answer at this time. For the moment, we can only tell you that he is here with us, so the family doesn't unduly need to worry," said the captain calmly but firmly.

"Wow, my God!" said Dermas, shocked and alarmed by what he had heard. The captain did not comment, he merely stared at him. Then Dermas became practical and asked, "Can we bring him clothes, food and other things he might need?"

"The accused is under investigation and interrogation, so everything he needs will be provided by us," said the captain with finality.

"Is there anything else we can do now?" asked Dermas.

"Nothing," was the curt answer of the captain. Then as an after-thought he added, "Depending on the circumstances, we will complete his interrogation within the next four to five days. Then you will be allowed to bring him things he needs. Until then, no other family member or friend is allowed to come and ask. If you have a telephone number, leave us your number and we will call you ourselves. Is that clear?"

Dermas nodded his head vigorously and then gave him the number of the bakery and the shop. The captain wrote down the telephone numbers.

Then, without even raising his head from his notes, he said, "We have finished!" Dermas went out without another word, with his head bent down.

The police had taken Habtom from the bakery. The two policemen were both plainclothes men and the workers did not suspect anything. When they asked him to accompany them to the station, Habtom did not give it much thought. He didn't say anything to anyone, because he was sure that he would return soon.

* 6 *

When he got out of the police station, Dermas went into a nearby bar and called Almaz at her shop. She picked up the phone instantly. Without any introduction or explanation, he hurriedly said, "There is something important we need to talk about right away. Go home and wait for me there. I will be there in 30 minutes."

Before she finished her sentence, Dermas had already closed the telephone. He had heard her starting to say, '"Did you find anything...." He purposely ignored her question. He knew that if he started telling her any information over the telephone, she would give him a hard time.

Dermas went straight to Almaz. She was already waiting for him. She didn't even give him a chance to sit. "What is going on Dermas? You closed the phone while I was talking to you! When you did that, my whole body shook! Anyway, is he ok?"

"Well, he is ok and he is also not ok," said Dermas.

"What? What has happened?"

"He is in police custody at the *Carscioli* police station."

"Police? *Carscioli*? Why?"

"He has been accused of a crime."

"Accused? Crime? Accused by whom?"

Dermas went on to explain everything the captain had said. When he was finished, Almaz said, "What do we do now? We can't just sit doing nothing! We have to try to find out information from somewhere else."

"That is why I am here, so we can discuss what is best."

Suddenly changing the subject, Almaz asked, "By the way, do you know if Habtom has any enemies or adversaries I don't know of?"

"Not that I know of. Except, of course, the situation with Tesfom and Araya, and I can't imagine any reason why they would accuse Habtom now!" said Dermas assertively.

"Wow! What a mystery!" said Almaz, sighing heavily.

It was Dermas's turn to ask, "Do you, by any chance, know anything I don't know?"

"I don't know of anyone that could do this," asserted Almaz.

"Since everyone is going to know about this soon, it is better if we ask our staff for details of anything they saw or heard," said Dermas.

"Yes, I think that is better. While we are at it, let's also inform and ask his friends if they know anything we don't know," said Almaz.

"Ok, we also need to tell the family soon, before this becomes common knowledge," said Araya.

"Ok, your parents should especially be told immediately. But don't tell that bastard Alganesh! She won't sympathize or help. She will merely celebrate her happiness with her neighbors over coffee!" said Almaz with rancor.

Dermas didn't agree with Almaz's statement, but he chose to keep it to himself. He didn't want to antagonize her. So, he merely said, "Well, Alganesh and the children are also going to hear it from other people, but if you say so, ok."

"Good!" she said, and then wringing her hands and sighing heavily added, "Oh my God! What a mystery! What a tragedy!"

"Ok, then let me leave you. I have to face my poor parents. I don't even know how to break this to them. They are both especially sensitive when it comes to Habtom," said Dermas, standing up.

"They are absolutely right. Remember that they are parents. Don't also forget that he is their first-born!" said Almaz.

Dermas was sure that Almaz had wanted to add, "After all, there is no one like Habtom." He was certain she had held it back at the last moment. He had heard that statement his entire life from her and the whole family. As always, Dermas kept his thoughts to himself. He merely said, "Ok then, I will see you," and left immersed in deep thought.

* 7 *

Dermas went straight to his parents' home. On his way, he started thinking about the best way of breaking the news to them. He knew Habtom's standing in the family hierarchy was going to make the handling more delicate. He collected his thoughts carefully and arrived at 7.30 pm.

Both parents welcomed their son with open arms. While chatting with them about trivialities, Dermas' mind was preoccupied by what to say and how to say it. All the ideas he had collected suddenly seemed inappropriate. He collected his courage and finally blurted out the words that came to his mind, "Habtom has encountered a problem."

Both parents were completely caught off guard. They both shouted, "What? What did you just say?"

"Habtom has encountered a problem," Dermas repeated, as if they hadn't heard him.

"What? What kind of problem are you talking about?", asked W/ro Lemlem nearly standing up from her chair, holding her head with both hands.

"Calm down," said Bashay coolly, pushing her back. Then he turned to Dermas and asked, "What kind of a problem are you talking about?"

"He has been imprisoned," blurted out Dermas.

"Imprisoned?" W/ro Lemlem stood up again. "Imprisoned?" said Bashay, standing up from his chair.

"Please sit down. Don't be excessively alarmed. It is not a big problem. Even if they imprison him today, he will come out soon," said Dermas trying to calm his parents.

Instead of calming his mother, Dermas's statement upset her further. "How could you say, this is not something alarming or worrying? Don't forget, it is Habtom that has been imprisoned!" shouted his mother.

Before Dermas could answer, Bashay saved him from the wrath of his mother by asking, "When did this happen and what is the reason for his imprisonment?"

Dermas went on to explain what the captain told him and what they knew up to that point.

His mother was not finished with him and asked a pointed question, "When you don't even know why he is imprisoned and by whom, then why were you trying tell us it is not alarming?"

Again, his father came to his rescue. He said, "I am sure he said so merely to appease and calm us."

Dermas immediately grabbed the life line his father had dangled and said, "Yes, that is why I told you so. Also, mother, I don't think I need to remind you that there are many things worse than imprisonment!"

"Well, in a way, you are right," said his mother softly, accepting the reality of what her son wisely pointed out.

Bashay was proud of what his son said," Well said, Izi Wedey! By the way, is there anything at all that you suspect could be a probable cause or a probable enemy?" he asked.

"Well, so far, Almaz and I could not come up with any cause or anyone who could do this," said Dermas confidently.

"Well, it could even be Grazmach's satanic son, Tesfom!" said W/ro Lemlem.

"Wow! Lemlem, how you rush to accuse and judge! How can you jump and blame him when we don't know the facts?", growled Bashay.

"As far as I am concerned, there is no one else we know who would want to hurt and ruin Habtom!" said W/ro Lemlem, sticking to her guns.

"What reason could Tesfom have to accuse Habtom? If he had any, he would have accused him while they were dissolving the partnership, not now," said Dermas with full confidence.

"What Dermas is saying is very rational and probable," said Bashay, siding with his son.

"You can think as you wish, but as far as I am concerned, he is the only one who could do this," said W/ro Lemlem. Then shaking her head and her eyes tearing added, "My poor son Habtom; to hear that you are spending your day and night in prison and that we can do nothing about it is a shame!" She raised her head and, in desperation again said, "Oh My God! Oh, Holy Mary! Help me! Where else can I turn to?"

Dermas was extremely touched by his mother's sadness and anguish. He knew his father was also suffering. He thus said, "Come on mother! Come on father! Don't be alarmed! Don't lose hope. Starting tomorrow, we are going to go around asking important people and friends for information and assistance. Rest assured; we will do our utmost. Until we know exactly what this is, it will be better to keep this information to ourselves. Allow me to go now," said Dermas, standing up.

"Ok, Izi Wedey, Go with God. God help you!" said Bashay. "Ok, Izi Wedey, let the blessed St. Mary accompany you and give you success," said W/ro Lemlem.

Dermas left his parents with a heavy heart.

* 8 *

On Friday, the 27th of February, Tesfom received a call from Colonel Habte. He told him that he would like to see him and Araya at 4.30 pm. Tesfom called Araya and told him the news. They both understood that the crucial and decisive time had come.

They went to the police headquarters at the appointed hour. The Colonel was busy and they had to wait for about 15 minutes, which seemed to them more than an hour. Finally, they were allowed to go in. Colonel Habte greeted them warmly, begging their pardon for keeping them waiting.

"We know that accidents, burglaries, fights, accusations and crimes are hard to predict and that emergencies suddenly pile-up out of nowhere. So, don't worry, we know your busy schedule and how emergencies crop-up unpredictably," said Tesfom.

"Thank you for your understanding. Anyway, let me get straight into why I dragged you in here this afternoon. After very cautious, hard, and concerted work, we have finally succeeded. The secret of our success was because we were able to pit them against each other. We separately told them that we had been following them for a long time; that we had many witnesses that were willing to testify; that there were people who saw them in the vicinity of the factory on the night of the fire; that Gebreab had said so and so; that Habtom has said so and so, etc. It took a lot of going to and for," said the Colonel.

He paused for a while to catch his breath. Araya's and Tesfom's faces were already beaming and glistening with joy. Then the Colonel continued, "Gebreab did not resist for long, he confessed comparatively quickly. However, Habtom was a harder nut to crack. Finally, we had to record part of Gebreab's confession on tape and make him listen to the part we wanted him to hear. Finally, he also succumbed and confessed."

"Wow, my dear Colonel, there are no words that could adequately express our gratitude. Thank you so much!" said Araya, his face glowing.

"Araya has said it all. We will never forget this deed. You are indeed a friend in need. Thank you so much!" said Tesfom with intense emotion.

"Come on, please guys, don't make it as If I did something out of the ordinary. I have already told you that our responsibility is to bring criminals to justice; I just did my job," said Colonel Habte humbly.

'By the way, I didn't go into much detail because you don't need to hear it all. However, one interesting finding was that the agreement was for Habtom to pay Gebreab 10.000 Birr for his criminal services," said the Colonel.

"What? What?" asked the two brothers in unison, nearly jumping out of their chairs.

'Wait, that is not the interesting part. The interesting part is that they were fighting bitterly because Habtom was insisting that because the factory was only half burnt, Gebreab's fee should be 5.000 Birr and not 10.000 as agreed!" said the Colonel.

"Amazing! Let alone agree to pay 10.000 Birr, Habtom is the kind of person, who does not even spend 100 Birr for anything. Yet, that he was prepared to pay that much, shows how much accumulated anger and hatred he had against us!" said Tesfom, shaking his head.

"Well, that is actually what eventually led to his downfall. It was because he was blind with resentment and hatred that he committed such an insane act!" said the Colonel, looking at his watch.

Tesfom noticed that the Colonel had looked at his watch. "We have already taken a lot of your time; it is time for us to leave. We know how busy you are," said Tesfom smiling and standing up.

"Yes, actually, I have a meeting coming up soon," said the Colonel standing up.

Both brothers again profusely thanked the Colonel and left.

* 9 *

Tesfom and Araya left the Colonel's office after 6 pm. Their faces were shining with joy and success. They were smiling, laughing, talking incoherently, and interrupting each other after every phrase. It was an indication of their state of mind and the relief and satisfaction that were overwhelming their feelings. Along with all the joy and merriment, Araya noticed that Tesfom was driving in another direction.

"Are you aware that you are driving in another direction? Where are you going?" Araya asked.

"I am driving in whichever direction I desire! Today is the

day when we have every right to go anywhere and everywhere we want!" shouted Tesfom.

Araya was taken aback by Tesfom's sudden burst of passion. "Initially, when I noticed that you were driving in the wrong direction, I was confused. I couldn't comprehend how you would lose your way. Then I asked myself, has my brother become drunk with joy?" said Araya smiling.

"There will never come a better day to get drunk on anything! We have worked and suffered for this and we deserve it!" shouted Tesfom again.

Tesfom looked and acted like he was already drunk. Before Araya could say anything, Tesfom added, "Today, I don't want to hear any argument. You are my younger brother and you will do whatever I tell you to do! You will go wherever I take you! You will eat and drink whatever I tell you to eat and drink!" shouted Tesfom again.

"Ok, no problem, we can proceed by mutual agreement," said Araya.

"Mutual agreement today will mean that you will do what I tell you to do! Although you are my younger brother, do you deny that for the last few months, I have been doing everything you have been asking me to do?" asked Tesfom.

"I don't deny that at all," said Araya.

"Then that is it! We have finished! End of subject!" said Tesfom, with finality.

"Ok, Tesfom Hawey, be happy! I will do whatever you say! Let alone celebrating with others, this is a secret that we can't even share with anyone else. So, you are right. We can only celebrate this victory with each other," cried Araya, agreeing with his brother.

"That is the only thing I want to hear!" said Tesfom, holding his right hand and shouting, "Give me five!" Araya obliged and both sealed their agreement with a firm handshake.

With Tesfom at the helm, Araya was not sure how the night would play out. He insisted they call both Embabba and Medhn and inform them that they were together and would be late. Tesfom reluctantly agreed. After that, he started not only driving their car but also driving their evening by taking full control of the night.

This was the first time Araya had gone out for entertainment with his brother. Araya occasionally used to go out with his friends, but it was always after a long time and they drank in moderation and always went home at a reasonable hour. So, he knew what it meant to go out and have fun, but it had always been in moderation.

As a young man, Araya had always feared and respected his older brother. Let alone go out with him, he was not even comfortable for his brother to see him out with his friends. But, today was different. For the first time, he was going out with his brother as an equal. Araya was glad to notice that Tesfom had started to enjoy his time with him, without any inhibition. This was the first time Araya was able to discover the other nature and side of his brother.

At first, Tesfom took him to a place he had never been and they heartily ate *Tsaeda* and *Keih Kulwa* and *Zilzil* (mild and hot minced stir-fried meat and fajitas, seasoned with Berbere and served with Injera). Tesfom ordered Heineken beer for both of them. Araya adamantly refused the Heineken and instead insisted on sticking with his local brand, Melotti beer. They ate slowly and drank their beer. Tesfom was jokingly telling him that this was in preparation for the night ahead.

Then they started their evening in earnest. They started going from place to place. Halfway during the evening, they went to the Babylon square, which had been christened 'Babylon square' because the whole square was composed only of Bars. They visited many of the popular Bars in the square.

After leaving Babylon square, Tesfom took him to places Araya had never been or seen before. They went to a bar near the *Monopolio* (Tobacco Industry; a popular bar near the post office; and then to secluded clandestine bars that offer their services to a few select patrons known as *Segreto* (Secret). These bars operate after the regular bars close their doors to the public.

Next, he took him to a *Segreto* in *Geza Banda Tilian*, in *Campo Pollo* and other areas. All the places they went where spots Araya didn't even know existed. It was easy to observe that all the places they went to looked as if they were just opening their doors for the long night ahead. They were all full of cigarette smoke, the smell of a cocktail of alcoholic beverages, loud music and loud and boisterous voices. Araya was finding it difficult to adapt to this new environment. Nevertheless, he decided to hang on so as not to spoil his brother's enjoyment.

As the night progressed, Araya was able to understand why his brother was so popular and had so many friends. Tesfom, under normal circumstances, was a very nice, decent and sweet person. Here he saw that during entertainment, his brother was even far sweeter, nicer and jollier. Moreover, he also saw that his brother was always willing to pay for anyone he knew and met. His conversations, anecdotes and jokes were very entertaining and amusing.

Araya clearly understood why there wouldn't be anyone who wouldn't love to go out with his brother. He told himself, "Instead of distancing themselves from my brother, those who enjoy going out and drinking would rush to be first in line, to buzz around and lick at the sweetness of his nectar." Araya marveled and smiled at his own analogy. He believed the inspiration was due to his great happiness and satisfaction at their victory.

They had a great evening and night. Even Araya admitted to himself that he had enormously enjoyed the evening. In terms of drinking, Araya could not proceed at the same rate as his brother. So, he took one shot, when his brother took two and would not even finish the portions that were poured. At midnight, he begged Tesfom to call it a night. He remonstrated with him that they had to go to work the next day. After much effort, Tesfom reluctantly agreed.

When the time for driving came, Araya was not confident

about his brother's state of soberness. After debating with himself, he decided to confront him about it. Araya suggested that he take the wheel by volunteering to drive Tesfom's car. Tesfom wouldn't even hear of it. He told Araya, "Don't underestimate your old brother, Araya. After such a night, I merely get a little high, but I never get outright drunk."

Araya begged him some more, but Tesfom refused. At the end, Araya decided to accept their fate. He sat beside his brother. When Tesfom started driving, he was amazed to see that he was in possession of all his faculties and was in fact driving very cautiously and carefully. He then settled down and started enjoying his brother's driving and jokes.

When they were half-way to his house, Araya suggested that they drive straight to Tesfom's house. He said he would walk home from there. Tesfom adamantly rejected the idea as totally unacceptable, seeing no reason why his young brother should walk after midnight when they had a car. Araya remonstrated that the fresh air and the walk would help him get rid of some of the effect of the alcohol and the tobacco. Araya did not want to divulge his real reasons for his request. He wanted to see his brother safely home. He had a suspicion that Tesfom might drop him and go back to drinking.

As if he could read his mind, Tesfom suddenly surprised him. He said, "What is your real intention, man? Did you enjoy and love the night we had so much, that you want to see me home and then go back to where we were?"

What? No! Come on, Tesfom! I was the one who suggested that we call it a night," said Araya defensively.

"If that is the case, then sit back and I will deposit you home and then I will head home," said Tesfom with finality.

Araya had no other alternative but to agree. Soon after, Tesfom dropped him off.

* 10 *

As always, Medhn was waiting for Tesfom. When she heard him coming, she opened the door for him. Since he had told her that he was with Araya, she had assumed they were at work. The moment he walked in; she could smell that he had been drinking. She was confused. She didn't want to ask him at that hour and create a scene.

Tesfom went straight to their bedroom. While she was checking on the children, she heard the telephone ring, which surprised her, because nobody called at that hour. When she picked up the phone, the voice said, "Don't call my name." At first, she was confused but then instantly recognized the voice and at the last moment, pulled back the name that was at the tip of her tongue. He asked her if his brother was safely home and when she responded in the affirmative, he promised to explain about their evening the next day and hang up the telephone.

* 11 *

The next day, Saturday March 1st, Tesfom called Hailom and secured an appointment. He arrived at Hailom's office at 10 am and was warmly welcomed.

As soon as they sat down, Tesfom jokingly said, "You attorneys claim to stand for justice, yet you sit in closed fortress-like offices, where no one can accost you without permission. We bankers don't even have doors to our offices; anyone comes in at will. In this instance, who is standing for fairness and justice, we or you?"

Hailom laughed heartily. Then he asked Tesfom if he remembered the hot argument, they had had long ago about the same subject. Tesfom didn't remember the incident, but Hailom reminded him that they had discussed how heads of departments, managers, directors, etc. work with their office doors closed. This allows them and their assistants to falsely claim the boss is busy or in a meeting, etc. which enables them to evade their responsibilities and deny service to people who need their assistance. They had recommended then that such bosses should either have offices without doors, or should not be allowed to close their doors, so that their work could be apparent and transparent to everyone.

Tesfom followed his friend's account with amazement, as if he was listening to it for the first time. He was amazed by his friend's capacity to recollect. They reminisced for a few minutes about the incident until Tesfom said, "Ok, let me get straight to business, so you can get back to your work."

Hailom was instantly all seriousness. He took a pen and a notebook and said, "Ok, great, go ahead,"

"I have good news. They have confessed!" said Tesfom.

"Wow! That is great news! Congratulations!" said Hailom, giving Tesfom a high five.

Tesfom explained in detail all the information the Colonel had given him. Hailom took notes and asked a few questions after Tesfom had finished. "Wow, this is really great, especially if after their confessions, they had to sign a deposition in front of a judge," said Hailom.

"Yes, the Colonel told us that they made them sign a deposition in front of a judge, asserting that they confessed without force or duress," said Tesfom.

"Great! In that case, the police will forward the case to the Attorney General. The state's attorney will study the case and indict them and then take the case to court and prosecute them. I know the state's attorney very well. Since I know the case very well, I will contact him," said Hailom.

"Thank you," said Tesfom.

"No problem. The Colonel has made our job easier. Now we will need to go to court merely to get the best deal for compensation and restitution," said Hailom.

"Will we also be able to present the case for compensation for the damages we suffered now?" asked Tesfom.

"No, we can't do that now. That can only follow after the criminal case is settled. The court has to first pass a sentence (verdict) and convict them of the crime. Then we can proceed with the civil case by filing a case for restitution of the damages," said Hailom.

"Oh, ok. Then if you can prepare the formal paper work making you our lawyer for the civil case, we could sign it as soon as possible," said Tesfom.

"Yes, no problem. The secretary will prepare it soon," said Hailom.

"Ok, then if we have nothing else, allow me to leave. I will go back to the office and you can attend to your clients," said Tesfom, standing up.

Hailom stood up. He said, "By the way, don't worry or stress yourself about signing formal agreements. My agreement with you is sealed by a handshake, not by signatures!" He then clenched Tesfom's hand hard and shook it several times.

Tesfom was touched by his friendship. "Thank you Hailom Hawey, I have no doubt about that! You are a true friend!" said Tesfom, shaking Hailom's hand vigorously several times.

* 12 *

Araya woke up much later than usual with a heavy headache. His head was throbbing and he was totally dehydrated. He was really hurting. This was something out of the ordinary for him. For the first time, Araya arrived at the factory two hours late.

They told him that Medhn had called twice. He knew she was worried and curious about what had happened. He called her and asked her forgiveness and explained to her how he was faring.

"Well, Araya, don't complain. You have actually fared well. Don't forget that you have tried to compete with professionals, but you are barely an apprentice!" said Medhn, laughing and then quickly added, "By the way, what was yesterday's thing?"

"Don't mention this until you hear it from him, but both Habtom and Gebreab have confessed to their crimes!"

"Oh, my God! That is a great relief! So, he must have insisted that you had to celebrate, right?"

"Yes. Actually, at first, I declined, but then, when he insisted, I didn't want to disappoint him," said Araya.

"Ok, Araya Hawey, thanks. Everything is clear now. I will let you go back to your work, ciao," said Medhn, hanging up the telephone.

"*Ciao*," said Araya.

* 13 *

When Tesfom went to the factory, he found his brother nursing his hangover. He made fun of him. He told him how yesterday's outing was a normal affair and that it was affecting him only because of his lack of experience.

Then Araya asked him about his meeting with Hailom. Tesfom recounted the contents of their discussion and the points the attorney had enumerated. When his brother finished, Araya said, "Then it looks like everything is in order. In that case, it is time that we update father and Medhn."

"Yes, I think you are right. By now, it is also possible that Habtom's family might already know about his imprisonment," said Tesfom.

"Then we should do it soon," said Araya.

"We don't have to do this together. If you want, I can pass by our parents this evening and tell them, and I can tell Medhn when I go home," Tesfom volunteered.

"That would be nice of you," said Araya, relieved.

With that, they passed on to other work-related issues.

* 14 *

Tesfom headed straight to his parents' home. Because Tesfom and Araya had been busy running around, they hadn't been to their parents for days. Grazmach and W/ro Brkti had missed their sons very much. Thus, when Tesfom came, they welcomed him warmly. W/ro Brkti still had no idea about what was going on.

As soon as he sat down, his mother said, "Luckily, I have already prepared the Shiro you love. We will eat dinner together."

"It is ok mother. I will just chat for a while and go. Medhn and the children will be waiting for me," said Tesfom.

"Nothing will happen to them if they eat alone for one day," said W/ro Brkti.

"Your mother is right. We can tell them, so they don't wait for you. Brkti, call Medhn and tell her that Tesfom is going to eat dinner with us," said Grazmach, concluding the subject.

Tesfom noticed that his father had intentionally closed the matter. He knew expressing further opposition wouldn't work, so he said, "Ok then, as you wish."

They ate dinner, chatting relaxedly. After dinner, his mother brought tea. While sipping their tea, Tesfom said, "I am here tonight, because I wanted to inform you about an important development. Father already knows the background to this new development," said Tesfom, and he started to briefly explain to his mother about how they found out that the accident at the factory was a sabotage.

W/ro Brkti, who had no clue about what was happening, went crazy. She put both her hands on her head, shook her head and interrupted him, "Oh, my God! Oh, my poor children! You suffered all this time because of the evil act of Habtom, the devil? I had opposed the whole idea of working in partnership with this person from the very start, but no one would listen to me!"

Grazmach did not seem happy with his wife's interruption and statement. But, without making a comment, he merely said, "Continue son."

Tesfom started to recount the train of events and as he was about to report the results of the police investigation, W/ro Brkti again interrupted him, "Oh, my God! My poor children! You were criticized and admonished so much as if the calamity was your fault, while the perpetrator was sleeping peacefully. It is very sad! We should never have gone into partnership with these people!"

"Come on Brkti, don't take us backwards. There is nothing we can change now, by regretting 'if we hadn't gone into partnership'," said Grazmach.

"I am not taking you backwards. All this would not have happened, if my opinion had been heard!" said W/ro Brkti, sticking to her guns.

"Saying, 'I told you so' after the fact does not change anything. Everyone is wise in hindsight. Please, Tesfom Wedey, continue," said Grazmach, with an edge of irritation in his voice.

Tesfom continued his narration. He told them that both had already confessed to their crimes and concluded by informing them that the next step was going to be suing them in court.

When he finished, Grazmach said, "The fact that they confessed is important in two aspects. It will make the legal battle less complicated and of shorter duration. It will also save you and us from being accused of implicating them without a probable cause and evidence. Otherwise, it is a very sad and tragic event."

They discussed the issue further and when they were finished, Tesfom departed.

Tesfom went straight home. He was not aware that Araya had already given Medhn a hint. He sat down and informed Medhn about the police investigation developments. Medhn listened as if she was hearing it for the first time. When he finished, she noted that it was an important development that would save them a lot of effort and time. They then concluded the subject and went to bed.

* 15 *

The captain of the *Carscioli* police station had strictly instructed Dermas that no family member should come to enquire about the case before the investigation was over. He had assured him that they would be informed at the appropriate time, but despite that warning, out of desperation, Dermas had continued to go and ask.

The response of the police was always, "Until he finishes his investigation, there is nothing we can tell you." More than the imprisonment of his brother, it was the "Why and by whom," that were bothering Dermas and the whole family. Everyone was under immense pressure and feelings of desperation. On Thursday afternoon, the 26th of February, Dermas received a call from the captain. He was told to immediately come to the station.

Before rushing to the station, Dermas spent a few minutes informing Almaz about the summons. When he arrived at the station the captain was busy and he had to wait, and the waiting seemed like an eternity. When he was finally called, he looked at his watch and was surprised to see that he had only waited for 30 minutes.

When he went in, the captain was busy working on a file. He acknowledged Dermas with a nod and, without lifting his eyes from the file, beckoned him to sit down. He continued leafing through the file and after a few minutes, looked straight at Dermas and said, "I am afraid, I don't have much good news about your brother."

"Eh! What?", said Dermas with terror in his eyes.

"Let me begin with the good news. Starting tomorrow, you can bring stuff that your brother will need," said the captain.

Dermas nodded and in a low barely audible voice said, "OK."

"Your brother has committed and confessed to a very serious crime!" the captain presented the tragic news.

"Serious crime? What kind of a crime? Against whom?" Dermas asked consecutive questions.

"We have ascertained that Habtom paid a conspirator to commit arson on a factory!"

"Factory! What kind of factory? Whose factory?" asked Dermas with trepidation, hoping he wouldn't hear what he was dreading.

"The pasta factory which initially you guys owned in partnership!"

Dermas put both of his hand onto his head and bent down, nearly touching the ground. Still with his hands on his head, he looked up and asked, "Are you trying to tell me that he confessed and accepted responsibility for this atrocious crime?"

"Yes!" was the only curt and firm answer the captain provided.

"I just can't believe that Habtom in his right mind would do this! I just can't!", shouted Dermas.

The captain ignored Dermas's statement, and instead, as if he hadn't heard him, chose to move to another subject, "There is something else I haven't told you."

"What can you ever tell me that is worse than this?" said Dermas, who was already numb.

The captain again ignored Dermas's comment and said, "Starting tomorrow, with police supervision and inspection, you can communicate with your brother in written form. Since the case will soon be going to court, in consultation with your brother, you have the right to nominate a lawyer who will represent him. After Monday, March the 3rd, the lawyer can come and consult with your brother."

To show that the meeting was concluded, the captain stood up and then curtly said, "We have finished."

Dermas understood that he was being dismissed. He had nothing more to say, so he bent his head and went out without another word.

* 16 *

Although Dermas was very conscious of everything he had heard, his mind refused to accept the reality. He kept telling himself, "This can't be real! This can only be a dream!"

He had hoped the fresh air outside would drive away the nightmare and replace it with another reality. To his dismay, nothing changed and he was forced to accept and swallow the bitter pill. Still, he kept telling himself, "How can this be? How?"

"*How can Habtom, who knows the pros and cons of any given situation in great detail, decide to go ahead with such a crazy plan? What is it that pushed and drove him to such a lethal and dangerous precipice? Habtom, who outgrew his childhood; Habtom who started with a tiny shop and succeeded in owning and managing several enterprises? Habtom, who despite barely finishing his elementary education, could stand up to and match and even excel educated and experienced graduates? Habtom, Habtom, Habtom...*" said Dermas in self-denial, enumerating an unending list of his brother's achievements.

All the enumeration and compilation did not help Dermas to resolve the answer to the riddle that was overpowering him. Soon, he realized the uselessness of his effort and decided to accept the facts without questioning. He was then able to shift his focus towards telling the tragic news to the family.

Dermas understood that it would not be difficult to tell Almaz. What was going to be most challenging was how he could tell his parents, something he found incomprehensible. He thought hard and deep about the best way of breaking it to them, without unduly hurting them. But, no matter how hard he tried, he couldn't come up with something sensible and realistic. "I've had enough!" He told himself. "Why am I troubling and distressing myself for a solution that does not exist? I should give myself respite. I will just say whatever comes to my mind." After his decision, Dermas felt slightly relieved.

He then went into a nearby Bar and called Almaz and told her to meet him at home. The moment Dermas entered, Almaz could read from his body language, that something was very wrong? She immediately put both of her hands on her head and said, "Things are bad, right?"

"Things are worse than bad Almaz! They have told me that Habtom, along with a conspirator, has admitted to committing a very serious crime," said Dermas.

"Crime?!" cried Almaz.

"Yes, crime! It would have been much more acceptable, if it had been some kind of crime on another person, but they are alleging that Habtom and his co-conspirator are responsible for burning the pasta factory!"

"Whaat? What are you saying? The pasta factory was burned by a combination of rain, wind, electricity and lightning!" said Almaz, incredulous at the preposterous allegation she was hearing.

Dermas went on to tell her all the information he had learned from the captain. Even when he finished, Almaz could not believe what she was hearing. She kept repeating, "How can this be? What problems did he have to push him to such a crazy decision? But one thing is true! When it comes to rancor, keeping score and enmity, your brother has no match! This could be the result of all that!" said Almaz bitterly.

"If indeed he has committed this, I will find it very difficult to believe that he did this while in possession of all his faculties!" said Dermas.

"Oh my God! Oh Lord! Habtom has made us the laughing stock of everyone! He has handed over full victory to Tesfom and his family! What are we going to do now?", asked Almaz, stressed out and anxious.

"Well, I guess, I have no option but go and break it to our poor parents," answered Dermas, who had misunderstood Almaz's question.

"I am asking you about what we are going to do, concerning Habtom!" said Almaz, raising her voice, with slight irritation.

"When we go to take stuff for him tomorrow, I am hoping he will send us a note and we will proceed from there," said Dermas.

The whole time, Almaz had not even once brought her hand down from her head. She shook her body and her head and repeated again, "Oh My God! This is unbelievable!"

"Ok, let me go now. Prepare everything and tomorrow we will go together," said Dermas standing up.

"Ok, I guess there is nothing else we can do now. My God! Habtom has sunk us all into a deep well!", said Almaz, standing up and seeing him off.

* 17 *

After talking with Almaz, Dermas felt as if a heavy object was lifted from his back. But this did not last long. The closer he got to his parents' house, the more he felt the pressure and the weight of the uncomfortable task ahead. After repeatedly telling himself that it was something that had to be done, he mustered all the courage he could marshal and knocked on the door.

While his parents were greeting him, he could clearly read that they were anxiously waiting for good news. However, instantly, W/ro Lemlem's maternal instinct kicked in. She saw that her son's body language did not augur good news. So, she asked, "Aren't we OK?"

"Habtom is OK, although in another sense, he is not OK. He is OK, because he is still healthy and alive," said Dermas, using the statement which he had prepared as a soft blow.

"What? What are you saying?", asked his mother anxiously, confused by Dermas's statement.

"The police have informed me that Habtom has admitted to committing a serious crime," said Dermas, trying his best to make the terrible news softer.

"Whaat? Admitted a Crime? What are you saying?" said Bashay.

"Crime? My son? Never!" said W/ro Lemlem fiercely.

"Well, they are saying that he and his conspirator have admitted to setting fire to the pasta factory,"

"The Grazmach family's pasta factory? No, that is impossible!" said his father.

"Impossible! Unless, the satanic Tesfom has framed him by his influential connections with the police. Otherwise, my son would never commit this!" said W/ro Lemlem angrily.

"Anyway, up to now, that is what they are saying," said Dermas.

"Ahh! Poor me! I had an inkling and a suspicion that something like this could happen. I even indicated loudly that Tesfom could be responsible, but I was ridiculed. Nobody listens to me in this house!" said W/ro Lemlem bitterly.

Bashay had no answer to his wife. So, he turned towards his son and said, "Just because they are alleging admission to a crime, it does not mean it is over. We will leave no stone unturned until we clear this up!" said Bashay, the veins on his forehead bulging and pulsating.

"As if his initial accusation of theft against you and your brother was not enough, he now wants to destroy Habtom by a false accusation!" said W/ro Lemlem.

"Father, mother, don't lose hope. We have been given permission to communicate with Habtom starting tomorrow. We will be able to understand the case in greater detail after we hear from him. Then we will devise a plan and a strategy on how best to deal with this," said Dermas, trying to give hope to his parents.

W/ro Lemlem had instantly progressed, from extreme anger, to extreme anguish and sadness. She had already started to moan and shed tears. Bashay was still holding his head with his hands and was shaking his body from left to right. Dermas felt bad and sad that his parents had to go through such anguish and pain. He wished with all his heart that he possessed the power to relieve them from their pain, but he felt helpless that he couldn't do anything.

Finally, he decided to leave rather than see them suffer. "Let me go now. If there is anything new, I will come and update you tomorrow," said Dermas, standing up.

"Since there is not much you can do, I think it is best if you go, son. After all, you are the one who is carrying the brunt of all this," said Bashay, sympathizing with his younger son's situation.

His mother did not even look up at him. She was still fighting with her tears. Dermas went out without adding another word.

Over the following days, the whole Bashay family and their close friends came to know of Habtom's imprisonment. However, there was one family that was not yet aware of the incident.

* 18 *

The first family Habtom established was the only family that was not aware of what was going on. Alganesh and her children still had no inkling of Habtom's predicament.

Medhn was worried that her main friend and neighbor and her children were still in the dark. She was repeatedly telling Tesfom how unfair it was that she didn't know and reiterated that they had a responsibility to tell her. Although he agreed with her stance, he still argued that it would be best if Alganesh came to know through the Bashay family. Medhn was so worried about the subject, that she even stopped going to see Alganesh, just to avoid her.

In accordance with their agreement, both Medhn and Alganesh had been closely observing Bruk and Kbret for a long time. Their observations led them to further worry about the nature of special relationship of the young couple. They had decided to confront them about their observation. Consequently, they had fixed an appointment for Saturday afternoon. Since Medhn's attention and concentration were wholly consumed by the Habtom case, she had completely forgotten about her appointment with Alganesh. Medhn became aware of the appointment only after Alganesh came on Saturday morning to remind her of their plans.

When they sat down in the afternoon with Bruk and Kbret, they strongly expressed their anxiety and concern about their relationship. They enumerated their observations and reasons for their concern and warned them that they were still too young to be embroiled in love. They insisted that this was the time in their lives when they should concentrate on their studies.

Bruk and Kbret adamantly rejected their observations and concerns. They assured their mothers that nothing had changed in their relationship, reminding them that their special relationship, closeness and care for each other was not something new; it had always been that way since they could remember. Finally, they solemnly assured and promised them that nothing would change in the future as well.

Medhn and Alganesh did not wholly accept their children's strong assurances and denial. However, they felt it was better to give them the benefit of the doubt, so, they decided to go along with their children. Nevertheless, they warned them to be vigilant and to examine their emotions at every turn. They finished by explaining to them how sometimes people fall in love unaware, without realizing it.

After the children left, Medhn and Alganesh agreed to continue their observation and follow up aggressively. Then they continued chatting about family and friends. From her friend's mood, Medhn was certain that Alganesh still had no clue about Habtom's imprisonment. Medhn was extremely worried by the situation and knew she had to talk to Tesfom urgently.

Alganesh noticed that something was bothering Medhn, but she decided not to mention it. She was certain that if it was something that she should know, then Medhn would tell her at the right time. Alganesh, who had no inkling of what was going on in Medhn's head, decided to leave her friend. Medhn saw her off.

* 19 *

When Tesfom came in the evening, Medhn wasted no time in confronting him about their delay in informing Alganesh. She insisted that they should tell her the next day. Tesfom did not resist much; he agreed that it was time that she knew. However, he insisted that Medhn do it herself; he begged her to excuse him from the task. Medhn sympathized with his aversion to the task and agreed to take the assignment herself.

The next morning, she told Alganesh that they had something important to discuss in private. They agreed to meet at 10 am, telling their children that they were not to be disturbed. Medhn decided to plunge straight into the subject. "Has anyone from the Bashay family, by any chance, visited or called you in the last week?" asked Medhn.

"None! No one would! All family members have ganged up on us. We have practically become lepers; no one wants to be seen near us. It has been this way for so long, even the children have gotten used to it. It has also been a while since their father had come to see them. The older children, don't even ask me about him; they understand that mentioning him hurts me. The younger ones used to, but now, even they have gotten used to it," Alganesh complained bitterly.

Medhn felt very bad, "I understand how much you are suffering Alganesh Habtey."

"Yes, but then, sometimes you can't escape your destiny, Medhn Habtey,"

"You are very wise and courageous, Alganesh Habtey. As you correctly said, when you can't change your destiny, it is wise to accept it with grace,"

"Well, when you have the responsibility of caring for innocent children, what else can you do? When my children have practically lost their father, I can't leave them without a mother as well!" Alganesh said wisely, though bitterly.

"In a way, your children are lucky! They have been blessed with a wise, dedicated and courageous mother. You are one of a few, who are able to be both a father and a mother to their children," said Medhn with admiration. She then quickly added, "How did we end up talking about this subject? Oh yes, actually, the issue I want to discuss with you, is related to this. I don't even know where or how to begin. Something terrible has happened. Initially, Tesfom even hid it from me," said Medhn, with hesitation.

"Oh no! Again? What has happened to Tesfom? Wow! How is it, that it is always the nice people who get the short end of the stick?" said Alganesh, unaware of the happenings, but sympathizing with Tesfom and his family.

"Oh no! This time, I am not talking about Tesfom. I am talking about Habtom! He has been imprisoned!" said Medhn.

"Imprisoned! Imprisoned? Does the whole Bashay family know about this?" asked Alganesh, incredulous at what she was hearing.

"Of course, everyone else knows!" asserted Medhn.

"Wow, this family's priorities and doings are astounding! However, that is to be expected. Anyway, why on earth has he been imprisoned?!" asked Alganesh.

"It is something very bad. The allegation is that Habtom with a co-conspirator were responsible for the fire in the pasta factory," said Alganesh, putting it as mildly as she could.

"What? What are you saying Medhn? This can't be real! How can a person do such a thing?" cried Alganesh, dubious at what she was hearing and yet at the same time believing it. She was certain that Medhn and her family were decent people, who wouldn't invent false accusations.

"Yes, it is absolutely difficult to believe and accept," said Medhn. Then she went on to recount the train of events in detail. She withheld the information that Tesfom and Araya had recruited informants to follow Gebreab and Habtom. She started her account from how the police suspected a factory worker by the name of Gebreab, and then how after cross-examination he accused Habtom, and how eventually both of them admitted guilt.

Alganesh couldn't comprehend what she was hearing. She kept repeating, "Oh my God! Oh my God! How can this be? How am I going to break this to the children? What am I to say to them?" she asked in desperation.

"Well, it would have been better if one of the responsible family members would tell them," Said Medhn.

"My dear Medhn, Habtom is not the only one who has abandoned me and my children. The whole family, including the parents have abandoned us. What worsened the relationship was that, after the fight between the two families, they wanted and expected me to break my relationship with you and your family. This, in their eyes, has made me a traitor. It is always sad that the one who stands steadfastly by his principles and sense of justice is the one who is condemned and ostracized. That is, I guess, human nature. But I always say, if that is the price you pay, then so be it!" said Alganesh bitterly but bravely standing by her principles.

"Yes, you are absolutely right Alganesh Habtey. It is sad, but that is the way of the world. Anyway, the best would be not to go into details but simply to tell them that Habtom has been imprisoned. Say that you still don't know the reason, and that you will tell them when you have reliable information. That should satisfy them for the moment," said Medhn.

Alganesh welcomed and instantly accepted the suggestion of her friend. After that they went on to chat about various other subjects. Soon after, they had to reluctantly break up their chat, because it was already lunch time. Alganesh went home and Medhn felt as if a weight had been lifted off her shoulders. She went back to her children very much relieved.

* 20 *

At the very time Medhn and Alganesh were chatting, Bashay Goitom was walking with his head down, immersed in deep thought. While walking, Bashay was talking to himself. Once in a while he gestured to himself and even emitted audible sounds and words, but he was not aware of his surroundings.

At one point, he looked up to see if he had reached his destination but was dismayed to see that he had gone two blocks past the house. He shook his head remembering an old Italian saying that was repeatedly told to him when he was young. Whenever his Italian boss sent him on an errand and he forgot something and had to go back a second time to fetch something, he used to tell him, '*Chi non cia testa, cia gambe!*' This literally translated means, "He who doesn't have a head, has legs!" which means: Since you don't have the brains, the memory and the presence of mind to perform your errand appropriately, then going back and forth several times to perform a single task shouldn't bother you, because it means you have been endowed with legs rather than brains! It was one of Bashay's favorite sayings, and he often used it to make fun of his children and his colleagues. Bashay would have quoted the saying to himself and laughed, if he was in a better state of mind. However, he was not in a good state of mind, so when he remembered the saying, he did not even smile, let alone laugh. He just shook his head with dismay.

Grazmach's house was in the *Addis Alem* zone, previously known as *Geza Banda Tilian*. It was situated two blocks away from the Coptic church of *Medhanie Alem*. It was when he came face to face with the church, that Bashay realized he had passed Grazmach's house by two blocks. Thus, he shook his head again, swallowed his pride and turned to walk back to his destination.

He arrived at Grazmach's house and knocked at the door. W/ro Brkti opened the door. Bashay, before even greeting her, asked, "Is Grazmach at home?"

W/ro Brkti didn't show surprise or shock that Bashay failed to greet her. She, more or less, knew why. Thus, as if nothing had happened, she greeted him warmly and profusely, "Good morning Bashay. Grazmach is taking a nap."

"That's OK, I can wait for him," said Bashay coming in, his demeanor unchanged.

"Please come in, I will wake him up. Until then, I will prepare tea," said W/ro Brkti.

Bashay didn't acknowledge anything, nor did he respond to the tea invitation. W/ro Brkti was certain that Bashay was very angry. She went without saying a word to tell Grazmach that Bashay was there to see him. She went back to the kitchen to prepare tea. While preparing tea, she heard Grazmach greet Bashay and after a while, she joined them with tea and bread.

W/ro Brkti poured the tea and offered them the bread. While sipping their tea, Grazmach started small talk, "So, how is Lemlem doing?"

"She is ok," said Bashay curtly.

"It has been a long time since I saw your daughters' *Lielti* and *Brur*. How are they doing?"

"They are ok," said Bashay, again in the same tone.

"It has been some time since I met anyone from our village. How is our village?"

"It is ok," answered Bashay curtly again. His demeanor seemed as if his whole vocabulary consisted of only three to four words.

The atmosphere became very tense and uncomfortable. To escape from the awkward and oppressive situation, all of them were doing their best to finish their tea as quickly as possible. As soon as the tea was finished, Grazmach asked W/ro Brkti to take away the tea things.

As soon as she withdrew leaving them alone, Bashay said, "I think you know why I am here!"

"Yes, I think I am aware of why you are here. I just heard yesterday about this sad development," said Grazmach.

"Is this a case you can just brush off by saying, 'I think I am aware,' Grazmach?! Is that fair?" asked Bashay with extreme sadness.

"No, it is not Bashay. Even If I tried to do that, which I am not, this is not something I can brush off easily. Excuse me Bashay Hawey, it was a matter of wrong choice of words on my part," said Grazmach.

"What is the intention of your children Grazmach? Do they want to completely erase my son from the face of this world?" said Bashay bitterly and angrily.

"Bashay, please, take it easy. Don't take it too much to heart."

"Take it easy? Take it easy? Is this an issue you can take easily and patiently? The last time we talked, you asked me to handle it patiently and coolly and I did. And now, where has that led us?" said Bashay, vehemently and angrily.

"Well, because we were able to handle it patiently and in a civilized manner, at least, we are now discussing our problems like close friends and family. If we had followed their way, we wouldn't even be talking to each other now," said Grazmach coolly.

"What you are saying might have made sense, only if by our handling we had resolved their differences and brought our children to an understanding. But we have achieved nothing and even far worse, your children are now trying to completely destroy my son!"

"Please Bashay, don't hasten to judge."

"I am not judging Grazmach. I am talking about the reality of what is happening! Is it fair Grazmach that you idly sit by, while your children are putting my son into prison? Though not biologically, even Habtom is also your son Grazmach! Is this just?" shouted Grazmach with exasperation.

"I can understand how frustrated you are Bashay. That is why, even now, you are rushing to judge. Let me ask you a question Bashay. How do you know or who told you that I am sitting idly by when all this has been going on?"

"Well, if you had done something, your children wouldn't have done what they are doing now!" said Bashay, still fuming.

"Why don't you ask me what I did?" said Grazmach, as coolly as he could.

"Ok, sure, why not? I can ask you now. What did you do Grazmach?" asked Bashay.

"If they had consulted with me before they went to the police, I would have advised caution and insisted that the two families talk about it first. However, you know that our children now don't value our point of view as much as they used to. They feel we are old and don't understand things as much as they do. The fact that they are informing us after the fact, is in their eyes, even a measure of their respect," said Grazmach, shaking his head.

"I think you understand that your children will not be satisfied with what they have done so far. They seem bent on completely destroying my son. Since you have bid me to ask you, can you tell me if you have done anything to avert and stop further exacerbation of the situation?" asked Bashay again.

"Allow me to answer your question by quoting what I told them. When they informed me of the imprisonment, I told them, "If you are accusing him and imprisoning him knowing that he is innocent, then I wish and pray that God make you pay for your evil actions." Furthermore, when they asked me to bless them, I refused to give my blessings and instead told them that, "I will only pray that the one with the truth on his side should prevail!" said Grazmach.

"Come on Grazmach! This is nowhere near telling them to stop their injustice and prosecution of my son!" said Bashay, further infuriated by his friend's statement.

"Well, to tell you the truth Bashay Hawey, except the Lord, no one knows who is right and who is wrong. You are passing judgement only because you are angry. Otherwise, you also don't know the truth of this matter. You know me Bashay, whenever I don't have all the facts, I do not and will not pass judgement, as to who is on the side of truth or wrong!" said Grazmach firmly, with slight irritation.

"Do you mean to tell me you can't even tell them we are family! Stop this!" asked Bashay, incredulous at the attitude of his friend.

"Well, Bashay, I am sorry, but once a case is in the hands of the police and the law, you can't stop it, even if you want to," said Grazmach firmly.

"That is all you have to say? That is, it?" asked Bashay.

"What I truly wish is, that Habtom had not committed any of this and that the law would find him innocent and free him. In that case, I would stand with you to make sure that Tesfom and Araya get the punishment they deserve. I wish that with all my heart!"

"Come on, Grazmach! You know that your son, Tesfom, is an influential person, who knows influential people. That is how he has actually managed to put my son in prison!" said Bashay.

"I believe and would like to believe that Tesfom is not that kind of a person. In that case, I don't think Habtom will find it difficult to prove his innocence in a court of law. If Tesfom is or turns out to be what you are saying, then I sincerely wish that he would face the full prosecution of the law as well as the wrath of God!" said Grazmach.

"Well, Grazmach, what you are saying is not within our control. However, because we are parents and friends and have been lifetime neighbors and partners, I had expected that we and especially you, would go between them and resolve this issue before it deteriorated further!" said Bashay.

"Bashay Hawey, what you just said is right and true and I sincerely wish with all my heart, that it was possible. I have always been truthful and blunt with you; I will not make a promise that I can't fulfill, just to appease you or momentarily make you happy! This case is completely out of our hands. There is nothing we can do to change its course. I can only hope and pray that God help our two families to get out of this quagmire! That is the only thing I can say and do!" said Grazmach with finality.

Bashay bent his head and stayed down for a few seconds. Then he looked up, shook his head, stood up and said, "It is OK,

Grazmach, *fa niente! Cie Dio*! meaning, it is OK Grazmach! There is God!"

Grazmach stood up without saying a word. Bashay proceeded to the door and Grazmach followed him. At the door, Grazmach said, "Have a good day."

Bashay did not look back. He responded, "Have a good day," and left.

For the first time ever in their relationship, Grazmach and Bashay departed without agreement and without narrowing down their differences.

* 21 *

While Tesfom and Araya were in a buoyant mood, anticipating better times ahead, the Bashay family were in great distress. Dermas and Almaz were preparing a draft letter to send to Habtom. They also prepared stuff that Habtom needed like food, slippers, towels, clothes, blanket and mattress.

They finalized all their preparations and were ready to go to the prison. The small note they had written read, "Dear Habtom, the whole family is OK. We are extremely worried and saddened by what has happened to you. Are you OK? Check out what we have brought and tell us whatever else you need. Please, provide us with information about the case and instruct us on what we have to do on our part. Accept greetings from the whole family. Yours, Dermas and Almaz."

They went to the prison and handed over the stuff and the letter to the police guard at the gate. The police accepted the provisions and the letter. He checked the clothing and meticulously checked the food by repeatedly poking at it with a fork. He then read the note and found nothing untoward and accepted it. He told them to wait for an answer.

After what seemed like a very long time to them, the policeman came back and handed them a very small folded note. They were in such a hurry; they unfolded the note there and then and read it. It said, "Greetings. I am ok. You have brought me everything I need. For the moment, I will not need anything else. I want you to immediately retain the best lawyer. Money should not be a concern; he has to be the best. Time is crucial. I want him to see me as soon as possible. Yours, Habtom Goitom."

After hastily reading Habtom's letter, they went back to the car without saying a word. Once in the car, they expressed their disappointment at Habtom's note. He didn't tell them anything new. After a while, they reasoned and agreed that it was unreasonable to expect Habtom to write about the case openly in a note that will be scrutinized by the police. They expressed their hope that they would be able to find out exactly what had happened, after the lawyer talks to Habtom.

Dermas and Almaz immediately started their enquiry to retain the best criminal lawyer in the city. After appropriate consultation with many, they finally chose an attorney to represent Habtom. They signed the necessary paperwork and agreed that the lawyer would go and talk to Habtom the next day.

* 22 *

After securing the lawyer, Dermas felt a slight sense of relief. After Habtom's imprisonment, he had neglected following up on their businesses. Now he found the time and the state of mind to return to taking care of his business responsibilities.

Over the last few days, Alganesh had been in Dermas's mind a great deal. He felt it was high time that Alganesh and her children were told about Habtom's imprisonment, so he decided to pay her a visit. He took this decision unilaterally against Almaz's wishes.

On Monday, March the 3rd, Dermas went to his brother's house. He greeted Alganesh and the children and sat down. The children were told the adults needed privacy so they soon left. Dermas began with an excuse, "I should have come earlier, but I have been running around and have been busy," he said. Then he hesitated for a while and, looking uncomfortable, quickly added, "I don't even know how to say this."

Alganesh looked at him without any outward sign or reaction. Her body language indicated that she was all ears and would continue to listen.

Dermas felt more uncomfortable and made clumsy movements in his chair. Though he waited, he soon realized that Alganesh was not going to give him a response. So, he decided to proceed and said, "Something extremely terrible has happened, Alganesh," he blurted out.

Dermas was certain that Alganesh would react and make a comment or ask a question. Alganesh continued to stare into Dermas's eyes, without any other body language or response. He was now very uncomfortable and confused. He asked, "Have you already heard?"

"About what?" was the only question Alganesh asked, without any other bodily reaction or comment.

Dermas's face became flushed, the veins on his forehead bulged and beads of perspiration could be seen on his forehead. He awkwardly uttered a sound of utter dismay and shock, "Oh, wow, strange!"

"What strange, Dermas? I utterly don't understand what you are talking about," said Alganesh.

Dermas's face and body instantly relaxed. He thought she was serious and took her words in earnest. He smiled and said, "You are right Alganesh. It is my fault; I have confused you. Anyway, Habtom has been imprisoned."

"When did he get imprisoned?" asked Alganesh.

He was again slightly confused. He had expected surprise or shock but her expression was blank. Anyway, because he had to answer her, he responded, "Last Friday."

"Four days ago?" she asked again.

"No, the Friday before last," said Dermas.

"So, does that mean, my children and I were not to be told for ten days?"

"Oh my God! Clearly you had already heard. Wow, Alganesh, if you had already heard, why did you have to put me through all that discomfort?" said Dermas.

"Dermas! Try to put yourself in our place. We were the only ones who didn't know, when every other family member had already been told. Imagine what we felt, when we had to hear about this through other people!" said Alganesh bitterly.

"It is only because I was busy running around, nothing else," Dermas dismally tried at an excuse, which he already knew would not work.

Alganesh did not want to let him off the hook easily, "How come everybody else knew despite your being busy? Dermas, this is the first family Habtom established and I am his first wife. I did not betray your brother; he betrayed us. Actually, let's forget about me and talk about the children. They are the first children he brought into this world. How can any of you not think or say, what will the children feel? They will not remain children forever; don't forget that they will grow soon and become adults, Dermas!"

Dermas was extremely embarrassed and saddened. He felt very uncomfortable and inadequate. The only answer he could muster was, "You are absolutely right, Alganesh Habtey; I am so sorry!"

Alganesh felt sorry for Dermas. Deep inside she knew that he was not the person most at fault and in control. Alganesh was kind and generous, so she said, "It is ok Dermas. I am sorry that I had put it all down on you. I know you are not responsible for this. I also know that you have been sand-witched in between. So, don't worry, I have nothing against you!"

Dermas felt great relief. He sighed a sigh of relief. He couldn't look at Alganesh's eyes. With his eyes bent, he again said, "I am so sorry Alganesh Habtey. Please forgive me."

After that, Dermas had expected her to pose questions about

the circumstances of Habtom's imprisonment. Instead, she just said, "it is ok Dermas, don't worry about it. Let me make you tea."

Dermas's face and body language showed immense relief. Standing up, he said, "It is OK Alganesh Habtey, let me go now. I am in a hurry."

Alganesh didn't say anything more. She merely said, "Ok then," and stood up.

She called her children to bid their uncle farewell. Dermas did not read anything into the young children's body language. However, he saw that the older children, merely threw their hands at him, without even looking at him. He felt bad and understood that he had failed them. He kept his emotions to himself and went out without saying another word.

Chapter 10
The High Court

As the trial of Habtom seemed inevitable and unavoidable, the Bashay family's rancor and grudge against the Grazmach family deepened in intensity. The relationship between Bashay and Grazmach started to drift and seemed to be hanging by a thread. The close friendship they had enjoyed for years was at its lowest. It was now confined to mere formal greetings.

The relationship between W/ro Brkti and W/ro Lemlem was far worse than those of their husbands. W/ro Brkti firmly believed that greeting another person was a responsibility that God imposes on all humans. Therefore, at the beginning, she tried her best to continue greeting W/ro Lemlem. However, W/ro Lemlem was so sore, that let alone failing to greet her in response, she wanted to show her that she didn't even want to see her. In the end, they even stopped greeting each other whenever they met in church. Their grudge and rancor blinded them so much that they forgot they were in the House of the Lord to practice and promote love, peace and to forget and to forgive.

Despite all this, there were others within the two families who were not affected by this climate of division and enmity. These were Medhn, Alganesh and their children. This was primarily because Medhn and Alganesh were very decent, fair and just human beings. On top of this, Alganesh and her children had never seen or encountered any type of negativity or hostility from their neighbors. On the contrary, they had always found Tesfom and Medhn very thoughtful, caring and helpful neighbors and friends. Moreover, they also knew that every problem and isolation Alganesh and her children faced, didn't emanate from the Grazmach family, but rather from the actions of Habtom, Almaz and the rest of the Bashay family.

For Alganesh's children, the question was not only about what was happening between the families, but rather the threat this friction brought to their valued intimate friendship with their friends and neighbors. The younger children, who remembered what their father had tried to do, saw this recent fissure between the two families as an opportunity to play with their neighbors at will and unhindered. Alganesh had properly explained to her older children what exactly had happened, so, they understood who was at fault and what actually happened. They also loved and respected Tesfom and Medhn and saw them not as neighbors but as their second parents. Moreover, they had also not forgotten how their father had unsuccessfully tried to separate them from their friends. Hence, they had no qualm about their friendship and relationship with Tesfom, Medhn and his children.

The main focus of hatred and rancor for Bashay and W/ro Lemlem were the 'two Satan's,' Tesfom and Araya. He and especially W/ro Lemlem, strongly believed that Grazmach's two children purposely and intentionally planned the imprisonment of their beloved son.

Alganesh became the second focus of anger and fury of the Bashay family in general and W/ro Lemlem in particular. After Tesfom's repeated "injustices," they expected her to show her anger and completely sever her relationship with that family. Thus, because she decided to continue her relationship with the family, they branded her as a Judas who colluded with the enemy. The fact that their grandchildren also sided with her, was an added headache to Bashay and W/ro Lemlem. They felt she was responsible for driving a wedge between them and their grandchildren.

Grazmach however, refused to be blinded by emotion and hatred. He kept his cool and his sense of direction. He was not unduly amazed or emotionally upset by W/ro Lemlem and Bashay's reaction. He believed that what they were feeling and how they were reacting, though not right, was a natural human behavior and response. He sympathized with them.

He used to repeatedly say to his wife and children, "*What they are feeling is natural human behavior that we would feel, if we were in their position.* They strongly feel that Tesfom and Araya have purposely and unfairly targeted Habtom. They feel Habtom's unfair imprisonment and the inevitable court appearance are caused by premeditated malice. *What they are temporarily feeling and doing, though wrong and misplaced, is natural. So, it is up to us to try to understand and sympathize with them.*"

His position on Habtom was also similar. He used to say, "If Habtom has truly committed this, I will not only be disappointed in him, but I will also feel very sorry for him. What on earth would make a person commit such gross outrage and crime, especially when he is blessed and gifted with more than his share? *Anyway, we shouldn't condemn and hate such a person, but rather pity him and his pettiness.*"

Whenever Grazmach expressed such views, Tesfom and Araya, who knew and understood their father well, did not mind him very much. However, W/ro Brkti would be furious and would scoff at his views.

* 2 *

While the climate of rancor, grudge and enmity between the two families was intensifying, the formal charge against Habtom and Gebreab was gathering steam.

The attorney general gave the go-ahead for the indictment of Habtom and Gebreab. The case was going to be tried at the high court, situated at the main Haile Selassie Avenue. Finally, the prosecutor finalized his preparations and took the case to court. The panel of judges who were going to review and rule on the case was assigned and the trial date was fixed.

From Habtom's family, Dermas, Almaz and Bashay were attending the trial. Tesfom and Araya had expressed their desire for their father to attend the trial. Grazmach however, insisted that, with the exception of Tesfom and Araya, no other family member should attend the trial. His reasoning and hope were that it might help to prevent the already inflamed feelings and passions from further worsening.

The court proceedings were near their final end. After the prosecutor and defense finished presenting the evidence and testimonies, the judge announced the day of the verdict. As that day drew closer, the Bashay family's tension and anxiety grew exponentially. On the day of the final verdict, Gebreab's family, as well as friends of Tesfom and Habtom, were also in attendance.

The chamber where the case was heard was on the 2nd floor, and the courthouse had a long flight of stairs. For Bashay and family, the courthouse and its stairs represented a hateful place that was on the verge of destroying them. Tesfom and Araya, on the other hand, were not even aware that the courthouse had stairs. In their enthusiasm, they took the stairs in two's, confident that the building was their savior and benefactor.

At the head of the courthouse, on a raised platform, there were three large prestigious looking seats that were reserved for the three judges with a large table in front of them. The court's registrar was seated on the far-right corner of the house, and in front and below the judges, the prosecutor and the defense attorneys were seated on the right and left side. Their documents were spread on the tables before them. The families, friends and concerned individuals who had come to witness the verdict sat far behind the prosecutor and the defense.

The two defendants were ushered into the court by a policeman. They were brought through the special tunnel that adjoined the court. They were made to sit on the dock reserved for the accused. Everyone was waiting for the arrival of the judges who entered the court house led by a police officer. Everyone was told to rise. The judges stood in front of their seats. The police officer stood in front of them on attention and saluted them. They bowed to him and then sat down. Everyone sat down. Complete silence fell in the court house.

The presiding judge in the center took out his eyeglasses and opened the file in front of him and called, "Defendants Gebreab Woldeyohanes and Habtom Goitom." The two defendants immediately stood up.

The judge started to read, "Defendant Gebreab Woldeyohanes, you were blinded by grudge, hatred and money and embarked upon destroying property through arson. That you have committed a serious crime was ascertained by evidence and testimony, as well as your own admission of guilt."

He turned his gaze towards Habtom and read, "Defendant Habtom Goitom, you were blinded by envy and hatred and you were bent upon destroying property through fire. You employed a weak person blinded by avarice to perform your evil design. You knew you had nothing to gain, except satisfying your evil spirit. Yet, you persisted and finally succeeded in your evil intention. That you committed this heinous crime was ascertained not only by evidence and the testimony of the first defendant, but also by your own admission of guilt."

The judge looked up from his file and facing both defendants said, "Hence, the court finds both of you, singularly and plurally, guilty of the charges brought upon you!"

Immediately, sounds of muffled cries and comments were heard from the audience. The judge immediately ordered the court to silence. Complete silence reigned in the court.

The judge then ordered both the prosecution and the defense to present their closing statements before a sentence was passed. The prosecutor and defense presented their statements. The judge then declared a half hour break for deliberation. The judges retired to their chambers.

* **3** *

After half an hour, the three judges returned from their deliberations. Everyone stood until the judges sat down in their respective seats. There was complete silence in the court. Every person was waiting with anticipation. Some were waiting with expectation, while others were waiting with trepidation. The presiding judge called out, "Defendants Gebreab Woldeyohanes and Habtom Goitom." The two defendants stood up.

"Both of you have committed grave crimes. However, since both of you don't have any previous crime record, the court has made limited consideration. In the case of the state against Gebreab Woldeyohanes and Habtom Goitom, the court has unanimously sentenced both of you to an eight-year imprisonment, to be calculated from the time of your imprisonment." The judge banged his gavel.

When the sentence was read, Almaz held her head in both hands and said, "Oh my God! What a desperation and tragedy!"

As soon as he heard the sentence, Bashay immediately felt dizzy, uttered a weak incomprehensible sound and his head instantly fell against Dermas. Dermas was so shocked by the sentence, that for a few seconds, he didn't realize his father's condition. When he noticed that his father had passed out, he woke from his shock and shouted, "Father! Father!" trying to wake his father.

Dermas's shouting drew the attention of Almaz and everyone else around him. Almaz looked down and saw the limp body of her father-in-law leaning towards Dermas. She instantly stood up shrieking, "Oh my God! Oh my God! What an additional calamity!"

By now, everyone had come nearer and many were already around Bashay. No one was taking any action. Tesfom pushed himself through the people standing around him and shouted, "Please give me a hand, we have to immediately take him to hospital."

Araya was already by his side. They tried to lift him on both sides, but they couldn't. All this time, Dermas was still standing by dumbfounded. Tesfom shouted again, "Dermas, come on, hold Bashay on the other side."

Dermas woke up from his dream. Tesfom and Araya held his head and Dermas and another man held his feet. They lifted him and carried him down the stairs. They passed the long corridor to the front door and then finally took him down the stairs that led out to the street. By this time, Almaz was right beside them. At the pavement, Tesfom shouted, "Dermas, where is your car?"

"It is behind the court house!" said Dermas.

"Ok, mine is nearer. I will bring mine!" shouted Tesfom and ran to his car that was parked nearby.

He brought the car. They put Bashay on the back seat with Dermas and Almaz and sped to the hospital. They drove through the main avenue and instantly arrived at *Iteghe Menen* hospital. When the gate was opened for them, they turned right into the emergency department. Bashay was 73 years old.

At the emergency department, every staff member started to dash and run around to save Bashay's life. After the medical team took Bashay, the family members had nothing else to do but wait. An eerie and uncomfortable silence fell between them. In their haste and shock, they had not even realized that they had come in the same car. Slowly, without even realizing it, they moved away from each other, until Dermas was standing with Almaz and Tesfom was standing with Araya. The silence was oppressive. They stood there without saying a word and each was soon immersed deep in his own thoughts.

After half an hour, a nurse came out and informed them, "Your father will live. He wouldn't have survived, if you hadn't brought him in time. He had a very serious stroke. For the moment, he will have limited paralysis on his left side but with time and exercise, he can regain his muscle strength. You will be allowed to see him one by one under supervision. You are not permitted to talk to him."

Dermas went in first, followed by Almaz, Tesfom and finally Araya. They saw him and came out instantly. When all of them were out, there was again an uncomfortable silence between them. Tesfom then said, "Ok, let's go, we will take you to your car,"

Without a word, all of them filed to the car. No one uttered a single word on the way. When they reached their destination, Araya opened the car door. Almaz got out first and walked away without a word. Then Dermas got out, took a step, hesitated and took another step and then suddenly turned back. He strode back towards them and then in a low voice, without looking at their eyes, said, "Thank you so much." He turned back instantly and walked back to join Almaz.

Tesfom and Araya looked at each other. Their body language showed they were looking forward to being alone.

* 4 *

Tesfom and Araya drove straight back to the factory. They were so shocked by the turn of events, that even when they were driving alone, they didn't say a word to each other. As soon as they arrived at the factory, Tesfom said, "What an unexpected turn of events we have had. What happened to Aboy Bashay is incredible!"

"Yes, it is completely out of this world. We were lucky father was not there. The event would have distressed him so much, it would have imperiled his health," said Araya, shaking his head.

"God really saved us today! Had he died; we would have been blamed for his death."

"Let alone them, even father would have felt we contributed to his death."

"Yes, of course. From the very beginning, father was extremely concerned about all this. He would have said, "I have repeatedly told you that rivalry and conflict drive away the grace and blessings you have and usher in misery, grief and sorrow." Although he would have said so initially, later on, when he cooled down, he would have told us, "Don't feel responsible for this, when we have done our best, whatever happens afterwards is always God's will! And...,"

Before Tesfom could finish his sentence, the telephone rang. It was Hailom. "Hi Tesfom, how is Habtom's father?"

"He has miraculously survived."

"Wow, that is great news. You had been telling us, that you did not wish for the maximum sentence, because you don't want the family to feel that you were doing your best to imprison Habtom for the maximum time possible. But now, this happens on the side! It is unbelievable!" said Hailom.

"Yes, that is true. But except for you, no one will know of this. So, they are still going to say that," said Tesfom.

"Well, you should expect that. Once people hate, whatever you do is always negatively interpreted. At least you should be satisfied that everyone was there to see how you reacted and rushed to save his life today," said Hailom.

"Still, people will continue to say, 'They nearly killed him,'" said Tesfom.

"Well, listen Tesfom. As long as you yourselves know that your conscience is clear, then you shouldn't bother about what people say. You can't control how other people will think and feel," said Hailom.

"Yes, actually, you are right. By the way, was there anything new in court after we left?"

"No, nothing. By the time you were going to the hospital, the court had already finished its work," said Hailom.

Tesfom concluded his telephone conversation with Hailom and immediately shared the highlights of the conversation with Araya. They then talked for a while about the court sentence and Bashay's episode. Finally, they talked about the importance of immediately updating Medhn, Alganesh and their parents. Araya volunteered to tell his parents. They agreed that Tesfom would tell Medhn and Alganesh. Both were extremely tired and agreed to retire.

*** 5 ***

Araya, though tired, went straight to his parents' house. His mother opened the door and before he was inside, asked, "How did it go?"

"It is good, mother," said Araya. He didn't want to go into specifics.

"How many years did he get?"

Araya had decided to inform both his parents at the same time. His mother's stance looked as if she was not going to let him in, lest he tell her. He had no choice but to tell her. "Eight years," he said, without providing any other additional information.

"*Assey* izi wedey! That is great news. It is only fair that evil and contemptible people get what they deserve!" W/ro Lemlem said, hugging and kissing her son.

Araya was certain that his father's reaction would not be the same. In fact, he was slightly apprehensive about it. When he saw his son, Grazmach greeted him warmly. After the greetings, he expected his father to ask about their day. Araya waited, but nothing was forthcoming. Grazmach kept quiet. Araya knew it was up to him. "The court proceeding has ended. They have sentenced Habtom to eight years in prison," said Araya.

"How sad! What a pity! I am so sorry for his wife, the children and the poor parents. They are the ones who will suffer for something they were not responsible for," said Grazmach, shaking his head gravely.

"Well, he got what he deserved!" said W/ro Brkti.

"So, should we be happy and celebrate because he got what he deserved? When God had provided us with more than enough, falling into this abyss because of rivalry and enmity is despicable!" said Grazmach angrily.

W/ro Brkti sensed her husband was very angry and frustrated. She decided not to say anything further. "Poor parents. Was Bashay present?" he asked.

"Yes, he was. In fact, after the sentence, he got sick," he said, deciding to break the news delicately.

"While in court? What happened?" asked Grazmach, sincerely worried and alarmed.

"As the sentence was read, he suddenly lost consciousness," said Araya and then went on and explained everything that happened. He then told them how he was saved miraculously.

Then Grazmach expressed his wish to visit him right away. Araya explained how they were not allowing people to visit him and promised to take him the next day.

"Oh, poor Goitom. Then his condition is serious. What a pity, may God be with him," said Grazmach, shaking his head and leaning down.

Araya felt that was the right opportunity to escape. He immediately got up and said, "Allow me to go now. I will come tomorrow to take you to the hospital."

His father did not respond; he merely acknowledged him with a nod, without even looking up. His mother saw him off.

* 6 *

When Tesfom arrived home, he told Medhn about the proceedings of the court, the sentence and finally Bashay's unexpected collapse.

Medhn was shocked by Bashay's illness. She also expressed her sadness about what the eight-year sentence will mean to the parents and especially Alganesh and her children. Tesfom agreed that it was going to be harsh, especially on Alganesh and the children.

Tesfom quickly changed the subject and asked Medhn to inform Alganesh about the sentence and Bashay's emergency admission. Medhn was apprehensive and reluctant to take on the role. Tesfom promised that if she could do that just this once, then in the next few days, he would have a serious talk with both Alganesh and the children.

Medhn agreed and decided to do it immediately. She picked a *Netsela* (shawl) and went to Alganesh. They sat in private and Medhn shared all the information she had received from Tesfom. Alganesh was extremely saddened and distressed by the whole incident. She could imagine the ramifications of what this would mean to her and her children. She couldn't believe the plummeting luck and destiny of her children.

Medhn saw the tears that were streaming down Alganesh's cheeks. Since she couldn't find words to console Alganesh, the only thing she could do was join her. Both wept and sobbed uncontrollably for several minutes.

Finally, Medhn managed to console her. They then discussed about the best and easiest way of breaking the news to the children. Further, Medhn informed her that Tesfom was going to have a talk with her and the children in the next few days. Moreover, she assured Alganesh and promised that she and Tesfom would be by her side and assist her in every way possible.

They then passed on to discussing the next day's visitation to the hospital. Under normal circumstances, Alganesh and Medhn would have gone together to visit Bashay. However, under the present circumstances, Medhn suggested that it was best, that Alganesh visit him alone. They agreed the scheme would prevent worsening of the friction and discord between her and the family. Alganesh was touched by Medhn's thoughtfulness, kindness and unflinching friendship. She thanked her profusely. Medhn went back home with a heavy heart.

* 7 *

Dermas and Almaz had not had an opportunity to talk to each other since Bashay's collapse. They got the first chance when Tesfom dropped them. It was Almaz who said, "What do we do now? Where do we go?"

"Let's first check if our attorney is still in the premises of the court. If not, we will call him," said Dermas.

They were told that the lawyer had departed a few minutes ago. They went home and Dermas called the lawyer. The attorney asked about his father and Dermas informed him how close a call it was, but that finally he had survived. They passed on to the sentence of the court. The lawyer told him that considering the severity of the crime and the fact that they had confessed, he had feared the worst. He further told him that he believed that the sentence levied was reasonable and he was satisfied with the result. They finished their call after agreeing that they needed to prepare for the civil case as soon as possible.

Almaz was waiting anxiously to know what the lawyer had said. When he recounted their conversation, she became furious, "He said, "The sentence levied was reasonable and I am satisfied with it?" Almaz shouted. Then she added, "Actually, he is right, because it is not, he, that will be caged for eight years; it will not be his wife that will drag herself daily to prison to deliver food!" said Almaz furiously.

"Well, for him, it is a job; it is just another case. We can't expect him to feel what we feel. In their professional careers, they see multitudes of cases, and they eventually become immune to any sort of feeling," said Dermas.

"People like him don't care about anything else except money! I didn't expect him to be saddened like us. As a minimum, I would expect him to express sympathy and not say, "I am satisfied'!" shouted Almaz again.

Dermas tried his best to calm her. After a while, she said, "What are we to do Dermas? Eight years of incarceration is unacceptable!" shouted Almaz.

'Well, there is nothing we can do Almaz. As you said, though it is not very easy to accept, at least we should be consoled that this did not involve life and death," said Dermas, trying to calm Almaz down.

"Come on, Dermas, there are times when death is better than such agony!" said Almaz.

"Come on Almaz, how can you say that? There is nothing comparable to death!" Dermas said with slight irritation. He refrained from sharing the words that had formed in his mind, "Spit it out, you stupid! How cruel can you be to wish death?"

Dermas felt that Almaz was already visualizing the bitterness of her life ahead. She seemed not ready to face it. Almaz woke him from his reverie. "Believe me, death is not worse than being the laughing stock of everyone for eight years," said Almaz, sticking to her position.

Dermas was extremely irritated but he did not wish to respond. Almaz then said, "I am sorry Dermas, I am giving you a hard time, because I am exasperated."

"Well, you are right. After all, what has befallen us is not a small thing," Dermas said. However, what he thought and wanted to say was, "Yes, but you stupid, don't you know that being exasperated and wishing the worst for another, are not the same things!"

He was relieved that such a cruel statement was not made in front of his father and mother, otherwise, he knew they would have gone mad. Then he remembered about his poor mother waiting alone anxiously.

They then passed to talking about his father and the imminent tragedy they had faced. They agreed that God had saved them from another great calamity. Dermas then told Almaz that they had to inform his mother before anyone else mentions it to her. He did not want to face his mother alone and begged Almaz to accompany him. She agreed.

They discussed how best to break the news to her. They reasoned, since when she doesn't see her husband with them, she will immediately ask about him, they agreed to start with Bashay's predicament.

Almaz shook her head and said, "She is going to be mad. She is going to give us a hard time."

"Well, of course, but there is nothing else we can do. My father is the only one she listens to, but now he can't even help himself," said Dermas sadly, shaking his head.

"Yes, she is really going to get mad. She can't accept anything, especially when it comes to Habtom," said Almaz.

Dermas didn't want to give her a response. He knew what that meant. That statement had followed him his whole life and he was sick and tired of it. So, Dermas merely said, "Ok, Let's go." They went out together.

* 8 *

In highland Eritrea, culturally it is the norm that the elder leads the way into a house and take a seat before the young. W/ro Lemlem was slightly astonished, when she saw Dermas and Almaz leading the way, instead of her husband. She was certain there was an explanation for it. While contemplating thus and while expecting her husband to walk in after them, she noticed Bashay was not behind them. She was slightly surprised and confused and immediately asked, "Where is your father?"

They were ready for that question. "He is coming. He is greeting some people he met on the corner," said Dermas, without stopping. Almaz followed him closely and both went straight into the house. W/ro Lemlem followed them reluctantly.

When they sat down, W/ro Lemlem sensed something was not

right. She immediately asked, “I don’t like the look on your faces. Are we OK?”

“Father is slightly sick,” said Dermas, using the well-rehearsed line.

“Sick? Where? What kind of sickness?” W/ro Lemlem shot, a consecutive series of questions.

“There were too many people in the court house and he felt suffocated and dizzy. We took him to the hospital,” said Dermas.

“Hospital? Oh my God! Then it is serious! I have to go see him,” said W/ro Lemlem, holding her head.

“No, it is not serious. They said he needs to rest properly, and hence should spend the night at the hospital. They just want to observe him. They have told us that since they have to take various tests and perform examinations, they will not allow visitors today. We will go together, tomorrow” said Almaz, coming to the aid of Dermas.

Dermas sighed a sigh of relief. He felt his father’s case had gone smoothly. He felt, since Almaz was already helping, the decision to bring her along was correct. He was apprehensive about their next task. As Dermas was occupied with his thoughts, the question that he most dreaded came. “What about Habtom’s court case?” asked his mother.

Both of them looked at each other, and froze for a few seconds. He hesitated for a moment and finally Dermas blurted out, “He has been found guilty and sentenced to imprisonment,”

“Sentenced to imprisonment? For how long?” asked W/ro Lemlem, already alarmed, holding her head.

‘It is bad, mother! We are hoping for some reduction later on but they have sentenced him for eight years!” said Almaz.

As soon as Almaz mentioned ‘eight years,’ W/ro Lemlem shot up, held her head with her hands and shrieked, “UUUYYY! UUUYYY!” She started to wail, and instantly tears started streaming down her cheeks. Almaz who had been in control so far, joined W/ro Lemlem.

Dermas tried to comfort his mother and to make her sit, but to no avail. He then tried to reason with Almaz, pointing out that she was there to help him. Nothing doing; he couldn't budge Almaz either. When he couldn't stop them, Dermas sat down, held his face and started weeping silently. His mother and Almaz wept and wailed for 15 minutes. Then they started to calm down. Dermas guessed the storm was over.

He got up, went to his mother and hugging her told her, "It is OK, mother. We have to accept this with serenity."

"Accept with serenity? Serenity!" What more do you think could happen to us, than this? Don't you see that their intention is not to punish him but to banish him from this world! Their intention is not to imprison him for a few years but to lock and frustrate him until his life passes away!" his mother shouted.

"Mother, mother, please" remonstrated Dermas, without any result.

"Oh, my poor son! I had warned everyone about Tesfom, more than a thousand times, but no one headed my warning! He has accomplished what he set out to do! Oh, my poor beloved son, what can I do to help you? Where can I go? To whom can I go? Oh God, I am helpless!" wailed W/ro Lemlem, her tears pouring anew, her torso weaving and heaving and moving from side to side.

Dermas was annoyed with himself that the words he chose to console his mother had infuriated her and drove her into further distress. He didn't know what to do. He became helpless and felt worthless. Almaz, who had become normal and had completely stopped weeping and wailing, started to wail and weep anew. He was disappointed that she was not helping him console his mother.

He started to observe her closely. That is when he started doubting her sincerity. Her first reaction when they heard the sentence at court, her second reaction when they discussed the sentence at home, and her third reaction now were totally different. These diametrically opposite reactions made him suspicious if what she was doing was genuine or just an act. "Is she acting to show my mother that she is really sorry, or is she expressing her real feelings?" Dermas asked himself.

While Dermas was contemplating thus, his mother started to slow down. He observed that Almaz also slowed down at the same time. He wanted to say something, but was scared lest it trigger another torrent of emotion. So, he kept quiet. After half an hour, his mother stopped and started wiping her face. At the same time, Almaz also stopped and wiped her face.

W/ro Lemlem, looking at Almaz said, "I am sorry my dear child that I put you into such an emotional turmoil and distress." His mother was expressing her satisfaction and contentment at Almaz's genuine reaction to the calamity that had befallen them.

"No, mother! We are the ones who are responsible for putting you through all of this. You are the kind of a mother who never deserves any of this!" said Almaz, further twirling and spinning her mother-in-law.

Dermas noticed that *Almaz was measuring and monitoring closely his mother's reaction and making sure that she was in the same footstep by synchronizing with his mother's every move. He marveled at women's general capacity of finely assessing and minutely monitoring people's feelings and emotions and responding accordingly. He believed that the gift when used appropriately was excellent and generally commendable. He also believed that to be useful to everyone, such a gift should be used sincerely and not faked or feigned.*

While Dermas was occupied by such philosophic internal monologue with himself, he heard Almaz add, "I am sorry mother that we are bringing you only distressing news. I am especially saddened that we are making you go through this torment!" said Almaz.

Dermas instantly saw that what he considered a double standard was having a great beneficial effect on his mother. She responded, "My dear children, none of this is your doing or your fault. You yourselves have been through quite a terrible day." Then she added, "Is there anything that can be done now?"

"It is ok mother; we will talk with the attorney and do everything that can be done. Allow us to go now. We have to go check the businesses. I will come tonight to check on you. Tomorrow, we will go together to the hospital," said Dermas.

"Ok, go with God my children," said his mother, getting up with a heavy heart and seeing them off.

* 9 *

Dermas did not want to unduly alarm and worry his mother. That was why he purposely downplayed his father's real condition. However, the next day, before they left for the hospital, Dermas explained to his mother the true condition of his father.

The two families arrived at the hospital at nearly the same time. Bashay's family arrived a few minutes before Grazmach's family. Alganesh and her twins arrived a little after both families. All of them were in the same hospital for the same reason - to visit a person that was close to all of them. However, the atmosphere between them was extremely strained and tense.

Any outside observer could read in the body language of everyone present that there was extreme tension between all of them. They were chatting in low solemn voices, grouped separately within strictly family lines. The main reason for this had nothing to do with Bashay's emergency hospitalization. The sentence of Habtom was hanging over them like a black menacing cloud.

The only person who seemed unaffected by the negative atmosphere was Grazmach. While the others could not even look each other in the eye, he went and greeted each member of the Bashay family. He expressed his sadness and disappointment at what had happened. When the time for visiting came, he made sure that Bashay's family, starting with W/ro Lemlem went in first, followed by Alganesh and her twins and finally himself and his family.

Everyone who was seeing Bashay for the first time was shocked by his condition. W/ro Lemlem was especially stunned and shocked. However, for Tesfom and the others who had brought Bashay to the hospital the day before, it was obvious that he had made substantial progress. The hospital staff attested to this. They further assured them that if his progress continued, then there wouldn't be any reason to keep him more than a few days. That was good news for a family that needed all the good news it could get.

After the visiting hours were over, the two families returned to the same family grouping as before. Bashay made steady progress. The Doctors were satisfied with his progress so that they decided to discharge him sooner than they had anticipated. They prescribed medicines that he would take at home, recommended an exercise regimen and sent him home. Exactly a week after he was admitted, Bashay came back home comparatively well and alive, though slightly disabled.

* 10 *

The Bashay family were in the most stressful and critical situation they had ever faced. After the sentence and Bashay's illness, they had to go daily to prison to bring Habtom food and also go daily to the hospital to visit Bashay. On top of this, they also had to take care of W/ro Lemlem, who was struggling to accept the double calamity that had befallen her son and her husband.

Dermas and Almaz were meeting regularly with their attorney. The first defendant, Gebreab, had no significant assets or property, so they knew that the bulk of the payment for the damages was going to fall upon Habtom. They also had to come up with a rough estimate of what this will mean and consider their best options. Dermas and Almaz were thus under a lot of stress.

The attorneys for both families had already started preparing for the upcoming civil case. Attorney Hailom had given Tesfom and Araya a list of the documents and accounts that would be needed, and they were both very busy sorting out documents and streamlining the accounts.

Tesfom and Araya also had to prepare a list of the damages: the prices of the items destroyed by the fire, the list and prices of each replaced item and its supporting document, the number of days and the income that was lost when the factory stopped total production due to fire, the number of days and the income lost after the factory started partial production etc. After they finalized everything, they handed all the documents to licensed auditor-accountants who audited and prepared the documents in a manner that was acceptable to the court. They attested its correctness and veracity, by signing and placing their official seal on the documents.

After a long and hard concerted effort, Tesfom and Araya finalized all the documents Hailom needed. Attorney Hailom also finalized preparation of the case file and paperwork to be presented to the court. When everything was ready, Tesfom and Araya officially submitted a civil lawsuit against the defendants. The court that was to oversee the case was the Court of Cinema Roma. After submission, Hailom immediately applied for a freeze of sale or transfer of the property of the defendants.

The name of the judge that was to preside over the case soon became official. The start date of the case was determined and the two attorneys started presenting their cases to the judge. The case continued for several sessions. At the end of the process, the two attorneys presented their final argument and the date for judgement was announced.

On the day of judgement, Habtom and Dermas were brought to the court by police officers. The two attorneys sat on opposite sides. Tesfom and Araya were seated on one side and Dermas and Almaz on the other. The judge prepared to read the ruling.

"That you had committed a serious crime has already been ruled by a higher court. Accordingly, you were convicted and sentenced. That you had to pay reparation for the damages you incurred is therefore obvious from your conviction. The responsibility of this court has therefore been to determine the exact amount of the reparation to be paid. This has not been an easy process and has taken time to compile and refine. To help us arrive at a fair and just figure, we have involved professional auditors and accountants. Finally, we have arrived at the exact figure of the reparation.

The judge paused for a moment, adjusted his glasses and then read, "On the case of defendants Gebreab Woldeyohannes and Habtom Goitom who have been charged singularly and plurally, the court has passed the following ruling. It has been judged that you will pay reparation in the amount of 78.000-Birr (seventy-eight thousand) for the damages incurred by the arson you committed," said the judge, banging his gavel.

Tesfom and Araya were not unduly surprised by the ruling. They had anticipated it during the weeks of court proceedings. Still, they were extremely happy that the case finally ended to their satisfaction. They didn't want to show any outward sign of victory or celebration to avoid further exacerbating the Bashay family's feelings. They therefore refrained from even openly congratulating their attorney.

Dermas and Almaz likewise, had anticipated the ruling from the court proceedings. When the ruling was read, Almaz did not show any outward emotion as on the day of sentencing. Since the ruling had been anticipated, they were not unduly surprised or distressed. Nevertheless, they still felt saddened at how much their family's fortunes had taken a tragic turn in such a short time. They could also imagine and foresee the hardship that their family was going to face in the days and years ahead.

* **11** *

After returning from court, Tesfom and Araya were sharing their victory and joy with family and friends. Contrarily, Dermas and Almaz were forced for the second time, to bring bad tidings to their family. While Tesfom and Araya were glowing with joy and success, Habtom was churning and fuming with extreme fury and frustration.

When such human dramas and tragedies are played out, it is natural that the victors become happy and joyous, while the losers become sad and dejected. Although most of us understand and accept this as the norm, Grazmach had a different view. Even when he heard about the civil ruling, he was not elated and did not consider the ruling to be a victory. First, because he felt that the so-called victory was achieved against a very close family; second, because he knew that although the perpetrator would pay for a share of his mistakes, the major part was still going to be shouldered by the other innocent members of the family.

More importantly though, Grazmach understood that the world's fortunes come and go and change at every turn. He knew nothing was permanent and that what goes up must eventually come down. He understood and appreciated that it was the law of nature that victory, defeat, happiness, sadness, comfort and adversity were all two sides of a coin. He knew they were elusive and temporary events and thus didn't permit himself to be enveloped and blinded by such fleeting temporary events.

Nevertheless, the rest of the two families, who didn't understand and fathom Grazmach's philosophy and wisdom, were engaged either in celebration or self-pity and frustration. Tesfom and Araya had already started calculating the amount of money they were going to receive and making plans. Dermas and Almaz, on the other hand, were fretting about how and from which source to raise the money for the damages.

Let alone see the far future, we human beings do not even have the capacity to predict what will happen in the next few seconds and minutes. At that juncture in their lives, each member of the two families thought they knew what was coming. But the truth was, none of them knew what was to become to the two families.

Chapter 11
Indemnity

Tesfom and Araya started deliberating on how to best use the reparation money. They already knew that 30,000- Birr, out of the total award of 78,000- Birr, was to be reimbursed to the insurance company, leaving them 48,000 – Birr. A part of that amount had to go towards paying part of their bank loan, while the rest was going to be used to rehabilitate the factory to its full working capacity.

While Tesfom's full attention was occupied with plans connected to the factory, Medhn was continually reminding and nagging him to talk to Alganesh and Habtom's children. Tesfom did not look forward to facing them. He continued to procrastinate by bringing up excuses, but after the civil court case was over, he had no more excuses.

He finally agreed to talk to them. They decided it would be beneficial to invite their eldest children to participate in the talks along with their peers. The twins of the two families were now 19 years old. The whole day, Tesfom had been thinking about how to handle the delicate subject.

Alganesh and her children arrived slightly ahead of Tesfom.

When he came in the room, the first thing he noticed was the happy and very close relationship between the youngsters. That gave him immense hope and strength.

After exchanging greetings, Tesfom wanted to avoid small talk, so he plunged into the subject, "It has been sometime since we planned to have this discussion. It was my fault that we did not talk earlier, and I ask your forgiveness. You have long been witnesses to the fact that our two families were not living as two families, but rather as one. Our parents were neighbors; we became working partners; we bought our houses together; we became close friends and Godfathers to each other's children. Your mothers have become very close friends and confidants, raising you together as brothers and sisters, and you have become very close to each other. The affection and love you have for each other is mostly thanks to Alganesh and Medhn. They deserve utmost appreciation and gratitude!" he said warmly. He paused for a while, noticing that all of them were nodding their heads.

Encouraged by their response, he continued, "However, we your fathers have not lived up to our responsibilities as parents. It is not uncommon for people to disagree and break their friendship and partnership. However, what is uncommon and sad is, that we were reduced to rivalry and enmity, finally ending up in court. It is sad that instead of becoming exemplary adults, we sank into such depths. However, sometimes in life, there are things that you can't change and undo. Hence, here we are in this deplorable situation. Who did what, how, and why etc. are all questions that I don't want to attempt to answer? Even if I tried, it would only be a subjective point of view. Therefore, I will not go into that."

He again paused, and when he was certain that he had their full attention, he continued, "What I want to talk to you about today is not about Habtom and myself. It is rather about the kind of relationships we will have with you now and in the future. Since your early childhood, to the best of my ability, I have tried to treat you like my own children. Even now, I give you my word that I will continue to treat you and care for you as my children. I also beg you to see me as your parent and give me the opportunity to prove my role as your parent," said Tesfom. He noted that Samson and Kbret were vigorously nodding their heads.

Heartened by their positive responses, Tesfom continued, "It will not be wrong for you to feel or think, "How can he dare to talk to us like this, when he is the one who has put our father in prison?" However, it has not been my desire to put Habtom in prison. In truth, I didn't put Habtom in prison; it is the law that did. It is unfortunate, and I feel sad that your father has been imprisoned because of a case and an incident also involving me. However, I assure you that I am still the 'Babba Tesfom' you have known your entire lives. I want you not only to see me as your father, but also treat me as one, by openly coming to me with your problems. I make a solemn promise, in front of your mothers, that I will stand by your side and do everything in my power to help you through any adversity that you may face," said Tesfom with conviction. He became slightly emotional and paused. He leaned down for a few seconds without uttering a word.

He quickly gained control and, looking up, continued. "Allow me to say a few words concerning your relationship with your family. I am aware, that the good relationship you have maintained with us has put you in an awkward situation. It has sandwiched you between us and them and has put you at odds with them. What we deeply wish for is that you continue to maintain a good relationship with your family. In this regard, we don't want you to worry about what we will think or feel in regard to how you react with your own family. In fact, we would like to help you maintain good relationship with your families. After all, whether we like it or not, our families remain our families forever. So, please, feel free to do whatever you feel is right, because we will understand and sympathize with you," Tesfom concluded, and he then turned his head to Alganesh.

"My dear Alganesh, I have been talking to our children in front of you. Now I also want to say a few words to you in front them. I want to give you my word that I will stand with you in your time of need, and I will do everything within my ability to help and support you. Thank you for your patience." Tesfom sat back, indicating that he had concluded.

Alganesh cleared her throat and said, "We have been truly blessed to have you and Medhn as friends and neighbors. Throughout our years together, you have been a true brother and a true sister to me and, more importantly, a true father and mother to my children. This is a fact that I and my children have witnessed throughout their lives. Whatever they don't understand and know now, they will come to know in due time," she said, pausing to look at the children.

Then she continued, "The things you said and the promises you made today in themselves attest to the kind of family you are and to what you mean to all of us. As if everything else was not enough, you had to also say, "If you maintain good relationships with your family, even at our expense, don't worry, we will understand you!" Who else would say that but you? So, we consider ourselves blessed that we have you as our friends and neighbors. Thank you so much. God bless you and God help us through the difficult times ahead," said Alganesh with emotion. As soon as she said the words, her eyes teared.

Medhn, who hadn't uttered a word said, "Honestly, we are the ones who should thank you for your understanding. We have been extremely worried, especially about what the children were going to think and feel. On the one hand, we tell them, consider us as your parents and on the other, they see their father being imprisoned with a case that is connected with us!"

"We understand your worry and concern, but what could you have done? There was nothing you could do, since he himself admitted to the crime," said Alganesh.

Tesfom did not want the conversation steered in that direction. He didn't think it was the right time to talk about specifics, so he quickly changed the subject. Turning his face towards Samson and Kbret he said, "If you have any questions, I will be glad to answer."

Both Kbret and Samson shook their heads. Then Kbret said, "We have no questions Babba Tesfom. However, we would like to thank both of you very much, not only for today, but for what you have done for us all these years," said Kbret. Her brother Samson, nodded his head fiercely in agreement. Alganesh beamed with pleasure.

Then he turned to his children and asked them, "Do you have any questions?" Bruk and Timnit shook their heads.

"Ok then, I think we have finished. I hope and wish that even in the future, we will sit down together as a family and discuss anything that comes up." Tesfom stood up and that was the end of their discussion.

* 2 *

While Tesfom and Araya were engaged in making plans on how to rehabilitate and build the factory, Dermas and Almaz were agonizing about how to pay the reparation money that had been ordered. They had a little less than 20,000- Birr in the bank and needed to raise another 58,000- Birr.

They started discussing the merits of which of their businesses should be disposed of first. It was on this particular issue that a misunderstanding and rift appeared between Dermas and Almaz in particular, and within the Bashay family in general.

When Dermas and Almaz began their consultation, Dermas initiated the discussion by saying, "Though we will consult with Habtom, the way I see it, I think the best option would be to sell the two building materials shops we own."

"Both of the shops! Why?" asked Almaz, not pleased with Dermas's suggestion.

"Well, because we can't collect the amount of money we need, by selling only one of them," said Dermas, as a matter of fact.

"Well, that is obvious but there are other options," said Almaz.

"What other options?"

"I think you will agree that the shop I run has more customers and is more profitable than the one you operate, right?" asked Almaz.

"I won't disagree with that, but we will still be short," said Dermas.

"Yes, we will be short, but in addition to that, we can sell Habtom's house,"

"Whaat?" shouted Dermas! Clearly, he hadn't expected that proposal. Then he quickly reigned in his reaction and coolly added, "Well, their residence..."

Almaz cut him short, "Wait. A residential house does not generate any income, but a business provides constant income that can help you repay your debts. If the house we were living in was not a rental house, I would have sold it," said Almaz.

"I understand your rationale, but there are other problems. Do you believe Habtom would agree to that?"

"Leave Habtom to me. I can convince him to agree to it," said Almaz confidently.

"Well, if it comes to selling the house, Alganesh has also to agree to it," said Dermas.

"Of course, but you are the only one who can talk to her,"

"Well, if it finally comes to that, then I can talk to her," said Dermas.

"Ok, great, then talk to her,"

"Ok, but before I talk to her, we must first ascertain whether Habtom will agree to it or not," said Dermas.

"What is the problem if you talk to her before we ask Habtom?" asked Almaz.

"I don't think she will accept the idea easily. As you know, she is a housewife who stays at home. She doesn't work or earn an income. The house is everything she has, and you also know that women in general have more attachment with house ownership.

So, I feel it would be best if we tell her that it is also Habtom's wish and decision," said Dermas.

"There are hundreds of jobs for women, but she doesn't have any capacity to do any kind of work," said Almaz, undermining and criticizing Alganesh on her way. Then she added, "Frankly though, I still don't see any problem with talking to Alganesh before consulting Habtom," insisted Almaz.

Dermas did not wish to respond to what Almaz had said about Alganesh's capacity. He was not surprised by her overreaction. He knew how easily she becomes furious at the mere mention of Alganesh's name. The truth was that Dermas did not have the courage to talk to Alganesh about the subject; nor did he have the desire. So, he was making excuses to escape that unpleasant task. Continuing to look as if he believed in what he was advocating, Dermas said, "Once she says no, it will be more difficult to make her say yes, even after Habtom's decision."

That blew Almaz's lid, she shouted, "If Habtom decides to sell it, she will have no choice. She will do it by hook or crook! After all, the house was bought by the sweat and toil of Habtom! She didn't contribute anything!"

Dermas again decided not to respond to the comments she made about Alganesh. He also didn't want to face Alganesh solely on the basis of Almaz's proposal. Since he could not find any more excuses, he finally collected all the courage he had and said, "I am not willing to talk to Alganesh before Habtom's decision."

Almaz was furious. She was about to say something and then seemed to hesitate and finally looked as if she had changed her mind. She merely said, "Ok, but if you had said that from the start, we wouldn't have wasted so much time on it!"

Dermas had expected much more fury. Although he understood the veiled criticism leveled at him, he had no problem with it. He was relieved that they had finalized the discussion.

As he was about to get up, Almaz opened up another line of discussion. "Listen Dermas, if Habtom does not agree to the sale of the house, or that damn Alganesh refuses to accept the decision, what other suggestion do you have?" asked Almaz.

"I don't think we have any other choice, except to sell the two shops," said Dermas.

"How about the bakery?" asked Almaz.

"Whaat? The bakery! Are you serious?", said Dermas, shocked and incredulous at the audacity of her suggestion.

"Habtom is the only one who knew how to properly run and administer the bakery. The other person who could have helped would have been your father, but that is impossible now. So, if we can't administer it properly, then why not sell it along with the shop you are running?" said Almaz.

"Please Almaz, understand that the bakery is not a mere business to us. It is an historical and sentimental heritage that is entwined with our lives. Especially for my father, it is his heart and soul. If father in his present condition heard this suggestion, he wouldn't even last a day. So, please, don't even mention this idea again!" said Dermas angrily.

Almaz was not impressed with his logic. "Listen Dermas, the situation we are in does not allow us the privilege of being led by emotional attachments or to lean on sentimental crutches. What this family needs to do now is to think objectively about the best practical avenue that will extricate us from the current situation. That should be the only consideration," said Almaz, standing firm in her position.

"Well, Almaz, that might be true for you, but it is not for us and our family. I am warning you, if my parents hear of this, they will be at odds with you,"

Dermas noticed that Almaz was not at all perturbed by his threat of how his parents would react. She immediately reasserted her opinion, defiantly saying, "We will see about that tomorrow, after we talk with Habtom."

"Ok," was the only thing Dermas could say. Then he stood up and left.

* 3 *

While going to his parents' house, Dermas was mulling over the discussion he had had with Almaz. The whole family had immense admiration and high regard for her. She had joined the family during its financial boom and blossom, so they knew her only in times of prosperity. Dermas started to have doubts about Almaz's authenticity. He told himself, "I really hope she doesn't turn out to be a wicked person, covered with glittering gold."

Whenever Habtom was mad at Alganesh, he used to describe his wife by telling Dermas, "You don't truly know her, she looks good on the outside but she is just wood covered with gold." Though Dermas never agreed with Habtom's assessment of Alganesh, he kept his opinion to himself. His internal response to his brother's comment was always, "Come on, Alganesh could never be like wood covered with gold. Even if anyone thought she was fake, she could only be true gold covered with wood." Dermas loved Alganesh's openness and honesty. She was not a wicked or ruthless person. Since she always spoke her mind with patience and conviction, there was no reason for Dermas to hate her.

Almaz, on the other hand, was too polished for his taste. He always felt she went too far to please everyone beyond what was required or necessary. He knew that if he was asked for tangible evidence to prove his case, he wouldn't have any. He didn't have enough objective evidence to convince even himself, let alone others. Yet, his feelings about her were always unchanged and firm.

Dermas had never shared his true feelings either about Alganesh or Almaz with anyone in the family. He always kept them to himself. Since Habtom's imprisonment, Dermas felt he saw a glimpse of who Almaz truly was. He observed that in every situation, she only cared about what she wanted and what was best for her, with no consideration for anyone else. In his mind, there was no comparison between her and Alganesh. He worried lest she create further complications in their family's present precarious condition.

As a final thought he told himself, "Under normal circumstances, it would have been prudent to discuss Almaz's preposterous proposals at least with my father. However, my parents are not now in a position and condition to carry other worries and burdens. So, I must handle this and follow it up by myself." Dermas was satisfied with his decision,

Being immersed in deep thought, Dermas did not realize that he had arrived at his parents' home. When he sat with them, he avoided the subject and chatted with his parents only about their health and general matters. With Almaz out of his mind, he enjoyed his parents' company and had a good time.

* 4 *

After the verdict, Habtom and Gebreab were transferred to the main *Sembel* prison. It was situated in the outskirts of Asmara, to the west of Asmara airport, near the St. Mary Neuropsychiatric hospital and the *Kidane Mehret* Coptic church. The prison was constructed on a flat field away from other institutions. It was surrounded by a huge high wall, topped by barbed wire fencing, with torchlights situated at various positions. It was manned 24 hours a day by policemen with automatic guns, who stood guard on top of the fences.

The main gate to the prison was made of a very sturdy and large metal frame. About 500 meters before the prison, there was a corrugated iron shed that was manned by policemen who reviewed the Id cards and registered personal information of visitors. In a second shed, the food brought by families to prisoners was thoroughly checked and combed by policemen.

Dermas and Almaz arrived at the prison at 9 am. They were there specifically seeking Habtom's decision on which particular business to sell. They finalized all formalities and stood in line. Since they still did not have permission to see Habtom in person, they handed over their personal notes to the policeman on duty.

Dermas wrote about his parents and the rest of the family, while Almaz wrote about the question of what to sell. They were told to wait.

Finally, they received Habtom's responses. He didn't like the idea of selling the bakery, so he rejected it. But, as to the sale of the house, he agreed with Almaz and gave her his support. He wrote that Dermas should inform Alganesh of the decision, adding that she had no right to reject it, because the house was his and not hers. He wrote that Dermas should reiterate and make that clear to her.

* 5 *

Dermas had deeply regretted that he had failed to inform Alganesh and her children about Habtom's imprisonment. Although he had not felt right about it, he had done so, because of Almaz's insistence. He had finally told her against Almaz's wishes, after which, he had made it his duty to inform her of every new development.

He was certain that the assignment he was given would not be as easy as both Habtom and Almaz had made it out to be. However, since he had to do it, he went to Alganesh with a feeling of unease. When they sat down alone, Dermas said, "You remember that in our last encounter, I had told you about the reparation money, right?"

"Yes, I remember clearly," said Alganesh.

"You also realize that in order to pay the reparation, we will need to sell some of the businesses," said Dermas.

"Well obviously, if there isn't enough cash, then you would need to sell something. However, you should understand that your brother has never given me any information about business or money matters. So, there is nothing I know about such things," said Alganesh openly.

"Yes, you are right. Actually, I am here today because Habtom asked me to talk to you," said Dermas, beating around the bush.

"That is strange! Since when does he say that? Your brother has always told me, 'You don't need to know; it is none of your business,'" said Alganesh with surprise and suspicion.

"Well, it is because you have to know about the proposed sales," said Dermas, still procrastinating, not finding the courage to say what he was supposed to say.

"Ok, I don't see anything wrong in knowing and in talking about it," said Alganesh.

"I had told you that the court had frozen the sale and transfer of the two shops, the bakery and this house. Habtom is now saying, "The businesses are important, because they provide us with income to pay our debts. So, as much as possible, the businesses should not be sold." Therefore, he is suggesting, that we sell one of the shops," said Dermas, hoping to break it to her as lightly as possible.

"Which shop?"

"The shop that I manage."

"Will the sale of the shop be enough to cover the reparation money?" Alganesh asked again.

"No, that is why he is saying, let us sell the shop and this house," said Dermas, finally relieved that he was able to get it out.

"This house! Did you say this house? Are you telling me, Habtom has decided that this house should be sold?", shouted Alganesh.

Dermas could only manage to say, "Yes," with a very low voice.

"There is a Tigrinya proverb which says, '*Anafra Kokah Zeyfelts, Ayhadanayn,*' meaning, "A person who doesn't understand how pigeons fly, can't hunt them." Do you understand what they are really saying Dermas? What they are really saying is, Almaz's shop and Habtom's bakery should not be touched; the shop you run and this house however, are expendable!"

"Well, what he is saying is also that Almaz's shop and the bakery are the most profitable," said Dermas.

"How about the house? What sin does the house have?"

"Well, he is saying, the house doesn't bring income. Further he is saying, we bought the house because we had businesses; we can sell it now to cover our debt; we can live in a rented house, and when all this is over, we can always buy another house," said Dermas, following the instructions he was given but still looking unconvincing.

Alganesh smiled wryly and said, "Let me tell you a story my father used to tell us, when we were children. "Once upon a time, a hyena found a lone fully loaded donkey in a deep valley. When it got closer, the hyena couldn't believe its eyes. The donkey was loaded with meat! When it saw this, the hyena roared with laughter and said, 'Oh my God! my dear donkey, you are meat; your load is meat; and instead of standing on top of a hill, where your cries for help could be heard, you are sitting on the bottom of a valley! Is this a joke or a dream? This is too funny to be true!' the hyena cried and roared with laughter again."

"I am telling you this story, not because of its direct relevance, but rather because of its reverse relevance," said Alganesh, looking at Dermas's eyes for a glimpse of understanding.

Dermas's eyes were blank. He just looked at her with an expression of confusion. She understood that she had confused him and decided to explain to him saying, "Let me say this in another manner. I am the only one in this family who cares for five children; I sit at home the whole day; I don't have a job; I don't have an income; I don't have a bank account or an asset; I depend on the goodwill of others for my monthly provisions; no one ever asks for my opinion on any important matter, and yet here I am, being asked to agree to sell the only guaranteed protection I and my children have! The only abode we have housing our six souls', whether in hunger or satisfaction; whether in sickness or health; whether in sadness or joy; or even whether we are scared or calm and confident. Mind you, this is the only abode we have! And yet, it has been chosen for disposal! How can any human being in his right mind come up with this? So, let alone talking about selling the house, even thinking about the very idea is a grave sin that should be condemned!"

Dermas, was very uncomfortable. He couldn't even look at her face. He looked down at the ground while Alganesh continued, "This house was the first property we ever bought and owned. This was way before the craziness of unnecessary expansion of businesses and way before the craziness of throwing away your own family and children got underway. Please tell me, have they or you thought, even for a minute, what will happen to me and to my children? Where are we supposed to be thrown away? Even thinking about it is shameful and disgraceful, let alone putting it into action," said Alganesh furiously.

"I am just passing on the message I was told to deliver," said Dermas, clearly looking embarrassed and mortified.

"Don 't worry Dermas. I know very well that you are not responsible for this. You are only doing what you have been told to do. I know for certain who came up with and refined this vile idea. After all, I am not a child, I am a 40-year-old woman and mother of five children. I may only be a simple housewife restricted to a house, but I possess enough sense to understand such machinations. So, don't worry at all Dermas Hawey," said Alganesh, excusing him from any wrongdoing and scheming.

Dermas's relief was soon evident in his facial expression and body language. His muscles relaxed and his face glowed and sparkled. "To tell you the truth Alganesh Habtey, I was sure you wouldn't accept it. I didn't even accept it myself," said Dermas smiling and finally coming clean about his feelings and belief.

"It is ok, don't worry Dermas Hawey. I know your good nature," said Alganesh smiling broadly.

They concluded the subject amicably and started chatting about other small issues. Soon after, Dermas bid Alganesh farewell and left.

* 6 *

Dermas knew that Almaz was anxiously waiting to hear Alganesh's response. For a different reason, he was also equally in a hurry to report the result of his encounter with Alganesh, because he had been elated that he had rightly anticipated Alganesh's response. He was also in a hurry to see Almaz's reaction.

When they met, he didn't get into the details of their conversation. He straight away told her that Alganesh had flatly rejected the proposal. Almaz went berserk. She was so mad that she didn't even ask what her reasons were. She went straight into abusive language, calling Alganesh all sorts of names.

After a torrent of abusive words, Almaz proceeded to question Alganesh's right to oppose the proposal. She said, "She had no right to have a say on a property where she didn't even contribute a single cent in its purchase. This was partially Habtom's fault, because he gave her too much leeway and freedom she didn't deserve. Habtom was too soft on her, that is why she now has the audacity to oppose his decision."

Dermas was careful not to antagonize her. He didn't dare defend Alganesh in any manner. He was even careful about his body language and just listened to her tirade with blank attention. However, on the inside, he was enjoying the scene. After she couldn't find anything else to say, Almaz cooled down.

Habtom was equally mad that Alganesh had the courage to reject his decision and order. He believed that she wouldn't have done that, if he were not in prison. He expressed his continued frustration by condemning and damning Alganesh and the day he was imprisoned.

In the following days, when Almaz realized there was no hope from Alganesh, she started anew her campaign to convince Habtom to sell the bakery. But he stood firm on his previous decision and continued to reject her pleas.

Almaz was frustrated and mad at all of them. She indirectly told Dermas that all of them, including Habtom, were not better than Alganesh. She explicitly told him that she was disappointed by their narrow outlook and their weakness in basing their decisions on subjective emotions, rather than on objective facts.

Finally, after taking out her frustration on everyone, Almaz reluctantly accepted the decision to sell the two shops. Dermas and Almaz immediately began concentrating on finding buyers who could pay the best prices for the two shops.

* 7 *

From the very beginning, Tesfom knew very well that he bore no responsibility for the fire that had gutted the factory. However, he knew also that the responsibility for not fully ensuring the factory was squarely on his shoulders. This had continuously troubled him, and after the accident, to soften and forget his frustration, he had gone back to his weakness: to drinking.

At the time, Medhn had conferred with Araya and suggested that they confront him before it was too late. Araya had not agreed with her assessment and told her that, since his brother was still under intense burden and pressure, it was better to let him be and to give him time. He told her how he feared that, if they put further pressure on him at this time, he might not be able to withstand it, which might actually worsen his condition. So, Tesfom had continued drinking with the lame excuse of "Being frustrated".

After the revelation that the fire was not an accident but caused by arson, Tesfom began to control his drinking. During the police investigations and the first and second criminal trials he was completely focused on the tasks at hand. He never drank, except on the days he christened as his basic rights, Saturdays and Sundays.

After the successful conclusion of the civil case, he started drinking again nearly every day. The excuse this time was the celebration of their victory. Medhn was very disappointed and saddened. She was inclined to try talking to him whenever he came home drank, which was at about midnight. But she knew that at that hour and in his condition, the conversation was going to be futile.

At midnight on Saturday, Tesfom came home fully loaded. She made a firm commitment to talk to him the next morning. She got up early and made sure the children had finished their breakfast before he woke up. Since it was Sunday, Tesfom got up late and then went to his children and passed time with them. After they told him that they had already eaten their breakfast, he went to Medhn and waited for his breakfast.

He was confused and surprised when Medhn came without bringing breakfast. He asked, "Haven't you finished making breakfast?"

"Yes, I have, but first I want to talk to you," said Medhn.

"You mean before breakfast? I also have an appointment," said Tesfom, looking at his watch and hoping to escape to his friends.

"This will not take time," Medhn said, sitting down in front of him.

Tesfom understood there was no way out and so prepared himself to listen saying, "Ok then."

"Listen Tesfom. You know that I have never accepted your usual Saturday and Sunday card games and drinking. We have implored with you to distance yourself from associating with such friends, without any success. However, what I have witnessed over the last ten days is a new trend, unseen before. You are drinking every night and coming home around midnight. What do you think you are doing?"

"Well, Medhn, this is a unique occurrence because of a unique situation. After the reparation victory, I was asked to invite everyone for three days. Then it was the turn of my friends to invite me for the victory. That is why this is happening, so it is strictly a temporary episode," said Tesfom.

Medhn shook her head, and said, "So, Tesfom, tell me, is this victory something you won only because of your effort and exertion? Or is it because it was God's will to bring the guilty to justice, so they don't remain hidden from their crimes forever? When God grants you such a victory, the right thing to do would have been to thank God for his bounty and grace. It is not right to celebrate a victory that doesn't belong to you! Even if you decide to celebrate, how can you celebrate it by drinking excessively and getting drunk?"

"Well, Medhn, come on. This is how everyone celebrates. How can you present it as if I am the only who is doing this?"

"My dear Tesfom, what is normal is to celebrate your joys and happiness with your own children and family. If you wanted to celebrate with your friends, then the other normal thing to do is to invite your friends to your home. Moreover, celebrating because Habtom has been imprisoned and has been ordered to pay reparation is not right at all. Wouldn't this be similar to how he acted when the factory was burned down? Isn't this getting down low to his level? Have you given thought to what people who notice this would say?"

"Habtom was celebrating not because he gained anything from the arson, but merely out of spite, just because a large part of our factory was destroyed. On the other hand, I am not celebrating because Habtom has been imprisoned or is paying reparations. I am simply celebrating because the perpetrators have been caught and because I will be able to collect reparations to rehabilitate our factory. So, don't compare the two. There is a huge difference between the two," said Tesfom.

"I understand and appreciate the difference Tesfom. But would any outside observer understand your actions? What is worse is, if they see you celebrating, do you think Habtom's family would understand? The other point that I fail to understand is what the advantage of getting drunk is? To whom is the advantage? To your health? To your family? To your finances? To any outside observer? Where is the goodness of it?" Medhn posed a series of tough pointed questions.

Tesfom had no answer to Medhn's strong and just arguments. Tesfom, when sober, was a very fair and just person, who could never cross a truthful and logical argument. Thus, he could only muster to say, "Well, you are right, it serves no one. We are merely doing it because we are used to it."

Medhn felt sorry for Tesfom. His condition and remarks made her think. She told herself, *"Other men wouldn't do or say what Tesfom had just done and spoke. Firstly, they would never give a woman the opportunity to be heard. If by some miracle she gets the chance and the woman speaks the truth, they proceed to threaten her, undermine and vilify her until she gives up. They expect to command respect, through fear and intimidation, which are the instruments of anyone without self-confidence. That is actually why I still respect him and still have faith in him and always hope that he will eventually change,"* Medhn thought, re-enforcing herself.

While she was thinking thus, she remembered a quote which Grazmach repeated often, "*Many people who have strength and power wrongly assume they are being "respected" by others, when they see other people below them doing their bidding and desires. However, anyone with strength and power is not necessarily "respected." That is fear. Respect is given freely. True respect is not something you gain because of your strength and power. When people fear you, you might get your way until you have the instruments of strength and power with you. However, once your power and strength are gone, your respect goes out of the window as well. Real and true respect is something you get because you deserve it, even long after your power and strength are gone. Real respect remains with you, even long after you are gone."*

She was so impressed by the depth of Grazmach's quote, that without realizing it, she smiled. When he saw her smile, Tesfom who was waiting for her to acknowledge his previous statement was confused.

"Yes, Medhn?" he asked, expecting acknowledgement and hoping that her smile meant her anger had passed and was about to excuse him.

Medhn was embarrassed and shocked that she had been far away with her thoughts. She quickly recovered from her lapse and said, "I was just thinking about how I should respond to your statement. Anyway, I understand the part where you said we continue to do it, because we have become accustomed to it. My desire and wish are actually to fight together and defeat this destructive habit forever."

Tesfom was extremely relieved, he stood up, hugged her and said, "No problem, we will soon put it under control!"

"I surely hope so. I always worry and fear, lest you hurt yourself," said Medhn.

"I understand how much you care and worry about me. Now please, Medhn, I am famished. Can I get my breakfast now?" asked Tesfom sweetly.

"Sure, give me a minute," said Medhn and ran to the kitchen.

* **8** *

Araya had also noticed his brother's upsurge in drinking. He had observed that Tesfom was interrupting work early at the factory and running away to his friends. He would come to the factory, barely work an hour and with the excuse of an appointment, he would run out.

They had been working for about an hour, when Araya noticed that Tesfom was putting away the files he was working on. When Tesfom started to excuse himself, Araya said, "What is with your appointments these days? They have become a daily affair."

"It is a temporary affair that is ongoing after our victory at the court. My friends are continuing to invite people every day. Then the others insist on securing their turn to extend an invitation to the rest. That is why it has been going around until now," said Tesfom smiling.

"Wow, that is not good. Taking daily turns for a drinking invitation is dangerous. At least, varying it with other kinds of invitations like food, soft drinks or coffee would have been better," said Araya.

"Come on Araya, that is not possible. Each one of us have loads of all the other stuff in our houses," said Tesfom.

It was Araya's turn to say, "Come on Tesfom, you all have also the possibility of stocking loads of drinks in your houses!"

"Well, you know, it is not only about the drinks. More than the drinks, we miss the noise, the jokes and the fun. You, being a man, can understand it to a certain extent. It is women who have no clue about this and hence don't comprehend what it means," said Tesfom, certain that he had a sympathetic ear in his brother.

"Let's be honest with ourselves, Tesfom. What would you have said, if they would say, "We now understand what it means to drink and enjoy; we will therefore join you!" or if they would say, "Since we can see that you guys are enjoying it and having fun, why not us?" Let's then assume that you have no other option but to accept. Then what would you say, if they start going to bars, leaving the children to themselves?" asked Araya.

"Wow Araya, don't say that!" was all that Tesfom could come up with.

"Why not? You know very well that women in the west, unlike our womenfolk here, join the men in bars and other drinking joints."

"Wow, I hope it never comes to that. Medhn and her kind do not only take care of our children, they also take care of us by their thoughtfulness and extreme consideration," said Tesfom, with conviction in his voice.

"Well, if you know that, then you should also know that we should at least, respect and take care of women like Medhn!" said Araya.

"You know that I respect Medhn very much," said Tesfom.

"Of course, you should! Medhn is a person who deserves the utmost respect. You should understand that she talks to you often because she loves and cares about you and doesn't want you to hurt yourself or get into unforeseen trouble," said Araya.

"I understand and appreciate that very much," said Tesfom.

"If you truly understand that, then it is not enough to only acknowledge it; you should act upon it!" said Araya firmly.

"Well, you are right, but it is not easy. Sometimes, I don't even understand it myself. Don't think that I forget even for a minute, what you and Medhn keep telling me often. However, whenever I want to get away from the card game and drinking, something pulls me back to it. When I occasionally succeed in getting away from it, instead of feeling good about my will-power, I get more depressed. So, it ends up being a lose-lose game," said Tesfom shaking his head.

Araya felt sorry for his brother. Under normal conditions, he knew Tesfom wouldn't have liked to admit to his younger brother such deep personal struggles. He desperately wanted to help his brother. He thought for a minute and then said, "If it is the noise, the jokes and the fun that you most miss, then why not sometimes join them without drinking?"

"Oh, that is impossible! Even If I would succeed, my friends wouldn't allow it. Let alone, not drink, even not drinking at the same pace is discouraged. They don't want anyone not drinking to join the group. They believe it spoils the fun," said Tesfom.

"Wow, this is...," Araya started to say, when Tesfom interrupted him.

"On top of that, if you don't proceed at the same pace, then you can't even understand each other's jokes and funny stories. I wouldn't understand theirs and they wouldn't understand mine," said Tesfom.

"Well, in that case, why don't all of you guys once in a while meet and chat and have fun without drinking?"

"Sometimes, we actually try to just sit down and chat without drinking. Then when one of us feels like drinking, he insists that we drink with him and we join him," said Tesfom.

"Wow, this is a dangerous association. It doesn't permit any sort of personal choice and freedom. Generally, any group is ruled by what the majority wants. It is quite strange that in your group, five to six persons follow the wish and whim of a single member," said Araya.

'Well, I agree with you on that. In any other situation, that is how things are. But, when it comes to drinking, that is the rule," said Tesfom.

"Wow, that is a strange and destructive rule. In that case, can you allow me to make a final suggestion?" asked Araya.

"By all means, go ahead. After all, although you are my younger brother, you are the one who is constantly guiding and advising me," said Tesfom sincerely.

"Thank you. I seriously feel you should take concrete steps to rectify this dangerous situation before it escalates further. I think you should do your utmost to change this rule. I feel the only solution to this is, to do your utmost to change the standing directive of "The majority has to abide to the wish of the few" to "The minority should abide by the wish of the majority." If after doing your best to change this, you do not succeed, then I highly advise you to pull yourself as far away as possible from this dangerous association. I now solemnly ask you as your brother, to give me your word that you will try your level best to do that," said Araya very seriously.

Tesfom saw how much his brother was trying to help him. He felt bad about it. After Araya finished, Tesfom looked down for several seconds. Then he looked up at his brother and solemnly said, "I give you my word, that I will do my level best."

"Thank you so much for giving me your word," said Araya, pleased by his brother's promise.

After they concluded the issue, Tesfom ignored his appointment and continued to work. When they finished their work, they left the office together and went to their respective homes.

While Araya and Tesfom were seriously discussing about lifestyle changes, the Bashay family were occupied by the far more critical and serious issue of how to get out of the financial quagmire that was bogging them down.

* 9 *

Almaz and Dermas were busy finalizing the transactions of the two construction materials' shops. When they were offered prices beyond what they expected, they sold the shops instantly. This enabled them to pay the reparation money without taking money out of their bank deposit.

Almaz was now 30 years old. Her children Haben and Mekeret were eight and six years old respectively. After eight years of a very comfortable life, this was the first time she had encountered such adversity and hardship. However, the rancor and frustration she felt was not primarily because of what had befallen them. It was due to the fact that it had all happened mainly because of Habtom's rivalry and stubbornness.

After the shops Almaz and Dermas administered were sold, the question arose about where each would work. The bakery was now the only business they had left. They discussed the issue with Habtom and finally agreed to jointly run the bakery. Almaz was to take care of finances, while Dermas was to be responsible for management and administration.

When Almaz started working at the bakery, Dermas and the workers immediately noticed that it was not going to be easy to work with her. The workers started talking and complaining about her. Dermas kept assuring them that her character was generally good and that what they were witnessing was a temporary frustration. He urged them to appreciate what the family in general and what she in particular were going through, due to the imprisonment of Habtom and subsequent loss of their businesses. Thus, he continued to implore them to give her time to adjust.

* 10 *

Tesfom and Araya received the money for reparation. They immediately paid the Insurance company its due. Since they had already calculated how much money they needed to rehabilitate the factory, they used the extra cash to pay part of their bank loan.

In a short while, they were able to return the factory to its original state. After the sentencing, they gave Tekleab the former position of Gebreab and put Weldeab in Tekleab's former position. They also gave them a hefty financial remuneration for the services they had rendered. Tekleab and Weldeab were very grateful.

Though Tesfom continued to make constant promises, he had not as yet made changes in his drinking habits and frequency. After the rehabilitation process was completed, he was running away to his group at every opportunity, leaving the major burden of the work to Araya. Araya was able to take care of the work without complaint.

The factory, made amazing gains; production and sales increased significantly. Customers who had distanced themselves due to Habtom's misinformation returned slowly. Though Tesfom still continuously expressed his admiration for Araya's efficiency and work ethic, he was not doing much to help his brother.

* 11 *

Tesfom and Medhn were now regularly helping Alganesh financially; she was extremely grateful to them. Although she needed their help, she was also feeling bad about being a burden to them. It didn't take long for Medhn to notice that this feeling was taking its toll on her.

Medhn discussed her concern with Tesfom. After conferring on the subject, Tesfom came up with the idea that they devise a way of helping her in a way that would also maintain her self-worth and self-confidence. After discussing various options, they agreed on buying her a sewing machine.

When they told her of their plans, Alganesh could not hide her happiness and relief. They decided to make her promise not to tell anyone, including her children, about the source of financing of the sewing machine. They agreed that she would tell everyone that the sewing machine was bought from her savings. She then registered in a sewing school run freely by catholic nuns. Before long, Alganesh became very proficient and started sewing for neighbors and acquaintances.

The little income she was getting from her sewing work became extremely important for Alganesh. It was not only important for her self-sufficiency, but also for her self-confidence and independence. The elders, Samson and Kbret, became proud of their mother's initiative and independence, which boosted their morale and confidence.

Alganesh was grateful not only for the overall help they provided her, but more so, for the intelligent plan to help her and her children regain their self-confidence. She was extremely touched by their humanity and true Samaritan aid. As her admiration and gratitude grew, Alganesh's friendship and love for Medhn and Tesfom blossomed further.

* 12 *

While so much was going on between the two families, Medhn and Alganesh had not failed to notice that the relationship between Kbret and Bruk was deepening. However, since more important and urgent events were going on, they didn't give it their full attention. Since Alganesh was more preoccupied with the distressful events that were going on, it was Medhn who had the time to notice the changes and to worry about it.

Thus, she frequently suggested to Alganesh that they should talk to the youngsters, before things got out of hand. However, because Alganesh had already so much on her hands, she kept postponing the confrontation. After a long time, she agreed to set up an appointment with the youngsters.

When they sat down together, it was Medhn who started the conversation by saying, "You might have guessed why we wanted to talk to you. It is not a new subject; we have already talked to you about it."

She looked at both of them. Bruk and Kbret did not show any outward sign of surprise, which revealed that they had indeed suspected the topic for their meeting. But except for their readiness to listen, both had blank faces that gave away nothing of their feelings.

Alganesh picked up from where Medhn left off and said, "The last time we talked, both of you vehemently assured us that the love between you two was that of a brother and sister, nothing more and nothing less. To be honest with you, both Medhn and I found it difficult to accept your strong assertion at the time. This was because with our natural gifts as women in general and as your mothers in particular, we have the capacity and unique opportunity to see and observe what others can't."

Alganesh signaled to her friend to proceed. Medhn took the cue and said, "We would like to beg you that whatever you tell us should only be the truth and the absolute truth. In short, we have to know your true feelings and where your relationship stands as of today. As your mothers, we feel that is the least we deserve."

Medhn sat back indicating that she had finished. The youngsters immediately understood that the ball was in their court. It was Bruk who started by saying, "To be honest with you, the last time we talked, we ourselves were not sure of where we stood, nor did we understand the real feelings we had." He paused and looked at both of them.

"Ok," said both Medhn and Alganesh, nodding their heads. They knew that the conversation was at a critical stage. Hence both of them sat on the edge of their chairs with great anticipation.

"At the time, we were not sure whether the brotherly and sisterly love was deepening or whether there was anything more to it," said Kbret.

"Since we ourselves were not certain, we couldn't confirm any suspicion you had at the time. However, what has happened since and our present condition is something we don't want to hide from you. We will tell you exactly what we feel, not only because of our extreme love for you as our mothers, but also because of the utmost respect we have for you as two amazing human beings," said Bruk, his voice slightly breaking and his face and body language showing extreme love and respect.

Kbret was nodding vigorously, underscoring her full agreement. Tears had already welled up in her eyes. The body language of the youngsters was enough evidence of the high esteem they had for their mothers. Both Medhn and Alganesh were touched by the scene before them. They instantly stood up, hugged their children and said in unison, "Thank you for your love, Izom Dekey. God bless you."

It took a while for the outpouring of emotion to calm down. Then Bruk continued from where he had left. "Let me continue. It is after our last talk that we slowly started to realize that we were indeed falling in love. At this time, we don't want to deny that we have fallen deeply in love," said Bruk and signaled to Kbret to proceed.

Kbret instantly took over. She said, "In the last months, we had on several occasions planned to take the initiative to openly talk to you. However, matters between our two families started getting from bad to worse and we never found an opportune moment," said Kbret, tearing up again.

"Oh God, our poor children," said Medhn and Alganesh

Bruk took over from Kbret. "While our families were in that kind of confrontational situation, there was no way we could talk about our love. So, we had to keep it to ourselves," concluded Bruk. Both youngsters sat back in their chairs.

Alganesh and Medhn started by thanking them for their honesty and candidness. They told them that it was important to examine the issue from various angles. It should not only be understood according to how it would affect them personally, but also how it would affect their siblings and the two families.

Finally, they told Bruk and Kbret that they needed time and privacy to fully digest the new information. They then asked them to step outside for a few minutes, so they could discuss the new implications of the issue. They promised to share with them openly all the contents of their discussion and the final recommendations they had.

Medhn and Alganesh began talking in earnest, thoroughly examining the issue from every possible angle. In the end they arrived at a practical conclusion and a common strategy to recommend. When they felt that they had discussed the issue thoroughly, they asked their children to join them.

When they were seated, Medhn said, "Your honesty, candidness, love, maturity and thoughtfulness have impressed us immensely. We are proud of you. We have discussed this thoroughly together and we want to assure you that we will support you all the way. The love you have fallen into didn't suddenly come out of nowhere. The life-time neighborliness, friendship and love between our two families have played a big part in it. And now, unfortunately, you are caught in the middle of the feud between our two families. If these were normal times and our two families were in a normal relationship, your love would have strengthened the closeness of our families. Unfortunately, these are not normal times. Whatever is going on though, we will still stand with you all the way."

It was Bruk and Kbret's turn to get up and hug and kiss their mothers. Their hearts were filled with happiness and gratitude for being blessed with two loving, understanding and thoughtful mothers. Kbret and the women shed tears, while Bruk's eyes welled up.

After a while, they controlled their emotions and extricated themselves from each other. Then Alganesh said, "Our ardent wish and prayer is that your love will somehow blow in the wind of love and friendship and bring reconciliation and peace between our two families. However, if our wish and prayers are to come true, there are precautions and strategies we have to follow."

She paused and looked at both of them and then added, "After a while, with Medhn's help, we will be able to explain this to your father, Tesfom. I am sure he will not give us a hard time. However, when it comes to your father Habtom, it will be another matter. As far as he and other members of the Bashay family are concerned, if things in the family don't improve, then none of them should have any knowledge of this. Otherwise, it is going to cause unexpected complications for you and will widen the rift between the two families. So, we have to tread cautiously and wisely."

They went on to discuss the details of how they should cautiously handle and shield the young people's love life. They finished by agreeing to meet whenever new issues and situations arose.

*** 13 ***

The repeated advice and pleading of Araya and Medhn did not bring any change in Tesfom's drinking predicament. They didn't know what else to do. If it was another person with no prospect, they would have given up long ago. However, in all other aspects of life, Tesfom was a very intelligent, responsible, fair and just person and so they didn't want to let that kind of intellect perish in alcohol.

On Tuesday, Araya and Medhn were talking about what other steps they could take. "What more can we say and do other than whatever we have done up to this point? Personally, I can't do anymore; the only thing left for me is tell Aboy Grazmach, so he can talk to him," said Medhn.

"Well, eventually that will be our last card. However, if father is told, I don't know and can't forecast what it will do to Tesfom. He has extremely high regard and respect for our father. He doesn't want father to be saddened on his account," said Araya with trepidation and worry.

"I know and I am very aware of that, Araya. I also know that there is a strong possibility that Tesfom might be at odds with me over this, forever. In fact, when I had once or twice threatened to do that, he had warned me that it will be the end of our love and relationship. But now, I am not thinking about what is best for me. I am thinking about what is best for him. I am at a point where I would prefer to save Tesfom's life and then confront whatever consequences come my way," said Medhn.

"I understand and appreciate your motives and thoughtfulness. You are willing to go that far because you love and care for him. By the way, do you know that father has equally high expectations of Tesfom? That will make it hard for father as well," said Araya.

"Of course, I do. That is what makes it much harder. Father will be extremely disappointed and saddened. He has on many occasions told me, "You know Alganesh Gualey, your marriage was a blessing for us; since your marriage, Tesfom has mended many of his ways. In truth, that was the other reason why I have so far avoided telling him," Said Medhn

"Yes, you are right. I have on many occasions also heard father refer to your marriage in those terms," said Araya.

"In short, I understand perfectly the disappointment and sadness both father and son will face. However, I fear, if we don't act now, the alternative will be much worse," said Medhn.

"Ok, I hear you Medhn Habtey. I am with you. However, I will beg you to give me one last chance. I want to tell him, "Since we couldn't help you; we have decided to tell father." Let me see what he will say or do," said Araya.

"Ok, but please, don't take too much time," said Medhn.

"I will choose an opportune time and at the latest, I will talk to him after this weekend," Araya promised.

They agreed on the strategy and timeline. They then parted.

While Araya and Medhn were agreeing on a timetable and a plan for a few days; what they had forgotten was that every day, life and time have their own schedule and plan.

CHAPTER 12
ITEGHE MENEN HOSPITAL

TESFOM WHO WAS now 46 years old, had already started to have a few gray hairs. On Saturday morning, March 1973, Tesfom ate breakfast and went to the bank. The whole morning, he was extremely busy and pressed for time. He was thus looking forward to his weekend of relaxation and rest.

After finalizing his daily work at the bank, Tesfom went home and ate lunch with his wife and children. As he was getting ready to go to the factory, Tesfom seemed in a buoyant mood. Medhn knew that since it was Saturday, he would go straight from the factory to his friends and would not be home before around midnight.

Medhn did not like to bring up a contentious subject, whenever Tesfom was about to leave. She felt it was a bad omen, to talk about anything that would disappoint or offend him. She didn't like to see him go with a scowl or a frown on his face. No matter what, she always wanted to see him off with a smile.

However, that day, something was pushing her to ask him to come home early without drinking. She itched to tell him, "Please Tesfom, why don't you just this once, not drink, and come back home in time." As much as she wanted to say that to him, her other self was reluctant; she hesitated two to three times. Finally, she decided to ask him. When he was right at the door, she called him, "Tesfom!"

Tesfom turned around and asked, "Yes, Medhn?"

Though she had decided to ask him not to drink, the words that came out of her mouth were however, not the words she wanted to say. Instead, she heard herself say, "Don't forget that tomorrow, we have to go to the family who have lost a daughter and pay our respects."

"I haven't forgotten it; we will go together," said Tesfom and left.

When the door was closed, Medhn could not understand what had pushed her to nearly say something she had never said or done. She was happy that she suppressed whatever it was that had pushed her and finally saw him off amicably and peacefully. Although she felt satisfied that she finally succeeded in suppressing her urge, however, that strange feeling still remained strong within her.

While Medhn was contemplating about the strange episode, her young daughter Hirieyti came running and started asking her about the sport's t-shirt she needed. Medhn started talking to her daughter. Soon enough, momentarily, she forgot her obsession about the unexplained strange feeling.

* **2** *

When Tesfom arrived at the factory, Araya was already at work. After exchanging pleasantries, Araya pulled out files that required their mutual attention. After a short discussion, they quickly agreed on a plan of action. Then they sat in their respective desks and started working on the files before them.

Now and then, Tesfom would bring up a funny or an interesting anecdote and would make Araya laugh. Araya noticed that his brother was in a great mood. He wondered whether his brother's mood was just due to the weekend or if it was due to the prospect of meeting his friends that evening.

He remembered the promise he had made to Medhn. He wondered if it would be best to talk to him then, while he was in a great mood. He thought of telling him, "We have lost all hope in you, and so, we have decided to inform father about your condition." However, he feared and was even certain that the statement would completely ruin his brother's mood.

He was torn between talking to him to uphold the promise he made to Medhn and sparing the brother he loved. Tesfom was still talking and making jokes, but Araya's mind was occupied by indecision. At one point, Tesfom noticed that Araya was not following him. "My dear Araya, where are you? You don't seem to be with me. I think you have something in your mind," said Tesfom.

Araya was Alarmed. He felt as if he was caught red-handed. Quickly he started denying it by saying, "No, no, I am with you! I am listening to you!" Then after a short pause, he added, "To be honest, I think I was carried away by the file before me for a little while."

After this, the idea of talking to Tesfom took backstage. Then he started making excuses for his new decision, by saying, "In the first place, why did I even think of talking to him today? After all, my promise to Medhn was that I will talk to him after this weekend. So, I have time." Although Araya was window dressing it, the reality and the truth was actually because he couldn't bear to see his brother's good mood crushed.

Tesfom continued talking, joking and laughing profusely. As the afternoon progressed, his jovial and cheerful mood was even more obvious. When Araya saw this, he said to himself, "I am glad I didn't destroy his mood. The weekend is always his; let him enjoy it."

At about 6pm, Tesfom put away his files and said, "I think I will call it a day here. People need to reward themselves for their hard work by resting and relaxing. I think you have worked hard enough; why don't you also call it a day?"

"Yes, you are right. I am nearly finished and I will also go after a while. You go ahead," said Araya.

"Ok, then, I will see you. Today is Saturday, so we will have fun," said Tesfom smiling.

"Sure, have fun, but since you are meeting your friends, please remember to talk to them about the solution we discussed last time," said Araya.

"Ok, sure. Bye," said Tesfom quickly, wanting to escape away before Araya could say anything more.

"Ok, bye," said Araya, shaking his head, looking at the closing door.

* **3** *

Tesfom went straight to Lalibela hotel. The whole group was already there. While he was at the door, he noticed that the card game had already started.

"Hi guys, when did you start?"

"We just started. So, you didn't miss much," said Werede.

"Ok, then why don't you start over, so I can join you?" asked Tesfom.

"No, we will finish this. It won't take much time. Until then, why don't you quench your thirst like the rest of us," said Werede.

Since all the others also kept quiet, he understood that none of them wanted to restart the game. So, he ordered a beer and started quenching his thirst. While he was waiting, he remembered Araya's talk. He felt this would be the best time to try to talk about the subject. He understood that after the night progressed, no one would willingly give him his ear. He also felt, even if they did, no one would be ready to seriously entertain the proposal.

Having reached a decision, Tesfom suddenly said, "Listen guys, I believe we have set up our pastime for the weekends satisfactorily.

However, I feel we have problems with our weekdays. We have to do something about it."

While Tesfom was talking, the attention and concentration of his friends was wholly on their card game. Hence, none of them were sure what Tesfom was talking about. They therefore looked at him strangely, confused by what he meant.

Tesfom was slightly taken aback by their looks. Still, he pushed ahead saying, "I am serious. I raised the subject because I want us to talk and do something about it," said Tesfom.

"I don't think anyone has understood what you are talking about. I, for myself haven't understood a thing. Has anyone?" asked Berhe, looking at each of them. All of them shook their heads.

"Hey guys, don't be fooled by him. He is doing this on purpose, so he can break-up the card game and get into it," said Werede.

"Oh, come on Werede, how can you say that? I am really serious!" said Tesfom seriously.

"Ok, if you are really serious, then explain to us what you are trying to say," said Berhe.

'What I am trying to say is that, since a long time, we have all agreed to set up Saturdays and Sundays as our days of enjoyment and drinking. However, nowadays, we have gotten used to drinking even on weekdays. This is because whenever one of us feels like drinking, he asks the rest, and wishing to oblige and accompany him, we join him. All of us eventually end up drinking," said Tesfom.

"So?! What are you trying to suggest?" asked Werede, showing more interest in the subject.

"Well, I am saying either let all of us promise not to drink during weekdays, or else let the one who insists on drinking, drink by himself," said Tesfom.

Tesfom felt relieved that he had finally voiced what he had to say. He was certain that they might not accept his views. However, he was satisfied that he had upheld his promise to his brother. He knew what he had done was much better than to say, "I tried," when he hadn't or procrastinate and make excuses of "I haven't talked to them yet." Therefore, Tesfom was prepared to face the indignation or even the condemnation of his friends.

Werede was now certain that Tesfom was serious. "Ok, before I give my opinion on the subject, I first want to ask Tesfom a question," he said and turned towards him, "Can you tell me exactly what friends or groups of friends mean to you?"

"Well, this is obvious. Friends mean to me exactly what we are to each other, and what we are as a group," said Tesfom.

"Great. Well said. If that is so, then people become friends or groups of friends because they have similar or same interests and leanings. As the British say, "Birds of the same feather, flock together," right?!" said Werede, smiling wryly.

"Yes, right. You should understand that we don't have any disagreement on the point you just raised. I am saying the exact same thing. Whenever there is a common interest or consensus, then let us be led by the common consensus. However, when there is no consensus, then let us be led by the interest and will of the majority. I am basically saying, why should the majority obey the desire of the few?!" said Tesfom.

"We are not obeying them Tesfom. We are simply following the minority to make them happy, because they are our friends." said Berhe.

"I am sorry, when I said "Obey," that was wrong of me. I meant to say follow. Like you, I also believe it is important to oblige and satisfy your friends whenever necessary. But it should only be whenever our help is important and useful. However, is what we are doing really helping our friends?" asked Tesfom.

"Of course, it is! Agreeing with your friend and joining him in his wish and desire is helping a friend," said Zere', who had so far not spoken.

"Come on guys, please don't forget that we are talking about encouraging and helping our friends to drink and to get drank.

We should know and understand what we are talking about," said Tesfom firmly.

"Wow, is this guy ok today? Is he himself?!" said Werede, whose body language showed shock at what Tesfom was saying.

"You know how he is; once he starts arguing about something, he never stops. He always differs with us on many subjects, including women, children and the like!" said Zere'.

"Yes, but today's is different. After all, he is arguing against the very thing that he most loves and enjoys," said Berhe smiling.

"Ahh! You guys, you never stop joking," said Tesfom, smiling.

When Werede saw Tesfom smiling, he said, "Here you go, that is better, that is more like you!"

Tesfom became serious again and said, "Guys, leaving aside the jokes, I am really serious about this. I am not sure if we will succeed to implement it or not but I seriously feel, we should genuinely think about this and take steps to remedy it."

"I think if we don't somehow conclude this discussion, this guy is not going to give us peace," said Werede.

"So, are you in essence telling us not to drink at all during weekdays?" asked Berhe.

"Yes, more or less. If one of us wants to drink, then we let him drink alone. Then he will either drink alone or decide not to drink," said Tesfom.

"Wow, what an audacity! This guy talks as if he does not beg us to join him, whenever he feels like drinking," said Werede.

"You are right there, but I have not been talking to absolve myself of this. All of us, up to now, have been in this together. So, I am simply suggesting, let all of us together get out of this quagmire," said Tesfom.

"This not fair at all. This will be like sitting together with a friend and yet feeling lonely and alone. Tell us the truth Tesfom, is this your idea or have you been sent to advance this new gospel?!" said Werede smiling.

'Come on, Werede! What does it matter, if the idea came from the sky or the ground or the East or the West; the important thing is the correctness of the idea and the fact that we are discussing it," said Tesfom seriously.

"Wow, I tell you this guy is not the same today. Can somebody please look behind his back, in case Medhn is with him?!" said Werede, standing up, going behind Tesfom's back and pretending to look if there was anyone behind him. All of them, including Tesfom, roared with laughter.

When the laughter died down, Berhe said, "Listen Tesfom, let's postpone this discussion to a weekday. We promise we will seriously discuss it then. However, today and tomorrow are our days and please allow us to enjoy it in peace!"

All of them unanimously applauded Berhe's suggestion. Then Tesfom said, "Ok, if you promise, I will agree to that. From the start, I think I was wrong to bring this up on a Saturday."

With that, they started concentrating on their drinking and card game. After that they continued playing and drinking, while at the same time joking and laughing. Halfway into the night, they stopped playing cards and started concentrating on their drinking.

As the night wore on, the drinks started to arrive faster, the jokes became louder and their utterances started to become slower and slurred. In the latter part of the night, Tesfom became the main resource of the jokes and anecdotes. He practically looked and seemed as the unannounced skipper of the team. Anyone who would have come at that hour, would not have believed if he was told, that before a few hours, Tesfom had been strongly advocating in favor of reducing drinking frequency.

It was now midnight. Most of them had enough. All agreed that they call it a night. Then someone suggested a last round for the road. The last round came and they drank.

When they were ready to leave, Tesfom said, "Come on guys, give me one more chance, I want to order another last round. Last of the last!"

They were all full, but as was their way, agreed to drink another round to satisfy Tesfom. By the time they finished Tesfom's round, it was already 1.00 am.

They finally quit and went out together. While the others soon left, Berhe and Werede stood chatting by the side of their cars.

When Tesfom got out, he realized that he was already past his normal time and understood that Medhn was going to get worried. He remembered their conversation of a few days and felt bad about it. Since he was already late, he quickly started his car.

* 4 *

Habitually, Medhn never went to bed until Tesfom was home safe and sound. Even when she felt very sleepy, she would doze and slumber on the salon but will never go to bed. She always wanted to open the door for him and welcome him.

Tesfom did not endorse Medhn's ways. He always insisted that whenever she felt sleepy, she should go ahead and sleep. Though he talked often about it, he never took any steps to correct his ways. Though he knew and understood that he was the cause, however, he still lacked the courage and determination to face his problem. This made him feel guilty.

Whenever he found her slumbered on the salon, Tesfom always used to admonish her, by saying, "Come on Medhn, how often do I have to talk to you about this. I don't want you to wait for me when you are sleepy. I don't like this. You are not helping me; you are just making me feel guilty."

"I know you don't like it and do not feel happy about it. However, it is not about you; it is about me. If I don't see you home safe, even if I go to bed, I can't relax and sleep well," Medhn repeatedly continued to say.

Tesfom continued talking and reprimanding her about, "Not sleeping" and about "How she was making him feel guilty." Medhn started to become exasperated and disappointed by Tesfom's all-talk, but no-action routine. She didn't like that he was continuing to reproach her, without making changes in his ways and his hours.

Medhn could not take it anymore. Then instead of the usual, "I can't sleep before you come home" routine, she started throwing at him a response that embarrassed him. Whenever he opened his mouth, she started saying, "Well, my dear Tesfom, if you really want me to sleep in time, and if you don't want to feel guilty, then the solution is easy. You will only need to mend your ways and come home on time."

Whenever she responded thus, Tesfom couldn't even look straight at her. He would look sideways and would stroll away without even attempting to respond. After such repeated discourses, let alone admonish her, Tesfom stopped even talking to her about "Slumbering on the salon."

Medhn was a decent, extremely loving and thoughtful person. Therefore, she did not count Tesfom's discomfort and embarrassment as a victory; nor did she see it as his failure or defeat. She saw it as a window of opportunity and as a chance and as proof that Tesfom had hope and could be saved. She used to tell herself, "*Whenever I point out an undeniable fact or a weakness, Tesfom does not try to argue or defend the indefensible, because he is a just and fair person. If he was any other man, he would have tried to argue and fight using any silly beat-up logic. He would even have denied me my right to express my views and my opinion on the matter." She would conclude by saying, "So, since, he admits his mistakes and weaknesses even to himself, I am sure there will come a day when he will be able to face himself and correct his ways."*

* 5 *

When Tesfom went out with his friends on weekdays, he would come home around 10 pm, but on Saturdays and Sundays, he usually arrived around midnight. Since Medhn had grudgingly accepted his ways, she will generally not worry until midnight.

However, on that Saturday, she started to feel uneasy early, around 11 pm. She constantly looked at her watch, but the minutes crept by very slowly. She asked herself, "What is wrong with me? Why am I feeling this way?" Although she tried hard to find an explanation for her feelings, she couldn't find any.

Though she tried every means to calm herself, there was still no respite to her feelings. When she couldn't find any explanation or solution, she started doing housework that was not necessary at that hour, just as a pastime. After a while, she noticed that it was already midnight. She was grateful for the housework that enabled her to sail through a whole hour.

She stopped her housework and sat down and waited, hoping he would come soon. It was 12.30 am and yet, Tesfom had not come. At that time, she became extremely worried. She forced herself to wait until 1.00 am. When Tesfom did not come by then, she became extremely alarmed and started thinking about what she could do. The uneasy feeling, she had all evening, compounded with the unusual late hour, took its toll on Medhn.

She felt her heart beat galloping, her hands shaking and her body becoming drenched in sweat. That is when she made a decision. Under her breath, she said, "It doesn't matter that people are sleeping, this is an emergency." She convinced herself thus and strode to the telephone. She put her index finger into the slot of the telephone and started dialing. The telephone rang, but there was no answer.

Medhn told herself, "They can't go anywhere at this hour; I am sure they are sleeping." She dialed again, but no one was picking up. Just when she was feeling hopeless, the telephone was picked up and she heard a voice different from the one she expected. For a moment, she was confused and thought she had dialed a wrong number. Finally, she understood that the voice was difficult to recognize because he was sleepy. She was now positive that the voice belonged to Araya.

So, she quickly whispered, "Araya, it is me, Medhn."

"Medhn! What is wrong? Why are you calling at this hour?" shouted Araya, with alarm in his voice.

"I am sorry Araya Hawey. I know it is an ungodly hour, but I am worried. Tesfom has not come home," she said apologetically.

"What time is it?" asked Araya and instantly looked at his watch, which read 1.30 am. He again asked, "Wow! Does he usually stay up to this hour?"

"Not really. Generally, he arrives at about midnight or a little later. There have been very few occasions when he came home at 1.00 am," she responded.

"Ok, then I will try to call the places they frequent and will get back to you soon," said Araya, already starting to worry.

"I am sorry Araya, that I had to call you at this hour," said Medhn.

"No, please don't say that. I will call you back," he answered, hanging up the phone.

Medhn held her face with her hands and paced around the telephone, extremely anxious and apprehensive. After five minutes, the phone rang and she sprang and picked it up instantly. It was Araya. He told her, "I just learned that they left a few minutes ago so, don't worry. Let's give them about half an hour, in case they chat for a while outside. If he doesn't come back by then, give me a call."

Although she said, "Ok," Medhn was not reassured by the news Araya brought, nor did her uneasy feeling go away.

* 6 *

Tesfom drove to the roundabout near Bar *Tre Stelle* and then turned towards *Clinica Igea*. He was about to turn right to the main Haile Selassie Avenue, when he changed his mind, saying, "Even if I am late," and continued straight ahead. Under normal circumstances, Tesfom did not like to drive on the main avenue and avoided it as much as possible.

Tesfom drove past the *Abu Habesh* high-rise building and the

Denadai building and drove straight towards *May Jah Jah*. He was aware that he was late and drove faster than usual. He passed the Datsun garage on his right and as he was turning right leaving the *Enda Finjal* factory to his left, he swung further left to the other side of the road.

Tesfom was shocked that he had gone too far left out of his lane. He knew that he was a very cautious driver, no matter his circumstances. Even a small loss of control was unlike him, and he reprimanded himself saying, "Hey Tesfom, what is wrong with you? You have never done this under any condition!"

He passed through the Bar Torino intersection cautiously and then drove past the Cinema Croce Rossa, straight down Yohannes 4th Street (formerly the *Viale Garibaldi.*) As he came nearer to the Mitchel Cots building, he saw something speeding straight towards the road he was driving on. It was coming from the Italian school intersection. At first, he thought it was a bicycle, but by its lights and its speed, he quickly understood it was a motorcycle and became alarmed. All this happened in seconds.

He immediately slammed on his brakes, but soon realized that, with their combined speeds, he was going to hit him head-on. He quickly swung the steering wheel, all the way to the left, missing the motorcycle by a few centimeters. However, his car was by this time totally out of control, careening across the street and speeding towards a huge electric pole and the side-wall of the Mitchel Cots building.

His brakes didn't hold and he helplessly saw his car and himself crash against the electric pole and the adjoining wall. The driver's side struck the pole with full force and then the front side slammed against the wall. Tesfom felt the steering wheel crush against his chest and his face being slammed into the dashboard. He immediately felt extreme pain in his left leg. He tried to move his leg, but soon found it was trapped. The driver's door was completely twisted and was entwined and squeezed against his body, making any movement impossible.

He felt extreme pain in his chest, forehead and left leg. Blood started streaming from his forehead down his face and onto his clothes. He slowly moved his left hand towards his left leg and felt something wet. Looking at his hand, he saw it was covered in blood. All this had happened within seconds, but for Tesfom, it seemed it had already been a long time since he crashed. He knew that if he didn't find help soon, his life would be in great danger.

The motorcyclist and his motorcycle were not touched. The motorcyclist put his motorcycle by the road and ran towards Tesfom. He saw that the driver's door was smashed against the electric pole and was completely twisted and curled towards the driver. He also saw that the windshield, front light and fender, were all smashed against the wall. He saw that the driver was bleeding profusely and instantly realized that the driver was in mortal danger.

He tried to open the driver's door but it was completely stuck. He could hear the driver moaning and weakly gasping from pain and quickly understood that if he was to assist him, he would need other people's help. He went back to the road and soon saw a car coming his way. He prepared to stop the car and noticed that the driver was slowing down. When he stopped, the driver got out and ran towards the crashed car, calling, "Oh my God, Tesfom, Tesfom."

The motorcyclist understood that the driver was a person who knew the injured driver very well. Together, they tried to open the driver's door by force, but it wouldn't budge. They tried to pull him through the other door, but they couldn't. Whenever they tried, Tesfom weakly cried out, 'My leg, my leg." While they were trying to pull him out, they saw that a lot of blood was pouring out of Tesfom. Blood was also dripping from the twisted driver's side of the car on to the floor.

When they saw that they were not getting anywhere, the cyclist asked, "Do you have any metal thing in your car, that could help us pry the door?"

"I am not sure if it will be useful, but I might have something," he said, going towards his car.

While he was opening the trunk of his car, the motorcyclist asked the driver, "I heard you call his name. Do you know him?"

"He is my friend. We were together a few minutes ago. Did you see the accident happen?" asked Berhe sadly, shaking his head in disbelief

"He had this accident trying to save me. Since it was past midnight, I didn't think there would be any oncoming traffic and I tried to drive straight through the intersection. When I saw him, I knew I was going to be hit. However, your friend had already seen me and instantly held his brakes and when the car would not stop, forcefully swung his car away from me. He missed me by a few centimeters, and instead crushed into the pole and the wall. I am so sorry, it is all my fault," said the motorcyclist, shaking his head sadly.

When Berhe opened his trunk, he didn't find anything useful. Thinking for a second, he said, "I will stand here and try to stop other drivers who might help us. Take your motorcycle and go to the Red Cross and ask for an ambulance. If they tell you the two ambulances are out, don't wait for them, just give them the address. Then in case we don't find enough people to help us pry the door here, you go to the *Pompiere* (fire brigade station) and ask them to help us pry open the car door."

The cyclist immediately said, "Ok," and ran towards his motorbike.

Berhe managed to stop a few cars that could help them. Everyone stopped and tried to help, but none of them had any equipment to pry the door. They collectively tried to pull the door, but without success. Tesfom was still moaning in pain and blood dripped from the car.

Berhe became desperate. When he was about to lose hope for his friend, he heard the sound of a motorbike. Turning around he saw the motorcyclist with another person on the back. The cyclist sprang from his motorbike and reached out to take a few tools from his passenger. Although he didn't understand what it meant, Berhe still gave a sigh of relief.

"All three fire brigade trucks were out, so I begged them to give us a person who could help," said the cyclist, breathing heavily.

"God bless you, man," said Berhe.

"Is the ambulance not here yet? I hoped they would be here by now," said the motorcyclist.

"Provided we can get him out, even if the ambulance doesn't come, we can take him in my car. We might hurt him further, but we won't have a choice," said Berhe.

The fire brigade technician, with the help of his tools and everyone present, went to work immediately. Within minutes, they were able to pry the door open. As they were expressing their relief, the ambulance arrived. They slowly and carefully transferred Tesfom to the ambulance. They could clearly see that Tesfom's injuries were far more extensive and serious than they had suspected. By now, he had lost consciousness.

The ambulance, sounding its siren and flashing its red lights, took Tesfom to the hospital. Berhe thanked all the people that had helped them. The cyclist wanted to go to the hospital with him, but Berhe excused him and insisted that it was not necessary. He asked him to take the technician back to the fire brigade station, and before they departed, they exchanged addresses and contact information.

Berhe drove his car to the hospital, and as he arrived, he saw them carrying Tesfom from the ambulance to the emergency room.

The doctor and his assistants rushed to save Tesfom's life. The doctor ordered the nurses to check his blood type, so they could immediately transfuse blood.

When the staff learned that Berhe was a friend of the injured, they asked him to sit down and wait. Sitting down, Berhe began to think about the night's unbelievable events. He remembered the discussion they had had and the strange topic Tesfom had raised. It was a subject he had never raised before and wondered at the coincidence. He then remembered he needed to inform Tesfom's family.

* 7 *

When Medhn had called in the middle of the night, Araya was drowsy, but now he was wide awake. He started thinking and talking to himself. "Medhn is right, I don't think my brother is going to change. I think it is inevitable; we need to tell father about it," he said. The telephone rang and interrupted his thoughts. He looked at his watch. Since, 30 minutes had not elapsed, he felt a sigh of relief. He picked up the phone. He was certain it was Medhn, calling to inform him that Tesfom had arrived.

When he answered, "Hello?" he was surprised and taken aback that it was not Medhn. It was a man's voice.

"Is that Araya?" asked the voice.

"Yes, who is this?" asked Araya, perplexed and confused.

"It is me, Berhe, Tesfom's friend," said the voice.

Araya was now extremely alarmed, he instantly asked, "Is Tesfom Ok?!"

"Did anyone call you before me?" asked Berhe.

"Medhn had called me because she was worried. Is Tesfom Ok?" Araya asked again, his alarm heightening.

"He is ok, but he had a car accident. We have brought him to *Iteghe Menen* hospital. I will wait for you here," said Berhe, trying his best to sound as normal as possible.

"No! Please don't tell me! Oh, my God! Oh, poor Medhn! All her fears have come true!" he cried and then realized he was practically talking to himself, while Berhe was waiting. Then he quickly said, "Ok, Berhe, thank you. I will be there." He put the phone in its cradle.

He didn't want to receive a call from Medhn before he was ready with some kind of a story. He needed to buy time, so he immediately took the telephone off its cradle and put it on the table beside him. He thought for a while about what to tell Medhn and soon formulated a story and was ready.

With his hands shaking, he called her. Medhn picked up the phone at the first ring and said, "Hello, hello," with desperation. When she knew it was Araya, she added, "I was just about to call you; Tesfom is not here yet. Did you get any news?" Her voice was full of both alarm and hope.

"Yes, I have got news. But these guys have gone berserk. They are crazy! I have been able to confirm that they have gone to another bar. I will now go there myself and bring him back. In the meantime, don't worry," said Araya carefully, lest she detect anything in his voice and manner.

"Oh, my God! This is crazy. I am sorry Araya Hawey that I had to put you through all this, in the middle of the night," said Medhn, gravely shaking her head hopelessly.

"Don't worry about that; I will see you soon," said Araya hurriedly, thankful that she hadn't detected anything.

He was satisfied that he had found a temporary solution to allay Medhn's fears. He knew that now he had ample time to go to the hospital and see for himself his brother's condition. He was so worried about what to do with Medhn that, up to then, he had not given much thought to Tesfom's accident.

Since the beginning, Embaba had been following the telephone conversations with curiosity and interest. However, when she heard of the accident, she was really shocked and alarmed. She wanted to go to the hospital with her husband, but Araya insisted that there was nothing she could do. She reluctantly agreed to stay behind.

Araya put on an overcoat and went out. While driving, he was extremely anxious and apprehensive, not certain in what condition he would find his brother. The more he thought of him, the more his heart raced and his hands shook.

He arrived at the hospital full of trepidation and fear. He stopped the car and half-walked and half-jogged to the emergency department.

TO BE CONTINUED IN THE SEQUEL:

"COVENANT
BETWEEN
MEDHN & ALGANESH"

Acknowledgement

After our retirement, my wife and I came to the US in 2016. Since then, our children have taken care of us and pampered us beyond our imagination. I was thus able to concentrate on my health and to devote my time to the task of writing, editing, translating and sharing my experience with Eritrean communities everywhere, virtually and over social media through interviews, speeches and presentations.

I would thus like to express my heartfelt gratitude to our children, Adiam, Winta, Semere, Seghen and their spouses Aron, Zerisenai and Mekdelawit. I would also like to express my heartfelt gratitude to my wife, Fana Tewolde, who made sure that I had all the time and atmosphere to focus on my writing and community engagement.

I would like to express my appreciation to my 11-year-old grand-daughter, Sina Senai, born and raised in the US, who is the first person to read the manuscripts of the two translated novels in a record 8 days. Her interest and enthrallment reassured me that translating the novels was the correct decision. Her fascination, impressions and appreciation of the novels, gave me hope that even among the younger generation, there are and will always be a few who enjoy reading.

I would like to express my heartfelt gratitude to Mrs. Jenny Wilder for reviewing the English translation and providing me with important feedback. She made detailed edits of my manuscript from beginning to end. Her contribution cannot be explained in a single sentence or a paragraph. Her input and imprint are evident on every page of my book. She was instrumental in streamlining and fine tuning the translation to bridge the cultural linguistic barrier. I am extremely indebted to her.

The beautiful and impeccable cover was designed and perfected by designer Ermias Zerazion from Australia. I would like to express my gratitude and appreciation for his patience, co-operation and perfection. I would also like to express my gratitude and appreciation to my tennis companion and former registrar of the High Court of Eritrea, Attorney Abraham Desta Ghebremedhin, for reviewing and editing the sections that deal with court proceedings and legal issues.

My eldest daughter Adiam, on top of doing everything to make our lives comfortable, has also been instrumental in organizing the promotion, book signing events and distribution of my books. I would therefore like to extend my appreciation and gratitude for her unbounded love, thoughtfulness and care.

I would also like to express my deepest gratitude to all those I have not mentioned by name above. These are all my family members, friends, former teachers, all Cathedral Pharmacy customers, all living and past authors, artists, their books, lyrics and poems, as well as the rich cultural heritage of the Eritrean community which directly and indirectly contributed to my works by playing a role into who I became and how I thought and reasoned. Although these books have been authored by me, the ideas, thoughts, depth and wisdom included in these pages mostly belong to them. I am merely a conduit giving expression to their wisdom.

Last but not least, I would like to thank the Almighty for gracing me with health and life to not only raise my children and hug my grandchildren but also achieve my dream and passion of sharing my experience and passing on the wisdom of the years to the next generation through my books and actual and virtual community engagement events.

Tesfay Menghis Ghebremedhin.

Epilogue

We have seen how Tesfom and Habtom's rivalry, obduracy and enmity adversely and negatively affected their families and themselves. Where will this madness end? Will they learn their lesson and mend their ways? Or will they be burned by the grudge and enmity they ignited and advanced?

We have followed how Medhn and Alganesh stood steadfast against all odds to protect their families and children from being engulfed by the fire their spouses ignited. Will their strong principles and strength of character prevail and save them from impending danger? Or will they succumb and fall victims to a rivalry and enmity they did not create?

How will the innocent children of both families, fare? Will they be permanently and negatively affected, traumatized and victimized? Or will they come out intact with their innocence?

How about the future of the elder twins, and especially Kibret and Bruk? Will the budding love affair between them flourish and heal the two families? Or will their love wither and dry up under the enmity between their parents?

What will Habtom's second wife, Almaz, decide? Will she try to heal the family's discord and enmity to bring peace and understanding? Or will she try to expand and enflame the controversy to save only herself and her children?

Will the brothers Araya and Dermas be absorbed into the fight and wallow in rivalry and enmity, or will they be strong enough to avoid being sucked into the madness?

Will this be the end of the woes and agony of the parents and heads of the two families, Grazmach Seltene and W/ro Brkti on one side and Bashay Goitom and W/ro Lemlem on the other? Or will they be subjected to further friction, disappointment, sadness and agony?

The answers to all these questions and riddles will be revealed in the next book, "Covenant Between Medhn and Alganesh," whose story line extends and runs for another eight years.

Author Tesfay Menghis Ghebremedhin

Tigrinya words

Abo=father, Aboy= my father
Ade=mother, Adey=my mother
Haw=brother, Hawey=my brother
Habti=sister, Habtey=my sister
Aerki=male friend, Aerkey=my friend
Mehaza=female friend, Mehazay=my friend
Wedi=Boy, Wedey=my son
Gual=Girl, Gualey=my daughter
Assey=A word used to express extreme satisfaction
Grazmach=traditional title
Bashay=traditional title
Ato=Mr
Woizero (W/ro) =Mrs
Woizerit (W/rt) =Miss

Italian words

Va bene= o.k
Veramente= Really
Proprio= Just
Dio= God C'e Dio= There is God
Stupida= Stupid
Ospedale= Hospital
Per favore= Please
Regina= Queen
Fa niente= It doesn't matter

Attachments-Book signing events

April 2019-Launching and book signing event of the first book, "**ህልኽ ተስፎምን ሃብቶምን**" in Seattle, Washington.

May 2019-Book signing event of the first book, "**ህልኽ ተስፎምን ሃብቶምን**" at the Eritrean Community Center in Santa Clara, California.

October 2019-Book signing event of the first book, "**ህልኽ ተስፎምን ሃብቶምን**" at the Eritrean American Center, Atlanta, Georgia.

December 2019-Book signing event of the first book, "**ህልኽ ተስፎምን ሃብቶምን**" at the Eritrean American Community Center in Boston, Massachusetts.

December 2019-Book signing event of the first book, in Wheaton, Maryland

Attachments-Interviews&Presentations

An interview conducted with Eri-Tv, on the Community Pharmacist's role in promoting health & awareness.

Interview conducted with the Voice of America, Tigrinya service, on Facebook & YouTube, about the first book, "**ህልኽ ተስፎምን ሃብቶምን**" *http://bit.ly/33pccio*

Interview conducted with Kebreab Yimesghen (Eri-Social Healing.) These six videos deal with life, work experience, family and other community topics. *https://www.facebook.com/kebreab.yimesgen/videos/10220156124463096*

Interview with Kebreab Yimesghen on YouTube, on how nutrition, exercise and life-style affect our well-being, health and longevity.

https://www.facebook.com/ariam.mehtsentu/videos/1024167892288019

https://www.facebook.com/kebreab.yimesgen/videos/10224642338068407

Interview with Raie Healthy Living on YouTube, on Pandemics, vaccines, the problems posed by social media, prevalent misconceptions & the value and true meaning of education.

https://youtu.be/DSOuAOV_VPY

June 2021-Keynote address-Eripco 2021 Semi-Annual General Meeting.

https://www.youtube.com/watch?v=0sQxvwCpnR0

Printed in Great Britain
by Amazon